The Vampire Countess

The Vampire Countess
(*La Vampire*)

by
Paul Féval

translated, annotated and introduced by
Brian Stableford

A Black Coat Press Book

Acknowledgements: I am greatly indebted to Xavier Legrand-Ferronnière, who found a copy of the Marabout edition of *Les Drames de la Mort* for me, and whose excellent periodical *Le Visage Vert* alerted me to the existence of Ignatz Ferdinand Arnold's *Der Vampyr*. I should also like to thank Bill Russell, for his invaluable assistance in researching German and French versions of Hoffmann's tales and for the translation of the Latin phrases, and Jane Stableford and David McDonnell for proofreading the typescript.

English adaptation, introduction and afterword Copyright © 2003 by Brian Stableford.
Cover illustration Copyright © 2003 by Ladrönn.

Visit our website at www.blackcoatpress.com

ISBN 0-9740711-5-3. First Printing. October 2003. Published by Black Coat Press, an imprint of Hollywood Comics.com, LLC, P.O. Box 17270, Encino, CA 91416.
Printed in the United States of America.

Table of Contents

Introduction

La Vampire (*The Vampire Countess*) by Paul Féval was first published in book form in a volume called *Les Drames de la Mort* (*The Dramas of Death*) issued in Paris by Charlieu and Huillery in 1856. It was the second of two linked novels included in that omnibus, the first being *La Chambre des Amours* (*The Love-Nest*). Both novels must have appeared previously as serials in a periodical, but I can find no indication of where and when. The internal evidence of *The Vampire Countess* suggests that it was most probably written and serialized in 1855, but I cannot be absolutely sure of that.

Les Drames de la Mort was reprinted in a two-volume edition in 1865. The notations contained in the catalogue of the *Bibliothèque Nationale* suggest that the first volume of the new edition was augmented by the addition of two prefatory essays, *Exposition* and *La Morgue* and there is one item of evidence internal to the text I have used which suggests that some slight amendments might have been made to the 1865 version of *The Vampire Countess* and carried forward into subsequent editions.

Les Drames de la Mort was reprinted twice more in 1866 and 1868. The first separate edition of *The Vampire Countess* was issued in 1891, and it always features in lists of the author's works contained in early 20th century editions as a one-volume item, with no mention at all *of La Chambre des Amours*. A new edition of *Les Drames de la Mort* was, however, issued in 1968 by Gérard et Cie. of Verviers and l'Inter of Paris, and a paperback edition followed in 1969 from the Belgian publisher Marabout. My translation has been taken from the Marabout edition, but I have compared the text with the 1891 edition–the earliest one I have been able to consult–and they appear to be identical except for a handful of obvious nd they appear to be identical except for a handful of obvious typographical errors which have been corrected in the Marabout edition.

The author of *The Vampire Countess*, Paul-Henri-Corentin Féval, was born in Rennes in 1816. He was the son of a lawyer and he trained for the legal profession himself after his father's death in 1827, qualifying as an advocate in 1836 while not yet twenty years old. In 1838, however, he abandoned his career and went to Paris, where he obtained work in a bank to support himself while he tried to build a career as a writer.

Féval's first literary success was a novella published in the *Revue de Paris* in 1841, *Le Club des Phoques* (*The Seal Club*). Many of his early stories were fantasies, often based in the folklore of his native Brittany. These were collected in *Contes de Bretagne* (*Tales of Brittany*; 1844) and *Les Contes de Nos Pères* (*Tales of Our Fathers*; 1845). Like many aspirant authors of the period, he soon became involved in the production of popular fiction for serialization in periodicals; the *roman feuilleton* was then approaching its heyday. Although he was always overshadowed as a *feuilletonist* by his more famous contemporaries, Alexandre Dumas and Eugène Sue, Féval ultimately became more prolific–and produced work of a greater variety–than either of them.

The term *feuilleton* derived from a line ruled across a sheet of newsprint, below which material could be set in advance of the news being filled in above it. The notion of *feuilleton* fiction eventually expanded its meaning, however, to encompass "literary supplements" like the ones published as Christmas issues of English periodicals like *Household Words* and part-work pamphlets akin to English "penny dreadfuls," thus being generally applied to all kinds of serial fiction.

The *feuilleton* first appeared in the *Journal des Débats* in 1800, but was not initially of any commercial significance; serial fiction did not make its appearance beneath the *feuilleton* until 1829, in the *Revue de Paris*. From then on, however, the importance of *feuilleton* fiction increased by degrees until it established sufficient popularity to become the principal weapon in a circulation war. Émile de Girardin made serial fiction the basis of the marketing strategy of *La Presse* in 1836 and his competitors were forced to respond, Armand Dutacq's *Le Siècle* responding to the challenge that same year.

The power of serial fiction as a circulation-builder was fully demonstrated in 1842-43 by Eugène Sue's *Les Mystères de Paris* (tr. as *The Mysteries of Paris*), which was quickly followed by *Le Juif Errant* (1844-45; tr. as *The Wandering Jew*). The latter was said to have added 20,000 to the subscription-list of *Le Constitutionnel*, whose total circulation at the time was less than 25,000. (Because the serials were read aloud in family groups and clubs and made available by commercial lending libraries, their total audience was much higher.) Even *Le Siècle*, the market leader, had a circulation less than 35,000 and *La Presse* was relegated–albeit narrowly– into third position by virtue of Sue's enterprise. Sue's most famous works ran in direct competition with *Les Trois Mousquetaires* (1842-43; tr. as *The Three Musketeers*) and *Le Comte de Monte-Cristo* (1844-46; tr. as *The Count of Monte Cristo*) by Alexandre Dumas, which were–and still are–his most popular works.

Féval made his debut as a *feuilletonist* with *Les Chevaliers du Firmament* (*The Knights of the Firmament*; 1843) in *La Législature* but moved into a slightly more competitive situation by working for *Le Courrier Français*, which serialized *Le Loup Blanc* (1843; tr. as *The White Wolf*). The editor of *L'Époque* commissioned Féval to write an imitation of Sue's *Mysteries of Paris* entitled *Les Mystères de Londres* (*The Mysteries of London*) under the pseudonym Francis Trolopp (Frances Trollope, mother of Anthony, was then a moderately popular English novelist).

Les Mystères de Londres set a pattern which was to dominate Féval's contributions to the *roman feuilleton* in building its plot on the foundation of a conspiracy which is part-criminal and part-political. It features the *Gentilhommes de la Nuit* (*Gentlemen of the Night*), whose leader is the mysterious Marquis de Rio Santo, alias Fergus O'Breane, the would-be liberator of Ireland. The conspiracy's plans are, however, thwarted by a young English nobleman, Frank Perceval, and a heroic Scot, Stephen MacNab. The story contains a strong element of irony and is full of flamboyant tongue-in-cheek Gothic touches.

The serial, which began in 1843 and ended in 1844, helped to boost the circulation of *L'Époque* considerably, though not as spectacularly as Sue's serial had boosted the circulation of *Le Constitutionnel*. Féval immediately began placing work in as wide a range of outlets as he could. *Les Aventures d'un Emigré* (*The Adventures of an Emigré*; 1844), also set in England, appeared in *Le Quotidien*, *Les Amours de Paris* (1845; tr. as *The Loves of Paris*) in *Le Courrier*, *La Fontaine aux Perles* (*The Fountain of Pearls*; 1845) in *L'Esprit Public* and *La Quittance de Minuit* (1846; tr. as *The Midnight Reckoning*) in *Le Journal des Débats*.

Although popular fiction did not carry quite the same stigma in Paris as "penny-dreadful" fiction in London, it was regarded with considerable disdain in literary circles, and the sheer pace of Féval's production won him a reputation as a hack. With the aid of hindsight, though, we can now recognize that he was an enterprising, ingenious and historically significant pioneer of several modern popular genres—as significant in that respect in France as Edgar Allan Poe was in America—but nobody knew that at the time, and conventional academic disdain for popular fiction has ensured that he has never received the credit he deserves, even in his native land.

Alongside his serials Féval began to write plays, and soon launched the first of several periodicals of his own, *Le Bon Sens du Peuple* (*People's Good Sense*), which was quickly followed by *L'Avenir National* (*The Nation's Future*). Both were founded in 1848, but that turned out not to be a good year for business enterprises. The so-called "year of Revolutions" did not blunt the French appetite for *romans feuilletons*, however, and Féval was soon able to increase the

10

flow of his work again. He often had several serials running simultaneously–but these Herculean labors eventually proved too much for him, and his health broke down in 1854, bringing an end to the first phase of his career.

The hiatus was not a long one. Féval's doctor was a zealous convert to homeopathy, and he provided treatment which at least did no harm–for which Féval, only too well aware that Paris was full of dangerous quacks, was duly grateful. The fact that Féval's subsequent attitude to homeopathy remained carefully enthusiastic and wryly ambivalent (as exemplified in *The Vampire Countess*) had much to do with the fact that he fell in love with his doctor's daughter, Françoise Penoyée, and married her. She was to bear him eight children, of whom the one named after him–born in 1860–followed the precedent set by Alexandre Dumas' similarly-named son by becoming a successful writer whose by-line was distinguished by the suffix *fils*. One is inclined to suspect that Françoise did Féval far more good than her father's prescriptions, but the necessity of keeping a wife and a steadily-growing family renewed the financial pressure that had driven him to exhaustion in the first place. He was soon writing just as furiously as before.

During the first phase of his career, Féval had produced several serials that were imitations of successful works by his more famous rivals, beginning with the Dumas pastiche *Le Fils du Diable* (1846; lit. *The Son of the Devil*, tr. as *The Three Red Knights*), but he was not a natural melodramatist and was always happiest working in the more light-hearted vein *of Les Mystères de Londres*. The most successful and most original works of the second phase of his career were all of this kind; the ingenious fusion of sarcastic humor and calculatedly casual melodrama was his principal contribution to the evolution of popular fiction in France.

Féval's influence would undoubtedly have been greater had he been more widely translated into English, but that was one respect in which he was signally unlucky. English popular fiction modeled on *romans feuilletons* was produced in great abundance in the 1840s, but the English literary marketplace was much more rigidly stratified than its French equivalent and the growth of functional literacy within the working class was slower. For this reason, English "penny dreadfuls" aimed exclusively at working-class readers tended to be a good deal cruder than the French serials, which aspired to a much broader and more sophisticated audience. Féval's awkward relationship with the world of English publishing began with the accident of his being commissioned to produce *Les Mystères de Londres*. It is hardly surprising that George W. M. Reynolds, who was to become the most prolific writer and publisher of English penny dreadfuls, felt perfectly entitled to write his own *Mysteries of London* in 1844–which provided his own big break–but equally inevitable that Féval would think himself a victim of plagiarism. Although there is no evidence of an actual feud between Féval and Reynolds, the fact that Féval made no secret of his opinion that English publishers were a crew of filthy pirates certainly did not help him to find honest translators for his work, and may have been something of a self-fulfilling prophecy. At any rate, the few contemporary translations of Féval's works that were published in London do indeed seem to have been pirated; more were published in the USA but those too proved transient and are almost impossible to find today.

Féval's work became much more distinctive when he recovered from his breakdown; he recaptured the versatility and spirit of adventure manifest in his earliest works, adding a conspicuous light-heartedness of manner and tone. Having established his own narrative voice, he scored his greatest success with *Le Bossu* (1857; *The Hunchback*; tr. as *I am Here! The Duke's Motto*; or, *The Little Parisian*). One modern reference book credits *Le Bossu* with having pioneered the sub-genre of "*romanesque humoristico-historique*," but contemporary commentators coined the term "*roman de cape et d'épée*" (*novel of cloak and sword*) to describe it. It was the ancestor of many modern mock-heroic epics, notably the adventures of

Zorro, whose career began in a strip cartoon by Johnston McCulley in 1919 before spreading to other media.

Although the phrase "*cape et d'épée*" eventually passed directly into English, its first translation was, of course, "cloak-and-dagger"–a term which came to be used much more widely for tales of criminal intrigue, on which Féval began to focus his efforts with increasing narrowness and coherency. His principal works in the emergent genre of crime fiction included *Les Couteaux d'Or* (1856: tr. as *The Golden Daggers*) and *Les Compagnons du Silence* (1857; *The Companions of Silence*), the latter of which formed a prelude of sorts to a series of seven melodramatic novels collectively known by the title of *Les Habits Noirs* (1863-75; *The Black Coats*), which he launched while serving as editor of *Jean-Diable*, a periodical whose name was derived from his earlier crime novel, *Jean Diable* (1860; *John Devil*; book 1863). This series tells the long and convoluted story of a vast conspiracy run by the prototype of all criminal masterminds, usually described only by his title, the "Colonel." One of Féval's employees on *Jean-Diable* was Émile Gaboriau, who went on to found the *roman policier*, which made the police rather than the criminals the primary focus of attention–the *Habits Noirs'* ultimate fictional descendants are nowadays to be found in Mafia stories.

In February 1865, Féval was elected President of the *Société des Gens de Lettres* but as a writer of popular fiction he was considered, somewhat to his chagrin, to be unfit for admission to the *Académie Française*. In 1875, the year in which he published the last novel in the cycle of *Les Habits Noirs*, his career hit the rocks. He lost an enormous amount of money through unwise speculation on the financial fortunes of the Ottoman Empire and was ruined. His response to this disaster was to make a considerable public fuss over his recantation of his profligate lifestyle and his conversion to ascetic Catholicism in 1876. As is often the way with converts, he subsequently became exceedingly zealous in the exercise of his new faith; he played a very active part in the movement to finance the building of the Basilica of the *Sacré-Coeur* at Montmartre.

Although Féval continued to publish new works as feverishly as ever, including a four-volume autobiography interpreting his life in the context of his conversion, they were marked by an exaggerated piety which was not much appreciated by his former audience. Much of his subsequent effort was devoted to the bowdlerization of those of his early works which warranted new editions. Some—especially those imitative of Sue, who was routinely accused of sadism as well as rabble-rousing radicalism—had won a reputation for encouraging immorality that Féval was now very keen to set aside by what he termed an "act of contrition."

Despite his hard work, Féval had hardly begun to reconstruct a viable economic position when he suffered a second disaster in 1882, when the person put in charge of his finances absconded with his money. He had to be rescued from destitution by a fund-raising committee chaired by the author Edmond About. The subsequent death of his wife redoubled the misfortune, from which he never recovered. He retired to a monastery and died in 1887. He left behind a massive body of work, including seventy-two novels—many of them very long—eighteen plays and a dozen volumes of non-fiction. He was, however, replaced in public view by Paul Féval *fils*, who wrote several sequels to *Le Bossu* and a good deal of other fiction in various genres.

In recent years, there has been a considerable revival of interest in French popular fiction of the 19th century. A special issue of the journal *Désiré* was devoted to Féval's work in December 1970 and a colloquium was held in his native town of Rennes in 1987, whose proceedings were published under the editorship of Jean Rohou and Jacques Dugast as *Paul Féval: Romancier Populaire*. Gradually, his most popular works are creeping back into print, and the significant contribution which he made to the development of French crime fiction, historical romance and supernatural fiction is becoming clearer to modern readers.

The Vampire Countess was not reckoned among Féval's most successful endeavors in his own day, and the author seems not to have thought much of it himself. He rewrote many of his early works after his ostentatious re-conversion to Catholicism in 1876, but *The Vampire Countess* was not one of them. It is possible that the reason for this omission was that he could see no way of reconciling certain highly sensational passages of the novel with his new-found piety, but it is equally likely that he simply did not think it worth the bother. Like the contemporary critics, however, Féval was not in a position to guess the likely import of his own innovations, and he may have underestimated the importance of some of the things he attempted to do in the novel.

A few other people do seem to have realized that it was an interesting work, however–considerably more interesting, in its way, than *La Chambre des Amours*, which is a straightforward historical swashbuckler enlivened (like *Le Loup Blanc* before it) with suggestions of lycanthropy. The 1891 edition must have reprinted it on its own merits, because six years were still to pass before Bram Stoker's *Dracula* was to usher in the new era in vampire fiction that extends to the present day.

By the time *The Vampire Countess* was written, Dumas and Sue had established an exemplary core of *romans feuilletons*, which put two elements at the heart of the enterprise: the popularization of French history, and the celebration of Paris as a cultural center. Although the medium was eventually to produce important pioneering work in the genres of crime fiction and supernatural fiction, such elements were initially subservient to these main themes.

In terms of the kinds of historical analysis they offered, Dumas and Sue were poles apart, Dumas being nostalgic for the days of royal glory while Sue was a forward-looking socialist; for Dumas history was a reservoir of fabulous tales of chivalrous derring-do, while for Sue it was a bloody record of terrible oppression and injustice. Féval, who was often called upon to imitate one or the other writer, or to attempt the impossible task of combining their key assets, had perforce to steer an unsteady middle way. One of the reasons why his serials seem so eccentric is that he was so often trying to be all things to all readers, and to amalgamate several different stories into a single whole. *The Vampire Countess* is a particularly chimerical work, because it not only seeks to combine Dumas' and Sue's contrasting attitudes to history, but also their very different attitudes to what would eventually become genres of popular fiction.

Although there was a strong element of horror in Sue's work, it derived entirely from naturalistic sources, in the tradition of the *roman frénétique* rather than Anglo-German Gothic fiction. In the absence of supernatural antagonists, Sue had perforce to make his human adversaries monstrous, which he did with great enthusiasm, employing sadistic criminals and cunning criminal conspiracies to generate the threats that faced his characters. Dumas, on the other hand, was much more enthusiastic about supernatural adversaries. His early Gothic romance *Le Château d'Eppstein* (1843; tr. as *Castle Eppstein*) features a standardized crumbling edifice in the Taunus Mountains of Germany, cursed by a prophecy uttered by Merlin and afflicted by a haunted "Red Room." It was rapidly followed by the premature burial story *Histoire d'un Mort Racontée par Lui-Même* (1844) and the novella *Les Frères Corses* (1844; tr. as *The Corsican Brothers*), a prototypical romance about a psychological bond between a pair of twins conjoined at birth but surgically separated. *Joseph Balsamo* (1846; tr. as *Memoirs of a Physician*) began a projected series of novels about a quasi-messianic immortal sorcerer whose Parisian manifestations were to include the famous lifestyle fantasist Count Cagliostro.

Féval was almost certainly commissioned to write *The Vampire Countess* because of the recent success of a play by Dumas called *Le Vampire*—a new and much-elaborated version of a classic whose earlier script had been cobbled together in 1820 by Charles Nodier, Achille de Jouffroy and the director of the Porte-Saint-Martin theatre, Jean-Toussaint Merle, to cash in on the *succès de scandale* achieved by John Polidori's *The Vampyre*, then widely misattributed to Lord Byron. (Both plays are referenced in the text.) *Le Vampire*'s second success following its 1851 premiere had, however, already proved difficult to transfer to the medium of the *roman feuilleton*. Long before the serial version of *Joseph Balsamo* had reached its conclusion, Dumas had yielded to editorial pressure to desupernaturalize it, and the subsequent items in the series it began had been sternly rationalized. Changing tack slightly, Dumas had begun in 1849 to write (or at least to collate) a mammoth part-work called *Les Mille et Un Fantômes* (*The Thousand and One Phantoms*) but it was never completed, most of the extant text being reissued in two volumes as *Une Journée à Fontenay-aux-Roses* (1849; lit. *A Day in Fontenay*, tr. as *Horror at Fontenoy*, Sphere, 1965) and *La Femme au Colliers de Velours* (1849; lit. *The Woman with the Velvet Necklace*, tr. as *The Pale Lady* or *The White Lady*), which contains the eponymous, oft-reprinted vampire story. Undeterred, he took a leaf out of Sue's book and started a novel about the Wandering Jew, Isaac Laquedem, which began serialization in 1852, but that too was aborted (the incomplete text was issued in book form in 1853).

In trying to combine Sue's and Dumas' attitudes to the supernatural in *The Vampire Countess*, therefore, Féval must have been aware that Dumas had already lost the contest and had failed to find a way of making the supernatural acceptable to the audience for serial fiction. Féval must have been torn between two impulses. On the one hand, he must have been tempted to favor Sue's example and place the entire melodramatic emphasis of his plot on criminal conspiracy and sadism (as he did for most of his subsequent career); on the other, he must have been tempted to see if he could succeed where Dumas had failed. It is hardly surprising that he appears to have tried to keep his options open—with the perhaps inevitable result that it is very difficult to figure out, at the end of the story, exactly what is supposed to have happened in it.

The end result of the unsteady application of these mixed motives and tactics is that *The Vampire Countess* is undeniably a mess–a patchwork that never achieves coherency. It must have seemed to many readers at the time–and even to its author–to have been a failed experiment, and a bad book. But it has virtues to counterbalance its failings, and there is a sense in which its even its failings are interesting. Today, we are far more used to "chimerical" texts which not only cross genre boundaries with blithe disregard for formulaic propriety but actually draw narrative energy from the chaotic clash of logically irreconcilable elements. *The Vampire Countess* does this by accident, not by design, but that does not mean that we cannot or should not appreciate its achievements in this regard.

The sheer impossibility of categorizing *The Vampire Countess*–it is in effect, a crime story with an ambiguous supernatural component grafted on to a domestic tragedy in order to serve as a protective vehicle for some mildly contentious political commentary, underlying all of which is the typical *roman feuilleton* nostalgia for Old Paris, which makes the city as much a character as a setting–emphasizes its status as an ancestor of a whole series of significant modern genres. It is important as an early crime novel, with several interesting and innovative features–including its hero's capacity to move from Clark Kent mode to Superman mode merely by holding a section of broken fishing-rod as if it were a sword. Even if all the scenes featuring its antagonist at work are delusory, it is important as a novel of the supernatural, because the scenes in which the vampire is active set several significant precedents as well as conjuring up a magnificently feverish quality. It is important, too, as a precursor of soap opera, not merely by virtue of its genre-compounding but by virtue of some of its set pieces–most importantly the sequence of written messages impotently hurled at a closed window by its hapless heroine.

Some of these factors cannot be fully analyzed without giving away too much of *The Vampire Countess*' plot, so I have placed a more detailed analysis of them in the afterword rather than discussing them here. In order to appreciate the novel fully, however, the modern reader does need to be attentive to certain aspects of its literary historical context, and some introductory commentary on the novel's background is necessary.

From a post-Stokerian perspective, *The Vampire Countess*' status as an important item of vampire fiction is compromised by the fact that the eponymous vampire is not a drinker of blood–but the novel's relationship with other vampire stories published in the same era is both obvious and interesting. The vampire's manner of predation is unique, but other aspects of her alleged nature are much more closely related to certain prior works of vampire fiction, and Féval's novel set at least two crucial precedents for vampire fiction to come.

Dumas' new version of the Jouffroy/Nodier/Merle play was not the only vampire story that had enjoyed some notoriety in Paris before Féval was commissioned to write his book. Just as the original play had been based on an English original, so its revival had probably been prompted by rumors of the success in England of the penny-dreadful serial *Varney the Vampyre* (1847). It is highly unlikely that Féval had actually read *Varney the Vampyre*, and it certainly had no influence on the plot of *The Vampire Countess*, but his awareness of the nature and progress of penny dreadful bestsellers is underlined in *The Vampire Countess* by a throwaway line which casually claims the plot of *The String of Pearls* (1846-47)–the tale of Sweeney Todd, the "demon barber" of Fleet Street–as an old legend of Paris. The third classic of penny dreadful horror fiction–whose success may also have played a part in Féval's commission for *La Vampire*–was, of course, *Wagner the Wehr-Wolf* (1846-47), by Féval's *bête noire* George Reynolds.

Varney the Vampyre and Dumas' play was presumably the inspiration of a *roman feuilleton* by the writer who was to become Féval's chief competitor once Sue was dead and Dumas had left the field, Pierre-Alexis Ponson du Terrail. *La Baronne Trépassée* (1853; *The Late Baroness*) was Ponson's first big success, and although its specific influence is not very obvious in the text of *The Vampire Countess*, Féval must have been keenly aware of the various precedents his new rival had set–especially its teasing ambiguity.

With vampires so much in vogue, it would not have been surprising if Féval had come up with the idea to write a vampire novel himself, but the hesitancy of *The Vampire Countess* gives the impression that he was in two minds about the propriety of the exercise throughout the time he was writing it, so it seems more likely that he was specifically asked to write a vampire story set in Paris. Having been commissioned to do that, however, he must have made up his mind that he would produce something distinctly different from the English school of vampire fiction, whose focus was on male vampires. Although the ancestry of *The Vampire Countess* does owe something to the two dramatic versions of *Le Vampire*, the change of pronoun acknowledges another chain of literary influences–about which more will be said in the afterword. What needs to be noted here is that Féval had already established an agenda of his own, into which he slotted the commission to write a vampire novel: the notion of writing a series of novels (of which only two were ever completed) with the overall title of *Les Drames de la Mort*.

The *feuilletonists* made several significant discoveries about the politics and economics of popular fiction, and the utility of series was one of them. Following the success of *Les Sept Péchés Capitaux* (*The Seven Deadly Sins*) in 1847-48, Eugène Sue had embarked on a series of novellas and short novels tracking the history of an ordinary family from prehistoric times to the present day, *Les Mystères du Peuple* (*The Mysteries of the People*), which kept him busy from 1849 until his death in 1857. His contemporaries inevitably followed suit; Ponson du Terrail was to score his greatest success with a series of picaresque crime novels starring a character named *Rocambole*, while Féval's longest series chronicled the adventures of *Les Habits Noirs*. There was, however, an interim period before it became obvious that crime stories offered the greatest scope for infinite series (because there is always another crime to be planned, executed and–if necessary–thwarted). It was in that interim that Féval happened upon the idea of a series telling the stories of individuals and groups featured in the expositions of the Paris Morgue.

Although mortuaries in general answered a legally-enshrined precautionary requirement to let corpses lie for a while before they were interred (the fear of premature burial, widespread in the 18th and 19th centuries, reflected the difficulty of finding reliable criteria of death), the principal function of the Paris Morgue was to display unidentified corpses so that they could be inspected by the relatives of missing persons. The practical difficulties of this process–which became obvious soon after its founding in 1722–necessitated the Morgue becoming a pioneer of refrigeration; by the beginning of the 19th century, when a thousand corpses a year had to be put on display, the temperature of the corpses was carefully controlled: after initial cooling to -15 degrees Centigrade they were stored at -2 degrees.

The necessity of opening the expositions to all-comers also demonstrated the macabre pulling-power of such displays; the Morgue became a place of popular entertainment, capable of drawing big crowds when an unusual number of corpses were delivered at the same time by some kind of catastrophe. The fact that some members of the crowd would indeed be relatives of the deceased, whose terror would give way abruptly to horror and grief when they found their loved ones, added considerably to the entertainment value of the spectacle for those crowd members who were there purely for recreational purposes.

The Paris Morgue was, in effect, the most significant ancestor of *grand guignol* theatre; it is easy enough to understand how the idea of writing a series of novels telling the back-stories of some of the corpses displayed there occurred to Féval. The idea of linking the series by means of a Morgue-keeper who also happened to be an expert swordsman must have seemed entirely natural, and the notion of setting one such story at the moment when the original Morgue, near the Châtelet, was being replaced by a new establishment on the Marché-Neuf must have seemed inviting even if Féval did not know of contemporary plans to replace the Marché-Neuf Morgue (it was closed in 1864). He certainly knew that the Morgue's functions had broadened out in the early part of the 19th century to retain and preserve bodies that were to be subject to *post-mortem* examination, so the alliance in *The Vampire Countess* between Jean-Pierre Sévérin the Morgue-keeper and savior of would-be suicides and the medical student Germain Patou has a definite symbolic significance; both men, despite the macabre aspects of their professions, are instruments of progressive Enlightenment.

I can only speculate as to the reasons why Féval abandoned the series after two novels, but *The Vampire Countess* certainly seems to have outgrown the prospectus, diversifying into too many other areas of concern. Féval realized quickly enough that crime fiction was far better adapted to the series format, but he must also have realized while writing *The Vampire Countess* that writing the back-stories of corpses puts a severe limitation on an author's ability to contrive the most crucial of all the standard devices of popular fiction: a happy ending.

The series idea was not the only agenda Féval was carrying forward in *The Vampire Countess*; he was also carrying forward his fascination with secret societies and–more importantly–his own idiosyncratic commentary on French history, as seen from the viewpoint of a Breton.

The Vampire Countess is set in 1804, in the days immediately before Napoleon Bonaparte–who had led the Consulate since the 18 Brumaire coup of 1799–declared himself Emperor. This was material that required careful handling if, as seems likely, the novel began serialization less than three years after Napoleon III was proclaimed Emperor in November 1852 (following a period of presidency instituted by the coup of December 1851). One of the consequences of this event was a period of unusually rigid censorship, so Féval's readers would have been acutely sensitive to the double implication of any comments offered by the serial as to the legitimacy or otherwise of the first Napoleon's institution as Emperor. (For this reason, one must assume that the careful disclaimer included in the novel's prelude is disingenuous.) Féval must always have intended to make the pursuit and arrest of Georges Cadoudal a significant element of his plot–and insofar as the affair of *The Vampire Countess* bears upon that matter, it also bears upon Bonaparte's assumption of the rank of Emperor. By prompting his readers to reflect on the circumstances preceding the former elevation, he invites comparison and contrast with more recent events, about which nothing could be said directly.

Georges Cadoudal, who was born near Auray in the *département* of Morbihan, was among the most important leaders of the chouans: the Breton insurgents who had fought against the Revolutionary army in the "Vendean Wars." After his ramshackle army was crushed by the Revolutionary forces, Cadoudal–financed by the British government–entered enthusiastically into several conspiracies against the Republic. The most notorious of these was the affair of the "*machine infernale*" (*infernal machine*).

The infernal machine was a barrel of gunpowder wrapped around with iron shrapnel–what would nowadays be called a nail bomb–which was supposed to explode as Bonaparte's coach went past on Christmas Eve 1800 (3 *Nivose* IX in the Revolutionary calendar), when the First Consul was taking his family to the opening of Haydn's *Creation* at the Opéra. Fortunately for Bonaparte, his coachman was driving very rapidly and had opened up a considerable distance between his vehicle and the one in which Josephine and her children were travelling; the bomb exploded a few seconds too late to kill Napoleon and a split second too early to kill his family. It did, however, kill twenty-six innocent bystanders, injuring a further fifty-two.

The bomb had actually been set up and detonated by two disaffected noblemen, Pierre Robinault de Saint-Rejant and Joseph-Pierre Picot de Limoelan, working in association with Cadoudal and his fellow chouan François-Jean Carbon. Napoleon's first instinct, however, had been to blame the Jacobins, and although Joseph Fouché–the ex-Jacobin Minister of Police inherited by the Consulate from its predecessor, the Directory–succeeded in securing the arrest of the two noblemen and Carbon, Bonaparte did not trust him. He created a new Prefecture of Police, appointing as prefect Louis-Nicolas Dubois.

The infernal machine was the second attempt to take Napoleon's life during an excursion to the Opéra. Another, earlier the same year, had involved the Italian sculptor Giuseppe Ceracchi (whose subjects had included several prominent American revolutionaries, most notably George Washington). Ceracchi had conspired with Joseph Aréna, Jean-Baptiste Topino-Lebrun and two lesser figures surnamed Demerville and Diana to deliver a party of three assassins into Napoleon's box, where they could stab him with their daggers, but in the event they were arrested in the corridor outside. As with the affair of the infernal machine, there are numerous references to this conspiracy in *The Vampire Countess*; the fact that Aréna had an equally-famous younger brother, Barthelémy, lent credence to Féval's invention of a vengeful brother for Ceracchi.

In 1802, Napoleon abolished the Ministry of Police, forcing Fouché into "retirement," although Fouché continued to command the loyalty of many of his former colleagues and spies. This too is a significant element of *The Vampire Countess'* background, which makes much of the assertion that the various factions of the police were so busy watching and plotting against one another that by 1804 they were incapable of efficient action against crimes and conspiracies committed under their very noses.

Georges Cadoudal fled to England to avoid arrest after the affair of the infernal machine, and was generally believed to be a spent force until news of yet another plot to kill the First Consul–involving two generals, Charles Pichegru and Jean-Victor Moreau–broke early in 1804. The ostensible justification for the new plot was Napoleon's intention to declare himself Emperor, and by an irony of fate, its revelation became one of the reasons offered to the French public for the necessity of the move. Moreau, who betrayed his collaborators, gave the information to his old acquaintance Fouché rather than Dubois, and Fouché's involvement in the affair enabled him to regain his position at the head of a revitalized Ministry of Police.

The action of *The Vampire Countess* takes place in the interval between Moreau's betrayal and Cadoudal's arrest, and insofar as it is a political fantasy, it concerns the rivalry between various ambitious men who are anxious to obtain the position that was ultimately secured by Fouché. Under the Empire, Fouché became the Duc d'Otrante, while two of his closest associates, René Savary and Claude-Ambroise Régnier, became the Duc de Rovigo and the Duc de Massa. Féval is presumably correct in his assumption that Louis Dubois must have been frustrated and annoyed by this reversal of fortune, although one suspects that Féval's scathing portrayal of the appalling vanity and ludicrous incompetence of the prefect and his associates may be a trifle harsh. His fondness for comparing the police to the legendary Argus Panoptes–the hundred-eyed sentry unsuccessfully appointed to guard Io by the Greek goddess Hera–is certainly overdone.

The fact that Georges Cadoudal obtains such sympathetic treatment in *The Vampire Countess*, in spite of his being in the pay of the British, presumably reflects the fact that Féval was a Breton himself, and must have known many people of his father's generation who were either chouans or Vendean sympathizers. (He was later to publish a story collection called *Chouans et Bleus*.) The careful ambiguity of the political judgments displayed in the novel is, however, typical of Féval's narrative method as well as being an understandable response to the political climate in which it was written and published. There is a telling symmetry in the fact that both of the glimpses of Bonaparte offered by the novel are second-hand narrations, one of them related by the not-entirely-reliable hero shortly before he offers his account of the vampire, the other by the exceedingly unreliable villainess shortly before she offers her account of the vampire.

The political satire of *The Vampire Countess* is unlikely to be of much interest to modern readers, but it is worth noting that the troubled and complicated situation Féval describes forms the background to most early French crime fiction, and sustains what was to become a staple of the crime genre: the idea that the police are absurdly incompetent and continually deflected by their stupid preconceptions from any objective analysis of any matters brought before them. There is no amateur detective in *The Vampire Countess*–Séverin may be far more heroic than Berthellemot and Dubois, but he is only a little more competent when it comes to the penetration of the mystery–and the setting of the novel might easily be regarded as a void of intelligence crying out for the application of a master of deductive reasoning. It is not surprising, therefore, that after compiling the awkward patchwork of *The Vampire Countess*, Féval went on to develop more sophisticated accounts of the battle between the evolving police forces of 19th century Paris and their cunning enemies, as well as more light-hearted historical adventure stories.

The background information given above is as much as the reader needs in advance of tackling *The Vampire Countess*, but it may be worth mentioning one more fact which is of some interest, even if it is probably irrelevant. As the novel's slightly promiscuous use of the term indicates, "infernal machine" became a very popular phrase after 1800. Its meaning broadened out to encompass many other allegedly ingenious contrivances, including the man-trap in which a certain Sergeant Bertrand was apprehended in Montparnasse Cemetery in 1849.

Although Bertrand was later called both a vampire and a werewolf, he was considered at the time to be a mere violator of graves and desultory cannibal–a ghoul, in effect. Bridging the gap between the publication in London of *Varney the Vampyre* and the production in Paris of Dumas' *Le Vampire*, the Bertrand affair might be reckoned another link in the chain of influences which led to the commissioning of Féval's serial. Given that Bertrand was incarcerated in the Val-de-Grâce military hospital, his case, along with Féval's novel, probably assisted in the inspiration of another mid-century vampire novel set in Paris and first published as a *roman feuilleton*: Léon Gozlan's *Le Vampire du Val-du-Grâce* (1862).

What is certain is that Bertrand's career was the explicit basis of a much later novel written in America by Guy Endore: *The Werewolf of Paris* (1933). Endore translocates the Bertrand affair to 1870 so that he can juxtapose it with the infamous Paris Commune, enabling him to propose that poor Bertrand's mental illness was a feeble and forgivable matter by comparison with an entire city caught in the grip of a murderous frenzy. What is one conscience-stricken werewolf, Endore asks, when politics and war make werewolves of us all? He was not the first person to make such a judgment. In *The Vampire Countess*, Féval suggests on more than one occasion that whoever and whatever Countess Marcian Gregoryi may be, the city of Paris can certainly be reckoned a metaphorical vampire which sucks the blood from its less fortunate inhabitants.

The narrative faults from which *The Vampire Countess* suffers are admittedly numerous. I have taken the liberty of making some very slight changes to the text in the interests of clarity and coherence–all of them indicated in the footnotes–but the object of the exercise has been to conserve Féval's work, so I have stopped far short of actually reconstructing the plot. I have explored some of the more puzzling aspects of the narrative a little more extensively in the afterword; again, I do not want to do it here because it would give away too much of the plot. It is, however, worth remembering that all the French and English serial writers of the period had, of necessity, to become experts in padding their chapters to fit the allocated spaces, and in letting their plots mark time while they sought for inspiration as to how to continue. Dumas was the master of this dubious craft because he was the most ingenious improviser; whenever Sue got stuck, he simply introduced a new character and a new subplot. Féval's main stock-in-trade was to make a game of his procrastinations, but this was always as likely to frustrate and irritate readers as it was to amuse them, and the modern reader will probably find some passages of *The Vampire Countess* a trifle tedious. It is, however, well worth persevering; although the glimpses of the vampire in action are fewer and further between than any modern reader could possibly wish, their peculiar setting makes their bizarre and vivid dramatic quality stand out all the more. Every one of them is a gem–or at least a spectacular item of paste–and nothing like them had ever been written before. They demonstrate as conclusively as anything he achieved subsequently that Féval, whether he was a "natural" melodramatist or not, had a flair for excess that has not been often matched, let alone surpassed.

Féval went on to write several more supernatural stories, and there are good reasons for preferring some of the later ones–and, indeed, some of the earlier ones–to *The Vampire Countess*. They are usually better organized, and the later ones tend to be much funnier. Although *The Vampire Countess* has an irrepressible humorous element, it is at its best when its satire is submerged beneath a melodramatic and erotic flamboyance that echoes the hyper-romantic fantasies of Gautier. There is certainly no injustice in the fact that Féval scored his greatest successes with works of a more relaxed and better-organized kind, but it would be a shame to let *The Vampire Countess* languish unread and unappreciated. Patchy it may be–but what gloriously gaudy patches its vampiric visions are!

Brian Stableford

Prologue

This is a strange tale, but it has a strictly factual basis. Nine-tenths of the material comprising the text has been furnished by the manuscript of Papa Sévérin. The opportunity has, however, been taken to add further intelligence to the information provided by that excellent man, which allows us to provide explanations for certain incidents that our honest children of the Tuileries regarded as frankly supernatural. These clarifications, by the grace of which this fantastic drama will present itself to the eyes of the reader in all its bizarre and somber reality, are derived from two sources. The first is an unpublished page from the correspondence of the Duc de Rovigo—who was, as everyone knows, the intimate confidant of the Emperor and who was entrusted, during the "retirement" of Fouché in 1802-1804, with the military control of the police force, which had been administratively reunited with the Department of Justice under the directorship of the great judge Régnier, later the Duc de Massa. The second, entirely oral source, consists of numerous conversations with the respectable Monsieur G***, the long-time private secretary of Comte Dubois, the prefect of police in the same period.

We shall not be much concerned with the tortuous internal political events of the period immediately preceding the coronation of Napoleon. Saint-Rejant, Pichegru, Moreau and the infernal machine are entirely irrelevant to our subject. It is scarcely necessary to note the passing of that huge man Georges Cadoudal, the Brutus of the royal family, as brave and resilient as any conspirator of old. International conflicts are of equal unconcern; in 1804 no one heard the distant fire of English cannon. The episode we have to relate, although a true history, is modest, having no reference at all to the intrigues of government or victories in battle. It is merely one page in the secret biography of that giant named Paris, whose life has seen so many adventures. Let us put to one side the five hundred volumes of diffuse *mémoires* which tell of the rights and wrongs of the great crisis of our Revolution, and turn our backs on the château where the crooked hand of good Monsieur Bourrienne [1] scribbles a few truths among the welter of well-paid lies, and plunge instead into the most thickly-wooded depths of the Parisian forest.

We hope that the reader will not have forgotten the touching and serene figure who is ever-present in the pages of our introduction. There is nothing in this book but stories; this preface is merely one more story, whose hero bears the name of Papa Sévérin. We are hopeful that the reader will remember another face, just as kind and handsome but in another way, less austere and more virile, more tormented and less peaceful: the cantor of Saint-Sulpice; the provost-of-arms who, in *La Chambre des Amours* gave the Baron de Guitry, courtier to Louis XVI, a salutary lesson in hand-to-hand combat. He too was a Sévérin: Sévérin, called Gâteloup [2].

That Gâteloup, who was almost an old man, and Papa Sévérin, who was still a child, played key roles in the earlier story; the one was father to the other. And if I may dip yet again into our fund of common memories, I would like to remind you of that dear little family of the Tuileries, comprising five children who did not resemble one another in the least, and to which Papa Sévérin was "dear Papa": Eugenie, Angela and Jean, who had come of age, while Louis and Julien were babies. To these five souls–who had been abandoned as orphans, but for whom the good Lord had provided the best of fathers–there had been presented, in the person of their parents, a lamentable history of suicide.

Indicating Angela, the prettiest of the young girls, and the one whose precocious pallor struck observers as a fatal sign, Papa Sévérin had said: "That one is bound to my family

---

[1] (see Notes page 333.)

three times over." He had added, on the day when the little girl first cast her avid gaze upon the blocks of ice in the Morgue: "She already has the idea..." For Papa Séverin believed in the transmission of a fatal heritage across the generations.

Our story will display the first of three Angelas [3].

Our story will also display a set of marble tables that are entirely new, untouched by any mortal contact. We shall see in the course of the narrative who it was that had the first use of the Morgue of the Marché-Neuf–all because of an adorable and impure demon, who revived for a moment, in the very heart of Paris and in the cradle of our "Age of Enlightenment," the blackest superstitions of the Middle Ages.

Chapter I
The Miraculous Catch

The beginning of our present century was far more legendary than is generally believed–and I am not talking here about the legendary immensity of our military glory, which wrote its opening pages in Republican blood to the triumphant fanfare of the *Marseillaise* before rolling out its marching songs amid the dazzle of the Empire and drowning its last chorus (a splendid cry!) in the mourning that followed Waterloo.

I am talking about the legends of the storytellers: of tales which soothe or excite companionable evenings; of things poetic, bizarre and supernatural, which the skepticism of the 18th century had tried to clear away. Let us remember that the Emperor Napoleon I was quite entranced by the foggy dreams of Ossian, passed through the academic sieve by Monsieur Baour [4]. That legend has been stiffened by starch, but it is still a legend. And let us remember, too, that the legitimate king of legendary lands, Walter Scott, was only thirty when the century was born. Anne Radcliffe [5], the somber mother of so much mystery and terror, was then at the height of her fame, the heart of a vogue that put all Europe to fright.

Fear was all the rage; darkness was in demand. A book of which one could make neither head nor tail could whip up a frenzy merely by describing a trap-door opening into a secret dungeon, a cemetery populated by phantoms at the hour "when the bronze bell sounded twelve times," or a confession packed from top to bottom with horrible and lubricious impossibilities.

It was the fashion. Such nonsensicalities were lavishly dressed in the grandiose language typical of that solemn epoch; it was all mixed up like a purée. The heroes–precisely cooked, according to a recipe, with "virtuous hearts" and "sensitive souls"—condescended to believe in "the sovereign master of the universe," and delighted to see a rainbow rise. The contrast between these philosophical preserves and sepulchral abominations formed a hybrid dish that was scarcely digestible but appealed nevertheless to the strange tastes of those pretty women who were so comically dressed, corseted under the bosom, with rings on their toes, their hips sheathed like folded umbrellas and their heads hidden beneath gigantic chicory-leaves. Besides which, Paris has always adored tales that disturb sleep, procuring the delicious sensation of gooseflesh. When Paris was still very tiny, it already had numerous stories to make one tremble, ranging from the conspiracy formed between the barber and the baker of the Rue des Marmosets for the sale of human *vol-au-vents* [6] to the gallant butchery of that house in the cul-de-sac Saint-Benoit whose demolition revealed numerous human bones lodged between the stone walls.

And in that regard, Paris has scarcely changed through the ages.

In the first month of the year 1804, there was a vague and ominous rumor circulating in Paris, born of the fact that miraculous catches of fish had been landed several times at the eastern end of the Ile Saint-Louis—on the south eastern side, to be exact, not far from the spot where the tritons of the Parisian elite now gather to bathe during the summer months.

It is a rare thing to find a shoal of fish in Paris. So many hooks, nets and diverse mechanisms are hidden in the water between Bercy and Grenelle that only gudgeons and imprudent barbels ordinarily come through the peril-strewn route. You will find neither carp, nor tench, nor perch there—and if the occasional pike is caught, it is because that freshwater shark has an exceptionally adventurous character.

At any rate, the fishy tribe made up a great windfall sent by Providence to the amateurs equipped with lines and every kind of net. As long as the day lasted, for a distance of a hundred paces—from the outlet of Bretonvilliers to the Quai de la

Tournelle, along the whole length of the Quai de Béthune–one could see a file of true believers, immobile and mute, casting their lines and following the floats bobbing on the water with eager eyes. To say that every one of them filled his basket would be misleading. Shoals of fish, in Paris, scarcely resemble those about our coasts, but what is certain is that every now and again a happy chap would land a big pike, or a barbel of unusual size. Gudgeons were abundant; chubs circled just beneath the surface; and one could see purple reflections in the turbulent waves which announced the presence of roach. All this in the depths of winter, when the habit of Parisian fish–who are as sensitive to the cold as marmots–is to desert the Seine in order to warm themselves who knows where!

On the surface, there was a great distance between the joy of the fisherman and the madness of the fish on the one hand, and the ominous rumor whose birth we have announced on the other–but Paris is a rationalist of the highest caliber; it readily connects an effect to its cause, and God knows that it sometimes invents very odd causes for the most vulgar effects. Besides, we have not yet said everything. It was not exclusively to catch fish that so many lines were suspending bait along the Quai de Béthune. Among the professional and habitual fisherman who went there every day, there were a number of laymen: imaginative and adventurous fellows who were in search of very different prey.

(Peru had gone out of fashion and no one had yet invented California; the poor devils who chased after fortune no longer knew where to lay their heads or search for a life of risk. Ingrate Europe does not know the service rendered to her by those magical blisters which declare themselves on the map of the world to be San Francisco, Monterey, Sydney and Melbourne. There were plenty of wars in those days, but in war one wins more blows than coins; model adventurers and "true seekers of gold" rarely make good soldiers in a pitched battle.)

Under the Quai de Béthune were to be found disinherited poets, broken-down inventors, ancient Don Juans–bankrupts of the love industry who had worn out their arms and legs in climbing ladders to women's bedrooms– politicians whose ambition had taken root in the gutter, artists insulted by renown (how cruel!), spurned comedians, inept philanthropists, neglected geniuses and lawyers of a kind which is to be found everywhere–even in prison, if they accomplish their duties with a little too much fervor. Nowadays, as we have said, all such bravos have gone off to such useful places as Sonora or Australia. But in the year 1804, they were kicking their melancholy heels in the troubled waters of the Seine, as if legend had placed a fantastic Eldorado in the depths of the river.

At the corner of the Rue de Bretonvilliers and the Quai there was a little inn, recently established, whose signboard had been sketched by a foreign student at the Academy of Fine Art. The board had two pictures juxtaposed within a single frame. The first picture showed Ezekiel–that was the innkeeper's name–costumed as a mudlark, tilting in one hand his wooden bowl, at the bottom of which pieces of gold could be seen shining, and holding up in the other a line whose rod, bent double, bore a marine monster of the kind described in the story of Théramène [7]. The second picture showed Ezekiel in his working-clothes, disemboweling the aforementioned monster in the privacy of the inn and taking from its belly a signet-ring embellished with a diamond which sparkled like the sun. It is necessary to add that the ring was around a finger and the finger attached to a hand; the whole ensemble had been swallowed by the monster from Théramène's tale, without preliminary mastication and with an evident relish to which further testimony was given by "its hindquarters folded in tortuous curves."

The two matching subjects had but a single caption inscribed in ill-formed letters, which said: *The Miraculous Catch.*

Perhaps the reader can now begin to comprehend the connection between the famous shoal of fish off the Ile Saint-Louis and the dark rumor rippling through Paris. We shall not begrudge, in good time, a chapter of explanations–but for the moment it suffices to say that all Paris knew the adventure of

Ezekiel represented on the board: an authentic, well-known and universally-accepted adventure whose absolute truth no one doubted.

Indeed, as everyone knew and could plainly see, it was with the produce of the sale of the jewel found in the monster's stomach that Ezekiel had built his inn. And when he had first discovered this Peru-in-miniature, this mother-lode of subaquatic riches, he had permitted the imagination of passers-by to weave an entire necklace of fanciful hypotheses around him. His name indicated an Israelite origin, and the high esteem in which the ancient children of God is held by the working-class is well-known. There was already talk of a vault in which Ezekiel heaped up his treasures. The other fishermen—the naive and adventurous alike—had arrived when the auriferous vein had already been skimmed: the poets, the inventors, the battered Don Juans, the fallen businessmen, the artists *manqués*, the broken-down comedians, the philanthropists at the end of their tether, the punctured geniuses and the lawyers, who had nothing for their supper but the leavings of that happy Ezekiel. They were not so much there for the fish—which really were extraordinarily abundant—as for that signet-ring, whose brilliant stone shone like the sun. They would willingly have dived in head first to explore the riverbed if the Seine, high, fast-flowing, discolored, and drawing foamy whirlpools along its course, had not defended the prowess of its kind. They carried wooden bowls to sift the mud at the bottom of the bank as soon as the water-level dropped. They scanned the waterline with feverish eyes while they waited, yearning to heap up riches from the watery depths.

Ezekiel, seated behind his counter, sold them spirits and carefully encouraged them in the opinion that provided his inn with custom. He was eloquent, this Ezekiel, and readily told them how he had seen with his own eyes, by moonlight, fish that fought over scraps of human flesh floating on the surface of the river. More than that, he also said that by lowering lines baited with Gruyère cheese and oxblood beneath the surface downstream of the sewer-outlet downstream of the sewer, he had caught one of those stout eels with fiery spots that are found in the Loire between Paimboeuf and Nantes, but are as rare in the Seine as white blackbirds in orchards: a lamprey, that cannibal fish which the patricians of Rome nourished with the flesh of slaves.

Whence came the abundant and mysterious fodder which drew such voracious hosts to this particular place? That question was asked a thousand times every day, with no lack of response. The answers came in all shades, but not one was either probable or good.

Meanwhile, the Inn of *The Miraculous Catch* and its keeper Ezekiel prospered. The sign was as fortunate as most things with double meanings. In effect, it pleased both the serious anglers who came to catch fish and that other, more numerous, category of fishers for chimeras: the poets, the painters, the comedians, the treasure-hunters, the businessmen impoverished by their wives and the lawyers. Every one of these hoped that a thousand-*louis* solitaire might attach itself to his hook at any moment.

And opposite the rank of fishermen, on the other bank, there was a rank of gawkers, who kept their eyes firmly fixed upon them. Gossips came and went; the superstitious crossed themselves. Enough falsehoods were fabricated there to quench the thirst of all Paris, incessantly seasoned with truths that were not common knowledge–I say truths, because I have been fully persuaded that beneath every popular rumor, however absurd it may seem, a real fact is always hidden.

The opinion most widely accredited, although it was not the most probable, could be summed up in a single word which strongly excited the imagination, equivalent to two or three of the darkest books of Madame Anne Radcliffe. The word in question was more ominous than the famous title *The Confessional of the Black Penitents*; it was more mysterious than *The Mysteries of the Pyrenean Castle, The Mysteries of Udolpho* or *The Mysteries of the Apennine Cavern* [8]: it had the ring of a knell, the odor of a tomb. This word, extremely appetizing to all unquiet, curious and avid spirits, to young men and women alike, to all who had a taste for terror and horror, was *VAMPIRE*.

Our education on the mournful subject of these funereal marvels has advanced little since the time of which I am writing. Several books have been written, of the sort which describe without explaining, which compile without abridgement, and which set out in fat volumes the pale tedium of their didactic pages–but it seems that the savants themselves, heroes of thought though they are, approach the redoubtable questions of demonology with troubled minds. In their company, the believers have the semblance of maniacs, while the incredulous remain steeped in that cold sweat called doubt, whose *communiqués* rain blows upon contagious boredom.

I have searched for, but cannot find among my childhood memories, the title of the prodigious book which first introduced my eyes to the word vampire [9]. That was no discouraging review-article, nor was it a slice of that banal bread whose crumbs fall from dictionaries; it was a poor German tale, full of vigor and ardor beneath its dress of starchy *naiveté*. It told–rather well, though timidly–stories so wild that I can feel my heart squeezed all over again.

I remember that it was in three little volumes, and that there was a copper-plate engraving at the beginning of each volume. They were not worth a great deal of money–but Lord God above, what trembling they caused!

The first engraving, as calm and pleasant as the prologue of an epic poem, represented... well, let's say Faust and Marguerite at their first meeting. There was nothing in it but a young man looking at a young woman, but it made the blood run cold, because Marguerite was obviously subject to the fatal magnetism that was spouting forth in invisible rays from Faust's eyes. Why shouldn't we retain those names, Faust and Marguerite? What is Goethe's masterpiece, after all, if not a splendid exposition of the eternal fact of vampirism–which, since the beginning of the world, has emptied and dried up the hearts of so many families?

So Faust looked at Marguerite. And there was a marriage, apparently: a country marriage, in which Margaret was the Bride and Faust chanced to be a guest. There was dancing on the lawn, among the rose bushes. The heedless parents and the groom–he had a bouquet at his side, the poor young bumpkin–were watching in open admiration as Faust waltzed with Marguerite. Faust was smiling; Marguerite's charming head was resting on his shoulder, cushioned on his Hungarian cloak.

And on the rosebush which grew in the foreground, there was a large twelve-sided net: a spider's web, at the center of which the monstrous creature–which is also a vampire of sorts–sucked the marrow out of an imprisoned fly at its leisure...

So much for the copper-plate engraving. Now, the text.

The pen paints less brightly than the crayon. There are the immense plains, overlooked by the ancient fortress of Ofen, beside that part of the Danube straddled by the modern city of Pest. From Pest to the Baconier forest, along the extent of the miry and turbulent river Theiss, there is the plain and nothing but the plain, as limitless as the sea. By day, the sun shines on that ocean of verdure, and the gentle breeze playfully caresses those immeasurable fields of maize which make up southern Hungary. By night, the moon slides over those mute solitudes. Down below, the towns contain sixty thousand souls, but there are no hamlets at all. The memory of wars against the Turks still causes the peasants to clump their homes together, sheltering like flocks of sheep in the fold, behind the corpulent tower topped with an oriental dome and armed with broken-down cannons.

It is night. The dead come to life in the Magyar lands as they do in Germany, but they come in chariots, not on horseback.

It is night. The moon hangs in a vault of blue, watching the galloping clouds pass by in profusion.

The flat horizon extends as far as the eye can see, punctuated here and there by a solitary tree, or a well-head looming up like a scaffold.

A wagon harnessed to four horses with flowing manes and tails passes as rapidly as a storm: a strange vehicle, set high on its wheels, half-Wallachian, half-Tartar. Its axles squeal.

Have you recognized the Hussar whose cloak billows in the wind? And that child, that gentle blonde girl? The dead are coming to life. The bell towers of Cegled have fled into the distance, with the towers of Kecskemet and the minarets of Szeged. Here are the proud walls of Timisoara, then, further on, Belgrade, the city of mosques...

But the wagon is not going as far as that. Its wheel has touched the marble slabs of the last Christian cemetery. The wheel breaks. Faust is on his feet, carrying the swooning Marguerite in his arms...

The second copper-plate engraving. Oh, I remember it well! It showed the interior of a lordly tomb in the cemetery of Petrovaradin: a long sequence of arches where the light of a single lantern was dying.

Marguerite was lying on a bed which resembled a coffin. She still wore her bridal dress. She was asleep.

Under the arches, vaguely illuminated, a long row of coffins which resemble beds supported lovely pale statues, laid down in eternal sleep. All of them were dressed as brides; all have wreaths of orange-blossom about their heads. All were white from head to toe, save for a spot of red beneath the left breast: the wound by which the Vampire Faust had drunk the blood from their hearts. And Faust, it is necessary to say, leant over the sleeping Marguerite: the handsome Faust, the admirable waltzer, the tempter and fascinator.

He was gaunt; without his Hussar's costume you would never have recognized him. The bones of his skull no longer had hair, and his eyes, his beautiful eyes, were gone from their empty orbits.

This was a cadaver, this Faust, and–a thing hideous to imagine–a drunken cadaver! He had completed his baleful orgy; he had drunk all the blood from Marguerite's heart!

And the text? In truth, I no longer know. That second volume was even less amusing than the first. The Hungarian vampire became bored at home, like the Spanish Don Juan, or the English Lovelace [10], or the Frenchman who is a heart-breaker whatever his name may be. All those villains killed contemptibly, like the cowards they were at bottom. They were worthless before their murders. For my own part, I have never been able to detect any great difference between poor Dumollard [11], the vampire of cooks, and Don Juan the great lord. The statue of the Commander [12] itself seems to me to be no more powerful than the guillotine–and if there is a villain capable of pleading the cause of three-quarters of those lost to the guillotine, it is Don Juan.

Let us pass on to the third copper-plate engraving, and a prize for memory will be awarded to me!

That one was the statue of the Commander, the guillotine, all that you could wish.

No one is ignorant of the fact that a true vampire is invulnerable and immortal, but in the same condition as Achilles the son of Peleus, who could only be wounded in one particular place and in one particular fashion. For example, the famous vampire of Debreczin [13] lived and died for four hundred and forty-four years. He would be living still if Professor Hemzer had not plunged into his cardiac region a red hot goffering-iron [14]. This is a well-known recipe which, at first glance, seems to be capable of doing the job effectively.

The third engraving showed Faust's own coffin, where he had probably rested for centuries, preserving the bizarre privilege of rising again on certain nights, resuming his Hussar's costume–always neat and very elegant–in order to go forth and hunt a Marguerite. Faust was there–the monster!– with his shining eyes and his moist lips. He had slept off the blood of Marguerite, who was lying a little further away.

The wedding guests had discovered his retreat–I don't know exactly how. A blacksmith's furnace had been brought in, in which a stout iron bar had been made red hot, and the bridegroom was thrusting it with both hands, with all his might, through the belly of the vampire–who could raise no protest.

And Marguerite was waking up in the background, as if the death of her executioner had restored life to her.

That was what was said and shown within my old book of three little volumes–and I declare that all the articles in academic collections have never told me as much about vampires.

I should add that the idlers of Paris, in the year 1804, had much the same idea as the book and I, as regards their opinions on the subject of the mysterious being that public anxiety had baptized *the Vampire* [15].

Chapter II
Saint-Louis-en-l'Ile

The vampire existed. That was the fundamental assumption and the certainty. Whether it was a fantastic monster, as some firmly believed, or some audacious band of malefactors gathered under that pretense, as more enlightened people thought, the vampire existed.

For a month there had been rumors of numerous disappearances. The victims seemed to be carefully selected from the population of rich visitors that an interval of peace had brought to Paris. There was talk of at least twenty foreigners, all young, all of them having marked their route to Paris by considerable expenditure, who had been abruptly eclipsed without leaving a trace. Were there, in fact, twenty? The police denied it. The police had declared that there was not a shadow of truth in these rumors, and that they had been put about by a mysterious opposition which was becoming stronger every day–but the more determined the denials of the police became, the more popular opinion hardened. In the suburbs, there was talk not of twenty victims but of hundreds–there, the existence of a shadowy charnel-house beside the river was confidently asserted.

No one, it is true, knew exactly where this charnel-house could be found. Indeed, it seemed to objectors to be a literal impossibility, for it was necessary to suppose that the river connected directly with the tomb in order to explain the phenomenon of the miraculous catch, and how could one admit the presence of a canal unknown to the people of the neighborhood? In the summer months, the level of the Seine sinks and the secrets of its banks are displayed for all to see. This was certainly a powerful objection, which lent its support to

43

the outrageous improbability of the idea itself: a secret dungeon in the 19th century!

The skeptics had a good laugh.

Paris saw no alternative but to imitate the skeptics. It laughed; it repeated over and over: it's absurd, it's impossible. But it was afraid. When country bumpkins are afraid, at night in sunken roads, they sing at the tops of their voices. Paris is the same; in the midst of its greatest fright it laughs, often and heartily. So Paris laughed while it trembled or trembled with laughter–because objections and rationalizations were powerless against certain items of evidence.

Panic developed gradually. Perhaps wise men were no longer believers, but the contagious disquiet took hold of them anyway–and the scoffers themselves fed the fever as they hawked their mockery around.

Two facts remained unassailable, though: the disappearance of several foreigners and provincials–a disappearance which began to excite a response of judiciary agitation–and that other circumstance, which the reader will judge as he pleases, but which impressed Paris even more vividly than the first: the miraculous catch of the Quai de Béthune.

There was, so to speak, a general preoccupation. Those who restricted themselves to a nod of the head acknowledging that there was "something in it" could pass for models of prudence.

Is it necessary to add that politics made its contribution to that concert? Never were there circumstances more propitious for the mingling of political melodrama with the imbroglio of private vice. Great events were brewing; terrible perils, recently averted, had left the administration fatigued and panting. The Empire, founded without much noise in the bedroom of the First Consul, afflicted the Prefecture of Police with the colics of its infancy. The Citizen Prefect, who can never have been a mastermind and who no longer called himself Comte Dubois, shuddered from top to toe every time a door slammed, thinking that he had heard an echo of that infernal machine whose explosion he had been quite unable to prevent. The somber inventors of that machine, Saint-Rejant and Carbon, had lost their heads on the scaffold but even in the depths of his disgrace, Fouché had murmured words that had reached the Head of State.

Fouché said: "Saint-Rejant and Carbon have left sons. Before them, there were Ceracchi, Diana and Arena, who left brothers. Between the First Consul and the Crown stand Republican France and Royal France alike. To make that leap will require a good horse—and Dubois is nothing but a donkey!"

The words were harsh, but the future Duc d'Otrante had a tongue of steel. There was more in the air than he-who-would-be-emperor wished to hear. As regards Louis-Nicolas-Pierre-Joseph Dubois, he was certainly no donkey, given that he dined on truffles and chicken—but he was a man prodigiously embarrassed. The cards had, in effect, been newly shuffled, and a conspiracy much more redoubtable than Saint-Rejant's threatened the First Consul.

The three or four police forces charged with the care of Paris, suddenly maddened by an invisible danger that each one sensed but of which they could find not the least palpable trace, collided in the night of their ignorance, injuring one another, thwarting one another's efforts, making reciprocal accusations with equal alacrity. Paris had such an affection for them, and such confidence in them, that the city woke up one morning saying and believing that the vampire, that connoisseur of cadavers, was the police!—that the young men who had vanished had paid with their lives for certain mistakes made by the police in happening by chance upon the pretended constructors of an infernal machine.

That day, Paris forgot to laugh—but it made amends the following day, when it learned that Louis-Nicolas-Pierre-Joseph Dubois had sent two hundred and fifty agents to surround the walls of the Madeleine, twelve hours after the end of a meeting held in broad daylight by Georges Cadoudal and his accomplices behind the walls of the half-built church. It seemed, in truth, that all Paris knew what Citizen Dubois did

45

not. Citizen Dubois passed through these events full of menace, like the eternal husband of the comedy who is the only one unaware of the romps taking place in his bedroom. He searched every place where nothing could be found; he threw himself about this way and that; he sweated blood; and, in the end, "threw his tongue to the dog" in desperation.

It was during the meeting at the Madeleine church that Georges Cadoudal proposed to ex-generals Moreau and Pichegru a bold plan to stop the future Emperor in his tracks. The word bold is that of Fouché, Duc d'Otrante. To Fouché's bold we may add the word simple.

Here is the plan, so well known as to be almost famous.

The three conspirators had a heterogeneous contingent of followers in Paris, which contained all the parties opposed to the First Consul, united by a communal passion and composed of resolute men. Contemporary memoirs estimate their nucleus at two thousand combatants, at least: Vendeans, chouans, national guardsmen from Lyon, Babouvistes, and old soldiers of Condé [16]. An elite of three hundred men chosen from among these partisans had been provided with uniforms like those worn by the consulary guard. The Head of State was resident in the Château de Saint-Cloud. When the guard changed in the morning–with the aid of information that was never fully explained–the three hundred conspirators dressed in regimental uniforms would take control of the château. It seems that they had already been given the orders. On awakening, the First Consul would find himself in the power of the rebels.

The plan failed, not by virtue of any action by the police–who ignored it until the last moment–but because of the irresolution of Moreau. The general was subject to moral qualms. He was afraid, or remorseful. The execution of the plot was put back by four days.

The execution of plots should never be postponed.

It is said that a Breton conspirator, Monsieur de Querelles, took fright at this hesitation, that he demanded and obtained an audience with the First Consul himself, and revealed every last detail of the plot. It is said that Napoleon Bonaparte mustered his military police, his political police and his urban police–Monsieur Savary, later Duc de Rovigo; the great judge Régnier; and Monsieur Dubois–in his study. He told them the curious tale of the conspiracy; he proved to them that Moreau and Pichegru had been coming and going in the streets of Paris like honest businessmen for eight hours, and that Georges Cadoudal, a fat man of jolly demeanor, was assiduously frequenting the *cafés* of the left bank after eating his dinner.

History does not record that this discourse was strewn with warm compliments for his three *chargés d'affaires* on the grounds of their clear-sightedness. The future Emperor gave thanks only to God, and his old friend Jean-Victor Moreau, whom he had always regarded as a good weapon badly loaded and inclined to misfire.

Moreau and Pichegru were arrested. Georges Cadoudal, whose corpulence did not prevent him from passing through the eye of a needle, remained free. And Fouché rubbed his hands, saying: "You see how things go wrong when I'm not there!"

The fact is that good policemen are rare, and Fouché was often at fault himself. What difference did it make that Argus had fifty pairs of eyes, given that he was myopic? The history of police blunders is interesting and instructive, but it is so very long and monotonous that one would get bored before it was halfway through.

We have several reasons for inserting this brief historical digression here, all of which pertain to our trade as a storyteller. Firstly, it helps to construct the frame within which the cast of our drama will move; secondly, it is useful to explain–if not to excuse–the inertia of the urban police in the face of those rumors which happened to coincide, within the city, with so much political gossip. The police had other things to do, and could not devote their full attention to the vampire. The police made themselves busy, searched, rummaged around, found nothing and were quite worn out.

On the February 28, 1804–the same day that Pichegru was arrested in his bed in the Rue Chabannais, at the home of the merchant banker Leblanc–a man passed rapidly along the Marché-Neuf, towards a little edifice which was under construction at the very edge of the quay, and whose scaffolding overhung the Seine.

The stonemasons plying their tools and their overseers obviously knew the man well, for they called out to him, saying: "Boss, won't you come look at how far we've got today?"

The man waved his hand at them and went on his way, continuing upriver.

The masons and their overseers smiled and exchanged knowing looks, because there was a young woman walking a few hundred paces in front of the man, her head enveloped in a mantle of black wool and her face hidden by a veil.

"That's three days in a row the boss has headed for the night-spots on this side," said a stonecutter.

"He's drunk again," added another.

"Listen here!" said a third. "Drink doesn't come into it. A man in his position has a lot on his mind. He needs a few laughs."

An old mason, whose jacket was whitened with plaster, murmured: "I've known the boss for thirty years; he doesn't laugh like everyone else."

Meanwhile, the man was moving on at a rapid pace. He was already lost to sight behind the hovels clustered on the Marché-Neuf, at the end of the Rue de la Cité. As for the veiled girl, she had completely disappeared.

The man was old, but he was tall and well put together, and he moved freely enough. He carried his freshly-laundered clothes, which seemed to mark him as a bourgeois, very well indeed. He had the appearance of a man who indulged in physical exercises of a kind usually reserved to members of the upper classes. Between the edifice under construction and the Pont Notre-Dame several men raised their hats to the man as he passed by; he was evidently well-respected in the quarter. He responded to these salutations with cordial and friendly gestures, but he did not pause for an instant. His course seemed calculated not so much to catch up with the young woman as never to let her out of his sight.

His quarry, whose legs were not as long as his, was going as fast as she could. She had no idea that she was being followed; at least, she never once turned her head to look behind her. Her eyes and her concentration were fixed in a forward direction. In front of her there was a proud and elegant young man, who was just crossing the Quai de la Grève. Was she following him?

The closer the man that the stonemasons of the Marché-Neuf called "boss" came to the Town Hall, the less numerous became the men who greeted him as if they knew him. Paris is full of celebrities whose fame does not extend beyond some particular street or some particular house-number. Once the man had reached the Quai des Ormes, no one offered him any further salutations. Meanwhile, "the boss" was enjoying a good view, whether he was bound for the night-spots or not. In spite of the dusk that had begun to restrict his visibility, he could see not merely the young woman but also the charming cavalier that the girl seemed to be following. That one turned on to the Pont-Marie, which he crossed in order to enter the Ile Saint-Louis; the girl did likewise; the boss took the same route.

The girl was slowing down noticeably, her breathing labored. This did not escape the attention of the boss, for when she sighed very heavily he murmured: He'll kill us! Must he take such pleasure in causing us such misery!"

The young cavalier was no longer visible. He had turned the corner of the Rue Saint-Louis-en-l'Ile and the Rue des Deux-Ponts. The girl was now waking with an effort so obvious that the boss made a movement, as if he wanted to throw himself forward to help her. But he did not give way to temptation, merely adjusting his pace in such a way as to have a good view of the course she steered after quitting the Rue des Deux-Ponts.

She turned to the left and unhesitatingly went through the door of the church of Saint-Louis.

Dusk had already fallen in the narrow street. In the shadow of the church, in front of the entrance, there was a luxurious carriage whose silver lanterns were lit.

The Republic slept, allowing the Empire to wake up. A small truce had been made with the extravagant luxury of the Directory [17], which put no proscription on aristocratic grandeur. The carriage halted at the door of the church of Saint-Louis was fit for a prince. It was splendidly equipped; the interior was furnished with exquisite elegance and the livery was spotless.

In those days, the Rue Saint-Louis-en-l'Ile was not in the least distinguished by any exceptional activity. The quarter was usually somnolent and almost deserted; it did not serve as an arterial road and offered no popular destination. An observer might have taken it for the main street of some market town a hundred leagues away from Paris. Nowadays, Paris has no deserted quarters. Commerce has taken possession of the Marais and the Ile Saint-Louis alike–dishonouring those magnificent old town-houses, some say, though others call it regeneration. In this respect, commerce has not quite made up its mind. It does not ask for rehabilitation; it is not afraid to get its hands dirty. It wishes to make money, and makes a mockery of everything else.

Under the Consulate, Paris had scarcely more that five hundred thousand inhabitants. The entire eastern part of the city was a desert, abandoned by the *noblesse de robe* [18] and having no local industry as yet. It was undoubtedly for this reason that the resplendent carriage stationed at the door of the church had attracted an unusual crowd of curiosity-seekers. You could easily have counted a dozen busybodies in the street, and an equal number of children. This twilight council was presided over by a doorman.

This doorman, typical of his species, had an austere philosophy, detesting all that was beautiful because he was frightfully ugly. He was preaching a sermon against vile luxury.

The street-urchins were staring at the gleam of the lanterns and prancing like horses. The old women were saying: "If Heaven were just, that kind of mud would stick to us, the world's poor."

"Please could you tell me," asked the boss of the stone-masons of the Pont-Neuf, "to whom that carriage belongs?"

The street-urchins, the old women and the doorman looked him up and down.

"It's not from around here," the urchins said.

"Is he working for the police?" one of the women asked.

"What's your name, pal?" the doorman demanded. "We don't have any truck with foreigners." The gentlefolk of Paris were foreigners to the insular inhabitants of this other world, separated from the rest of the universe by the two arms of the Seine.

Just as the boss began his reply, the door of the church opened—and he fell back three paces, letting loose an exclamation of surprise, as if he had seen a ghost.

It was, at any rate, a charming phantom: a young and very beautiful woman, whose blond hair fell in graceful curls about an adorable face. This woman was on the arm of a young man of twenty-five or thirty, who was definitely not the one who had recently been followed by our young girl. Certain aspects of his costume suggested that he was German.

"Ramberg!" murmured the boss.

The delectable blonde was already seated in the cushioned interior of the carriage, and the young German took his place beside her. A soft and musical voice issued the command: "The hotel!"

And the carriage-door closed.

The fine horses immediately broke into a trot, setting off in the direction of the Pont-Marie.

"That's a *ci-devant* [19], I tell you," the doorman said.

"Not at all!" one of the women replied. "It's a duchess from Turkey, or somewhere else."

"One of Pitt's spies, or maybe Coburg's [20]."

The street-urchins, to whom a few small coins had been thrown, ran after the carriage crying: "*Vive la Princesse!*"

The boss remained quite still for a little while. His gaze was lowered, his pale forehead was furrowed with thought.

"Ramberg!" he repeated. "Who is that woman? Who will give me the key to the mystery...? Baron von Ramberg was supposed to have left eight days ago, and it's only two weeks since Comte Wenzel disappeared... the girl I saw him with was a brunette, but those were exactly the same features..."

Without further troubling the little assembly, which was now examining him suspiciously, he mounted the steps of the church pensively, and went through the doorway.

The church seemed to be quite empty. The uncertain gleam of the last rays of sunset coming through the windows scarcely penetrated the shadows. The lamp that was never extinguished shed its eternally-faded gleam upon the high altar. There was not the slightest noise to indicate a human presence in the nave.

The boss was, however, absolutely sure that he had seen the young girl enter the church—and if the girl had come in, there must be some trace of the person she had been following.

The boss had already passed along one of the aisles, peering into each of the side-chapels, and was halfway along the other when he was touched by a hand extended from behind a pillar. He stopped, but said nothing, because the human creature who was there, hidden in the deep covert behind the pulpit, placed a finger upon its lips and drew him towards a confessional situated a few paces away.

The boss knelt down, assuming an attitude of prayer. Immediately, the door of the confessional opened, and a young priest whose tonsure was a white clearing in the middle of a black forest of hair made straight for the altar of the Virgin and prostrated himself before it.

After a brief prayer, during which he struck his breast three times, the priest kissed the stone beyond the balustrade and went into the vestry. The shadow then emerged from its hiding-place and said: "Now we are alone."

It was a child–or so, at least, it seemed, for its head did not reach as far as the shoulder of its companion, although the voice had a virile ring to it and what little that could be seen of the features contradicted the slightness of the figure.

"Have you been here long, Patou?" asked our man.

"Monsieur Guardian," the shadow replied, "Doctor Loysel's lecture finished at precisely three o'clock. I was here at twelve minutes past, and it's a long way from the School of Medicine to Saint-Louis-en-l'Ile."

"What have you seen?" asked he who was here addressed as Monsieur Guardian and previously as "the boss."

This time, instead of replying, the pretended child swept a hand briefly through the shock of hair bristling on his strong head and murmured as if talking to himself: "I would have come sooner, but Professor Loysel was giving a lecture on Samuel Hahnemann's *Organon* [21]. During the eight hours that the discourse seemed to last, it was not so much a lecture as a deluge. This Samuel Hahnemann is so often insulted at the School that I am beginning to think of him as a great scientist..."

"Patou, my friend," the guardian interrupted, "you student doctors are all chatterboxes. This Samuel–who must be a Jew, or some German jabberer, since his name ends in mann– is irrelevant. What have you seen? Tell me!"

"Ah, Monsieur Guardian," Patou replied, "the strangest thing, on my word of honor! The policemen would certainly be amused, because the only time I have played the spy I have been entertained like an angel! What a lovely woman!"

"What woman?"

"The Countess."

"Ah!" said the guardian. "She's a countess!"

"That's what Abbé Martel called her. Did you think that I meant your Angela, poor sweetheart, when you asked 'What woman?' "

"You have not seen Angela?"

53

"That I have... very pale, with tears in her lovely eyes."

"And René?"

"René too... even paler than Angela, but with a mad gleam in his eyes."

"And have you discovered...?"

"Patience! In a sickbed, he who expresses the clearest symptoms never finds a cure. There are savants and there are doctors: those who profess to know, and those who heal... I will give you the facts: I am the savant; you shall be the doctor, if you can figure out the key to the charade... or charades, for there is more than one disease in this, I'm sure of it."

A clink of keys sounded at that moment from the side of the vestry, and the verger began his rounds, saying in a raised voice: "The doors will soon be closed!"

Save for the guardian and Patou there was no one in the church. The guardian moved towards the main door, but Patou held him back and set him to walk in the opposite direction. As they passed the little basin close to the side door, the guardian dipped the fingers of his right hand therein and offered the holy water to Patou–who refused with thanks, laughing.

The guardian crossed himself soberly.

"I have not yet investigated its properties," Patou said. "Yesterday I made fun of Samuel Hahnemann; today I would willingly put his name on my hat. When I have completed my medical studies, perhaps I shall study a little theology and become a monk. He interrupted himself to add, while indicating the door: "Monsieur René went out this way, and Mademoiselle Angela went after him."

The guardian was thoughtful. "Perhaps you need reasons for all your studies, Patou my friend," he said, rather tiredly. "Personally, I have never studied anything but music, fencing and men..."

"That's no excuse!" said the medical student.

"It's too late to study the rest," the guardian concluded. "I'm the past, you're the future. The past knows what you don't. Doubtless you only believe that which you can understand; for myself, I wish to believe because it's good to believe. I believe in the God who created me; I believe in the Republic that I love, and in my conscience, which has never deceived me."

Patou jumped on to the pavement of the Rue Poultier and performed a series of four *entrechats*, of which one would not have thought his short limbs capable. "You, boss, are as innocent as a child, as muscular as an athlete and as silly as a pretty girl," he said, then burst out laughing. "Your ideas are all mixed up. I have a little nephew who said to me the other day: I love mummy and apples. Just like you! That little blonde countess has put ideas into my head. What a subject for dissection!... I'm studying the particular diseases of women at the moment, and I have a great need of someone... someone as young and as well-proportioned as that... a magnificent specimen... how would you like to have that in your blessed vault, Monsieur Jean-Pierre?"

Chapter III
Germain Patou

It was almost dark. A single slow and heavy footfall sounded on the pavement, so old yet almost virginal, of a melancholy street where no one passed by and whose open shop-fronts were never illuminated. This solitary tread was that of a poor cripple who lighted one smoky match after another as he went along, for the sake of their miserly gleam. The cripple limped along in his rags like some miserable boat stirred by the swell. He was singing a comic song, as mournful as a dirge.

Patou and the man whom we have previously designated by such labels as the boss of the stonemasons of the Marché-Neuf, Monsieur Guardian and Monsieur Jean-Pierre went down from the side-door of the church of Saint-Louis towards the Quai de Béthune. In the shadows, the difference between their heights became fantastic; Patou seemed to be a dwarf and Jean-Pierre a giant.

One day we shall rediscover that dwarf enlarged, not so much physically as morally. We shall see Doctor German Patou, wearing the name of Samuel Hahnemann on his hat like a cockade of his own free will, producing miracles like those which once caused the founder of the homeopathic school to be stoned in Leipzig, but which later caused a colossal bronze statue of that same Samuel Hahnemann to be erected in the very center of the main square of that very same city, his birthplace. If all the petty persecutions which have halted for an instant, then added prolific fruit to the cause of progress through the centuries, were to be summarized in a single phrase, we might call them "triumphant calvaries." Doctor Germain Patou had a role to play in that bizarre and terrible comedy that we have already published under the title *Numéro Treize* [22].

The boss replied thus to his final question: "Little man, you don't always give the items of my business the respect they deserve. I don't like jokes about that subject–but I'd rather that than irony, and it's said that the profession you've chosen hardens the heart a little. I knew you when you were a child. I haven't been able to do all that I wished for you..."

Patou interrupted him by pressing his hand urgently. "Stop right there!" he said, and continued with a deep emotion that seemed even more astonishing than the fourfold *entre-chat*. "You've given me bread twice over, Monsieur Séverin: bread for the body and bread for the soul. It's thanks to you that I'm alive; it's thanks to you that I am a student; if I out-shine my comrades at school, it's because you have opened to me that somber amphitheater next to which you sleep, as calmly and mercifully as the incarnate bounty of God..."

A tear fell upon the boss' hand. "You're a good little chap," he murmured. "Thanks."

"I will be whatever the future requires," Patou replied, drawing himself up to the full extent of his meager height. "I don't know what that is–but I can reply for the present, and I tell you that at a sign from you I would throw myself into water or fire, as you please!"

The boss leaned over him and kissed him, repeating in a low voice: "Thanks, little chap. I'm too embarrassed to tell you exactly what sort of trouble I'm in, but I sense that I shall soon have need of all those who love me... tell me what you've seen."

They resumed walking side by side, and Patou began his story.

"When I arrived, after school, Abbé Martel was alone with the fat horse-trader. They were talking about this and that–the arrest of Pichegru, I suppose, since the Abbé said: 'In a few short days, the unhappy man has tarnished the glory of many glorious years.'

" 'Well, I don't know,' the fat horse-dealer replied. 'That depends on one's point of view!' Then he added: 'Monsieur l'abbé, you know that I don't meddle in politics. My business comes first, and if it happens that I can do something for the First Consul, you know what my response will be.'

" 'May God preserve us,' said the abbé, making a large sign of the cross. Afterwards he gave the horse-dealer the address of someone whose name I didn't catch but who is staying 'at her house in the Chaussée des Minimes.' And he added: 'That one's an angel, or a saint.'

" 'All as you wish, Monsieur l'abbé,' the fat merchant replied, with the air of a merry confederate, 'provided that it buys me a pair or two of my beautiful Normandy horses...' "

"He didn't mention his nephew?" asked the boss.

"Not that I know of," Patou replied, "but I hadn't heard the whole of their conversation... and Professor Loysel's lecture was still rattling round my head a little. What a jolly chap that Hahnemann is! A veritable angel, not to say a saint–it must be the blonde Countess. You haven't seen her as I have. It was already dark, and exquisite perfection requires broad daylight. You'd think those eyes were two sapphires! A mouth that's a smile, a figure that's a dream of grace and youthfulness, translucent hair all a-gleam with light, cheeks..."

"Little man," the boss put in, "I am here to find out about René and Angela."

"Right, boss!" exclaimed Patou. "I seem to be lit up like an armful of dry wood. I don't want to come across as a lovesick fool, but it's certain that if the devil could put temptation my way, that creature... enough–it's not important. Let's get to Monsieur René de Kervoz. I think that Monsieur René de Kervoz has the same opinion as me, and that your poor Angela has found that out before us.

"I want to report the pure and simple truth of what I've seen. It isn't much, but you're a clever one, boss, and you'll be able to crack the case easily enough.

"After the fat horse-merchant had gone, Abbé Martel went back into the vestry and I took up my post behind the pulpit. A light footstep caused me to turn my head; a dazzling vision passed before my eyes. It was the blonde angel. Word of honor, I never imagined anything as lovely...

"The angel crossed the threshold of the vestry, leaving behind her a perfumed breeze that betrayed the presence of Venus–that's Virgil. When she came out again, Abbé Martel followed her. He's a good priest, very venerable, although he occupies himself a little too much with politics. He was still talking politics as he reached the confessional, saying: 'My daughter, the First Consul has done much for religion; I fear that you'll become mixed up in all these intrigues and conspiracies.'

"The beautiful blonde wore a strange smile as she replied: 'Father, this very day you shall know the secret of my life. A fateful destiny weighs upon me. Don't be suspicious of me before I've told you about my unhappiness, and the hope that remains to me. I'm a member of a noble and powerful race; death has reaped a harvest all around me, leaving me alone in the world. The letter I have brought from the Archbishop of Gran, the vicar-general of His Holiness in Hungary, has told you that I seek protection and a family in the Church. Conspiracies fill me with horror, and if I lose the last chance I have of heartfelt happiness, my intention is to seek peace in a cloister.'

"Abbé Martel's confessional opened, then closed. I heard nothing more..."

At this point, the medical student stopped abruptly, transfixing his companion with eyes that gleamed in the darkness.

"Boss," he asked, "do you understand any of this?"

"Keep going," replied the guardian, whose head was bowed thoughtfully.

"If you understand it, that's all right!" said Patou. "I'll go on. A quarter of an hour or thereabouts went by. The Church of Saint-Louis-en-l'Ile doesn't have many visitors. The first person who came in was the German swell. He went straight to the vestry, where Abbé Martel and the divine blonde soon joined him. There was a conference in the vestry lasting more than twenty minutes, after which the delectable blonde went to kneel before the altar of the Virgin, while the German and the Abbé took their places in the confessional... one has to go to confession before getting married, isn't that so, Boss?"

The guardian made no reply. Patou continued: "Monsieur René de Kervoz came in while the German was making his confession. Angela was close behind him. You decide whether I had my eyes and ears in my pocket! René de Kervoz hurried across the church. It couldn't have been the first time that he had a rendezvous in that place, or at least in some similar place. My blonde goddess heard the noise of his footsteps and turned around. She put a finger over her mouth. Kervoz stopped as if bewitched. They thought that they were alone. Angela–pale, exhausted, almost fallen into a swoon, but with eyes afire and breast heaving–hid herself only a few paces away from me, behind the same pulpit. Darkness had already fallen; Angela didn't see me. When she sank to her knees, no longer able to stay on her feet, I could have touched her just by extending my hand. I remained quite still, but my heart was touched by the muffled sound of the sobs heaving in her bosom.

"The other two believed themselves to be alone. Neither one suspected my presence–and the altar of the Virgin could not be seen from the confessional where Abbé Martel was listening to the German. The figure of the unknown beauty seemed as if it were painted, illuminated as she was by the last rays of daylight passing through the stained-glass windows. Behind me, poor Angela murmured in a voice drowned by tears: 'My God! My God! How beautiful she is!'

"Kervoz wanted to speak, but an imperious gesture closed his mouth. The queen of blondes smiled like a Madonna. She whispered a few words which didn't carry to me, but it seemed to me that her finger was indicating Abbé Martel's confessional. The interview would only last a minute longer. The hand of my unknown beauty extended to point towards the side door and René, obedient as a slave, left the church by that route. Angela, poor child, groaned as she rose to her feet and set herself once again upon his trail.

"Just at that moment, the German's confession came to an end. My unknown–for she's mine too, boss, and though I'd be a very ugly moth, I'd gladly burn my wings in that diabolical or celestial flame–my unknown rejoined von Ramberg, and they knelt down one beside the other. Before departing, they both bowed down before the confessional, from which a blessing was pronounced.

"That's all, save for the detail that I heard a double offering fall into the poor-box, heavy and loud. You know the rest better than me, since you came in that the moment when they left together...

"Now, boss," the little doctor said, fixing his companion with eyes bright with curiosity, "If you see things clearly, tell me quickly what that charade was all about, for I'm burning to know. Is it nothing but a love-affair? The old story of one lovely woman playing around with two lovers? Are we on the track of a conspiracy? Is the priest a victim of deceit or an accomplice? Everything in this is bizarre–including the fat horse-trader, who seemed to me to be a menacing and terrible figure when seen from behind...you aren't answering, boss."

The guardian was indeed silent and pensive.

They had stopped at the end of the Rue Poultier, by the parapet of the quay that faced the wine-dock. The moon, rising behind the trees of the Ile Louviers as if attracted by the tall poplars of the Mail Henri IV, struck the stream of the Seine obliquely with its rays, forming a long spectral trail of moving spangles. The Ile Louviers is no more, alas, and the giant poplars of the Arsenal have been felled. To the west, all along the river, Paris merrily lit its candles, its lamps and its streetlights. To the east, the darkness was almost as intense as night in open country, for the Ile Louviers and the Mail hid the Arsenal quarter, and on the other side of the Seine one's gaze would have to go as far as Ivry, beyond the Botanical Gardens, to encounter a few glimmers of light.

One solitary gleam, vivid and red, attracted the eye to the corner of the Rue de Bretonvilliers. It was the tantalizing lantern of Ezekiel's hostelry: *The Miraculous Catch*. There was not a soul on the quay, but the silence was occasionally disturbed by sudden rumbles mixed with bursts of laughter. The noise came from the river, and to discover its origin it was only necessary to lean over the parapet. The fishers for miracles were at their posts in spite of the advanced hour. There was a line of men on the bank, tightly pressed together, casting their hooks with patient zeal. The shouts and laughs were occasioned by those petty incidents that constantly enliven the fishing along the river Seine, where the hooks find more old hats, drowned boots and carcasses of dead cats than sturgeons. Every discovery of that kind brings transports of joy.

The medical student, who was evidently a cheerful soul amused by everything, listened momentarily to the hustle and bustle at the bottom of the wall. He had the air of one who understood quite well the kind of place and the kind of occupation that brought them all together. After a minute or two, he raised his head to look at his companion again, and repeated: "You aren't answering, boss."

The guardian had put both elbows on the parapet, and he was looking down over it.

"Do you believe in this, Patou?" he asked, pointing at the rank of fisherman, who had just that moment fallen silent.

"I believe in everything," the little man replied. "It's less tiring than doubting. Besides, last week I bought a beautiful femur here, which might have been dissected and prepared by a laboratory assistant."

"Ah!" said the guardian. He added: "It was brought out of the water, this femur?"

"It hadn't been down there long," Patou replied, "and nothing will dissuade me from the opinion that there was some deviltry involved in putting it there... but that's not a reply to my question. Do you know any more than I do, or not?"

The guardian sat on the parapet and raised his hat in order to wipe away the sweat that bathed his knitted brow.

"What happened back there," he said, "is as mysterious to me as to you. That's why I don't understand why I'm afraid." His voice was full of emotion as he went on: "I wouldn't wish any evil upon the First Consul: I like him, even though I suspect him of wanting to take over the Republic... but the First Consul is well-defended if he were attacked; it's not him I'm thinking about. Angela, René... those two children are my heart's blood... I would give my right arm to know..."

"A valiant arm!" said Patou. "That would be too dear a price."

"It may be a love-affair," the guardian continued, "involving only two conspirators... or it may one of those dark villainies which take advantage of our troubled times for their achievement. Something is going on... and I feel that it's something bloody and menacing. I'd have to get to the bottom of it before I go to the Prefect of Police!"

Patou let out derisive laugh, which did not express much confidence in that august magistrate.

"I'll go higher, if need be," the guardian went on. "One of my three German friends has already disappeared. If Ramberg disappears, it will be into the same hole. Once warned, foresight should enable me to avert the second–but that woman is beautiful, and her eyes make one dizzy..."

"Do you think...?" Patou began. His mouth was still open.

"I'm afraid!" the guardian said, for the third time.

The little man murmured: "It's true. Her eyes make one dizzy... I'm beginning to understand."

There was a sudden explosion of cries on the river's edge.

"Hold hard, Colinet!"

"Steady, Colinet! Don't let go!"

"Colinet, your fortune's in hand! Reel it in!"

Our two companions got up onto the parapet and looked to see what was happening.

By the light of the moon, they could see that the fishermen had broken ranks to surround one wretchedly-dressed man, who was trying with all his might to pull his line out of the water.

"It must be a whale to pull that hard!" Patou muttered.

"Or an entire cadaver," said the guardian.

Others came to the aid of Colinet, the man whose line was taut. With considerable skill and effort, the object he had hooked was lifted from the surface of the water and illuminated by hastily-lit torches of straw.

A mighty burst of laughter echoed along the deserted river bank from Notre-Dame to the Quai de la Râpée.

"Bravo, Colinet!"

"Colinet has all the luck!"

"Colinet's fished up a clown, with a clay ball!"

The object was indeed a clown, dressed from head to toe in the traditional costume of an Italian comedy buffoon. It was not a drowned man of flesh and blood; for whatever reason, someone had played a joke on the solemn rank of fishers for miracles, by placing a mannequin stuffed with straw and sand in their favorite spot.

The noise on the riverbank took some time to die down. Colinet, desolate with shame, bundled up the rags in which the mannequin was dressed and asked for a bid in excess of forty *sous*.

Patou had laughed along with the others, but then he became pensive and said: "Whoever made it must have had a motive."

"Little man," the guardian said, brusquely, "I don't need you any longer. Go back to the house for the present—my wife is alone there, and probably anxious. Angela must have returned by now. If you know a good remedy for chagrin, make up a prescription...say that I will be home late. Goodnight!"

Patou, thus dismissed, meekly took himself off in the direction of the Pont-Marie. The guardian, alone now, began to walk slowly towards Ezekiel's inn, at the sign of *The Miraculous Catch*.

Chapter IV
The Heart of Gold

If the Lady of the Camelias, that posthumous photograph taken by the charming and implacable poet Alexandre Dumas *fils*, had taken a timely passage on a clipper operated by the Australian General Company, she would have been cured of her pulmonary phthisis and would now be a prominent presence at all the parties of the *trois-quarts-du-monde*, in her capacity as the Baronne de *N'importe quoi* [23]. She would be terribly rich; she would have the contemporary world at her feet; and she would dole out her memoirs to her contemporaries in ten instructive and amusing volumes that would embody the very heart of the 19th century.

This century must be a veritable California for the priestesses of love, whether they be ten *louis* ladies of the camellias from the Eldorado of ancient Peru or one *sou* wallflowers from New South Wales. They no longer break down coughing as soon as they come to battle, now that Marlborough, Colomb, Cortes, Pizarro and Captain Cook have discovered and conquered for their benefit two-fifths of the world and Monsieur Benazet has founded a sixth [24]. Do you ever see them spit blood at the sound of gold being shoveled up? Are they ever lacking in any gambling-den, whether glittering or humble?

God preserve us from comparing Ezekiel's sordid inn to those marvelous fields of gold that surround Melbourne, the Paris over the sea, or to the Romanesque "placers" of the Vermilion Sea, or even to the gentle paradise of Baden-Baden. Gambling-dens differ by several orders of magnitude. We only wish to observe that all gambling-dens, disgusting or magnificent, attract these flower-girls as wool attracts mites. They flourish there; the atmosphere obviously does them good. There were wallflower-women in Ezekiel's inn, which was a gambling-den. That poor field of gold of the Quai de Béthune attracted adventuresses from the Cité and from Saint-Marceau, who came to see Midas in rags bet the indigent windfall drawn from the ooze of that Pactolus [25] on the turn of a dirty card, laughing the while. Ezekiel was the only one who won a little silver therefrom; whether the tale of the first wreck retrieved from the river–the diamond ring–was truth or fiction, Ezekiel certainly made a tidy profit.

Ezekiel was a tall, thin fellow, whose hair and complexion were yellowing. He had a spare figure, a vacuous gaze and a bloodless smile. His guile was hidden beneath a thick layer of innocence. You all know these parochials–half Norman, half Jew–who are a match for the Auvergneans themselves when it comes to rascality [26]. Before becoming a capitalist, Ezekiel had been a fisherman himself; he knew from experience how to arrange a rendezvous with the fish by laying bait beforehand in the appropriate place. Had he prepared a place here not for fish but for dupes? That idea had not yet occurred to anyone.

The only surprising thing in the story of Ezekiel was the unusual good luck with which he had overcome the material difficulties opposed to the initial establishment of his inn. Then, as today, the Quai de Béthune presented a rigid and monumental alignment. There was no room for anything but a hut. On the far end, in the neighborhood of the Hôtel Lambert–which nowadays lends its name to the female baths–a few cottages could be found, but their backs were turned to the spot consecrated by the first find. Given that the Casino had to be close to the shore, there was no better choice than the corner of the Rue de Bretonvilliers, except that the two corners of that street were formed by the rectangular stone walls of two devilishly huge town-houses, as thick as ramparts. The real miracle, for Ezekiel, was to have obtained permission to assault one of those angles and hollow out his hovel within the thickness of that noble masonry, like some impudent larva rounding out its resting-place in the healthy wood of a great tree.

But Ezekiel had obtained that permission. The inn of *The Miraculous Catch*, a sort of irregular cavern, insinuated itself into the bowels of the battlements, only taking up about a third of the height of the ground floor. Since the Marais has gained the favor of industry, a number of its remaining town-houses have followed this example, opening their own flanks like pelicans, not for charity but for avarice. The floor of Ezekiel's inn was a little lower than street-level. One could eat, drink and play there, buy fishing-line, rods, hooks, bait–everything one needed, in a word, to catch fish furnished with signet rings.

The house in question was owned by a respectable old man, Monsieur d'Aubremesnil: and old parliamentary councilor, who was no exile but lived at Versailles. The only part of the property that was occupied was a lodge situated at the end of a big garden, whose entrance was on the Rue Saint-Louis opposite the grounds of the Hôtel Lambert. This lodge had been leased some months previously by a young woman of rare beauty, who lived alone and devoted herself to good works.

When our man, the "boss" of the stonemasons of the Marché-Neuf, arrived on the threshold of the semi-subterranean hovel where the brave Ezekiel was master after God, he hesitated, so repulsive and obscene was the appearance of the cavern.

Paris threw such soiled garments away a long time ago. Paris, despite the exaggerations of certain pen-painters, is one of the least dishonored places in the universe. That which has become a monstrous exception in today's Paris is encountered everywhere in the best parts of London, that Babylon of glacial debauchery and immodest ennui–but the mores of Paris, in 1804, still bore the shameless stamp of the Directory.

The lantern of *The Miraculous Catch* did not light the interior very well. Inside, there was a hazy half-light, swarming with scarcely-veiled nudities. Half a dozen women were

67

there, wallowing on wooden sofas covered with a few strands of straw, drinking, playing or watching the play of an equal number of men, who belonged to the most abandoned class of idlers.

It was not French, to tell the truth, any more than Paul Niquet's stupid and cold "nights" are French [27]. Such hideous things are best regarded as the borrowed hopelessness of English degradation. London alone is a frame favorable to such unremitting horrors, where vice adopts the physiognomy of torture and wretches amuse themselves as if they were suffering in Hell. In Paris, vice always retains a healthy portion of braggadocio, but in London serious and committed perdition swims in the mire as naturally as fish in water. Whoever has penetrated by night the "spiritshops" of the old district of Saint Giles, or even the "gin palaces" crowded together in the midst of the fashionable area around Covent Garden, would recognize the truth of this saying: in Paris, horror is an eccentric fashion; in London, it is the fruit of terror [28].

The guardian hesitated as the fetid exhalations emerging from below caught him by the throat, but his hesitation did not last. He was a man well used to overcoming obstacles.

I know another vault, he thought, *where the air is worse still.*

And he entered, smiling sadly.

Although his costume certainly did not give him the appearance of a nobleman, and even an honest businessman would have looked with disdain upon the coarse material of his clothing, there was such a contrast between his bearing and that of the regulars in *The Miraculous Catch* that his appearance caused quite a stir.

It was not unknown for an honest man, excused by his passion for fishing, to enter Ezekiel's establishment by day. It served, as we have already observed, as a shop for fishing equipment of every kind. After nightfall, though, the hovel showed its true face so clearly that the most valiant of sightseers would have taken to his heels after a single glance into the interior.

"Look at the lamb!" said one of the wallflowers.

"More like a sheep," riposted a rogue fit for the gallows, who was playing a hand of *foutreau* (a noble game which is a derivative of *bouillotte*) [29] and whose hooked nose had a drogue, or pair of wooden tongs, jauntily posed across it. "Old mutton–and tough! D'you want to see to him, Ezekiel?"

Ezekiel had needed no urging; a dog follows its nose. He came towards the guardian suspiciously, his pipe in his mouth.

"What do you need, Citizen?"

"Wine," the boss replied, taking a seat.

"My wine isn't good enough for a gentleman of your sort," Ezekiel said.

The women burst out laughing, and the men cried: "The gent's lost his way."

The boss took off his hat, which was far from new, and put it on the table. His balding head did, indeed, give him the appearance of a gentleman–and the impression was sealed by the facile frankness of his big blue eyes–but there was something else there too. This sheep had an indefinable something of the wolf about him. His neck was broad, his movements expansive and supple; despite the placid manner he affected, there was something about him that spoke of muscular strength and athleticism. The men came to feel ill at ease under his gaze, and the women stopped jeering.

"Give me your wine, such as it is, friend," he said to Ezekiel, "And be quick–I'm thirsty."

This time the innkeeper obeyed, muttering. By the time he came back with a full half-pint pewter jug and a moist glass, the rogues and their princesses had resumed their revels.

"Sit down here, friend," the guardian said to Ezekiel, touching a stool with his foot, "so that the two of us can have a chat."

"Do you think I have the time to chat...?" Ezekiel began.

"I don't know whether you have the time, friend, and I don't care. I need to talk to you. Have a chair."

"And if I don't want to...?" the innkeeper said.

"If you don't want to," the boss interrupted him, while filling his glass, "we shall have to speak loudly about a subject you would rather discuss quietly." He drank.

Ezekiel sat down.

"The fact is, friend, that your wine is detestable." the boss continued, calmly. "How much did it cost you to obtain permission to deface d'Aubremesnil's town house with this corner-cupboard?"

Ezekiel lowered his large eyelids as a glimmer of anger flared behind them.

"And what cemetery have you profaned," the boss went on, "in order to give so much dead flesh to the fish hereabouts? You see, friend I know that you're not a tiger–merely a jackal."

The innkeeper's wrath fought with an evident terror. Both emotions were betrayed by the contraction of his features and the pallor of his lips. "Who are you?" he demanded.

"I am the man who comes and goes by night along the river," the guardian replied, "but I don't hunt the same game there as you do. We ran into one another on the night you became rich."

"Ah!" said Ezekiel. "So that was you." He added, in a dull voice: "There was a dead man in your boat too!"

The guardian nodded his head gravely in agreement. Then he took a six-*livre pièce* from his pocket and deposited it on the table.

"I'm not rich, friend," he said, "and I've no desire to harm you. I'll leave here as I entered if you will let me know the name of the woman you paid. You're nothing but a blind instrument; no misfortune will come to you through me..."

The innkeeper had lowered his head. He stepped back suddenly and grabbed his stool by one foot in order to brandish it over his head.

"Help me, lads!" he cried. "This is one of Cadoudal's agents. He came here to buy men to kill the First Consul! His head must have a high price on it–let's go for it!"

This accusation, so patently absurd and completely un-related to the subject of the conversation it had interrupted, was not all that surprising. The moment was prepared for war. The hour had arrived in Paris when the first-comer might have killed a passer-by accused of having thrown cholera powder into the Seine. The regulars of *The Miraculous Catch* leapt to their feet and threw themselves forward to bar the door.

The boss was smiling. "That's not the way I'm going," he murmured.

He got up in his turn and calmly replaced the wide-brimmed hat on his head. "Friend," he said, moving to the table where the gamblers had been seated, "that was a pretty good trick–but you don't know who you're dealing with, and it will take something much more powerful to embarrass me... make way!"

So saying, the boss snatched up the lamp from the table. As the innkeeper lifted his stool, he brushed it aside with a single movement of his hand, and went by.

The innkeeper took several backward steps, tottering, only stopping when he ran into the wall.

"That's some strength!" said the women, admiringly.

All the men had armed themselves with whatever came to hand; several of them had knives.

"If you can knock this mad dog down," Ezekiel snarled, "you'll get a big reward from the police."

The boss, meanwhile, lifted the lamp up high, then ran into the back of the room. There was some fishing equipment there: rolled-up nets and bundles of rods. He threw the rods aside without overmuch ado, and uncovered a door which he tested with his foot. The door yielded; it was not locked and it opened outwards.

"Knife him!" cried Ezekiel, hurling himself forward recklessly. "He knows too much. He mustn't get out alive!"

The boss turned around at the exact moment when the innkeeper reached him, well-supported by the others. The lamplight illuminated his extraordinary calm figure, which brought the surge of his assailants to a halt.

The boss handed the lamp to Ezekiel, who took it mechanically. "I've seen what I wanted to see," he said, "and I'll be on my way."

"He's a madman!" cried one of the women, seized by pity at the sight of him, still smiling and self-confident.

"Shut the street-door," Ezekiel ordered, "and finish the job."

"Now, now," said the boss, taking a fishing-rod and breaking it over his knee, snapping off the length necessary to provide a swordstick. "I've told you–you don't know who you're dealing with!" His smile broadened, and his eyes brightened.

As soon the street door closed, the boss was attacked from three sides at once: by Ezekiel, who had lifted his stool in both hands to aim a blow at his head, and by two ragamuffin bandits, one of whom lifted a weapon to stab at his side while the other thrust a club into his stomach.

There was a dramatic transformation. The boss' entire body took on a new character, boldly and swaggeringly youthful. His posture grew straighter, his chest expanded and his face lit up. No one present would have been able to say exactly how the three attacks were avoided. The boss' head had scarcely leaned to the left to let the stool pass by when his half-rod described two semi-circles, one of which sent the club flying through the air while the other struck the hand that held the dagger a sharp blow. The wounded men let out howls of pain and rage.

"Make sure that lamp doesn't go out!" the devil said, cheerfully, "or I won't be able to see well enough to punish you gently–that would be so much the worse for your heads!"

Ezekiel promptly moved to the rear. He armed himself with a long-handled gaff and took rapid account of his forces.

"La Meslin!" he cried, "The rogue has crippled your man for life. The women must get into the fight... if he wasn't so thin, I'd swear to you that it was Cadoudal in person. I bet my head on the guillotine that he's worth a thousand *écus* at the préfecture! Grab brands from the fireplace, my lovelies! Let's burn him! It's time to set the house on fire!"

La Meslin was a tall, broad-shouldered woman, who was already on her knees beside her stricken man. She got up again and pounced like a lion upon the fireplace, where the cooking-pot was simmering. She seized a burning brand and repeated: "Let's burn the beggar! Let's burn him!"

The men split into two groups, putting up their knives and cudgels, like the infantry who withdraw from the field while the gunners let fly. The hovel was full of smoke and flame; the six shrews hurled their torches.

The boss jumped to one side and the burning projectile launched by la Meslin sailed past his arm. The terrible cane described half a dozen circles, and for one long minute the interior of the inn was an indescribable turmoil of cries, blows, curses, falls, grindings of teeth–and a single pistol-shot.

Once the minute had run its course, this was the situation: our singular friend, the boss of the stonemasons of the Marché-Neuf, was standing in the dead center of the room, about which smoking brands were scattered in every direction. He had a black smudge on his right cheek, and a large burn on the back of his overcoat, but no serious wound had been inflicted on him.

On the floor of the inn the nets, ignited by the embers, caught fire.

Ezekiel no longer had the long-handled gaff, whose broken pieces were scattered on the ground; by way of compensation, his face bore a magnificent purple bruise and his toothless mouth was spitting blood.

La Meslin's man was rolling in the dirt, still clutching the discharged pistol in his hand. His frizzy hair had not protected his skull, which sported a wide cut.

The other bandits kept their distance, and the terrified women were huddled in a corner–except for la Meslin, who was trying to lift her lover's broken head.

Not a single word had been exchanged by the lone man and the many assailants laying siege to him.

At that moment, the lone man–whose eyes had lost their fulgurant gleam and who now seemed as calm as if he were strolling in the gardens of the Palais-Royal–put his cane under his arm and plunged his hand into his pocket.

"It's the devil himself!" moaned Ezekiel.

"You're ten against one," howled la Meslin, who got up, drunk with rage. "If we all attack him at once, my man will be avenged..."

She stopped, stifling an exclamation; the knife that she had snatched from the ground was no longer in her hand. "Ah!" she said, fixing the boss with a stupefied stare. "It's far worse than the devil... why didn't I recognize him? That's Monsieur Gâteloup!"

The name of Gâteloup was murmurously repeated in every corner of the room. La Meslin's lover opened his eyes and stared.

The boss had taken his hand out of his pocket and was calmly securing the object he had taken from it to his button-hole. At first glance, it seemed to justify Ezekiel's accusations, for the chouans of Brittany wore a similar sign on their hats or their chests, and Georges Cadoudal would have had one in his pocket–but long before the Breton chouans, the Brotherhood of Parisian masters-of-arms had consecrated that sign for its professors and provosts to carry on the left sides of their breastplates. It was a heart embroidered in gold and framed in a rosette of scarlet ribbons. Each master added to it a distinctive mark, which was a sort of blazon making his name known to initiates.

Now, the boss of the stonemasons of the Marché-Neuf was a local celebrity in his capacity as a good bourgeois, hats being raised to him all the way from the Palais de Justice to the City Hall. But in another capacity–as an adversary of scuffling revolutionaries, as a life-saver, as a leader and governor of men–Gâteloup's fame was universal, particularly among the poor. Good men loved and admired him; villains were in awe of him. In past times of danger–during the civil war, when he had played a role both terrible and benevolent–he had made himself recognizable by means of the badge that labeled him a master-of-arms: a heart of gold in a knot of red ribbons, within which a Saint Andrew's Cross was prominently marked out in black. This signified "I am Jean-Pierre Sévérin, called Gâte-loup" in exactly the same way that, in former times, gold *fleurs-de-lys* on a field of azure had signified Bourbon, coupled crystals Rohan, and six blue eaglets with crosses in their mouths on a field of gold Montmorency.

In ancient conflicts, there was no shame in a brave man retiring from the fray before a stronger foe. Achilles' chariot rode through battles without encountering any adversaries, save for those too myopic to recognize quickly enough the flamboyant shield presented by Hippodamia [30]. The rogues assembled in *The Miraculous Catch* were not imbued with any chivalric prejudices, but there was not a single hand that retained its weapon, and La Meslin pointed at her man as she said: "Ah, Citizen Gâteloup, I owe you an apology. You could have knocked me out if you'd wanted to."

"That's true, girl," the boss replied, "and if I'd put my name in my buttonhole, fear alone would have knocked you all out. Put out the fire, Ezekiel. The rest of you, make way."

Two or three buckets of water were thrown upon the nets which were slowly being consumed by fire. Ezekiel, a smile upon his lips, approached the conqueror. He was the worst of rascals, for he hid his rancor under an obsequious and flattering manner. "My dear master," he said, "we must have been out of our minds to think that there is any Parisian who could wish to kill Citizen Bonaparte. For myself, I see the traitor Cadoudal everywhere... and as for that door, it opens into the cellar where I keep the poor wine that you found so awful."

The boss put his hand on Ezekiel's shoulder.

The innkeeper seemed about to collapse, as if a weight too heavy to bear had descended upon him. "Don't hurt me," he murmured.

"Listen," said the boss. "Are you a man who can reply frankly and honestly to questions that are put to you?"

"As for that, master," Ezekiel exclaimed, "you can ask anyone. I'm always as frank as frank can be. Hand on heart! Ah, if I'd had an ounce of malice, my business would have been ruined long ago."

"You're working for a woman?" the boss said, in a low voice.

"For a woman?" Ezekiel repeated. "What an idea!" Then he added, winking his eye in a confidential manner: "Well then, yes. One can't hide anything from you, master. For a woman... and we try to put a spoke in the wheel of any villain who want to kill the First Consul... is that against the law?"

The boss' hand weighed even more heavily upon the innkeeper's shoulder, but at that moment a noisy and joyous clamor was heard through the street door.

"A godsend! A godsend!" was the cry. "Open up, Citizen Ezekiel!"

"There has been a miraculous catch!"

"And a successful hunt," added other voices, seemingly more distant.

"We have the fresh fish," said the fishermen.

"And we the game," said the hunters.

"Open up, Ezekiel. Look sharp about it, old man!"

"May I open it, good master?" asked the innkeeper, looking at the winner of the recent battle respectfully and submissively.

The boss made a gesture of consent.

The door swung on its hinges, and a numerous company entered, loaded with booty. The four who came in first, four strapping fellows, were carrying between them a little basket where there must have been at least fifty gudgeons. Behind them came the happy owner of the straw mannequin. In third place, two street-urchins were triumphantly holding up an old pair of trousers, in the pocket of which one had found a six-*liard pièce* [31].

"Look what we've caught!" was the cry. "Shut up shop, Ezekiel, there's nothing left in the river."

"I know who's playing these tricks on me," the inn-keeper replied, sadly. "It's the enemies of the First Consul!"

He was interrupted by a new wave of arrivals, shouting: "Look what we've found!"

On a makeshift stretcher of fishing rods, they were carrying some unfortunate poor child, unconscious or dead.

As soon as the lamplight fell on the face, which was white but still lovely, the boss of the stonemasons of the Marché-Neuf let loose an anguished cry.

It was a name: "Angela!"

Chapter V
The Boundary-Marker

In the first chapter of this story, we observed a young man, handsome and elegant, walking alone along the Quai de la Grève. Then, behind him, a charming young woman, also alone, who seemed to be following him at a distance. Then, finally, an old man, dressed as a bourgeois but nobly set-up, who was apparently following both of them. In the course of our narrative, we have discovered the name of the young man, René de Kervoz, and the name of the young woman: Angela. Those who have read the previous episode in this series, *La Chambre des Amours*, will already be familiar with the old bourgeois.

After the mysterious and almost silent scene which took place towards nightfall in the Church of Saint-Louis-en-l'Ile, featuring the dazzling blonde who was addressed as Madame la Comtesse, Ramberg the German, René and Abbé Martel–the scene of which the medical student Germain Patou and Angela had both been silent witnesses–René de Kervoz had left first. Angela had followed soon after, as if she were making for the Place du Châtelet.

She seemed very weak; she staggered along slowly and painfully–but poor wounded hearts possess a terrible courage.

The darkness was not yet total when René de Kervoz left by the side door that led to the Rue Poultier. Instead of turning towards the Quai de Béthune, as Germain Patou and "the boss" would later do, he went back towards the Rue Saint-Louis. His pace was also slow and uncertain, but not because he was enfeebled.

Those who knew him, if they could have looked him in the face at that moment, would have been astonished to observe the fierce redness that had replaced the usual pallor of his cheek. His eyes burned beneath his tightly-contracted eyelids.

Angela, poor gentle child, had grown up in the company of two good and simple hearts: her adopted father and her mother; the only two friends she had in the world. She knew nothing of life. She could not see anything of René's face; in consequence, she could not read the book of his physiognomy–but who knows from where she obtained her second sight? Hearts sick with love have their own witchcraft; that which she could not see, Angela divined.

The passion which distressed the features of René de Kervoz had its dolorous and woebegone echo in the soul of Angela. She had no thought for herself; her mind was full of him. Was she suffering? Sometimes it is happiness that crushes one thus, but the dread of happiness is almost as great as the dread of suffering. Angela was not yet entirely a woman. Girls love differently than women; Angela was halfway between a woman and a girl.

René turned the corner of the Rue de Saint Louis and went towards the section of the Quai d'Anjou which faces the Ile Louviers.

It was not the first time that Angela had followed René. She was entitled to follow him, if such a right is conferred by the most sacred of all promises: the contract of honor binding a man to the pure child who is given to him. Angela was the acknowledged fiancée of René de Kervoz, his wife before God.

Never had she seen so much before today.

That which she had suspected in her heart for some time had tonight become a bitter certainty. René loved another woman, and not as he had loved her: gently and reverently. Oh, what happiness she had lost!

René loved another woman: loved her with fervor and with anguish.

Halfway along the Rue Poultier, at the eastern turning to the Quai d'Anjou, a monumental wall formed the corner of the

Rue Bretonvilliers, on the other side of which was the inn of *The Miraculous Catch*. The block of properties between the two streets formed the eastern extremity of the Ile; it comprised Bretonvilliers Lodge and the Aubremesnil house, with their gardens. These two buildings, separated only by a magnificent avenue of trees, belonged to the same owner, the old parliamentary councilor who has already been mentioned. Beyond these noble dwellings, there were several smaller houses forming a facade along the street. Bretonvilliers Lodge, which was the only remaining wing of a much older house–perhaps some sort of manor-house of the era when the Ile was still in the Paris countryside–was wedged in by the wall, and even projected into the road for several feet (which would be the cause of its subsequent demolition). It had only two stories; the first with three windows overlooking the street; the second, much higher, with five. The whole was surmounted by a peaked roof. There was no doorway on the ground floor. One gained access by a door in the wall to the right of the facade, which led into the gardens.

It was on this door that René de Kervoz knocked.

The deep and hollow voice of a barking dog, which seemed as if it could only come from the mouth of a giant, responded to his call. An old woman dressed in a strange costume came to open the door. She barred René's way, saying to him: "The owners are away."

"*Salus Hungariae,*" René responded, pronouncing the Latin words in the Magyar fashion.

The old woman looked him in the face, seemingly hesitant. "*Introi, domine,*" she said, finally, "*sub auctoritate dominae meae.*" Which means: "enter sir, by the authority of my mistress." She too spoke Latin with a Hungarian accent.

The door closed again. The resounding crack of a birch-rod put an end to the barking of the guard-dogs.

Angela was too far away to see or hear this. By the time she arrived at the door, all was silent inside. She stopped still, as downcast as a statue of Discouragement. She did not weep. It never entered her head to knock on the door. Why had she come, anyway? Alas, they do not know, these pour wounded souls. They come to catch a glimpse at the very foundations of their unhappiness, not to fight. When the idea of fighting occurs to them, they nearly always push valor to the point of madness, but the idea of fighting usually comes to them too late. They remain so long in doubt! They cling so hard to the cherished illusion of hope!

Angela remained standing before the door for some time, her heart oppressed, her eyes half-closed. No noise came from within. The outside was equally silent, for night had fallen and the sound of the lamplighters' footfalls had ceased. Only one murmurous sound, confused and intermittent, came from the side of the Quai de Béthune, where the inn of *The Miraculous Catch* was still open.

Facing the door through which René had disappeared, at the corner of a house whose windows were all dark and which seemed as uninhabited as most of the dwellings in this miserable district, there was a granite boundary-marker encircled with iron.

Angela sat down on it.

From there the windows of the ancient Bretonvilliers Lodge could be seen. They too were dark, enormously high and strangely lit by the moon, which sent its rays obliquely upon them as it rose out of the shadow to its zenith in the south. Mechanically, Angela's gaze fixed itself upon those three gigantic lattices, behind which huge muslin curtains could be discerned. She saw, as one sees things in a dream, one of these curtains part and a head appear. The moon's rays could only pick out its outline, and that vaguely. It was a young head, a well-beloved head whose face and features Angela saw night and day, whose mouth had said to her: "I love you!"

Oh, and that smile! And that hair, so soft that a chaste kiss ruffled it as easily as her own.

René! Her entire soul, her first, her only love!

It was René. It was definitely René. Why was he in this place? And alone? Who was he waiting for?

Who was he waiting for?

The moon was obscured; the shadow concealed the smile which perhaps did not even exist. For Angela, at least, René smiled, ever so gently–and through those accursed panes, René looked at her with such tenderness.

Could it be? If René had seen her, if René had recognized her, he in that house and she in the street, on that boundary-marker, René could not have smiled. Oh, surely not. He was good, he was noble. He would have been ashamed, remorseful, afraid.

But what did it matter whether it was possible or impossible? The time comes when the mind no longer makes judgments; fever takes over. Angela reached out her poor tremulous hands towards René and began to talk to him in a low voice. She said those soft things to him that loving children say to one another over and over again in order to enchant the best hours of life. Her heart recited from memory the litany of youthful tenderness. How she loved! How she was loved! Could it be, dear Lord, that those solemn oaths that once gushed forth from one soul to another, to form an indissoluble bond, were meaningless?

Could it be? For there was more between them than solemn oaths, and René was noble and good. We have only said it once; she repeated it to herself a hundred times. She did not feel the iciness of her hands, or her little feet freezing on the moist pavement of that cold February night. She only knew that her brow was feverish.

One night, the previous autumn, the night air had been so mild and so inviting that they had gone for a walk along the Quai de la Grève, and then along the riverbank as far as the Pont-Marie. There were flowers and a lawn around the towpath inspector's cabin; René wanted to sit down; he was weak then, and ill; Angela laid her scarf out on the grass for him. She placed herself so close to him, so happy and so beautiful that René had tears in his eyes. He said to her: "If you stopped loving me, I should die."

Angela had made no reply, because the thought had never entered her head that René could ever stop loving her. It was a wonderful evening, whose memory could never be effaced. While passing over the Pont-Marie, Angela had suddenly caught sight of the great elms.

But now, whispering, as if René had been right beside her, Angela said in her turn: "If you stopped loving me, I should die."

The moon was obscured, and the facade of Bretonvilliers Lodge fell into shadow. It was impossible to see René's silhouette in the high window–and yet Angela saw it still. In the pitch blackness, she divined a beloved form; but René was no longer smiling. His face was sad, thinned down, wrought with emotion, as it had been on the night of the walk along the riverbank, and it seemed to Angela that the distance between them vanished; she climbed up, he came down; both of them were supported by an antique balcony, one within and one without, and they exchanged murmurous words, intermingled with long kisses.

Suddenly, Angela started and woke up–for that really had been a dream. The black facade had changed: two of the great windows were vividly illuminated.

Angela had not been mistaken. René's silhouette was outlined in shadow in the luminous depths. He had not left the window. Angela stifled a cry, because another silhouette stood out behind René's: a feminine form, young and admirably graceful, which Angela recognized at first sight. "The woman of the Church of Saint-Louis!" she murmured, clasping both hands to her heaving breast. "Her again!"

She tried to stand up, but could not. She had wanted to throw herself forward in defense of her happiness. In the midst of her confusion, however, one thought surfaced. "The door has not opened since René went in," she said, "and that woman could not have preceded him, because she left the church in the company of... how did she get in there?"

The feminine shadow neatly defined by the light that shone behind her was projected on to the transparent curtain.

Her slender figure could be seen, and the fine details of her coiffeur, where the light played upon the moving curls of her hair.

"Her hair!" Angela repeated. "Her blonde hair! There has never been anything like it. I believe I can make out its glints of gold... she is too beautiful. Oh René, my René, love her not! One cannot have two loves. If you stopped loving me, I should die..."

The image of two hands clasping was cast on the revealing curtain.

Angela stood up, galvanized by a terrible anguish. "But before dying," she said, "I shall fight! I am strong! I have courage! And who will ever love him as I do? He is mine..."

She slumped down again on the boundary-marker. On high, behind the muslin curtains, an attentive arm wound around the slender figure. Again, Angela stammered; "I am strong... I shall fight..." But she broke off, the words caught in her throat.

She pressed her icy hands to her forehead.

"It's a dream–a frightful dream!" she said. "I want to wake up..."

Her voice was strangled. The shadows on the curtain turned towards one another, presenting their profiles: two young and handsome profiles. A heart-rending pain clutched at Angela's bosom. She had an anguished wait, for it was only slowly... so very slowly... that the two mouths came together for a long, ardent kiss.

Angela fell to the pavement, an inert mass. Her disordered hair fell from her hood as it slipped from her shoulders: beautiful hair, softer than that of the enchantress herself.

The silhouette of the woman drew back first and flew away, while a resounding burst of laughter came through the windows. René's shadow followed it. Then the third window in the facade was suddenly illuminated. The two shadows passed by it, interlaced, before vanishing–but Angela saw no more of that. Her inert body was stretched out at full length.

There was nothing between her poor forehead and the pavement but her scattered hair.

Half an hour later, a group of idlers came by, having left the edge of the Quai de Béthune. No shadows were displayed on the windows of Bretonvilliers Lodge now. The idlers, who were going home with their fishing-baskets empty, came upon Angela's body. The hunt was more profitable than the fishing: around Angela's neck there was a gold cross, a present from René de Kervoz.

The idlers immediately began to argue over who should have the gold cross. It was soon decided that they should take it to Ezekiel's inn, where the Jew would doubtless be able to value the object and purchase it, so that they could divide the money between them.

They had reckoned without the boss of the stonemasons of the Marché-Neuf, Monsieur Jean-Pierre Sévérin, called Gâteloup. He took off his overcoat to drape it over the icy limbs of the young woman. Upon his orders, which no one dreamed of disputing, four porters made a litter on which Angela was deposited on a mattress. Then the boss said: "Let's go!" And the porters marched off without even asking where they were going.

In the end, the hunt proved to be worth even less than the fishing on the Quai de Béthune that night.

When La Meslin had led away her injured man and the rogues of both sexes had departed, Ezekiel barricaded the door. That brave fellow was anxious, and in a rather bad humor. While extinguishing the magnificent lantern that was the glory of his establishment and the neighborhood, he said: "That's a game to break one's bones. If anyone were to find out that all this is to distract the dogs, and hide the vampire's hole..."

He shivered and looked around. "Every time I pronounce that name," he muttered, "I get gooseflesh. I don't believe in them, but all the same, there must be something in it... and I would love to see for myself the mine dug out in the flesh of such a beast when a red-hot iron is plunged into its heart. That would be amusing!"

His smile was both sensual and villainous.

He used his feet to kick away the half-burned nets encumbering the back door and opened it, still thinking aloud. "It's not easy to fill a pot with small change!"

Beyond the door was the dark passage that had been glimpsed by the boss, which led to a stone stairway. After the descent of the stairway, the corridor went up again to a second door, which opened into a large garden. As soon as Ezekiel had opened that second door, a bellowing roar sounded in the distance; the reader will immediately recognize the voice of the giant dog which guarded Bretonvilliers Lodge.

"Everyone knows the devil in the country from which these people come," Ezekiel said to himself. "That dog has the voice of a demon."

He passed beneath a dark row of lime trees, cut into a hedge, which extended towards the Rue de Saint-Louis-en-Ile. The watchdog's barking soon became so violent that the frightened innkeeper came to a halt.

"Hola! Goodwife Paraxin!" he cried. "Hold back your dog, or I'll smash his head with a pistol-shot!"

A burst of laughter burst forth from the nearby thicket and made him jump.

"The dog's chained up, you old French Quaker." The words came from behind the trees. "There's no need to be afraid–and as for the pistol, it went off in your place, down below. Was it something to do with your fish?"

Before Ezekiel could reply, a woman as tall as a man, dressed in Hungarian costume, stepped into a shaft of light that the moon had directed into the avenue.

"Good evening, Ezekiel," she said, in barbarous French that she pronounced with difficulty. "One can't speak to you Parisians in Latin, you're as ignorant as slaves. Have you something to tell us?"

"I want to see Madame the Countess," the innkeeper replied.

86

"Madame the Countess isn't here," Paraxin said. She towered over Ezekiel by a head now that she was close to him. "She's busy this evening."

"She's eating someone?" the innkeeper asked, his curiosity mingled with horror.

Paraxin patted him gently on the head. "She's eating two."

Ezekiel recoiled in spite of himself.

The big woman laughed derisively. "What do you have to say?" she asked again.

"I have to say," Ezekiel replied, "that all this can't go on. Everyone's talking. There are two people on the track, and the charade of the Quai de Béthune has gone to the wire. It will all be over in a fortnight."

"It will all be over in a week," the big woman corrected him. "The money's coming and the account will be paid. Those who stick with us to the end will have their fortunes made. Those who lose their nerve before then will be fattening the fishes. Is that all?"

Ezekiel remained silent.

"What are you thinking?" the Hungarian demanded, abruptly.

"Goodwife Paraxin," the innkeeper replied, "I think I'm afraid. Your threats frighten the life out of me. I can't hide it, because you're looking at me like a devil incarnate..."

The Hungarian tipped his chin with her finger.

"But I'm even more afraid," Ezekiel went on, "of the dangers that surround me on every side because of you. What will it profit me to have lots of money, if I lose my head?"

Madame Paraxin slapped him heartily between his shoulders and cursed him in Latin. Afterwards, her tone became serious as she said: "We've drawn attention away from you, brave man, have no fear of that... do you see that light down there?"

They had arrived at the end of the avenue, and the tall shadow of Bretonvilliers Lodge was silhouetted against the sky.

"Yes, I see the light," Ezekiel replied, "but what does it mean?"

"It means, my son, that there is a handsome young man there, in the process of burning himself in the candle-flame. Thanks to that moth, we have two or three weeks of safety, should we desire it."

"Who is the moth?"

"Georges Cadoudal's very own nephew, my lad–who will sell us, for a smile... or for a kiss, or something a little dearer... the secret of his uncle's hiding-place."

Chapter VI
The Isolated House

The room was very large, and so high-ceilinged that one might have thought it a hall in some ancient royal palace. The tapestries were faded, dulled by decay, but they must have been very beautiful when their colorists had found harmony in the subtlest nuances and played games with the solar spectrum in order to obtain their skillful effects–such games that, for example, their paint-brushes gave a marvelous co-ordination even to the costume of a mendicant. The lamp enclosed in a globe of Bohemian glass–which was not frosted but engraved in imitation of the semi-transparency of opal–hardly clarified that vast expanse, endowing every object with a discreet and almost mysterious light. It was impossible to make out the paintings on the ceiling, or even those on the panels, which were cut into octagonal *cartouches* according to the fashion characteristic of the epoch of Louis XIV. A few muted glints of polished gilt could be glimpsed here and there. In front of the two large windows, drapes of damask silk displayed a multiplicity of capacious folds, with soft curtains of Indian muslin behind them.

The general impression made by the room was of space and austerity, but above all of sadness–which is almost always the case with works of the Middle Ages that the 17th century attempted to refurbish. It was through the windows of this room, behind the Indian muslin curtains, that Angela had first seen René's face lit by the moonlight, then the two shadows whose amorous combat the glass had betrayed.

Now there was no one here–but the vibrant light that passed through the half-open door from the neighboring room, which had no casement overlooking the street and was the last to be lit, indicated the route to be taken in order to rediscover René de Kervoz together with she whom Germain Patou had called the queen of blondes: Abbé Martel's radiant penitent, the unknown of the Church of Saint-Louis-en-l'Ile.

The jealousy of women who are profoundly in love is rarely mistaken. There is a subtle and sure instinct in them, which picks out the preferred rival. Angela had recognized the profile of her rival on the muslin curtains, and we have explained how it came about that Angela, within that moving silhouette, had even divined the delicate gold which hung in delectable curls over the forehead of the stranger.

Let us now pass through that half-open door from which the alluring light is shining.

This was a much smaller room, and the threshold dividing the two chambers might have been accounted a distance of six hundred leagues, separating the Occident from the Orient. On the far side of that threshold, in effect, was the Orient: a carpet as thickly-piled as a lawn; heaps of cushions; perfumed candles. You might have imagined that you had entered one of those enchanted boudoirs where the wealthy daughters of southern Hungary competed in magnificence and luxury with the Queens of the Thousand-and-One Nights.

The contrast was striking and complete. On the right hand was the melancholy and slightly mildewed stiffness of a grandiose era; on the left of the partition sprawled the voluptuous luxury and semi-barbaric sumptuousness of the Ottoman frontier, as if one might open the casement and see the minarets of the white city of Belgrade on the horizon. In the first room, it was cold; here there was a soft warmth, adrift in tepid currents charged with odorant languor.

The light of two magnificent lamps, modified by two cupolas of rose crystal, fell upon an ottoman surrounded by exotic arborescent shrubs in full flower. A young man and a young woman were there: two creatures as beautiful as any in creation. The young woman was stretched out on the ottoman; the young man was at her feet, seated on cushions. They had cast the two silhouettes on the muslin: René de Kervoz first, whom Angela would have known among a thousand–and so far as the woman was concerned, Angela had not been mistaken in identifying her profile as that of the blonde foreigner. The features offered, indeed, a perfect parity: the same eyes, the same smiling and haughty mouth, the same exquisitely delicate face–except that the beautiful blonde hair, so brilliant and vaporous, had existed only in Angela's imagination. The young woman on the ottoman had beautiful hair, to be sure, but it was blacker than jet.

A single glance was sufficient to see that in spite of the very close resemblance, that this was not the mysterious Countess of Saint-Louis-en-l'Ile.

At the precise moment when we entered the boudoir, she was touching that adorable black hair saucily, and she said, smiling: "I never would have thought that anyone could have mistaken one of us for the other: she so blonde, me so dark... least of all my handsome Breton cavalier, who claims that my image is graven on his heart!"

René, lost in a sort of ecstatic contemplation, made no reply. He lifted a graceful little hand to his lips and relished a long kiss. "Lila!" he murmured.

She leaned over him and stroked his forehead lightly, saying: "My name is soft in your mouth."

That stirred a memory; a cloud passed over René's face. Once, that poor child who had given him her heart–Angela, his fiancée–had said to him: "In your mouth, my name is as soft as an assurance of love." He had loved her a great deal, and had fought against the passion for another that had now overtaken that love, as a kind of madness. He loved in spite of himself, in spite of his reason, in spite of his heart; he was in the grip of an irresistible fascination. These observations may provide an excuse to those who believe in spells and charms.

Angela was devout. About two weeks before, on the evening of February 12th, René had accompanied her to the evening service at Saint-Germain-l'Auxerrois. While Angela prayed, René had dreamed of the impending joy of their undoubted union. There had been a woman kneeling not far from them. René saw two gleams of light beneath her veil–but I do not know how the light of the altar candles could possibly have penetrated the shadow where the unknown was. René felt a vague unease. His gaze returned to Angela, who was praying in such a saintly fashion. He was fearful and remorseful, and only obtained relief by the effort which he made to refrain from turning his eyes again towards the unknown.

He left with Angela and escorted her to her door. Their homes were close to one another; he left her to go to his own– but for some reason he could not have explained, he retraced his steps to the church. At the door he hesitated, for he understood that it would be a kind of treason even to cross that threshold. Anyway, she would soon be leaving.

She!

René went in, even as he said to himself: "I shall not go in."

Their paths crossed as he reached the basin of holy water. In spite of himself, René's finger plunged into the marble bowl. The hand of the unknown touched his; a chill went to his heart.

That was all. She left.

René remained where he was, immobile, saying: "I shall not follow her." A voice distracted him, murmuring the name of Angela within him and saying: "It is she who is happiness; the other is extravagant caprice, fever, torment, the fall..."

Why is it always thus? René threw himself after the unknown. His heart raced, his head burned.

There was no one in the square, bordered by small houses, which separated the front of Saint-Germain-l'Auxerrois from the as-yet-unrestored Louvre. A singular thing, requiring explanation, was that René had not even seen the person whom he was pursuing in spite of himself. He knew nothing of her but the glimmer of her gaze and the vague profile outlined by the light descending from the altar. When their hands had touched at the basin of holy water, the unknown's face had been hidden behind her veil. That it was a young woman of marvelous beauty he had certainly decided, but he could not have put any detail to the impression with which her severe but very elegant costume had left him. She carried it wonderfully, and while she moved away, René had admired the noble gracefulness of her walk–but can so little inspire love, especially when the heart is already bound, firmly and seriously?

René was honor personified. He came from a land where honor was everything. He had been raised from childhood in a simple and strict family, to which political passion alone had access. Even political passion had slept for some time in the Kervoz manor-house, situated between Vannes and Auray. René's father had fought as well as he could, but he had laid down his arms abruptly and without afterthought as soon as the gates of the parish reopened to worship [32]. There were two kinds of chouan in Brittany: the King's chouans and God's. When the last rites are administered to the old granite house which blesses births, marriages and deaths, it will be utterly devoid of the ranks of the rustic army. René's father had said to his son: "The past has gone; the future awaits judgment." He was one of God's chouans. But René's mother had a brother who was one of the King's chouans. There was talk of him sometimes in the manor-house near Vannes. He ran through Europe, conspiring and raising up the enemies of those who had taken the place of the King. His name was notorious. He had sworn loudly to engage himself–alone and outlawed though he be–in a sort of single combat with the First Consul, who was surrounded by so many soldiers and defended by so much glory.

All those who have been educated in our universities ought to be embarrassed when they are called upon to pass judgment on an action of this kind. Common sense says that the true name of such a tournament is assassination–but the University, for eight fatal years, has taken the trouble to teach us all other names, Latin or Greek. Everyone remembers the classical admiration of his professor for the dagger of Brutus. "In open senate, messieurs, in open senate," our own said to us–who, however, accepted from Caesar a salary of a thousand

93

écus a year, no more and no less. He added: "He was certainly a *vir fortis et ubicumque paratus* [33]. The fellow had pluck! In open senate, messieurs, in open senate."

Cassius, the collaborator, also reaped his fair share of eulogies. And there still remained something nice to be said about all the citizens from Harmodius and Aristogiton [34] to the friends of Paul I of Russia [35], who engaged in precisely the kind of tournament that Georges Cadoudal proposed to the First Consul. Since Caesar has written a book, of course, Brutus's dagger receives a little less praise in our colleges–but Caesar's book is very young, and we who would be elevated by the University to an amorous respect of the man and his instrument retained a certain embarrassment in repudiating the admiration imposed upon us: "In open senate, messieurs." Applaud–or look out for your salary. Perhaps a day will come when the University, converted to less ferocious sentiments, will help Caesar to correct the proofs of his book. We hope that on that day, Brutus' dagger–definitively put into retirement–will rust in the groves of academe. So let it be! But I ask of heaven and earth how the University, before its conversion, could possibly reproach the sword of Georges Cadoudal?

René de Kervoz, Cadoudal's nephew, was not involved in his desperate intrigues. In Paris he was enrolled on a course at Law College, preparing himself for a career as an advocate. We should add that his uncle took great care to keep him away from the dangerous path he had adopted for himself; there was a sincere affection between them. Of the conspiracy of which his uncle was the leader, René knew that which everyone knew–for the police, as we have already said, were in the position of those husbands who are the only ones ignorant of their misfortune. In Paris, the Cadoudal affair was the secret of the comedy; everyone was talking about it.

As far as anyone could say, the whereabouts of the terrible Breton were a mystery, but the mystery–and this is perfectly certain–lay entirely in the chronic blindness of the police. We have seen something similar in our day, and only people who do not know that chronic myopia can affect the hundred eyes of Argus will believe that in certain epochs the police partake in the weaknesses of the University in regard to the toolshed which served Brutus.

Cadoudal knew and approved of his nephew's love for Angela. He had formed a relationship, under an assumed name, with the adoptive family of the young woman and wished to serve as a father to René for the marriage. We should add that he had discussed the conditions of the contract, in good faith, with Jean-Pierre Sévérin, called Gâteloup, the boss of the stonemasons of the Marché-Neuf. Jean-Pierre held Monsieur Morinière in high esteem and amity. (Morinière was the assumed name of Georges Cadoudal.)

Cadoudal had said to his nephew: "Your Angela will make the most delectable *comtesse* that was ever seen. Me, I'll have a cracked head one of these days, there's no doubt about it–but when the king returns, you'll be made a *comte* as a memorial to me, and devil take me if the nephew of old Georges is not as noble as any marquis in the universe!"

René had replied: "I love her for what she is. She will be the wife of an advocate, and I shall try to make her happy."

And they discussed the wedding reception. Georges in Paris was like a fish in the sea, so well did he calculate the somnolence of the police. Memoirs of the time–the memoirs of policemen most of all–avow that he came and went easily, pursuing his occupation just as you or I, and living quite happily. Caesar must sometimes regret that he is not guarded by a simple poodle.

While leaving the Church of Saint-Germain-l'Auxerrois, René de Kervoz looked all around him, his expression troubled and his chest constricted. It was the name of Angela that came to his lips, as if he sought in their holy affection a refuge from his madness.

He was mad already. He sensed it.

At the corner of the Rue des Prêtres-Saint-Germain, a form was disappearing. René took the steps in one bound and ran after her. An elegant carriage was standing at the junction where the Rue des Prêtres opened into the Place de l'Ecole.

The carriage door opened, then closed again. The horses set off at a rapid trot.

René had not seen the person who had climbed into the carriage, and yet he followed it as fast as his legs could carry him. It was certain that the carriage contained his unknown woman.

The magnificent horses drawing the carriage trotted for a long time. Sweat inundated René's brow. He was short of breath but not of courage, and he did not pause in his pursuit. The carriage followed the Quais as far as the City Hall, then went back up the Rue Saint-Antoine, in which it came to an abrupt halt. The doors remained closed; the footman alone got down, knocked on a door, went in, came out again and resumed his place, saying: "Go! The doctor will come."

René had taken advantage of the pause to regain his breath. When the carriage set off again, he continued following it. What did he want, though? He would not have known how to answer that question. He went on, drawn by an irresistible force.

The carriage stopped twice more, in the Rue Culture-Sainte-Catherine and the Chaussée-des-Minimes. Twice the footman got down and got up again without having any communication with the interior of the carriage.

After leaving the Chaussée-des-Minimes, the carriage went back to the Rue Saint-Antoine. At that moment the clock on the Church of Saint-Paul chimed ten o'clock.

This time the journey was long and very hard on René. The horse-drawn carriage hurtled up the Rue Saint-Antoine at full speed, crossed the Place de la Bastille and continued through the Faubourg Saint-Antoine without slackening its pace. There was then a large empty space between the last houses of the Faubourg and the Place du Trône. The Rue de la Muette was nothing but a narrow causeway bordered by marshland.

The carriage finally came to a halt in front of an isolated dwelling in the region neighboring the Rue de la Muette. There was no light in the windows of that dwelling, which was approached by a side-road across the fields. In front of the door, on the far side of the driveway, a wall was falling into ruins, allowing one to see through its breaches a field of fruit-bearing bushes: raspberries, blackcurrants and gooseberries, overgrown by a few meager cherry trees.

René was a good runner; even so, in spite of his efforts, he had finally been left far behind by the galloping horses. He saw the carriage turn in the distance, then come to a halt, but it was too dark for him to make out what happened at the door of the house.

When he arrived at the entrance to the side-road, the carriage, retracing its steps, set out once again for the Faubourg Saint-Antoine. The windows in the two carriage-doors were now pulled down. René was able to dart a glance into the interior, which seemed to him to be empty. The coachman and the valet were still at their stations.

The carriage went back along the road which had brought it and vanished into the Faubourg.

René hesitated. His reason, reawakened for a moment, rebelled energetically against the absurdity of his conduct. He asked himself once more, with sudden anger against himself: "What am I doing here?"

He was from a land whose superstitions were obstinate. The idea occurred to him that someone had cast a spell on him—and he said to himself, determined to put an end to the sorry escapade: "I shall go no further!"

But the same words are always spoken. Those on whom "spells" are cast, of the sort that already had Angela's fiancé in its grip, always do the opposite of what they say.

René turned into the side-road and marched directly towards the solitary house whose outline was vaguely picked out by the light of the cloud-enshrouded moon. The house looked like an abandoned factory.

It was cold, the wind whipping along a fine drizzle of rain which made the ground moist and shiny.

René made a tour of the house, which had neither a garden nor a courtyard. On further consideration, it had the air of

97

one of those unfinished buildings–the fruits of unsuccessful speculation–which remain in a state of disrepair without ever having been occupied by their owners. It had large windows, all with their shutters closed.

René came back to the facade facing the driveway. On this side, as on the others, the windows were closed. In front of the door, grass was growing around and over a little flight of three steps. René looked at the casements. The closed shutters did not let out any light. He listened. The silence and the solitude would have allowed any sound, no matter how faint, to be heard. None reached his ears. He finally stood on tiptoe in order to see better. So dark was the night that any fugitive light could easily be seen at a distance. He scanned the wall that comprised the face of the house.

Nothing–and while he stood there, he repeated to himself like some poor maniac: "She has cast a spell on me."

The cold rain soaked into his light clothes. He trembled with fever, but he continued to stand there.

Just now we were with a poor child chilled to the depths of her heart, who also waited, interrogating the mute facade of a Parisian house–but Angela, seated on her moist boundary-marker before Bretonvilliers Lodge, knew what she wanted. She came in search of her destiny. René did not know what he was doing. At that moment, he had no idea–not one!–in his empty head. There was only an illness that set his veins afire, while a shudder wormed its way under his skin. He sat down on the damp grass, hiding among the bushes. The moon, disengaged from its veil of cloud, lit the countryside brightly.

The sound of midnight, struck by the bell of the Church of Sainte-Marguerite, was carried on the nocturnal wind from afar. At that moment, a strange harmony seemed to emerge from the ground. It was one of those solemn and evenly-cadenced songs which enable German exiles to be recognized in every part of the globe.

René came out of the half-sleep which had numbed his mind and body. He listened, thinking that he was dreaming.

As he left his retreat to approach the house again, ears pricked for the slightest sound, the noise of a carriage came from the Faubourg Saint-Antoine. He squatted down in the bushes again.

The carriage stopped at the end of the driveway. A man got out and came to knock on the door of the isolated house.

"Who are you?" asked a voice from the interior, in Latin.

The newcomer replied, also in Latin: "In the name of the Father, the Son and the Holy Spirit, I am a Brother of Virtue."

And the door opened.

Chapter VII
The Hiding-Place

The moon, momentarily disengaged from its veil of clouds, shed its light directly on the door of the isolated house, so René could see the person who opened the door from within. It was an old woman with a manly figure, with hard, tanned features. She was wearing the peculiar and beautiful Hungarian costume which nomadic dancers introduced to our theatres a long time ago. The figure of the newcomer, on the other hand, remained invisible. René could only see his back, where the collar of his capacious cloak met the wide brim of his hat.

The old woman said something to the newcomer in a low voice. He turned around quickly, as if his gaze were striving to penetrate the shadows in the direction of the raspberry field where René was hidden. It was all over in an instant; René only saw that the face was young, framed by long, seemingly white hair. Then the door closed and the house became silent again–but midnight must have been the hour appointed for a reunion or a rendezvous, because, in the space of little more than ten minutes, three more carriages came from the Faubourg, releasing three mysterious persons. Each one knocked at the door like the first, was interrogated in Latin as he had been, and replied in the same language.

René was able to observe that they had a particular way of spacing the raps when knocking on the door: six blows in all, divided into three, two and one.

When the last one had gone in, the surroundings remained quiet for half an hour. The city was asleep now, and it no longer emitted that constant murmur which nowadays fills the Parisian countryside until one o'clock in the morning. The rain had stopped. The moon shed its cold light across the whole expanse of the flat and dreary terrain.

René had not budged while all sorts of confused thoughts were born and died in his brain. Not once did the idea of going away occur to him. He was brave, as nine in every ten young men of his age are; it is hardly surprising or noteworthy that there was no fear in him–but he was also discreet and scrupulous in all things touching on matters of honor. Given his character and his education, he was bound to be scrupulous, all the more so given the particular situation of his family. Evidently, there was a mystery here. According to all appearances, the mystery related to political intrigues. What right had René to remain in his hiding-place within reach of that mystery? Similar conduct has a name which is repulsive to esteem and inspires hatred, more or less, in the overhasty judgment of ordinary men: a name which is an explanation and must often serve as an excuse, because the spy, that soldier of dolorous and inglorious conflicts, is more often than not required to put his very life at the service of his obscure vocation.

René was not a spy. One becomes a spy out of passion, duty or for a salary, but René's existence was completely outside politics. The ideas that still enfevered those of his country and his race had never been instilled in him. He belonged to that transitory generation which reacted against the violence of great movements: he was a thinker, perhaps a poet; he was neither a chouan, nor a Republican, nor a Bonapartist. From the political viewpoint, the meeting that was taking place behind those mute walls had no special interest for him. That particular passion was lacking in him; he neither debated, nor even recognized, the duty that arises for everyone as soon as news of a conspiracy reaches his ear, which the opinion of the greater number characterizes simply thus: to act or not to act; to fight for or go against.

Neutrality is shameful. René, however, remained neutral–not for want of courage, but because, at certain times and after certain disturbances, patriotism simply does not know which way to turn. Parties have an interest in denying such subtleties, but history speaks too highly of the intolerance of rationalizers, and sometimes confesses that there is a time for asking oneself, amid the crowd of drunken egotisms: where exactly is the fatherland?

René stayed where he was, and did not even ask himself the question of what eventual use he might make of this knowledge. The memory of the infernal machine crossed his mind, and left him in his moral somnolence. That was of no importance to him; it seemed to him to belong to another world, full of romantic and puerile preoccupations.

Someone had cast a spell on him.

He thought of her, and of her alone. She was there. What was she doing? He was there for her. He stayed there to see her come out, as he had seen her go in, and to follow her again–it did not matter where.

One ominous thing: the thought of Angela came to him again and again, but he chased it away brutally, as if escaping the tyranny of an obstinate refrain. The thought of Angela, the object of pursuit, becoming soft and patient; of poor beautiful smiling eyes, moist with tears... and René thrust it away as if it were a living being that spoke to him angrily, saying: "Don't you know that I love you?" He loved her. Perhaps he had never loved her more. The dreams awakened by that evil night displayed her to him, adorably beautiful and good.

Have you ever known one of those unhappy souls–those damned souls–who furtively let themselves out of a house where cherished children and a much-loved wife are asleep, to go off who knows where, to play, to drink absinthe, to make themselves dizzy, to find a slow and ignominious death? Such madmen are numerous–innumerable, in fact. It is said that theirs is a disease endemic throughout the human species, although it is the exclusive property of human nature.

They are found among the common people–and for such as they, terrible speculators have recently built those almost-sumptuous palaces where billiards can be played at a discount and alcohol sold at a cheaper price, to appeal to the poor. And when the poor, releasing the dream of light and drunkenness, return to the miserable hovels, where their families ask for bread, the drama howls so frightfully that the pen stops and does not dare go any further...

They are found among the bourgeoisie, who have other entertainments. Each class, indeed, seems to have its particular mirage, its special dementia. They leave behind in their homes a fresh pure wife, educated and spiritual, good and young and they go through the back door of a low theatre to find a creature crouching who is old, ugly, ignorant, coarse and stupid. There they are loved; here they are mocked–and with both hands they throw the future of their children into the lap of this Armide [36], whose tobacco-perfumed clothes still bear the imprint of another lover: the love of her heart, some dirty villain who beats her violently! A conqueror! A hero! A brute!

They are found among artists and students. These have no family; it is their own lives that they sacrifice, their noble and virile youth, to go–you know where–to drink the greenish idiocy which Circé [37] pours out for two *sous* in every corner of Paris, the city mounted on the extreme summit of civilization.

They are found in the magistracy and the army: two great institutions of which one cannot speak without provoking someone or something, and regarding which we must therefore remain silent!

They are found among the nobility and the rich, those twin aristocracies–rivals today–who concur in their vices as they do in their virtues. They demolish, with savage fury, all that it is in their interests to safeguard. Sometimes their unnatural orgies cause sudden scandals in the city, which examines itself fearfully to whether it has, by any chance, been transformed overnight into Sodom or Gomorrah. On other occasions, the ghastly audience of an assize court listens, with bated breath, to a terrifying calculation of the number of hatchet-blows it requires to kill a duchess. Again, on other occasions...but why go on?

And even if we were to go higher than dukes, do you suppose there would be no cause for outrage? Profound sadness is no insult–and human folly, extended to that degree, inspires more sadness than anger.

René underwent that heart-rending delirium which is our universal lot. La Fontaine [38] said as much, smiling, as he described that ill-advised dog which lets go of its prey for a shadow. And to tell the truth, La Fontaine's dog still had more sense than us, for the shadow did resemble its prey. As for us, how often do we abandon the most beautiful prey for a hideous shadow? How, then, can we refuse to believe what the naive take for granted? Spells are cast, that's certain: on the poor; on the bourgeoisie; on artists; on students; on magistrates; on generals; on dukes; on millionaires–and all the rest.

René was under a spell. So he went after this woman blindly, fatally.

It took a long time, for his intelligence was harassed by the conjunction of the two ideas: the woman and the conspiracy. When he had married these two ideas, an extravagant joy surged within his heart. "She is a conspirator!" he said to himself. "I will be a conspirator too." Against whom? For whom? The question was never raised. He was incapable of judging the folly according to the principles which guide wisdom.

René's numbed head set to work incontinently. This was a fortunate coincidence, he decided. While he was thinking about it, another troublesome hypothesis occurred to him. Conspirators are not the only ones who hide their activities; evildoers are naturally inclined to the same mysterious ways. René shivered, but the thought did not stop him. He put an end to it by pronouncing two words cherished by lovers and madmen: That's impossible! And he continued his mental labor. Six blows reverberated, distributed thus: three, two, one. To the Latin question this response, which he already knew by heart, was made: "In the name of the Father, the Son, and the Holy Spirit, I am a Brother of Virtue."

This was René's reasoning. That formula would get him into the house. Once in the house, perhaps there would be other tests. But the luck which had thus far served René so strangely, would serve him still. "I shall see her," he said to himself. And that word alone set his whole body a-tremble.

Meanwhile, time had passed. A great black cloud was coming towards Paris, its approaching edges already silvered by moonlight. The subterranean song that had hurled René abruptly into the land of illusion was not renewed. Nothing could be heard from the house, which was still dark and gloomy, but a mixture of almost imperceptible noises was audible across the plain. The hearing of Europeans, ignorant of the secrets of the prairie, is affected in much the same way when redskin savages creep up on a sentry under cover of pitch darkness. The noise was coming from behind the house, but then it was divided and somewhat dispersed, turning around the buildings and losing itself in the distance, before coming together again, as if from a different direction. At that moment, it seemed to be coming from the very enclosure where the raspberries, blackcurrants, gooseberries and little Montmorency cherries grew in fraternal harmony. One could not say that René paid much attention to these noises. He perceived them nevertheless, for he had spent his childhood in Brittany and he was a hunter. There was a moment when he dreamed of the great chestnut trees which grew between Vannes and Auray. He saw them from his hiding-place, and heard poachers sliding towards him beneath the trees–but his thoughts always came back to her. He was under a spell.

When the great cloud with silver borders bit into the moon, the bell-towers of Saint-Bernard, Saint-Marguerite, the Quinze-Vingts and Saint-Antoine were sounding the first hour. An animal–or a man–was evidently a few feet away from him in the thicket. Fat game is rare in the marshes of the Faubourg Saint-Antoine. René, giving way to the obsession which tyrannized him, and not wishing to believe in the evidence of his senses, had just set himself to march towards the house when these words, spoken in a very low voice, were whispered in his ear.

"I can't see him any more–where is he?"

Indeed, the darkness had become so absolute that René had disappeared completely into the bush within which he was crouching. The dream lost its grip on him. René immediately recovered all his composure. He was not armed. He remained immobile and waited.

The noises had ceased for several seconds when a cry for help, long and shrill, sounded to his left in the gooseberries. René, taken by surprise, had no idea that it might be a ruse, and came to his feet to hurl himself to the rescue.

There was derisive laughter in the shadows, and a violent blow, dealt to the head of the young Breton from behind, threw him back stunned into the bush from which he had emerged.

For a second or two, unknown figures danced before his dazzled eyes. He was in the midst of a great commotion, which entirely surrounded him. A torch was lit by a running figure coming from the house, whose open door disgorged a dim light. By the light of the torch, René saw a huge black silhouette: a colossal Negro whose white eyes gleamed. We speak positively, because it would be monotonous and impractical to keep telling the story while using doubtful terms—but it is certain that René had profound doubts about the evidence of his senses. All this had become, for him, an improbable nightmare.

Everyone knows perfectly well how much can be seen in the narrow space of two seconds, when the troubled eye is dazzled and perceives all objects as fantastic forms. That there was a Negro there was no doubt: a Negro with rolling eyes and a sharp dagger, such as might be seen at the door of a wax museum. There was a thin, pale man, thinner and paler than a corpse; he seemed very young although he had white hair. There was a Turk, shaven-headed beneath his turban—and others whose faces and costumes seemed so bizarre as to be beyond the bounds of possibility.

None of this could be real—unless our Breton had fallen into the midst of a masquerade. And the carnival was over.

Those violent shocks which, according to popular usage, light "thirty-six thousand candles," can evoke other phantasmagorias too. But René did not only see these figures; he heard them too–and what he heard tallied marvelously with the strange setting of his dream. All of these different disguises spoke different languages. Although René understood none of these diverse languages, he recognized Latin pronounced in the Hungarian manner, and he had already heard Italian and German being spoken that night. All these idioms were speaking of death, and one exclamation–"Flatten the bleeder!" [39], pronounced in the jabbering argot of the London cockney–constituted a summary of the general opinion.

The Englishman continued talking, while brandishing one of those scourges made from whalebone, copper and lead which John Bull has baptized a "life-preserver," from which René had undoubtedly received the blow that had floored him. The Negro, bending down in the grass on one knee, was already drawing back an arm to hit him when a woman's voice, soft and musical, set René's heart pounding in his breast.

He could not see the speaker, and yet he recognized her, by the sound of a voice he had never heard.

She was very close to him, though hidden by the crowd of strange shadows which pressed him on every side, when she said: "Don't hurt him. It's him!"

Chapter VIII
The Narcotic

For a moment or two, René's head was full of darkness and confusion. The wound on his head was giving him so much distress that he could not focus. He thought he saw a hand seize the frizzy hair of the Negro and pull him backwards. Then a knotted handkerchief was passed over his eyes, blindfolding him and his mouth was gagged. Every possible precaution was taken before he was seized by his legs and shoulders, and placed on some sort of stretcher.

The only sense remaining to him was hearing–but the effort of trying to make sense of the surrounding voices lent them a bellowing quality and he seemed to be drowning in a confusion of languages. Even so, he clung to one near-lucid thought while he languished: she!

He had heard her.

She had saved his life.

She had said: "It's him!"

Him? Who? Was she mistaken? Had she lied?

The few words pronounced by the woman's voice, so soft in spite of their imperious quality, proved to be the last as well as the first. René listened as hard as he could, but in vain; she said no more.

His strength ebbed away little by little; the top of his head was horribly ablaze. After being carried a few paces, he lost consciousness. The last word that he heard and understood seemed to him the most incredible of all: it was the name of his uncle, Georges Cadoudal.

It was a spring-like morning at the end of winter. A sky as blue as midsummer was visible through the foliage of a miniature thicket of tropical plants. The bed on which René was lying looked out over a large garden, planted with tall trees stripped of their leaves. To the right was a conservatory from which warm and discreet perfumes emerged; to the left, an open door displayed the shelves of a library. The bed was old-fashioned, and its twisted cornerposts supported a square canopy of damask silk, as thick as velvet. The walls, fully paneled with plain moldings, had an almost monastic appearance, which contrasted sharply with the smart and entirely modern decor of the conservatory.

René had slept deeply and peacefully. He woke up to find himself lying on the bed. His head was heavy and a little empty, but it did not feel painful. This was what he saw at first glance–and perhaps, without that view, as explanatory as the illustrations that our distant childhood adds to every future text, it would have taken a very long time to fish out the bare truth from the confusion of his memories.

In the conservatory, through the panes of glass, he perceived the Negro–the giant Negro–who was smoking a corncob pipe stuffed with tobacco, stretched out at full length under a flowering palm-tree. The Negro was looking up contentedly at the tortuous flight of the smoke of his pipe and seemed to be the happiest of blackamoors. His slothful languor was not in the least suggestive of ferocity. He no longer had the pointed and diabolically sharp-edged dagger that had come so close to making the acquaintance of the young Breton's side.

In the same room as René, not far from the window which looked out over the garden, the young man who was very thin and very pale, and whose hair was completely white, was sprawled in an easy-chair with his feet up, reading. He was wearing a sternly elegant business suit.

René did not see anything else at first. But another sensation, more vibrantly exciting than the view itself, made his tired and still-enfeebled eyelids close again. Through the open door of the library a song could be heard, accompanied by the strains of a harp.

(The harp was fashionable then, and every young woman yearned to have her portrait painted in the pretentious costume of Corinne, with her feet on a pedal and her fingers extended like ten spider's legs, strumming arpeggios as solemn as phrases by Madame de Staël on the most theatrical of all instruments [40]. The guitar came next, in the terrible decadence of the last years of the Empire, providing a languorous transition to the migraine that abuse of the piano has given to the world. Of the three instruments, the most hateful is surely the piano, upon whose clattering keyboard even the English ended up learning to play. There will be nothing after the piano, for it is the most accomplished expression of musical tyranny. The guitar makes less noise; the harp is beautiful.)

The voice audible through the library door was singing a bold, wild song, punctuated according to the unexpected and halting cadences of the Slavic rhythm. The voice accentuated each near-barbaric melody with incredible passion. The voice was sonorous, far-reaching, full of vibrations that wrung the soul. It was corrosive, if it is permissible to intrude such a verb into the technical language of dilettantism. If that voice had not been singing, moving René to the most profound depths of his heart, he would already have opened his mouth to ask where he was—but he remained under the charm and held his breath.

He did not know where he was. Nothing that he had seen through the windows was reminiscent of the flat terrain surrounding the house at the end of the by-road off the Rue de la Muette. There were tall trees here and high walls beyond them, draped with ivy.

At the precise moment when the voice stopped singing, a side door opened. The tall woman in the Hungarian costume, who had come out of the isolated house with a torch in her hand on the previous night, came into the room, carrying a cup of chocolate on a tray. The sound of her footsteps caused the pale, thin young man with the white hair to turn his head.

"Salut, Domina Yanusza," he said, with pretended affection and respect.

110

The old woman acknowledged the greeting in a stiff and formal manner. "I'm a servant, not a mistress, Doctor Andrea Ceracchi," she replied, in Latin. "Would you like to speak to me once without laughing–you, who should have been weeping ceaselessly since the moment when your brother fell beneath the hand of a tyrant?"

The Italian's features contorted spasmodically, and he pursed his thin lips.

"Laughter is sometimes more bitter than tears, Goodwife Paraxin," he murmured, replying in the Teutonic Latin which allowed them to communicate with one another.

"For myself, Doctor," she said, with a strange emphasis, "I neither laugh nor weep. I hate. It's said that General Bonaparte will proclaim himself Emperor. If you let that happen, there will be no more time."

"I'm ready!" the man she had called Andrea Ceracchi assured her.

René remembered that name, which belonged to one of the two Romans implicated in the plot of the *Horaces* [41]–the companion of Diana and Aréna; a young and handsome man whose stoical death had lasted eight hours, while Paris and the world were agog: the sculptor Giuseppe Ceracchi.

Yanusza shook her grey head and growled; "It would be better to be active than ready, Sir Doctor." Then she resumed her measured path to the door. Her tread was firm; she did not glance at the bed where René lay motionless.

When Yanusza had gone, the Italian doctor remained still and pensive for a moment, then he dipped a piece of bread in the cup of chocolate, which he immediately pushed away. "Everyone has a taste for blood here!" he said, in a deep voice.

After a few minutes René's eyelids became heavy again, and irresistible sleep sought to reclaim him. The Italian's last words reached his ears, but slid over his understanding. Then, all of a sudden, there was a loud noise inside the house. It came neither from the conservatory nor from the library. René thought hat he heard a cry similar to that which had startled him on the previous night, when he had hidden in the raspberry bushes in front of the isolated house. He tried to fight the urge to sleep, but his whole body was growing more and more numb, and it seemed to him that the Negro–who had got up from his seat in the conservatory–was staring at him.

It was from the white eyes of the Negro that sleep came. It arrived in an almost-visible flux, that strange sleep. René felt it climbing along his veins, and he experienced a sensation of being slowly submerged in a bath of liquid opium. He retained the use of his eyes and ears, but only to see and hear impossible things, of the sort that opium-dreamers discover in their intoxication.

Two men entered the conservatory by a door that communicated with the interior of the house. They were carrying something long, which put René in mind of a shrouded cadaver. The Negro smiled, displaying a long row of dazzling teeth. At the same time, a vision–a delectable and radiant vision–illuminated the room. A woman with an adorable smile bounded from the library door. Her blonde hair was shining brilliantly, as if she were crowned with an aureole.

"Count Wenzel is about to depart for Germany," she said.

René recognized that voice, which crushed his heart so voluptuously. Sleep enchained him more and more securely. The impotent defenses that he raised exhausted him to the point of anguish, and he thought: "All this is a nightmare."

The name of Count Wenzel struck a chord in him. He had heard it spoken by Angela's adoptive father, and he knew that Count Wenzel was a young German gentleman who was on the point of contracting a marriage in Paris. That brought his thoughts back to his own marriage: the marriage so passionately desired, so recently awaited with impatience, which now filled him with dread: the marriage which was, however, the fulfillment of a sacred duty.

He was astonished to conceive, in parallel with his dream, such clear ideas followed by such righteous reasoning. He was astonished, too, by the particular sense that his intelligence attached to those few words, apparently the most straightforward in the world: "Count Wenzel is about to depart for Germany."

To him, they embodied some indefinable threat. Beneath the harmony of that voice there was something coldly, pitilessly mocking.

He thought: "I must remember all this and seek the advice of Angela's father."

The ravishing blonde, her smile sparkling with childish gaiety, sat down beside the Italian, lightly smoothing the folds of her dress. Her entire person was inexplicably radiant. Her dress shone when she shook out its graceful pleats, just as her hair glinted with every movement of her smiling head. She turned her back on the conservatory. René still had not taken his eyes off the long package that the two men had deposited at the Negro's feet. The Negro placidly finished his pipe.

"My brother is not yet avenged," said the Italian in a low voice, "and I shall soon run out of strength."

"In a few days," murmured the blonde, "it will all be finished. You have my word."

Her eyes abruptly turned sideways towards the bed, and René said to himself: "That one is evil. It is not she!"

"Is he asleep?" the woman asked, in a low voice and with a certain anxiety.

"He's never stopped sleeping," replied the Italian. "The dose of the drug was just right... what do you want with him?"

"Our safety and your vengeance," the young woman replied.

The Italian's eyes glowed with dark fire. "Countess," he said, slowly, "I was twenty-two when my brother died. On the following day, I had hair as white as an old man's... I wanted to kill myself, but a man saved me and told me that he too had changed, in a single anguished night, a forest of black curls into a white mane... That man advised me to go overseas and forget. You have murmured the word vengeance in my ear: now I wait."

The young woman seemed to grow larger, and her transfigured beauty expressed an indomitable force.

"Others are waiting just as you are, Andrea Ceracchi," she replied. "All that I have promised I shall deliver. I have gathered around me those whose hearts have been broken by that man–and have I not worked hard already for our communal cause?"

She was interrupted by a dull noise from the conservatory, which sent a shudder through her body. Ceracchi could not have become paler, but his features altered and he closed his eyes.

René, whose gaze went in spite of himself to the conservatory, saw the Negro upright next to a square hole that had opened among the pots of flowers. He wore a sinister smile.

The long package had disappeared.

"You wish to avenge your brother," the young woman continued, in a different tone. "Taïeh wants to avenge his mother." She pointed over her shoulder at the Negro, who was occupied in closing a large trap-door over which he slid a pot containing a Yucca plant. "Toussaint-Louverture [42] is dead, as Ceracchi is, having died more slowly under the torture of captivity. Taïeh does not ask for an account of the price to be paid for his vengeance. Osman has come from Cairo with a poisoned dagger hidden in his turban, but it will be no ordinary dagger that kills that man... It requires blood and gold: a flood of blood and gold. It requires a hundred weapons obedient to a single will. It requires a will, a mission, a destiny... as the blood runs, the level of gold rises day by day. The Brothers of Virtue are ready–and here am I, whom destiny has appointed. Will Andrea Ceracchi be the first to lose confidence? Have I stopped? Have I retreated...?"

She paused, because the Italian was on his knees kissing her hands. She was so marvelously beautiful that her face seemed to be giving off sparks.

"I have faith in you!" said the Italian, with quasi-mystical devotion.

The extended hand of the young woman was pointing at René. "That one will furnish us with the ultimate weapon," she murmured.

A swarthy head encased in a turban appeared at the library door.

"What is it?" asked the doctor.

"Baron von Ramberg wants to see Countess Marcian Gregoryi," was the reply.

On the evening of that same day, René de Kervoz re-entered his study, weak but no longer sensible of his wound. He retained a vague memory of a certain unhealthy dream that had occupied an entire night of terrible fever, then a day when the nightmare had taken on impossible proportions. The more effort he made to clear away the confusion from his memory, the more muddled the dream became with absurd misadventures, simultaneously displaying to him the living cadaver of a young man with white hair, a Negro couched among flowers, a maddeningly beautiful woman smiling amid the liquid gold of a fairy's tresses, an open trap-door, a human body wrapped up in a shroud... then there was the termagant who spoke Latin, and the Turk who had announced the arrival of Baron von Ramberg, and the woman with the penetrating voice who had said: "Count Wenzel is about to leave for Germany!"

He also had memories more recent and more precise, in which one could actually believe, even though they were even more romantic.

Towards the end of the day, René had suddenly seen a woman appear at the head of his bed, in that vast room in whose objects were already disappearing into obscurity: a woman who seemed to be keeping watch over his sleeping body; a woman whose face was as calm and gentle as the face of a Madonna, bathed by magnificent waves of hair blacker than jet.

This woman resembled the strange and dazzling vision which had passed through his dream: the voluptuous fairy whose radiant blonde hair had shaken as she tossed her insubordinate head–but it was not the same woman. Certainly not! René could feel it in the profound beating of his heart. This was she: the unknown of Saint-Germain-l'Auxerrois.

When René woke up, she put a finger over her beautiful mouth and said to him: "Someone may be listening, and I am not mistress here..."

"Is it the other one who is the mistress?" René interrupted her.

She smiled. Her smile was an enchantment.

"Yes," she murmured. "It's the other one. Don't speak. You were wrong to follow me. One should never try to penetrate certain secrets. I have saved you twice. You are healed, but be careful." And before René could make any reply, she closed his mouth with a caress. "You must get up and get dressed," she continued. "It's time to go."

She glanced towards the library door, which was still half-open, and added, in a tone so low that René could hardly catch the meaning of her words: "You will see me again. It will be soon, and in a place where I shall be able to listen to you. In the meantime, I repeat, you must be careful. Don't try to question the one who is coming, and submit to all the demands that are made of you."

René's hand felt a furtive pressure, and he found himself alone again.

An instant later, a man came in. He was holding two torches. René saw his clothes on a chair beside his bed.

The newcomer helped him to dress, but said not a single word. When René was ready, the silent valet gave him a silk handkerchief rolled up like a cravat and made him understand with a gesture that he must place the blindfold over his eyes.

"Why?" asked René, disobeying the orders of his protectress for the first time.

"I cannot speak French, sir," the man with the handkerchief replied, in English. His guttural accent immediately revived René's memories; he had already encountered this bravo who did not speak French. It was the throaty voice which had advised the Brothers of Virtue, in English, to "flatten the bleeder!" Nevertheless, René let himself be blindfolded.

A few moments later, he climbed into a carriage, which immediately moved off at a trot.

After ten minutes, the carriage stopped.

"Should I get out?" René asked.

No one replied. He removed his blindfold, and was astonished to see that he was alone. A coachman opened the carriage door, saying: "I've brought you the length of the Rue de Dragon as far as Châtelet, Monsieur. The fare is paid. Will there be a tip?"

Chapter IX
Between Two Loves

As chance would have it, René de Kervoz was due to go away for a while on the day after the evening when he had accompanied Angela to mass at Saint-Germain-d'Auxerrois. For this reason, his absence went unnoticed by those who loved him. We will discover in due course exactly what his position was with respect to the family of his fiancée. They were people of humble origin but good heart, who had earned his respect by their actions.

Once he was alone again, René presumably tried to wrestle against this new element which threatened to take over his life. His life was already consecrated to an undemanding and pleasant duty; there was no place in it for adventures. It was necessary that the romance whose first chapter had drawn him so far had to be violently ripped apart at a time when a shadow still remained upon his reason, so that it might become his whole existence. Thus it was. René did not win his wrestling-match; the image of Angela was ineffaceable from the profoundest depths of his heart, but he turned his maddened gaze towards a mirage.

He was cherished too tenderly for the malaise of his heart and spirit to pass unnoticed by those around him. His character altered; his changed habits excited mistrust and awoke disquiet. René saw this, and suffered from it–but he had already slid so far downhill that nothing could stop him. The spell, moreover–since it is agreed that he was under a spell–would neither let him rest nor permit a truce. The fascination, once begun, was unstoppable; the romance continued, the pages added to its prologue extrapolating a plot full of mysteries and narrative twists.

During an illness that he had recently endured, René had been tended by an apprentice doctor who was a friend of his father-in-law: an amusing little man named Germain Patou, who had spoken rather irreverently about his profession. This Germain Patou had discovered a German pathologist named Samuel Hahnemann, who had replaced the voluminous poisons of the traditional pharmacopoeia with a new kind of quackery–which, Patou claimed, could work miracles. The little man could have passed for a madman readily enough, but even though he was not yet any kind of doctor, he cured–seemingly without rhyme or reason–all those who fell into his hands.

The next day but one after the nocturnal scuffle in which René had received the blow to his skull, Patou chanced to visit him. René showed him the wound, saying that he had fallen backwards after slipping on the pavement. The wound still carried a small dressing that had been put on it while René was asleep in the mysterious house.

Patou had no sooner seen the injury than he cried: "That's enough to kill an ox!" He immediately put the dressing to his nose. "*Arnica montana,*" he said, reverently. "The vulnerary of the master [43]. Comrade, you have been bandaged by a true believer; would you care to give me his address?"

Embarrassed, René told him that he would have done so if he could. In the meantime, Patou unfolded the dressing. It was a handkerchief of the finest batiste, in the corner of which was an embroidered coat-of arms, capped by a crown which marked it as the escutcheon of a count.

"Well, well!" said Patou. "Have you read in the newspapers the story of Szandor's tomb, discovered on an islet in the Sava, upriver of Semlin? It's very curious. Personally, I love vampires, and my belief in them is cast iron. Besides, it's the fashion; it's not just a question of vampires. Journals, books, people talk of vampires every day. I know a man who causes boats to move with neither sails nor oars, by the power of steam: his name is Citizen de Jouffroy [44]. He's a marquis and as mad as Samuel Hahnemann. He wrote a melodrama entitled

119

Le Vampire. It brought down the house at the Theatre Saint-Martin! For myself, I would give Professor Loysel's wig to see the vampire who is devouring half of Paris at this very moment... but to get back to the story: in Szandor's tomb, there was a vampire which emerged at night, swam across the Sava and laid waste to the country as far as Belgrade. That vampire was a count, as was proved by the inscription on the tomb. He had been buried in 1646... and this is the funny thing: Count Szandor had the same Latin motto as the Citizen Count or Countess of 1804 who lent a handkerchief to bandage your wound."

So saying, Patou laid out the batiste on the table, where the embroidered letters stood out whitely. The motto which ran around the escutcheon was: *In vita mors, in morte vita*!

"An appropriate motto for a vampire!" Patou exclaimed. " 'In life, death; in death, life!' To conclude the story of Count Szandor: after a sojourn of a hundred and fifty-eight years in the tomb, that gentleman still had the most luxuriant black hair, almond eyes and lips as red as coral. He was, however, toothless. A red-hot iron was plunged into his heart: a surgical method which appears to be the generally-accepted treatment for a vampire... Had I been in their place, myself, I would have chatted to the fellow for a while, in order to find out what he thought; I would have given him a thorough examination from top to toe; I would have taken care of him, to be sure, according to the Hahnemann method, and he would have been able, once cured, to give us a first-hand account of the Thirty Years' War, except for the last two years..."

When Patou had departed, René took up the embroidered handkerchief, and touched it to his lips.

The next day, he received a letter in unfamiliar handwriting, which made his heart beat faster. The large seal of black wax carried the same escutcheon as the embroidered handkerchief, and the same motto: *In vita mors, in morte vita*. A shudder ran through René's veins, but then he smiled proudly, thinking: "Our time has outgrown these superstitions."

The letter said:

"One desires to have news of a wound which has given sleep to the wounded but insomnia to another. This evening, at six o'clock, one will pray for the wounded at the Calvary of Saint-Roch."

There was no signature.

The letter had been delivered by a strange messenger: a Negro wearing the uniform of the musicians of the Consular Guard.

That day seemed very long to René, and for the first time those who loved him noticed that he was troubled.

At five o'clock, he arrived on the steps of Saint-Roch. For the next hour, he waited in vain for the carriage that he hoped to see. When six o'clock chimed, feeling battle-weary, he went through the church to the Calvary displayed on the back wall of the chapel of the Virgin Mary.

There was a woman there, kneeling before the mystic rock.

René approached her. There was an imperceptible movement behind the woman's lowered veil, but she did not turn around.

The woman whose austere and somber costume allowed an exquisite figure to be detected, seemed perfectly fitted to a twilight as devout and humid as the chiaroscuro cleverly contrived for the cause of art by pious painters. It was as if she were part of the tableau. She seemed to be deeply immersed in her prayer, unaware of anything else.

"Answer me, but in a whisper," she said, in a soft and stately voice. "We are not alone."

René looked around. There was no one in the chapel–no one, at least, that he could see.

"Are you better?" she asked him.

"My only suffering is of the heart." he replied, in spite of himself.

Again there was silence. The veiled woman seemed to be listening to sounds that were not reaching René's ears.

"Can one have two loves?" she murmured at last, in a tremulous voice.

"Oh!" he said. "I love only you!"

She started in surprise and got up, crossing herself ostentatiously before turning to leave.

"Don't follow me," she ordered, hurriedly.

She walked away rapidly.

René, rooted to the spot, immediately heard the dull and heavy tread of a man fall into step with the light noise made by her fairy feet as they brushed the flagstones of the chapel. When he finally turned his head, there was no longer anything to be seen. The enchantress and her cavalier had gone out of a door by the Calvary.

René, intoxicated and insane, set forth on their trail. He left by the exit that led to the Passage Saint-Roch.

It was empty.

"Intoxicated" and "insane" were the right words. He headed home in a state of feverish excitation. Something had seized control of his brain: a center of action far more powerful than the organ of vague aspirations we call the heart. Since the world began, the heart has always been vanquished by the brain. When the fever dies down and the hour comes for repentance and expiation, a voice is sometimes heard pronouncing the pitiless phrase: "It is too late!"–but the observation is useless, for it never prevented any crime or ill-fortune. Such is life.

Before going home, René had to knock on the door of Angela's adoptive father. There are proprieties to be observed, and the brave man had never done anything but good to him. There was goodness and noble calmness in that house: the holy serenity of the family.

The grandmother was rocking an infant in her arms–for René de Kervoz was much more engaged than the common run of fiancés. The white-haired father was reading, while the daughter sewed, thoughtfully and sadly. But have you ever seen the magical transformation that the first rays of spring produce in the desolate winter countryside? Here, René was the sun; his entrance generated an epidemic of smiles. The mother gave him her hand, the father set aside his book, the young woman rose happily to her feet and came to him with open arms.

René did his best to be worthy of that welcome, which was always the same and whose dear monotony was now his greatest joy. It is said that the cruelest torture, for a man who is drowning, is the sight of the riverbank.

Here was the riverbank, and René was drowning.

The grandmother put the sleeping baby into his arms. René kissed her, with an ache in his heart, and could not look at the child's mother—not that he had any cowardly thought of abandoning these poor creatures. We have said that René was an honorable man, and the consciousness of wrongs that he had already done them was breaking his heart. He knew full well that he was dragging them with him down a slope of irreparable unhappiness—but he was powerless to stop himself, or lacked the will.

There was still no inkling of this within the house; we know, in fact, that René's absence the previous night had passed unnoticed. No disquiet had yet been awakened in these good souls—but it was to be born that very evening.

When René made ready to leave at the usual hour, the mother went to sit down, discomfited and sad for the first time in months. The boss went silently to his study and Angela remained alone next to the little one, weeping as she kissed the child.

Unhappiness had come to that formerly tranquil house. Henceforth, the least symptoms would be perceived and passed through the sieve of an affection already roused to jealousy. That evening, Angela remained seated by the window for a long time, watching the other side of the street, where René's light was not extinguished until very late.

René was thinking of her, too—or, rather, René believed that he was thinking of her, for it was her image that he conjured up as a safeguard. But within that image he saw his madness, his vertigo, his fate: the other; the one whose name he still did not know; the one who had used a terrible science to wind him around with the threads of guilty passion; the one who had the irresistible allure of the unknown, the attraction of romance, the seductiveness of mystery.

The obsession continued through the following days. It seemed that there was a purpose at work, surrounding him with a vague net whose bait–always set at a distance–persistently fled his hand, but then showed itself again, to prevent discouragement or fatigue.

He received letters summoning him to rendezvous–if one may thus describe brief and fugitive encounters, where the presence of an invisible third person always prevented conversation.

He was loved. The persistence of these rendezvous, which never led to anything, was manifest proof of that. They were the obstinate gambles of a captive wrestling against her jailer–unless they were nothing but an audacious and pitiless mystification. But how could it be a game? What object could there be in such prolonged mockery? On the one hand, there was a poor Breton squire, an obscure student; on the other, a great lady–for René never had the shadow of a doubt that his unknown was a great lady. She had to thwart such redoubtable surveillance. She did her best. What enslavement is more complete than that of a noble position?

Whenever René received a written summons, he ran. At one time, it was in a crowded street in which he met a carriage whose closed blinds allowed a glimpse of a white hand which spoke mutely; at another, it was in the Tuileries, where the wind lifted the corner of a veil just far enough to display an ardent smile and two languishing eyes. Most often, it was in churches–then a few words would be let slip, and the giving and receiving of holy water would permit a brief hand-clasp.

And René's fever only became worse. His desire, ceaselessly stimulated and never satisfied, became a state of torment. He became thinner, and paler.

Angela and her parents suffered the repercussions. Sometimes her mother said: "The marriage has been too long delayed. The waiting has made René ill; the wedding will cure him." But the boss shook his white head, and Angela's smile was melancholy.

Angela often went out, and was gone for some time. If you could have encountered her in one of her solitary walks, you would have thought she was not going anywhere in particular–but she always had a goal. Every time the furtive meetings between René and his unknown took place, Angela was somewhere nearby, her eyes dry and burning, her bosom oppressed. She was determined to find out what was going on. If she knew anything, she never gave any indication. She did not say a single word to her parents, or to her fiancé. She always gave him the baby to kiss: the baby who was also becoming thin and pale. But when she was alone with the tiny creature, she opened her heart, certain that her words would not be understood. She said: "The wedding day is getting closer, but which of us will hear the bells?"

As quickly as the days passed, however–by means of a peculiar process with which all psychologists are familiar–René acquired a clearer retrospective perception of the confused events which had filled that infamous night of February 12th. The general impression was ominous, and full of terrors which extended into the day of the thirteenth, spent in the house that had a large garden and a conservatory. In the conservatory, René saw once again, more distinctly now, the square hole, and the two men carrying a human-shaped burden, and the black man smoking his pipe beneath the flowering bushes... and he heard the voice of the woman who said, with cold irony: "Count Wenzel is about to leave for Germany!" In René's thoughts, that phrase had a double and sinister meaning. The oblong package which had been thrown into the hole: that was Count Wenzel.

If things had been other than they were–if René de Kervoz had still passed his evenings in conversation in the home of his future father-in-law, the boss of the stonemasons of the Marché-Neuf–he would have heard the name of Wenzel spoken more than once. He would then have been able to gather precious intelligence, for there was often talk of Count Wenzel in the home of Jean-Pierre Sévérin, called Gâteloup. Count Wenzel was one of a trio of young Germans who had been students together at the University of Tubingen: Wenzel, Ramberg and König, three wealthy, happy young men. But René no longer chatted with Angela's parents. He went there every day out of duty; he suffered, he witnessed their suffering, and he withdrew in despair. The idea that a murder had been committed remained, therefore, locked in his confused thoughts.

One might go further, and say that he was entertaining the thought of a series of murders. This was the impression he had formed. The trap-door hidden under the potted plants had served this purpose more than once–and that was the most plausible excuse he could offer to his conscience for the passionate desire that he entertained towards his unknown.

For him, in fact, the mysterious house contained two women: one blonde and one dark. He had seen them with his own eyes: "the Countess" and she who had no title at all; the bloody-handed woman, upon whom any and all crimes naturally devolved, and the angel of his salvation.

On the evening of the day on which our story began by displaying those three persons filing along the Quai de la Grève–René first, then Angela following René, then the white-haired man following Angela–the emotions which René had experienced in the mysterious house returned to him like an echo. It was then, at Saint-Louis-en-l'Ile, that his unknown failed–for the first time–to turn up for an assignation.

René had been waiting for more than an hour when the young man with the cadaverous figure, whose hair was completely white, came out of the vestry with a priest whom René had never seen before: a middle-aged ecclesiastic with an honest and serious face. The sight of the young man struck René like an actual blow, and the name overheard in his dream came to his lips: Andrea Ceracchi!

Andrea Ceracchi and the priest passed close by René, who was hidden in the shadow of a pillar, saying: "She will

126

come tomorrow. The thing must be done quickly, because the Baron von Ramberg is under considerable pressure to return to Germany."

These words, and the tone in which they were pronounced, seemed the most natural in the world–but before René's eyes the trap-door opened, and was covered again by flowers, and it seemed to him that he heard the ominous echo of those other words: "Count Wenzel is about to leave for Germany."

She must have been telling the truth, he thought.

And the following day, as we have seen, he returned to the Church of Saint-Louis-en-l'Ile. No rendezvous had been arranged this time.

Whether René had really been deceived, or whether he had affected to misunderstand, he had accosted a woman who was not waiting for him: the blonde madonna so admired by Germain Patou, who was there for another purpose entirely. After exchanging a few words, he had gone out of the side door and had set out for the old Bretonvilliers Lodge, where he had been told to go.

One corner of the veil, at least, had been lifted; the blonde had agreed to carry a message to the brunette.

During the rather long interval which René was obliged to spend alone, in the large upstairs room, he interrogated his memories one more time, seeking to discover whether this house was the one to which he had been carried, drugged and unconscious, after the night of the twelfth of February. His memory remained mute so far as the fixtures and fittings were concerned, but his general impression was that this was not the place. Places do not only have a visual aspect, they have a flavor; René remained convinced that the room in which he had lain could not be any part of this house.

Lila! He knew that name at last! And it was the blonde who had betrayed the brunette's secret.

Astonished, and perhaps afraid–for he had caused some slight disarrangement of the subtle plot that she had been weaving at the Church of Saint-Louis–she had said, "Go to

Bretonvilliers Lodge and knock six times, spaced like this: three, two, one. When the door is opened, say these words: *Salus Hungariae*. You will be let in, and I promise that my sister Lila will come to meet you."

Lila! What torrents of harmony a name can unleash!

Lila came. René was at the window, where poor Angela watched him from below, detecting his much-loved figure in the darkness. For several seconds, René's eyes had chanced to fix themselves upon a blurred form: the form of a woman slumped upon the boundary-marker at the corner. To be sure, he did not see it, in the precise sense of the term–the shadow was too dense–but remorse, like hope, gives rise to illusions. A cold sweat bathed his brow; the name of Angela died on his lips. We repeat, however, that he did not see her. For him, the woman on the boundary-marker carried a baby in her arms; he saw the little child more distinctly than the woman.

But Lila came, and then René saw nothing but Lila. Angela–the true Angela, for, alas, the other was nothing but a vision–fell dying, while René forgot everything in a kiss.

The first kiss...!

Chapter X
Tête-à-Tête

Hours passed, measured by the hoarse bell of Saint-Louis-en-l'Ile. The last sounds from the street were the footsteps of the men who were carrying Angela to *The Miraculous Catch*. We rediscover Lila and René where we left them, sitting beside one another on the ottoman in the boudoir, holding hands and gazing into one another's faces–and we shall say once more that it would have been difficult to find any couple younger, better looking or more graceful.

Lila had just pronounced the words that had caused René's expression to cloud over: "My name is soft in your mouth." These words will serve as the point of departure for the relation of a long and bizarre episode. They struck the only remaining dolorous chord in René's heart. As chance would have it, Angela had pronounced the same words, in almost the same manner, on another occasion, the memory of which was now revived as cruel remorse.

"Lila," said René, after a silence that the young woman had not interrupted, "ignorance weighs heavily upon me. I live in a state of fever and anguish. It is necessary to explain my affliction to others, but you know my story... the story of those twenty-four hours whose imperfect memory remains with me like a painful enigma. You know it even better than I do. I need to know."

"You shall know everything," the charming creature replied, her large eyes expressing reproach. "Everything that I know, at least... but I hope that curiosity is not all that has brought us together."

"Make no mistake," Kervoz was quick to say. "My curiosity is the product of love: a profound and ardent love."

She shook her head slowly, and her beautiful smile was stained by sorrow. "Perhaps I deserve that," she said. "There is a proverb in my homeland which says that one should never play games with the heart. To begin with, I was playing with your heart. The first time my gaze summoned you, I did not love you..." She took his hand in spite of his resistance and put it abruptly to her lips. "But love has come," she continued. "Don't punish me! I am not only mistress, but also slave. Love me well, for I shall die if I do not feel loved–and above all, René, I beg you never to judge me with your reason, for I have sacrificed my liberty to a sacred cause. Judge me only with your soul!"

She put her head on René's shoulder, and he kissed her hair. Intoxication possessed him as he felt her body quivering in his arms. He fought against that long-desired joy, without knowing why, and appealed to Angela for help–but there are flowery perfumes more penetrating and more powerful than liqueurs, which make the head spin; they intoxicated him.

"Did you know me, then, that first time?"

"Yes," she answered. "I knew you... and I was there because of you."

"At Saint-Germain-l'Auxerrois?"

"I had gone there before because of you, but you had not noticed me... I knew that you were not yet the husband of that lovely child who always accompanied you..."

René's hand pressed down on her lips.

"You don't want me to speak of her," Lila said, in a tone that was docile and sad. "Oh, I would not have said anything against her. You have tears in your eyes, René... you still love her..."

"I would give the better half of my life," the young Breton replied, "to love her forever."

Lila pressed herself passionately against his breast. "Then let us never speak of her again," she continued, in a tone so soft that one might have reckoned it a song. "Since I hoped to be loved, I pray that she will be well..." She stopped, and resumed: "Let's talk about us. I was sent to you."

"Sent? By whom?"

"By those who have the right to give me orders."

"The Brothers of Virtue?"

She lowered her head as a sign of affirmation.

"And what do they want with me?" asked René.

"Nothing from you...but everything from another."

He wanted to interrogate her further, but she closed his mouth with a hurried kiss. "You were nothing to us," she went on, "who became everything to me... have you read that strange book by Cazotte [45] which tells how a demon fell in love with a handsome youth with a virtuous soul? I'm not a demon... oh, how I wish I could be an angel for you, René, my beloved René! But perhaps there is a demon among us..."

"The blonde?" Kervoz exclaimed, in spite of himself.

"My sister?" she said. "Isn't she beautiful? But what's the matter?"

René's hand had seized hers convulsively. He was very pale.

"There is one explanation I need to have," he said, firmly. "I insist on it. There was blood, was there not, in the seemingly simple words: 'Count Wenzel is about to leave for Germany?' "

"Ah," said Lila, who became pale in her turn. "You were not asleep, then?"

"You hoped that I was asleep?" René said, excitedly.

"Not I," she replied, in a tone so melancholy and so persuasive that Kervoz's suspicions were deflected from her as if by an enchantment. She added, while fixing the candor of her beautiful eyes upon him: "Never be suspicious of me. I feel for you as if my own heart were beating in your breast!" Then she repeated: "Not I. I thought of nothing but healing you, but the others... I would scarcely have been able to save you if the others had known that you were not asleep."

"And why were you in that den, Lila?" René asked, mistrust and pity mingled in his tone. She stiffened so proudly that the young Breton kissed her eyes in spite of himself. "Have I offended you?" he stammered.

"No," she replied, recovering all her softness, "you could not offend me–but let me say this to you, René: there are things about which the nephew of Georges Cadoudal should only speak with great care."

René drew back along the ottoman as enlightenment struck him. "Ah!" he said. "It was the nephew of Georges Cadoudal that you were ordered to seek out."

"And to find," Lila confirmed, smiling. "And to attract him to me by any means possible."

"Then why so much mystery?"

"Because, like Cazotte's poor demon, I allowed myself to be captivated. I will no longer work for them unless you are with them. I set you free from any obligation. I love you, and there is nothing more within me but that love."

"Perhaps," said René, hesitantly, "I have neither the same sentiments nor the same opinions as my uncle, Georges Cadoudal."

"That is of scant importance to me," Lila replied. "Your opinions will be mine, as will your sentiments. I know that you are fond of your uncle; I am sure that you would not betray him..."

"Betray him!" Kervoz said, indignantly. Then, as Lila opened her mouth, he said: "You still haven't replied to my question about Count Wenzel."

In a very low voice, Lila said: "I don't want to say anything about that subject."

"I want the truth!" Kervoz insisted.

"You command, I obey. The secret societies of Germany are as old as Christianity, and their strict laws have been perpetuated across the ages. The men of iron who executed upon Charles of Burgundy [46], surrounded though he was by a hundred thousand soldiers, the secret sentence of the rope and dagger are still with us. The Brothers of Virtue originated in Germany. Its traitors are punished by death."

"And Count Wenzel was a traitor?" Kervoz demanded.

"I don't know everything," Lila replied.

"Does your sister know any more than you?"

"My sister is a Rosicrucian of the thirty-third palace," Lila replied, not without a certain emphasis. "She has been master of the Buda kingdom [47]. There is nothing that she does not know."

"And you, Lila? What are you?"

She enveloped him with her charming gaze and let herself slide to her knees as she murmured: "Me? I am your slave! I love you. Oh, how I love you!"

René's heart went out to her. The words of love that he longed to utter could be read in his eyes. Meanwhile, he said: "Lila, what is the meaning of the words Baron von Ramberg will soon be leaving for Germany too? Will there be yet another murder? Is there still time to prevent it?"

The young woman's eyelids lowered, causing the delicate arches of her eyebrows to contract slightly. "I don't know everything," she repeated. "You're cruel!" Then, putting René's hand to her heart, she went on: "Don't ask me what I don't know. Don't ask me about foreigners or enemies. Georges Cadoudal is going to die too, and I can only think about Georges Cadoudal, your mother's brother."

René had sprung to his feet before the end of the sentence.

"Will my uncle be in the power of the First Consul?" he stammered.

"Yesterday, your uncle still had two companions," Lila replied. "He confronted Napoleon Bonaparte proudly, a real threat. Today your uncle is alone: Pichegru and Moreau are in prison."

"God help them!" said René, thinking aloud. "They were both great warriors, and no one knows the dictates of their conscience... but that might perhaps be the salvation of Uncle Georges, who will now understand the madness of his enterprise..."

"His enterprise is not mad," Lila put in, her tone firm and resolute. "He is even more reckless than you think. Georges will never confess to madness. Don't argue–what good would it do? You know him, and you know it's true. If Georges Cadoudal could make his escape as easily as I may lift my finger to demand your silence–for I must talk and you must listen– Georges Cadoudal would not run away. His enterprise might seem dubious, seen from the stern viewpoint of honor, but is itself pursuing a matter of honor. He meets all threats with a murderous mouth and bloodshot eyes, like a boar driven back by the hounds...but even if he wished to flee–and you must understand this–flight will henceforth be impossible. Paris is guarded like a gaol, and any attempt to leave will ensure his capture. Your uncle's safety lies in the hands of one man."

"What man?" demanded the young Breton.

"That man is named René de Kervoz."

That man set off across the room with a purposeful stride. Lila's eyes followed him, smiling. "I must love you very much," she said, as if the thought had slipped unthinkingly from her lips. "It seems that each passing moment delivers me more completely to you. I am in a hurry to be finished with everything but you. It is no longer for those who sent me that I am here, nor for Georges Cadoudal, but for you... Come back!"

Her words–half-caress and half-command, stopped him in his tracks. He came back, anxiously. She said to him: "See: you have stopped loving me already!"

Kervoz's fiery expression was reply enough. Lila took his head in her hands and stuck her mouth to his lips, murmuring: "So when shall we speak of love?"

René trembled. He was drowning in her eyes. She was beautiful. She was charm brought to life, voluptuousness incarnate. "Have we time to save him?" he asked.

"Someone is already watching over him," she replied. "At least, someone is already on the track of his pursuers."

"But who are these men, exactly?"

"The Brothers of Virtue," the young woman replied, her smile broadening and her voice becoming serious, "are those who will restore to Georges Cadoudal his lost strength. Two powerful allies have been taken from him but a thousand will take their place. I have no authority, Monsieur de Kervoz, to reveal the secrets of the society to you... but you shall see whether I love you, René, my René... For you, I shall lift the veil, at the risk of terrible punishment..." Kervoz wanted to stop her then, but she seized both his hands and continued in spite of him. "Those who plough their furrow through the crowd leave blood and hatred behind them. In order to climb to great heights, it is necessary to tread on many heads. From the square of Saint-Roch to Aboukir, General Bonaparte has advanced by degrees. Every step on the staircase that has carried him is made of human flesh... don't argue with me, René; if you love him, I shall love him too; I would love Satan if you ordered me to do it. Besides, for my own part, I don't hate the First Consul. I fear and admire him—but those who were my masters before I gave myself to you hate him murderously. They have all been violently separated from those they loved, who have been pitilessly crushed in the course of his ascent. You have glimpsed some of them through the haze of your fever; your memories are vague but I will make them clearer—and that which you have not seen I shall show you.

"Our leader is a woman; I shall leave her until last. Next, after my sister, Countess Marcian Gregoryi, is a young man whose ghastly features are crowned with white hair. When God makes twins, the death of one sweeps away the life of the other. Giuseppe and Andrea Ceracchi were twins. One of the two paid with his life for an audacious attack; the other is a living corpse who only breathes for vengeance.

"As Mahomet led Seïd [48], so Toussaint-Louverture, the Christ of the black race, had a satellite soul. You have seen Taïeh, the ebony giant who would devour the heart of his master's assassin's. You have seen the Welshman Caernarvon [49], who embodies all the rancor of vanquished England, and Osman, the mameluke of Mourad Bey [50], who has been on the trail of the victor of the Battle of the Pyramids since Jaffa. Osman is like Taïeh: a tiger who must be kept chained. There are many others you have not seen. Glory wounds the envious to the utmost depths of their obscurity, just as the sun's rays make myopic eyes bleed. The ranks of the avengers are swollen by the jealous. Behind the battalion consecrated by hate, we have that immortal multitude which already existed when Athens flourished, and voted the exile of Aristides [51] because happy Aristides dazzled too many gazes.

"We have the Lucullus [52] of the Directory, bitterly regretting his fall, and the diamonds which decorate the toes of his half-naked muse in the shameful arrogance of his box at the comedy; we have the slender means of muzzled Mirabeau [53], the ruined chivalry of Coblentz [54], Vendean swords, September daggers. We have it all: the angry past, the jealous present and the fearful future; the Republic and the Monarchy; France and Europe. The poniards of the New World come to us, and the gold that will grant access to the house of Tarquin [55], where everyone haggles over the price of their tottering devotion.

"But this is no Tarquin. Tarquin was a hereditary monarch; this is a Caesar, who invariably exposes himself to danger in putting his foot on the first step that leads up to the throne. Perhaps General Bonaparte is invulnerable–but his crown must be set on a bare head and there is no breastplate over his imperial mantle. His best armor, in any case, is the simple title of Citizen, which he is discarding voluntarily. Jupiter troubles the spirits of those who want to kill him: but look at him, devoid of armor!"

Lila stopped and passed the fingers of her beautiful hand over her brow, over which her jet-black locks trickled. While she was speaking, her voice had become strangely sonorous, and her speech was so powerfully punctuated by the gleam of her large eyes that René was disconcerted. For the second time, he asked: "Who are you, Lila?"

She smiled sadly. "Perhaps..." she murmured, instead of answering the question. "Perhaps Jupiter wants to slay the last demigod who still has the power to bring about the weary decrepitude of the world. Is this man too great a target for us? You think I'm exaggerating, René–and indeed, my countrymen are often dreamers–but I always remain within the bounds of reality. I am Lila, a poor daughter of the Danube,

136

already well-tried by suffering, but on whom destiny seems at last to smile, since she has encountered you on her path through life. I'm telling you the truth.

"It would be insane, however, to think that among so many who are with us there remains no vestige of those who are traitors to us. We are the members of the resuscitated Vehmgerichte [56] of old Germany, recruiting the magistrates of our mysterious tribunal throughout the world. This tribunal is composed of all the enemies of the hero–and one party of his friends.

"We did not want Pichegru and Moreau: they, and only they, have fallen because our hand did not support them. But Countess Marcian Gregoryi has looked favorably upon Georges Cadoudal; it's thanks to her that he has so far avoided the fate of his accomplices. His would be the most cruel fate of all, René, for there are standards to be maintained with regard to two illustrious generals who so often led the armies of the Republic to victory, whereas the rebellious peasant–the chouan, the brigand–must be cornered and beaten down like a mad dog."

René bowed his head. He obviously needed to think. His reason, captive like his senses, was still capable of revolt.

Lila did not give him time to explore the question. "It only remains to tell you about my sister," she said, abruptly, knowing perfectly well that this would reawaken his lapsed curiosity. "About my sister and myself–for her higher destiny drags me in its wake, and I am nothing but my sister's shadow.

"We are the two daughter of a magnate of Bangkeli. Our mother, at sixteen years of age, fell victim to the vampire of Uszel–whose tomb, as large as a church, was found to be full of skulls that had belonged to young women and adolescent girls.

"You French don't believe in that sort of thing, but that's the story, and I'll tell it to you as it was told to me by my father. He was a colonel in the Black Hussars of Bangkeli, in the cavalry of Prince Charles of Lorraine, the Archduke of Austria. The vampire of Uszel–whom the people who live on the banks of the Sava call 'the beauty with changing hair' because she sometimes appeared brunette and sometimes blonde to the young people who immediately fell under her spell–was, during her mortal span, a Bulgarian noblewoman who shared the crimes and debauches of the banate of Szandor during the reign of Louis II, the last of the Jagellons of Bohemia [57] to reign in Hungary. She spent a pleasant century in her coffin– and then she woke up, opened it and used her own hands to excavate a subterranean passage, which led from the depths of her sealed tomb to the bank of the Sava.

"In the faraway lands that are afflicted by these mysterious scourges which you have relegated to the rank of fables, everyone knows that each vampire enjoys a special dispensation to do evil, which it exercises under a particular condition: a rigorous law whose infraction condemns the monster to abominable tortures.

"The particular gift of Addhema, as the Bulgarian noblewoman was named, was to be reborn as beautiful and young as love itself every time she could apply to the hideous bareness of her skull a living head of hair. I mean a scalp, torn from the head of a living victim. This was why her tomb was full of the skulls of young women and adolescent girls. In much the same fashion as the savages of North America who strip the flesh from the heads of their vanquished enemies and carry their scalps away as trophies, Addhema selected and carried off to her sepulchre the most beautiful and happiest faces she could find, so that she might tear from their heads the prey that would secure a few days of youth–for the spell only lasted a few days: as many days as the years of life that remained to the victim. At the end of this period, a new murder was necessary, and a new victim.

"The banks of the Sava are not as populous as those of the Seine. I have no need to tell you how rapidly young women and adolescent girls became rare in the vicinity of Uszel... you're smiling, René, instead of quivering." She was smiling herself, but within that gaiety, which seemed to be an obedient concession to the young man's skepticism, there was an adorable melancholy.

"I'm listening," said René, "but I'm amazed by the path you have taken, under the pretext of talking about love."

"You don't want to talk about love, Monsieur de Kervoz!" Lila murmured, her smile tinged with mockery.

René did not protest; he merely said: "The banks of the Seine have no need to envy the shores of the Sava. We too have a vampire."

"Do you believe in it?" Lila asked, immediately adding: "A strong-minded fellow like you would be ashamed to believe in it!"

"How did you come upon this strange motto: *In vita mors, in morte vita*," murmured René, instead of replying to her question.

"Death in life," Lila intoned, slowly, "life in death: it is the motto of the human race... It was handed down to us by one of our ancestors, the Ban [58] of Szandor, who was also accused of being a vampire. We are a strange family, as you will see..."

She suddenly broke off and stood up, so proud and so beautiful that the young Breton's eyes sparkled. "René, René, I am the one who has set aside love, and I am the one who will bring it back. I am not afraid of your coldness. In an instant, you will be prostrate at my feet!"

Chapter XI
Count Marcian Gregoryi

The hands of the boudoir clock stood at ten o'clock. There was a profound silence within and without Bretonvilliers Lodge. The distant murmur of the living city could scarcely be heard. René and Lila were sitting next to one another on the ottoman. René had kissed her eyes in response to the amorous challenge that sprang forth from Lila's pupils. He too knew that she was certain of victory.

"It is necessary that you should know everything, Monsieur de Kervoz," she went on. "Your Breton superstitions are not the same as our Hungarian superstitions, but what does that matter? Fables or realities, these premises of my story will end up as incontestable facts, on which the life or death of a relative dear to you depends–and on which the life or death of the greatest man of all might also depend. I shall go on.

"Every time that Addhema, the vampire of Uszel, came to re-enliven the cold bones of her skull with the aid of the hair torn from the young head of a living victim, she gained a few days–sometimes a few weeks but sometimes only a few hours–of new existence: one week for every seven years that the victim would otherwise have lived, one month for every thirty. It was like a terrible game, whose prize might be great or small. Addhema never knew in advance–but what did it matter, after all? The hours won, whether numerous or few, were always hours of youth, of beauty, of pleasure–for Addhema became again the splendid courtesan of yesteryear, with all her fiery passion and irresistible power of attraction. That was her gift.

"I want to tell you the condition imposed with respect to that gift: the law that she could not infringe without incurring the penalty of suffering a thousand deaths. Addhema could not surrender herself to a lover before having told him her own history. In the middle of a conversation of love, she had to bring up the strange story that I have just told you, speaking of dead girls, of scalps torn away, and relating with exactitude the bizarre conditions of her death in life, her life in death. I employ the past tense, because she once broke the rule governing her hideous resurrections, and that was while she was bearing the blonde hair of our mother. Love made her forget her strange duty. She received the kiss [59] of a young Serb, as beautiful as the day itself, before having sought and found the opportunity to set out her supernatural history. The evil spirit withdrew at the very moment when she stammered words of tenderness, and the young Serb recoiled in horror at the sight of his mistress restored to her real condition: the cadaver of an old woman, fleshless, icy cold, totally bald and already turning to dust.

"Her true self was reawakened–for during her hours of punishment, every vampire is forced to tell the truth. The Serb heard these words, which seemed to rise up out of the ground: 'Kill me! My greatest torture is life itself. The hour is favorable–kill me! In order to kill me, my heart must be burned.'

"The recent mourning in the house of the Magnate of Bangkeli, where an inconsolable spouse and two babes in the cradle remained, had made a great noise throughout the land. The Serb mounted his horse and came to find our father, who was in the midst of the funeral celebrations. Our father took all his friends and relatives with him and they went to the tomb of Uszel, for the cadaver of the vampire had already disappeared from the home of the Serb.

"The tomb of Uszel was demolished, and our father, having put the blade of his own saber into a fire until it was red hot, plunged it three times, withdrawing it each time, into the heart of Addhema the Bulgarian.

"We grew up, my sister and I, in the sad and seemingly-empty castle. We lacked all maternal caresses, and were rocked to sleep with the tale of these ominous mysteries.

There was a song whose words were: One day for one year, twenty-four hours for three hundred and sixty-five days. At the final minute of the final hour, the hair dies, the spell is broken, and the hideous sorceress flees, vanquished, to her vault...

"My sister was in her sixteenth year and I was nearly fifteen when our father hoisted the red banner above the towers of Bangkeli. At the same time, he sent his Czechs to the homes of his tenants along the river. There were four of them: one carried his saber, the second his carbine, the third his Hussar jacket, the fourth his jatspka [60]. That night, there were two hundred fully-equipped and armed Hussars camped around our ancient walls.

"My father told us to pack our clothes, our jewels and our poniards, and we departed in a carriage that very same night, bound for Trieste. The regiment–my father's two hundred tenants comprised the regiment of the Black Hussars of Bangkeli–took the same road on horseback. The rendezvous was at Trevise. Archduke Charles of Austria was there with his general staff. Bonaparte had already completed two-thirds of the crushing Italian campaign, which would conclude in the very heart of Germany. Our army had changed its general four times and had withdrawn, no longer counting the battles it had lost. Even so, there were celebrations in Trieste, where twelve regiments newly-arrived from the Tyrol, Bohemia and Hungary presented a magnificent spectacle. Prince Charles swore to annihilate the French at the next encounter.

"My sister and I had never known anything other than the wild shores of the Sava and the austere solitude of the castle. The first three days were like a dream to us. On the fourth, our father said to my sister: 'You are to be the wife of Count Marcian Gregoryi.' My sister did not say yes or no; it was not a question but a command.

"Marcian Gregoryi was twenty-two years old. He wore his bright Croatian uniform heroically. That same evening, Prince Charles made him a general. He was handsome, noble, richer than a king, loving and joyful. My sister and he were married on the day when Bonaparte crossed the Tagliamento [61]; on the following day the great battle took place which annihilated the Archduke, his hope and his glory, and opened a passage into the Tyrol for the French. We were separated from our father. Count Marcian Gregoryi looked after us. We passed the night in an inn near Udine. My room was separated by a simple partition from the one where the young spouses were to sleep. About midnight, I heard my sister's voice loudly raised. I thought at the time that it belonged to another woman, for I did not recognize that imperious tone.

"She said: 'Count, I have nothing against you. You are brave, and you must have met many women who would admire your noble figure and handsome face. I have obeyed my father, who is my master and who said to me: This man will be your husband. But my father, while departing from Bangkeli, also said to me: Pack your poniard. My poniard is in my hand. It is my liberty. If you take one step towards me, I will kill myself.' Marcian Gregoryi begged and wept. Can you guess why I took the side of Marcian against my sister?"

Lila broke off for a moment, combing her slender fingers through René's hair. "Oh, there is no need to be jealous. Marcian Gregoryi is a long time dead. At the end of that month—March 1797—the French, driving us constantly before them, entered Trieste. On the twenty-fourth of March—or the sixth of Germinal as it is now called—my sister and I were together in a country house situated a league from Chiusa [62]. That night, my sister came to find me. I never saw her look more beautiful. Her outfit was dazzling, and pride was shining in her eyes. She embraced me, kissed me on the lips and said goodbye. I had no time to question her. Two minutes later, her galloping horse was raising clouds of dust from the road. I followed her course as best as I could from my window, although she was already becoming lost in the darkness. In the distance, from several different directions, the roar of cannon could be heard.

"Yanusza, who had wet-nursed both of us—the old woman who let you in this evening—came up to my room and sat down in the doorway. 'My master's older daughter is on the road to her death!' she moaned, tears in her eyes. She silenced my questions; loud hoofbeats sounded in the courtyard. The ringing voice of Marcian Gregoryi ordered: 'Full speed!' And for the second time, the road disappeared behind whirlwinds of dust. Marcian Gregoryi took the same direction as my sister.

"Several leagues away there was a simple tent, pitched on the edge of a grove of ash-trees, surrounded by bivouac fires. In front of the tent, the French general staff were conferring in low voices. Inside, a young man of twenty-six–pale, thin, puny, his hair cut square above a powerful forehead–was asleep, his head propped up by a rolled-up map. A letter signed Josephine was open on the table, bearing a French postmark. He was easily able to sleep; he had worked terribly hard since daybreak. An entire army guarded him: soldiers and generals alike. He was the hope and the glory of the universally victorious French Republic. His name was Napoleon Bonaparte, and his sleep was peaceful. In order to get to him, an enemy would have to get past an army of thirty thousand men. Even so, he was suddenly woken up by a hand placed on his shoulder. A man he did not know–an enemy–was standing over him, saber in hand: a tall man, strong, young, endowed to the highest degree with the masculine beauty of the Magyar race, whose eyes spoke a terrible language of wrath and hatred.

" 'General,' he said, coldly, 'I am Count Marcian Gregoryi. My forefathers were noblemen before the birth of Christ our savior; no member of my house has ever been anything but a soldier. I do not want to assassinate you. I beg you to take your sword in your hand in order to defend yourself, for my wife has betrayed me for you, and one of us must die.'

"One is enfeebled when one has only just woken up, but Bonaparte was not afraid. Nor did he call out, although he could hear the murmur of watchmen all around his tent. If he had called out, he would be dead, for the point of Marcian Gregoryi's saber was upon his breast. 'You have made a mistake, or you are mad,' he replied. 'I do not know your wife.'

Calmly pointing to the open letter, he added: 'There is only one woman for me, and that is my wife.'

" 'General, you are lying,' was Marcian's response. And without sacrificing his striking-position, he took from his jacket a similarly open letter, which he presented to Bonaparte. The letter was written in French; my sister and I, like all Hungarian aristocrats, had spoken French since infancy, as well as our mother tongue.

"The letter was addressed to Marcian Gregoryi and it read:

" 'Monsieur le Comte,

" 'You will never see me again. A caprice of my father's has thrown me into your arms; you did not ask me whether I loved you before taking me for your wife. That is unworthy of a man of courage, and equally unworthy of a man of honor. Your sin is its own punishment. Only one thing would have made me surrender myself to you: force. I love force. If my husband had subdued me violently on the day after the wedding, I might perhaps have been an obedient and worshipful wife. You were weak; you retreated in the face of my threats. I do not love those who retreat; I despise those who give way. I am the master of my own fate; I am leaving. There is no point in looking for me. He is a man who has never retreated, never given way, never weakened: the conqueror of all your faults, as young as Alexander the Great and destined, like him, to put the whole human race beneath his heel. I love this man and I admire all the hatred and all the disdain that he has for you. I tell you again, there is no point in looking for me, unless you dare to follow me into General Bonaparte's tent.'

"The signature was my sister's.

"The French general read the letter to the end. Perhaps he hoped that one of his lieutenants might chance to come into his tent, but he took not a second longer than was necessary to read the letter.

" 'Monsieur le Comte, he said, his voice as calm as his expression, 'I will provide, if you wish, the means for you to leave my camp. I have heard it said that jealousy is a dementia. I tell you again that I do not know your wife.'

" 'And I tell you again that you are a liar,' Gregoryi growled, through clenched teeth. At the same time, the forefinger of his left hand extended convulsively, pointing to the rear entrance to the tent, which was situated behind Bonaparte.

"Bonaparte turned and saw a woman of marvelous beauty, wearing an opulent Magyar costume, whose incomparable blonde hair was adorned with long *torsades* [63] of sapphires. He let out a cry of astonishment, for he saw that he was lost, this time: condemned to death by the mere presence of this woman.

"What happened next was quicker than a flash of lightning. Marcian Gregoryi was not the man to release his prey. He had demanded a fight, and had been refused; although he was master of the situation, by virtue of his drawn sword, a delay of one second would make him a slave. The French general's cry would bring a hundred swords. Marcian Gregoryi aimed for his rival's heart and drew back his arm to drive the weapon home—but before the saber-point, thrust in such a manner as to cleave that vulnerable breast, had completed half of its trajectory, a convulsive movement of the arm snatched it back.

"A flash had illuminated the gloom of the tent; an explosion had reverberated through it. The saber fell from Gregoryi's hand as he was struck down. My sister had taken aim too; a bullet from her pistol, shattering her husband's skull, saved the life of General Bonaparte.

"Generals, officers and soldiers came in from all directions at once, to see Bonaparte standing upright, a little pale, but quite cool. To his right was a man bathed in blood, to his left that dazzling woman, whose half-uncovered bosom was palpitating, and who still had a smoking gun in her hand.

" 'Citizens,' said Bonaparte, 'you are a little late. It appears that the tent of your general and commander-in-chief is not very well guarded—be more vigilant in future.' And when the consternation had died down, he added: 'I fell asleep; that was a mistake, because we have work to do. I have been woken up... Citizens, that man must be tended with the utmost care, if he still lives; if he is dead, he must be honorably buried. He was not an assassin.' He made a gesture of dismissal to those who surrounded him, then said: 'Citizens, make ready. I shall reassemble the council very soon.'

"The body of Marcian Gregoryi, who was no longer breathing, was carried away.

"My sister was left alone with General Bonaparte. You have only caught a glimpse of her, and seven years have passed by. I do not know any woman who could be compared to her. She was a hundred times more beautiful then, and the man that she had come to save certainly could not look at her with indifferent eyes. General Bonaparte had a large and handsome Swiss watch placed upon the maps which covered his work-table. He consulted it, and said: 'Madame, speak quickly, and try to justify yourself...' Does that astonish you?"

Lila broke off at this point, in response to a gesture of surprise which René had not been able to suppress.

René had not ceased for an instant to listen with intense interest. "Yes," he murmured, "that astonishes me. Your story grips me, because I believe it to be true... that woman is going to Georges Cadoudal as she went to Bonaparte..."

"Not at all," Lila interrupted, dryly. Her rapidly-lowered eyelids hid the glint which, in spite of herself, illuminated her eyes. Only her mouth expressed a nuance of disdain. She added, in the tone of a dreamer: "Do not compare them; no comparison is possible. Georges Cadoudal can never be anything but an ordinary man, Bonaparte is a giant. Hatred is more clear-sighted that you imagine, and my sister increases hatred as she increases admiration. The magnet that drew her towards Bonaparte was glory; the force that draws her towards Cadoudal is vengeance. Let me continue, I beg you, for I have almost finished and have made haste to arrive at that which concerns us.

"My sister refused to justify herself; she had come with other intentions. Perhaps she said so, for I have never encountered a heart as bold as hers. Her words fell upon an ear of marble. Her gaze, which no one could resist, was blunted by lowered eyelids. I cannot tell you the details of what happened; my sister never confided them to me. I read the meaning of her silence; I translated the gleam in her eye and the tremor of her bloodless lips. My sister never forgives.

"The hands of the watch marked out two minutes; then General Bonaparte called out again, saying: 'Citizens, take your places, the council is open... I order that Madame la Comtesse Marcian Gregoryi should be conducted, under escort, back to the Austrian front line.' "

Chapter XII
The Windowless Room

"No one in Prince Charles's army," Lila went on, "knew how Count Marcian Gregoryi had died. My sister and I were taken to the convent of Varasdin. It was occupied by cloistered nuns of the Order of Saint Vladimir, but its walls were not sufficiently high, nor its bars sufficiently solid, to contain the will of my sister.

"During the brief and victorious Tyrolean campaign, Bonaparte experienced many hazards unrecorded by history, save for two or three which now seem like chapters of a romance in the middle of the great epic of his life. The hand of Countess Marcian Gregoryi was in them.

"Our father died before the end of the century, and my sister became her own mistress. I did not know how to resist her. She completely dominated me–a mere girl–with the hauteur of her hatred. We owned estates as extensive as a province on the banks of the Sava; all of them were sold, with the sole inexplicable exception of the sterile field where the tomb of the vampire of Uszel was situated, which my sister kept. That desolate field still belongs to her. We left for France after the treaty of Campo-Formio [64]. In the midst of the triumphs which Bonaparte the conqueror received in Paris, there was one enemy gaze which followed him like a malediction.

"One man soon stood up against the young general radiant with glory: one man who seemed to have sworn to put an abrupt end to his soaring fortunes. That was director Rewbell [65], the arrogant puritan who recited his Genevan litanies with an Alsatian accent. Rewbell had an Egeria [66] to support him in that unequal struggle of mediocrity against genius. In a villa situated on the heights of Passy lived a young woman whose reputation for extraordinary beauty grew in spite of the peaceful retreat where she concealed herself. The puritan Rewbell came to visit her every night. My sister, the brilliant Countess Gregoryi, became the mistress of Colmar's advocate to appease her hatred.

"It was like trying to catch an eagle in a spider's web. Bonaparte broke the threads of those petty intrigues with a single flutter, and fearful Egypt woke up one morning to see a French army covering its shores. The villa at Passy to which Rewbell went at night fell vacant again. An English ship carried us to Alexandria.

"All those who are destined to dazzle or dominate the world are born under a lucky star, that's certain. Bonaparte's star appeared to me in Egypt, where he might have died a hundred times. My indefatigable sister spent all her days and nights setting useless traps. He proceeded along his historic path entirely unaware of the pitfalls over which his marching feet were passing.

"What can I say? As I became a woman, he grew in my eyes until he seemed a god. It wasn't love; I was far too conscious of the enormous gulf which separated us–and besides, my heart's destiny was to wait for you, and to beat for no one but you. No, it wasn't love. What I had for him was a timid and respectful admiration, but–I don't know how to tell you this, René–the worship that forced me to my knees was mingled with a secret horror. I am the daughter of a dead woman.

"I see that terrible thing called vampirism–a kind of life that is dependent on the blood of others–everywhere. And with what is all that glory made if not blood? With blood, it is said, the alchemists created gold; they needed it by the barrel. Glory, more precious than gold, requires torrents. And one man floats upon that red ocean: the vampire supreme, who has multiplied his own life with a hundred million deaths.

"In my soul, I became a deserter to my sister's cause. Perhaps there was a secret charm in the depths of my weakness to protect the providential march of that giant. I protected him, that's the truth: the fable tells us, smiling, what even the humblest of animals can do for the lion, king of beasts. I protected him in the long marches across the sands of Egypt. I protected him during the crossing, and while he fought that other battle, in the Conseil des Cinq-Cents [67]–the battle where coolness seemed to be temporarily abandoned–I still protected him. There was a moment then, I assure you, when the famous grenadiers would not have known how to defend him. And woe betide him who allows himself to be too often defended by soldiers anywhere else but in the field, which is where soldiers belong!

"My sister asked herself whether some demon was protecting the life of that man, but her conspiracy went stubbornly on, indefatigably. On the tenth of October, in the year 1800, my sister put a dagger into the hand of Giuseppe Ceracchi, a young sculptor who was already famous, whose chivalrous soul she had intoxicated. Aréna, Demerville and Topino-Lebrun had sworn that Bonaparte would not see the end of the performance of *Horaces* put on that night. An anonymous letter warned General Lannes [68]. I wept over Ceracchi's death, but Bonaparte was saved.

"Three months later, on the twenty-fourth of December, at the moment when the First Consul's coach turned the corner of the Rue Saint-Nicaise into the Rue de Rohan on the way to the Opera, a young boy cried out to the coachman: 'Go faster, if you want to save your life!' The frightened coachman whipped his horses, whose rapid course carried them over an obstacle placed in their path. That obstacle was the infernal machine! Who do you think that 'young boy' was?

"I have been watching over him ever since.

"I have told you the secret of my life, René, for I cannot defend myself against my sister. With one word you can destroy me. Day after day, in ceaseless opposition to my sister, I have kept him safe. I do not love her; she terrifies me–but she remains sacred to me, and I would lie down in the doorway of the room where she sleeps to make sure that she sleeps safely. Before being arrested, Moreau and Pichegru received warnings; it was I who warned them. They held their course; they are lost."

There was a long silence.

"What do you want from me?" René de Kervoz asked, finally.

"The means of saving your mother's brother, without compromising the security of the First Consul. I want to have a meeting with Georges Cadoudal."

René said nothing.

"You don't trust me," Lila murmured, sadly.

"I would trust myself to you," the young Breton replied. "What you've done so far was done well, and in your story–to which I listened without missing a single word–I have perceived the energy of a righteous and praiseworthy soul. But my uncle's secrets are not mine to give away."

She got up, smiling. "It's your decision," she said. "I have already given this man I do not know–and it was for you, only for you–the gift of a few precious hours that should have been devoted entirely to us. By to us, I mean to our love. I have explained everything that you wanted to know; there is no more mystery for you in the strange adventure of the isolated house where you heard the Brothers of Virtue mentioned for the first time... and take note than in doing that, I have not betrayed my sister to you. My sister is one of those whom it would be madness to attack. Whoever goes against her will be broken. She too has her star!" She clapped her hands softly, and continued: "Trust will come when you have seen how far my love for you will go. In the meantime, not one more word on these matters which have stolen an evening of happiness from us. It is nearly midnight. Give me your hand, René, and let us both put into practice the chorus sung by German students: 'Let us rejoice while we are young...' "

While she was speaking, a curtain moved slowly aside, revealing another room where dewy candles gave out a sweet light. In the middle of this other room, a light meal was neatly set out on a table. There was a recess in the far wall, where ruffled curtains of Indian muslin stood half-open, displaying

152

the bed within. There were only two chairs set before the table. There were flowers everywhere, and the fire burning gently in the hearth exhaled odorous incense.

When René crossed the threshold of this room, Lila seemed even more beautiful–but his passion was cooled by a certain vague dread. The memory of the bizarre story which he had heard was glimmering in his eyes. Lila had told the tale with an indescribable charm, and yet René was still tormented by a doubt, whose source owed more to instinct than to reason.

Strangely enough, the part of the story that had struck him most forcibly was the hazy episode of the vampire. René had always responded with a scornful smile to anyone who asked him whether he believed in vampires, female or male–and yet he could not dislodge that striking image from his thoughts, in spite of its absurdity: the bald corpse, resting in the tomb for centuries, then waking up young, ardent and lascivious as soon as a living head of hair, still moist with warm blood, covered the horrible nudity of its skull.

He stared at the undulant ebony of the marvelous black hair that crowned Lila's face–that face sparkling with youth and charm–and he said to himself: Those whose heads of hair were torn away by the dead woman looked like this. And he shivered–but the shiver penetrated into the marrow of his bones when another thought occurred to him, which he tried in vain to resist: And by the same token, the dead woman must have looked like this when she had torn their hair away! The dead woman! The vampire! Sometimes dark, sometimes blonde, according to whether her last victim had hair of jet or gold!

Lila filled the glasses from a bottle of Tokay: a topaz liquid which filled the exquisitely-cut Bohemian crystal with wild sparks. Together, they moistened their lips with that nectar. Then Lila proposed that they should exchange glasses, saying: "It is my country that produces this liqueur of princes and queens. In Semlin, near Belgrade–at the place where the Sava, always Christian, is lost in the Danube, which ultimately becomes Muslim–young girls sing the ballad of Amber, while

153

each lover plucks a pearl of Tokay from the lip of his mistress with a joyous kiss."

A single golden tear trembled upon the coral of her mouth. René drank it, and it seemed to him that the drop of ambrosia was intoxication itself, and pure sensuousness. His temples throbbed; his heart was cramped by a spasm of anguish and delight. He looked at Lila, whose wide eyes were languishing, transformed by caresses. She was as beautiful as those dreams of an Oriental paradise whose doors are opened by smoking opium. A supernatural aura extended itself around her. Her long eyelids released a spring of sparkling prayers.

René was still struggling. He tried to pronounce Angela's name in the depths of his soul, but the wine was passion, forgetfulness, folly. It shone like a flame in the jeweled cups, and like a flame it burned.

"Another pearl upon your lips," he murmured, wishing that he might never, ever be able to awake from the adorable fever of this beautiful dream.

Lila filled the cups for a second time. Their mouths met again. René, swooning, slumped back into his chair. Lila seized him again in a sudden embrace: "But you do not trust me!" she said.

René saw that her eyes were brimming with lovely tears.

"I love you!" he stammered. "Oh, how I love you!" Then, exalted to delirium: "Haven't you told me what you want? Isn't your mind as heavenly as your beauty? You are the angel sent down by the mercy of God to fight against the demon. Everything I have is yours, including my conscience! Georges Cadoudal is a hero struck blind; you will save him because of the blood of my veins which now runs in yours, and you will prevent him from destroying the destiny of the century. I put his life in your hands. Listen..."

And he spoke, giving away the secret of the retreat that allowed the Breton conspirator to remain hidden while showing himself and moving about Paris, like those werewolves of legend who had a magic lair.

Lila obeyed. She listened–and every word was engraved upon her memory.

The molten candles had all been extinguished. Nothing but a nightlight, suspended from the ceiling, now illuminated the solitude of that room, so joyously voluptuous a short time before, imprinting an almost funereal aspect upon its tremulous brightness.

The protective muslin curtains hung motionless, closing off the alcove.

Within the alcove René de Kervoz was sleeping–alone.

For how long had he slept?

The table had been cleared; the fire was dying in the hearth. Various noises could be heard outside in the distance: the great murmur of a city waking up. And much closer–surely it must be an illusion, for the birds in our gardens do not sing at night!–a concert of little chattering birds could be heard.

It was dark, pitch-black.

Oddly enough, though, a sliver of bright light passed between the bottom edge of the closed door that was opposite the alcove and the floor. It seemed like reflected sunlight.

It was by that door that Lila and René had entered the dining-room. Was there daylight beyond? It did not show through any window in that strange room. How long had René been asleep there?

It had all been one long dream rather than slumber, that must be made clear: a delicious, intoxicated, adorable dream, which had then become feverish, and then sad, dismal and full of fearful omens.

René had remained conscious throughout, vaguely but incessantly. He heard and he saw–or perhaps only believed that he heard and saw.

His dreams, which he reckoned happy dreams or horrible nightmares, had proceeded thus:

How beautiful, young, ardent and divine she was! What fond words they had exchanged! And what silences, a thousand times more eloquent than words! That was the first hour.

René remembered having contemplated going to sleep, with her charming head, bathed in black hair, resting on his bare arm. Then there undoubtedly had been an interval of true sleep, of which he retained no memory or sensation–then a sort of awakening: a hard, acrid kiss, a broken voice which said, "You are the only one I have ever loved; you shall not die!" These words remained in his mind; he heard them over and over again, like an obstinate refrain. What did they mean? Then again... but who is astonished by the absurdity of a dream? Everyone knows full well that the impressions received in a waking state return to trouble sleep. There was that hideous story of the vampire of Uszel, the bald cadaver relieved by young heads of hair.

Lila, grace incarnate, the enchantress. Lila was the cadaver.

René saw her change while he slept: change rapidly, passing through all the successive stages of degradation which separate exuberant life from death... from that frightful death which hides its ruin in the depths of a tomb.

That rosy cheek had turned ghastly white, and then the bones had burst through the corroded flesh.

But why attempt the impossible? That which René had seen, no pen should dare to write.

One fact alone must be noted, because it was connected with René's *idée fixe*. While that astounding transformation had taken place before his very eyes, the black hair–that splendid head of hair–had slowly detached itself, like a clinging parchment shriveling up in a fire. Then a sort of fissure had appeared above the face, extending around the temples. The dried-up skin corroded, revealing a frightful skull...

René wanted to run away, but his body was leaden.

He wanted to cry out, but he no longer had a voice.

She got up. Lila–was that still her name? Her legs collided with one another, rattling like a skeleton's, producing a resonant echo that congealed the blood in his veins. The hairpiece was still clinging to the crown of her skull. She went to the fireplace. The hairpiece fell into it, yielding up black smoke.

René saw no more, except for an inert form, stretched out on the carpet in front of the fireplace. A voice which came from who knows where–from everywhere and nowhere–cried out in agony: "Yanusza! Help!"

The old woman who spoke Latin appeared. She came to the bed, laughing derisively and muttering incomprehensibly. In passing, she stirred the inert mass with her foot, making a dry sound.

The old woman bent over René and felt his breast roughly.

"Why hasn't she killed you, then?" she said.

At the touch of those rude, cold fingers, René made a desperate effort to recover the use of his muscles, but he remained paralyzed.

The old woman cleared the table unhurriedly. Then she extended the tablecloth on the carpet and slid the groaning, collapsing mass into the center of the cloth before tying the four corners in a knot. By this means, she made a package, which rattled like a sack full of ivory chesspieces.

She threw it over her shoulder and went out, bent over beneath her burden.

The next-to-last noise that René heard was that of the latch closing the lock; the last was the grinding of two solid bolts sliding home on the other side.

When René finally awoke–for he did wake up–his head was heavy and all his joints were aching. He sometimes felt like that after excessive indulgence at the table; on the previous evening, however, he had eaten nothing at all. All he had done was empty two of those marvelous Bohemian glasses of that Hungarian ambrosia, Tokay wine.

His first thought was for Angela, and the sensation of loving her just as he had before was a great joy, impregnating his whole being. His second thought was for Lila–and he recalled, for a quarter of a minute, the voluptuous subsidence that had been the beginning of his slumber; but these vague delights were cut through by a *frisson* which chilled the marrow of his bones: the memory of his dream.

Was it a dream?

What else but a dream could explain the black madness of those confused adventures?

And yet he was here, in this bed.

Where had Lila gone?

By the flickering light of the lamp, he consulted his watch, which was on the night-table. Its hands stood at eleven o'clock. He thought it had stopped. He put it to his ear. It was ticking...

Eleven o'clock! He was certain that he had heard the twelve strokes of midnight at the moment when Lila's story concluded.

It was eleven o'clock in the morning!

But why was he still surrounded by darkness? Was he truly in the somber realm of the impossible?

He leapt out of the bed. His clothes were there, scattered carelessly on the floor. He could not remember having taken them off. As he began to get dressed, his eye fell upon the ray of light that crept under the door. He felt a chill, and his eyes made a rapid tour of the room, searching for a window.

There was none.

For the first time, the idea occurred to him that he was a prisoner. But it was so improbable! In the middle of Paris!

He was ashamed of himself, and he smiled scornfully, saying: "It's a continuation of the dream." He went on dressing, not wanting to see that mendacious luminous ray, not wanting to hear the noises from outside, not wanting to understand, or to think, or to reason. There are some things that are beyond belief.

When he was fully dressed, he tried to open the door, but in vain. A cold sweat bathed his temples.

He called out. The dull voice seemed to strike the walls of the room and rebound, choked off. No one replied. He climbed up on the table and unhooked the lamp, whose oil was almost exhausted. He looked for a way out. There was none.

When he came back towards the hearth, something caught his eye: a scrap of parchment, to which adhered a few black hairs, half-burned. He collapsed upon the floor, his heart squeezed by extravagant terror, thinking: "The vampire! Was my dream a reality?"

The lamp suddenly flared up, illuminating a coat-of-arms above the mantelpiece, stamped with a comtal crown, around which ran the motto: *In vita mors, in morte vita.*

Then the lamp went out.

René put both hands to his insurgent heart. Words echoed in his ears: "The vampire! The vampire!"

And as his hard-pressed reason searched for objections, saying: "Would she have dared to tell me her own story?" his memory replied: "That's the rule! She obeyed the law of her infernal existence and told me her own story!" He let out a horrible cry, leapt to his feet, and flung himself madly at the door–but the door was as solid as a wall

It took him an hour to exhaust his vain efforts. When he finally fell, utterly worn out, it seemed to him that moist and icy lips touched his mouth, and he lost consciousness just as the carillon of Saint-Louis-en-l'Ile sounded the mid-day Angelus [69].

Chapter XIII
The Secretary General

Two days later–which is to say, on the third of March 1804–
the whole of Paris was excited by reports of the Moreau-
Pichegru-Cadoudal conspiracy, which, it was said, had very
nearly succeeded. Shortly before nightfall, the Secretary General of the Prefecture of Police was notified of the fact that a
man insisted on speaking in confidence to his superior, Monsieur Dubois.

Moreau and Pichegru were behind bars, but Georges Cadoudal remained at liberty, and all attempts to discover his
hiding-place had come to nothing. Citizen Dubois, who would
become a Comte under the Empire, had run the Prefecture of
Police since the 18th Brumaire; he had done his best work in
the *Théâtre Français* Affair and the Carrousel Affair, but the
First Consul had a rather low opinion of him even so, and
certainly did not think of him as a wizard.

There were even more police forces in those days than
we have mentioned, and the Prefecture's police were very
strictly controlled: firstly by the general police under the great
Judge Régnier; then by the castle police, led by Bourrienne,
and the military police, at whose head was Anne-Jean-Marie-
René Savary, Duc de Rovigo; and ultimately by the counter-
police of Fouché–who, despite having retired to private life,
alternating his residence between his château at Pont-Carré
and his house in the Rue de Bac, still had an eye at every key-
hole.

Monsieur Dubois was persuaded that his future influence
and fortune were dependent on the outcome of the Cadoudal
Affair. He was then a man of forty-eight, well-proportioned,
well-dressed and moderately good-looking, although his face

promised little more than the man was capable of delivering. The aforementioned notification was sent just as he had put on his gloves to go home, and it did not prevent him from going about his own personal business. He had for his Secretary General a brave old man moldering in the bureaux, whom he had selected less for his strength than for his own amusement. Citizen Berthellemot, an overripe fruit of the reaction against the Directory, was possessed of considerable pretensions, the greatest possible respect for bureaucratic traditions, a profound worship of routine and a slight hint of erudition. He coveted the position of the Citizen Prefect, who coveted in his turn the rank of Citizen Judge. Berthellemot was a tall, gaunt man of remarkable propriety, wearisome formality and excessive loquacity. He was as pompous and finicky as all vain men; he was over fifty, to his bitter regret.

Monsieur Berthellemot was alone in his huge office overlooking the Rue du Harley-du-Palais when Divisional Inspector Despaux came in to announce the arrival of a stranger who insisted on speaking to the prefect of police.

"What sort of man is he?" asked the Secretary General.

"A tall, hearty fellow, grey-haired but half-bald, with the serious and resolute manner of one whose youth is not entirely past and who keeps his hands in his pockets. I have a vague idea that I have encountered him somewhere in the Palais Quarter, near the Cathedral."

"Monsieur Despaux," the Secretary General said, sternly, "an employee of the police must not have vague ideas. Either he knows, or he doesn't."

"In that case, Monsieur, I don't know."

The Secretary General looked a him disapprovingly, but Despaux was much stronger than his superior, and faced up to the stare without flinching. Talleyrand [70] once said that one must go to England to find heads who are stronger than their deputies; he had a rather spiteful tongue.

"Will you see him, please?" Despaux asked.

The Secretary General hesitated. "Not so fast, Inspector," he replied. "Steady as you go! It's obvious that no responsibility rests on your shoulders, but I can see much further than the end of my nose." Despaux bowed coldly. Berthellemot continued: "We have come to a wretched pass, do you know that? The Septembrists are agitating in the shadows, and the Babouvists are simply the devil incarnate."

"They are old friends of Monsieur the Prefect," Despaux said, calmly, "and Monsieur the Secretary General."

"You are mistaken, Monsieur!" Berthellemot said, solemnly. "I have always shared the opinions of the First Consul... and the prefect and I intend to sweep the bureaux clean."

Despaux smiled. "If Monsieur the Prefect wishes to dismiss me, temporarily or permanently," he said, "I have an offer from the secretary of Monsieur Fouché, who arranges excellent fishing-parties down at Pont-Carré. I'll send you a basket of trout, Monsieur Berthellemot."

The Secretary General frowned. He crumpled the letter that he had in his hand in a sudden fit of anger. "Watch what you say, Inspector," he said through clenched teeth. "I have the good grace of the First Consul... I arrested the most dangerous man of the century... when I say 'I', I mean Monsieur the Prefect."

"Cadoudal?" Despaux put in, still smiling.

"Pichegru! I am determined to stifle all this scandalous noise that has arisen concerning the supposedly anti-libertarian measures that Napoleon Bonaparte has taken to ensure the security of the State. I am determined, Monsieur... when I say 'I', you understand... and although we have found it necessary to demolish the Bastille, Inspector, the Congerie is still standing...and if a man like you, who knows too much, is contemplating a shameful desertion... for I tell you, Monsieur, in case you do not know it, that the First Consul distrusts the old Ministry of Police... and there's a reason for that!"

"Impossible!" said Despaux. "That good Citizen Fouché...!"

"I beg you to remember that the word citizen is regulated by official usage, Monsieur Despaux. And I shall not be far away, my dear Inspector, if I am content with you—and in memory of the excellent relationship that has always existed between us–I shall not be far away from thinking seriously about your promotion. When I say 'I', it is understood that I refer to my superior, Monsieur the Prefect."

Inspector Despaux made no reply, but merely smiled. "Does Monsieur the Secretary General wish to receive the man who is waiting?" he asked.

"Ah! He's waiting... I had forgotten... I don't think that I'm at the service of everyone who happens along, Monsieur Despaux. If I gave you specific instructions to interrogate him...?"

"He will refuse to answer me."

"He has said so?"

"Very clearly."

"Your personal recommendation, Monsieur Despaux, is that I should receive him, in the absence of Monsieur the Prefect?"

"Monsieur Secretary General," the Inspector replied, "it is hardly for me to give advice to my superiors–but in the circumstances in which we find ourselves..."

"They are diabolical circumstances, Monsieur."

"It might be that the revelations of this unknown..."

"Then he has come to reveal something to me?"

"I believe so... and if the revelations concern the conspiracy... you know that we are no further advanced than on day one..."

"Monsieur," Berthellemot interrupted him, "my line of inquiry... and when I say 'my line', I mean Monsieur the Prefect's... our line of inquiry is always determined in advance, independently of the opinion of this one or that one. Great events are in the making–very great events. I know a great deal that I cannot tell you, believe me... France needs a master: I have never varied on that point. Who shall live shall see. As soon as you spoke to me about this man, I was fully intent on seeing him. If he has evil designs on my person, my duty is to risk my life...and when I say 'my life'... but no matter... in the service of His Majesty..."

163

"His Majesty!" Despaux repeated, without overmuch astonishment.

"Did I say 'His Majesty'? That's proof of the high regard I have for the First Consul... Be careful, Monsieur Inspector... perhaps chance will permit you to lift your gaze far above your sphere today... would you please put two men on watch... and send in the man who has come to talk to me about Georges Cadoudal."

The Secretary General pushed back his chair back and got to his feet. With a solemn gesture, he dismissed Despaux, overruling the Inspector's intended objection to the final words. Soon afterwards, the sound of heavy boots marching into the next room were heard. It was the two agents taking up their observation post. Then the usher introduced the mysterious unknown by the far door.

Monsieur Berthellemot was still standing up. He looked the new arrival up and down, taking stock of him with the exaggeratedly profound stare of the actors who play Messieurs de Sartines and de la Reynie [71] in theatrical melodramas. That stare is sufficient in itself to put the most vulgar rogue on his guard. I swear on my honor that neither Monsieur de la Reynie, who was a man of great merit, nor the good Monsieur de Sartines, who was not much better at his job than Monsieur Berthellemot, ever condescended to use that stare; it was, however, a great success in the theatre. No self-respecting comedian would ever choose another role when he had occasion to disguise himself as a police lieutenant.

The stare did not seem to make any impression whatsoever on the singular person who came in, and who turned politely to offer his thanks to the usher. Monsieur Berthellemot folded his arms across his chest. The unknown greeted him amicably and politely.

"Come in," said Monsieur Berthellemot.

The unknown obeyed.

Inspector Despaux's description had been a good one. The man was indeed a "hearty fellow"–or, at least, must have been once. He was now an old hearty fellow, so far as appearances were concerned. To judge by the wrinkles on his face and the color of his hair, he was well past his prime. He was dressed in black, very formally but rather poorly. It will be remembered that we employed similar expressions in describing the costume of Papa Sévérin the first time we encountered him, on his wooden bench in the Tuileries. He was tall and seemingly strong. His features were heavily emphasized but calm and chiseled, carrying the scars of more than one battle: some sustained in conflict against disorderly passions, others merely the legacy of the eternal war of man against misfortune. When he had come two-thirds of the way from the door to the desk, he bowed politely and said: "It is to the Prefect of Police that I desire to have the honor of speaking."

"Impossible," Berthellemot replied, solemnly. "Besides which, Monsieur the Prefect is me; we are one."

"In that case," said the gentleman, "for want of the organ-grinder... I thank you all the same for granting me an audience."

Berthellemot sat down and stuffed his hand inside his jacket; then, crossing his legs, he took up a paper-knife, which he examined very attentively. "Well, my man," he said, affecting an air of distraction, "I hope that you have something worthwhile to tell me."

The stranger put his hand–a robust hand, but very pale–upon the back of a chair. When the Secretary General's eyes expressed surprise, he simply said: "I've been running all around Paris today, Monsieur Civil Servant, and I don't have the means to run around in carriages." He sat down–but there was not the least effrontery in the action. While sitting down, the unknown retained his attitude of respect and courtesy.

Monsieur Berthellemot wondered whether this was a man of importance badly dressed, or merely some poor devil ignorant of his offense against the profound respect that was owed to himself, Monsieur Berthellemot, as the alter ego of Monsieur Dubois. He was a lynx by profession, but myopic by nature; he had sharpened the version of Monsieur de Sartines' stare that he had discovered in the theatre, but he could not resolve this dilemma. "My friend," he said, "this time, I will tolerate a familiarity which it is not my custom to extend to agents."

"I'm not an agent, Monsieur Employee," the stranger replied, "and I thank you for kindness. I recognize you, now that I look at you. In the days when there were Jacobin clubs, you spoke loud and long about equality, fraternity and so on. You have done well out of it, and I congratulate you. While you were preaching, I was practicing–which brings less reward. Since you have closed the clubs, where you have nothing more to do, I keep to my old habits; I continue to speak frankly to my inferiors, my equals and my superiors alike."

Humility is not generally a fault of newly-elected leaders. During the era of the Consulate, Paris was full of petty Brutuses turned into enraged patricians. To tell the truth, the hatred of the aristocracy easily gives rise to an immoderate desire to kill the aristocracy, in order to step into their shoes. Monsieur Berthellemot belonged emphatically to that category of bourgeois conquerors who push the wheels of revolutions while they have everything to gain, but who put the brakes on very abruptly as soon as they have something to lose. You all know how things are–it is needless to say more, or to insist.

"Friend," Monsieur Berthellemot said, disdainfully, "I know you too. The constant happiness which accompanies the measures I take, which are as skilful as they are beneficial, distresses the enemies of the First Consul."

"I am loyal to the First Consul," the stranger put in, unceremoniously. "Loyal to the man as well as the rank."

"So you say. You speak highly of yourself, friend. Take care! I warn you that a man like me is never caught napping. I would only have to say the word and your insolence would be severely punished." He rapped on his desk three times with the paper-knife that he had in his hand: a *coup de théâtre* which he evidently expected to call forth a rapid response.

The two large doors of the side-entrance swung back, to reveal two evil-looking men standing in the doorway.

The stranger smiled as he saw them. "Well, well!" he said, softly. "Laurent and Charlevoy! Poor chaps! I didn't expect to see you, of all people, here. How are you?"

Expressions of embarrassment spread across the faces of the two agents. We would be lying if we said that they looked like princes in disguise.

"Do you know this man?" demanded the Secretary General.

"In a manner of speaking, yes," said Laurent. "Everyone knows him, Monsieur Berthellemot."

"Who is he?"

"If Monsieur the Secretary General had asked him," murmured Charlevoy, "he would already know, since he isn't one for hiding."

"Who is he?" repeated Monsieur Berthellemot, stamping his foot.

The stranger raised his hand to impose silence on the two agents and turned towards the magistrate. He replied with a modesty that was almost majestic: "Monsieur Civil Servant, I'm no one important. I am Jean-Pierre Sévérin, successor to my father, the guardian of the vault of exposition and confrontation, duly appointed by the Tribunal of Paris."

Chapter XIV
Citizen Bonaparte's Fencing Lesson

There are names which can bring about sudden changes. That of Jean-Pierre Sévérin, official keeper of the Morgue, did not appear to produce any extraordinary effect on the Secretary General of the Prefecture of Police. "So you say, Monsieur Sévérin," was all that Berthellemot said, in a tone that was not quite devoid of mockery. "I am dealing with a government employee, or so it seems... you may go, messieurs, but remain within earshot."

The two agents disappeared and the door was closed again.

"Monsieur," the Secretary General went on, his tone severe, "I do not see how you can take the attitude that you have adopted relative to me. I am here in place of the prefect!"

"I haven't adopted any attitude," replied Jean-Pierre Sévérin. "I've been myself for forty-five years and I've no intention of changing. It isn't me that led the conversation astray."

"Please let's say no more about it, Monsieur Morgue-keeper," Berthellemot interrupted, brusquely. "My time is precious."

"Mine too," said Jean-Pierre.

"What do you want with me?"

"I want to do you a favor, and ask one of you."

"Does it concern an important matter?"

"I don't know of any matter more important than the one it concerns."

The Secretary General let go of his paper-knife, and his face became flushed. He had a sudden vision of receiving intelligence of great importance to the State, while his superior was away gadding about. He saw himself as the Prefect of Police. "Why didn't you say so?" he exclaimed, in a voice that was now tremulous with impatience. "You will be richly rewarded, Monsieur Sévérin! You can name your own price..."

"Monsieur Civil Servant, I don't want a reward."

"As you wish, Monsieur Sévérin, as you wish... do you know where he's hiding?"

"Where he's hiding?" repeated the guardian of the Morgue. "You mean, where he is hidden." When the Secretary General looked at him uncomprehendingly, he added: "Where they are hidden, in fact, because there are two of them: a young man and a girl."

Berthellemot furrowed his brow; then he seemed to be struck by a sudden idea. "Is there more than one of you, Sévérin?" he said, abruptly opening one of the drawers in his desk.

"It's not a very rare name," the guardian replied, "but in my family I only know of my son and myself."

"How old is your son?"

"Ten years old."

The Secretary General read the piece of paper that he had taken from his drawer, attentively. "Have you ever heard talk, recently or otherwise," he said, "of a man of the same name... of a Sévérin... who has the nickname Gâteloup?"

"That's me," the guardian replied. "Gâteloup was my nickname when I was a fencing-master before the Revolution."

Monsieur Berthellemot experienced a brief shudder, which he immediately repressed. "Ah!" he said, looking at his visitor warily. "So you have more than one profession, Monsieur Official Guardian."

"I have many professions, Monsieur Civil Servant."

"And perhaps you still have more than one string to your bow, Monsieur Gâteloup?"

"Monsieur Senior Civil Servant," the other corrected him, meekly.

Berthellemot repeated: "And perhaps you still have more than one string to your bow, Monsieur Gâteloup?" He spoke in a pointed manner: the cunning manner of de Sartines.

Jean-Pierre Sévérin took an old hunter watch from his waistcoat pocket and consulted it. "If Monsieur Senior Civil Servant wants me to get on..." he began.

Berthellemot interrupted him. "Have no fear," he said, striking a pose that would have earned him a hundred *livres* a month in any theatre that had a part for a comical aristocratic father. "Keep calm, Monsieur Official Guardian. You will be getting on, in no uncertain fashion!" He sat back in his chair and went on: "Sévérin, called Gâteloup, do you think that the First Consul chooses his servants at random? If he has entrusted to me the important mission of standing in or making up for Monsieur Dubois, it is because his keen eye has discovered in me that certainty of vision, that coolness, that discernment which the annals of the police force only accord to certain out-of-the-ordinary magistrates. You have tried in vain to deceive me. I know your game–you're a conspirator!"

Jean-Pierre fixed him with his great blue eyes, which had taken on a child-like quality. "Rubbish!" he said.

"Monsieur Berthellemot continued: "Yesterday, at half-past nine in the evening, you were seen and recognized engaged in conference with the traitor Georges Cadoudal, in the Rue de l'Ancienne-Comédie."

"Rubbish!" repeated Jean-Pierre. "And if the traitor Georges Cadoudal was recognized," he added, "why isn't he well-and-truly locked away?"

"I defy you," said Monsieur Berthellemot, majestically, "to penetrate the depths of our schemes!"

Jean-Pierre was no longer listening. "It is, however, true," he said to himself, "that at half-past nine yesterday evening I was at the crossroads of the Théâtre-Brulé–or the Odéon, if you prefer. There, I chatted to Monsieur Morinière about matters which are no concern of yours... but I swear that I do not know anything about the traitor Georges Cadoudal."

"Don't try to wriggle out of it..." Berthellemot began. And when Jean-Pierre suddenly frowned, he added: "I'm talking to you for your own sake. It never pays, in the end, to play games with the administration–especially when it is represented by a man such as me, whose attention nothing escapes, and who can easily read minds. You informants have the habit of taking short cuts in order to double or triple the price of an item of intelligence. It's your way of haggling. I don't approve of it."

When he paused to draw breath, Jean-Pierre said to him discontentedly: "You're quite right to disapprove of that sort of thing, Monsieur Senior Civil Servant! A little while ago you accused me of conspiracy, now you take me for a spy!"

Monsieur Berthellemot never lost his smile of imperturbable complacency. "That's the difference between us," he went on. "We feel our way along, we go to the right and the left, beating about the bushes... every bush, my good man, might hide an infernal machine!"

"Beat about your bushes then, Monsieur Senior Civil Servant," said Jean-Pierre, settling himself into his chair, "and shout out a warning when you find a machine... when you've finished, we can talk, if you want to."

All great men have a particular gesture which they use in times of mental distraction: a pout or a tic. Archimedes, at such times, leapt from his bath and ran naked through the streets of Syracuse–that would no longer be tolerated; Voltaire, more sensitive to the cold, restricted himself to throwing his snuffbox into the air and catching it skillfully; Machiavelli chewed his lip; Talleyrand amused himself by turning the skin of his eyelids inside out. Monsieur Dubois, the prefect of police, did nothing of that kind; thanks to the long practice he had put into the exercise, he obtained from each of the joints of his fingers a little click, with which he diverted himself and annoyed others. When everything went to plan, he could produce, at three per finger, thirty little explosions–although the little ones sometimes only yielded two. Monsieur Berthellemot imitated his superior in everything from which his superior derived benefit. When the Prefect was not there, the Secretary General could sometimes obtain as many as thirty-six cracks, thinking to himself: "I can do much better than the Prefect!"

Today, while disarticulating his fingers, Berthellemot said to himself: "This is a dangerous man, as deep as a well. It's necessary to get round him, so to speak, and I'm the man to do it!"

"My dear Monsieur Sévérin," he resumed, with great condescension, "you are not the first to have come here. You've received a good education, that's obvious, and you have a very decent way of presenting yourself. The job you have is mediocre..."

"It suits me," Gâteloup put in, rather rudely.

"Very well... we have certain funds at our disposal here, for the purpose of rewarding loyalty..."

"I don't need money," Gâteloup put in, again. Then he added, with a smile which advertised his gentility: "Monsieur Senior Civil Servant, you are beating the wrong bushes."

"At last!" Berthellemot exclaimed. "What have you to tell me, my good man?"

"It's not my fault that Monsieur Senior Civil Servant doesn't know it already," Jean-Pierre replied. "I came here..."

But the demon of interrogation took hold of Monsieur Berthellemot again: "Allow me!" he said, in an authoritative tone. "I suppose it's up to me to guide the conversation. We shall not go astray... you say that the suspect you were with in the Rue de l'Ancienne-Comédie was called Morinière..."

"He's not a suspect," Jean-Pierre put in.

"You deny that he is Georges Cadoudal?"

"Wholeheartedly."

"Then who is he?"

"A horse-trader from Normandy."

"Ah! From Normandy... I'm taking notes, never fear... the fact is that there are a lot of horse-dealers in Normandy... and why, if you please, Monsieur Sévérin, are you keeping company with horse-dealers?"

"Because Monsieur Morinière is in the same situation as me," Jean-Pierre replied.

"Be careful," said Monsieur Berthellemot. "You'll make things worse for yourself. What situation are you in?"

"The situation of a man who has lost a child."

"And you came to the prefecture...?"

"So that the Prefect could help me to get her back–that's all!"

There are men who can wear two pairs of spectacles. To the stare of Monsieur de Sartines, which he used routinely, Monsieur Berthellemot added the stare of Monsieur Lenoir. Argus himself could not have done more. "Is that likely?" he muttered. "I'm taking notes... oh yes, the Prefect will be very embarrassed."

"And if that is not your business, Monsieur Senior Civil Servant," Jean-Pierre added, as he made ready to get up, "I shall go elsewhere."

"Where will you go, old boy?"

"To the First Consul's residence, if you please."

Monsieur Berthellemot leapt up from his armchair. "The First Consul's residence!" he repeated. "My good man, do you think that anyone can simply go to the First Consul's residence, just like that?"

"I can," Jean-Pierre replied, simply. "Now, you must give me a straight answer, yes or no–without losing your temper–as to whether it is your job to help people in need."

The question, thus posed, manifestly displeased the Secretary General, who took up his paper-knife again and whetted it on his knee. "Friend," he said, between clenched teeth, "you have already taken up a great deal of my time, which is dedicated to the public interest. If you ever pretend that I have not received you with kindness, you will be guilty of an outrageous slander. Understand this: I do not have a 'job;' I am a senior civil servant in the most important ministry of all, closely akin to the priesthood! I give you fair warning that I shall flatly deny any accusation you may make that I have refused you my help. Can you blame me for the precautions with which I surround the precious life of our master? Explain to me briefly, clearly and categorically, without any detours, ambiguities and circumlocutions, exactly what your complaint is. I am listening."

"I came to ask you..." Jean-Pierre promptly began–but Monsieur Berthellemot interrupted him with a gesture whose familiarity stood in almost touching contrast to the somewhat haughty gravity of his bearing.

"Wait! Wait!" he said, as if an idea had suddenly crossed his mind. "I'm a little lost. Let's clear things up while we can. How does it come about, my dear Monsieur Sévérin, that you have been to the First Consul's residence? If it's a secret, of course, I shall not insist in the least–that goes without saying."

"It's not a secret," Jean-Pierre replied. "It happened once under the Convention..."

"We do understand one another, my dear Monsieur Sévérin? I am not forcing you. At least..."

"Monsieur Senior Civil Servant," Jean-Pierre interrupted, in his turn, "if I did not wish to reply, you certainly could not force me. I never say anything I do not wish to say."

"A brave man!" exclaimed the Secretary General, with an admiration whose sincerity cannot be guaranteed. "A truly brave man... go on!"

Jean-Pierre continued his story. "Towards the end of the Convention–in fact, to be more precise, I think it was during the first days of Vendémiaire year IV, or the 23rd or 24th of September 1795–a young man in bourgeois dress, sickly and pale of face, came into my fencing-school..."

"What fencing-school?" Monsieur Berthellemot asked.

"I had been married for three years then, and I had a young son. As Saint-Sulpice, whose doors had been shut, had no need of cantors, I had the idea of opening a little academy in a room at the back of what had formerly been the d'Aligre house in the Rue de Saint-Honoré. But most of the people who would normally go to schools of swordsmanship were as far away, at that moment, as those who would normally have come to the church, and I could not earn my daily bread."

174

"Poor Monsieur Séverin," Berthellemot put in. "I can't tell you how much your story interests me."

"The young man in bourgeois dress of whom I spoke had a military bearing..."

"I know it well, my dear Monsieur Séverin. Like Caesar! Like Alexander the Great! Like..."

"Like Napoleon Bonaparte, Monsieur Senior Civil Servant. Nothing gets past you–you have guessed that it was he."

Berthellemot stuck his right hand inside his shirt and said, with conviction: "True–you are more perceptive than most. Those to whom the First Consul awards important positions are not selected at random. I am not here by chance!"

"So," Jean-Pierre Séverin resumed, "the young Bonaparte, not yet a general but in charge of a brigade, attached–I don't know why–to the Ministry of War thanks to Monsieur de Pontécoulant [72], malcontent, feverish, tormented... a poor scabbard employed by a magnificent foil... went straight into the first fencing-school he came to, in search of a physical fatigue that might pacify his nerves and dull his intelligence."

"Do you know that you express yourself very well, my dear Monsieur Séverin?" the Secretary General said.

"I had never seen him before," Jean-Pierre continued, "and had never even heard his name spoken, but I happen to be a bit of a magician." Berthellemot abruptly sat down again, and Jean-Pierre went on: "You don't believe in magicians– well, no more do I. Even so, Monsieur Senior Civil Servant, some very strange things are happening in Paris at the moment, and the reason for my presence in your office has to do with matters touching on the supernatural, or very nearly so... But let's get back to the young Bonaparte. I had something of a shock when I saw him. He smiled and took a foil, which he put *en garde* in an inexperienced and almost maladroit fashion. 'Are you Citizen Séverin, called Gâteloup?' he asked me.

" 'Yes, Citizen General,' I replied–I am not mistaken here; I called him Citizen General, although I cannot explain why.

" 'Captain, my friend,' he corrected. 'Do you think I'm too old for my rank?' Citizen Bonaparte was then only twenty-five, and did not look a day over twenty. I no longer remember what reply I made, although I have tried hard. He went on: 'Antoine Dubois, my doctor, has ordered me to do some exercise. I don't like walking–it takes too long–and I can ride a horse for twenty-four hours without getting tired. Are you a man who can stiffen my muscles and rattle my bones for twenty minutes a day?'

" 'Yes, Citizen General.'

" 'Captain, I tell you... and how much would it cost me? I'm not rich.'

"We agreed on a price, and had to begin right away–in those days, and ever since, he didn't like to wait. I didn't just tire him out–I ground him down so fine and so well that he asked to be let off, and fell breathless on my bench. 'Parbleu!' he said, laughing and wiping sweat from the fringe of hair that hung down over his great forehead. Madame de Beauharnais would laugh out loud if she saw me in this state!' I was nearly as tired as he was–I, who have arms of iron and hamstrings of steel!–and couldn't speak. 'Well, master!' he said, suddenly getting to his feet, 'I've spent more than twenty minutes. I'll pay you, and see you tomorrow!'

"He plunged his long, slender hand abruptly into his waistcoat pocket, but it came out empty; he had either lost or forgotten his purse. 'Look at me!' he said, blushing slightly. 'I've come here under false pretenses, and I'll be obliged to ask you for credit!'

" 'General,' I replied, 'you have deceived no one.'

" 'That's true. Do you know me?'

" 'No, on my honor.'

" 'Then how do you know...?'

" 'I know nothing.' He raised an eyebrow. 'Sire...' I continued."

"Sire!" exclaimed the Secretary General, who was listening with avid attention. "A fine word! You called him Sire, my dear Monsieur Gâteloup!"

"Monsieur Civil Servant," said Jean-Pierre. "I'm telling you what happened. I have promised to tell you the story, not to explain it. Citizen Bonaparte did exactly what you did: he repeated the word Sire, and he stepped back several paces, saying: 'Friend, I'm a Republican!'

"I continued regardless, speaking like the ancient pythoness, possessed by a spirit that was not my own. 'Sire, I too am a Republican. I was a Republican before you and I will be a Republican after you. Never fear that I shall exact too heavy an interest from Your Majesty for what I do today.' "

"You said that?" murmured Berthellemot. "Before the thirteenth of Vendémiaire! It's curious, to say the least–extremely curious."

"Not long before... it was the fourth or the fifth."

"And what did the Emperor–I mean the First Consul... I mean, Citizen Bonaparte–say in reply?"

"Citizen Bonaparte stared at me. The pallor of his thin and hollow cheeks became even duller. 'Friend Gâteloup,' he said, 'ordinarily I don't like visionaries or madmen... but you seem to be a good sort, and you've given me a good work-out. Tomorrow!' And he left."

"But he came back?" Berthellemot asked.

"No–never."

"What! Never?"

"There was no time. He had not recovered from his stiffness when the thirteenth of Vendémiaire arrived. He commanded the artillery in the square of Saint-Roch. A great deal of blood was shed there–French blood. The young brigade-commander was promoted to general by the Directory; he had no more need of the protection of Monsieur de Pontécoulant... I followed his career at a distance; I listened whenever he was talked about, and he was soon being talked about everywhere... how can I describe it? He frightened me, and the fear was mingled with hate and love...

"The following year, he married Madame de Beauharnais, who would have 'laughed out loud' had she seen him in the state to which I reduced him in my fencing-school. Then he left for Italy, as the commander-in-chief of the army."

"And you have not seen him at your fencing-school since?" asked the Secretary General, who quite forgot his actor's pose in the grip of his curiosity.

"I have not seen him there since," Jean-Pierre confirmed.

"Ought I to conclude that he is still in your debt?"

"Not at all. He has paid me."

"Generously?"

"Honestly."

"What did he give you?"

"My fee was a six *livre pièce*. He gave me a six *livre pièce*."

The Secretary General puffed out his cheeks and breathed like Aeolus [73], while cracking his fingers. "No! To say the very least... it's impossible."

"What was impossible," Jean-Pierre Sévérin said, slowly, whose head became stiff in spite of himself, "is that I should have accepted more."

"Why?" Berthellemot asked, naively.

"I have told you, Monsieur Executive," Jean-Pierre replied. "I was a Republican before General Bonaparte was a Republican; I am a Republican now that the First Consul is only just a Republican; and I will still be a Republican when the Emperor is not a Republican at all."

Chapter XV
The Rue de la Lanterne

The Secretary General of the Prefecture took up his pose again, and tried to put on all his charm.

"So, dear Monsieur Sévérin," he said, "we sometimes pay a little social call on our old schoolmate, do we?"

"Sometimes," Jean-Pierre replied. "Not often."

"And we never ask for anything?"

"As a matter of fact, I always ask for something."

"And we are not refused?"

"I have not been refused yet." He added, as if talking to himself: "Even though my last request was for six thousand *louis*."

"The devil you say! Six thousand *louis*! There's a lot of six-*livre* fees in that, my dear Monsieur Sévérin!"

"When you pass over the Marché-Neuf, Monsieur Civil Servant, take a look at the little building that is under construction there...."

"The new Morgue!" exclaimed Berthellemot. "I know about that! They didn't want to follow our plans..."

"Because they didn't conform to mine," Jean-Pierre put in, modestly.

"Good, good, good!" the Secretary General said, in triplicate. "I am, in truth, very pleased to have made your acquaintance. We're neighbors, my dear Monsieur Sévérin... when you have need of me, don't stand on ceremony; I'll introduce you to the prefect."

"You've known that I have need of you for an hour and a half, Monsieur Civil Servant," Jean-Pierre put in, softly.

"Agreed, neighbor, agreed... don't worry... agreed–what a pretty word!–agreed."

"What is agreed?"

"Everything–it doesn't matter. We're like two fingers of the same hand. Oh, mercy! It's not Republicans like you that terrify us... I don't remember ever having encountered a man whose conversation was more interesting and lively... but we don't need to have anyone listening in, do we? Laurent! Charlevoy! In here, my good fellows!" The side door opened immediately, displaying the two agents with their hats in their hands. "Go to the restaurant and see if we're there, Citizens," Berthellemot said to them, "and on the way warn Monsieur Despaux that I shall be putting him at the disposal of Monsieur Séverin tomorrow, for a very serious and very urgent matter, which concerns a devoted friend of the Consular Government."

"May I interrupt, Monsieur Civil Servant?" asked Jean-Pierre.

"Of course, my dear neighbor. Wait a minute, you two!"

"I simply want to make the observation," Jean-Pierre said, "that it isn't tomorrow but this very night that I require your assistance."

"Do you hear, Laurent! Do you hear, Charlevoy! Make sure that Monsieur Despaux doesn't leave the Prefecture, and remain close at hand yourselves... do the whole night-shift, if necessary... Go! There are people for whom one cannot do too much."

When the two agents had disappeared, Berthellemot resumed: "See, my good friend and neighbor! Everything is arranged, lubricated, oiled as if by an expert mechanic. The First Consul knows very well that I am the soul of this enterprise; he would have liked to promote me to responsibilities more in keeping with my abilities, but the excellent Monsieur Dubois has such great need of me. Then again, I'm so very attached to this poor little city of Paris, whose tutor and guardian I am...the mischief that she makes for me puts me to so much trouble, but I'm in love with her all the same...ah yes! Now that we are alone, we can talk... When you next see the First

Consul, I hope that you'll tell him how eagerly I have put my-self at your disposal..."

"May I explain to you why I am here, Monsieur Employee?"

"Yes, yes, of course," Berthellemot assured him. "Make yourself at home. Except, you know, leave out the petty de-tails–we don't want to waste time in idle chatter. I do hate tittle-tattle! I can explain the most difficult case in a minimum of words–that's my *forte*... Take your time! Collect yourself. He's just like that–I mean the First Consul! He must have been struck very sharply by that bizarre incident: a man who called him Sire and Your Majesty when the Convention was at its height... and do you know, often people placed in these posi-tions... eccentrics...might have more influence than the most important functionaries... I am all ears, Monsieur Séverin..."

"Monsieur Senior Civil Servant," Jean-Pierre began, "although I have no desire to tell you much of my own history, it is necessary that you know that I married a little late in life."

"And how is Madame?" asked Monsieur Berthellemot, amiably.

"Quite well, thank you. When I was married, in 1789..."

"A great day!" put in the Secretary General.

"...She had," Jean-Pierre continued, "an adopted child, a little girl..."

"Do you want me to take notes?" interrupted Berthel-lemot, petulantly.

"It's not necessary."

"Hang on–it's always for the best. My memory is so full! And while we are here, just the two of us, good friends, my dear neighbor and colleague... for we are, in the end, both salaried employees of the state... let me tell you something that will astonish you: I'm not like the First Consul at all!"

Jean-Pierre was not as surprised as Monsieur Berthel-lemot had hoped.

"I'm not like him," Berthellemot went on, "in the sense that, for myself, I have the slightest belief in any of these machinations... I'm not superstitious...By no means!... Other

181

than the Supreme Being, whom we admit because he is not embarrassing, I can't believe in any religion, deep down... But, see here, it's incontestable that certain deviltries exist. I have an old aunt who has a black cat...don't laugh, that cat is astounding! And I defy you to explain philosophically the care that it takes to hide itself away in the deepest cellar whenever there are thirteen at table... Do you know the tale of Monsieur Bourtibourg? It's very curious. Monsieur Bourtibourg had lost his wife to a feverish relapse. He was a tidy and thrifty man, who kept his cook on to save himself from running wild in night-spots. Do you disapprove of that? Opinions are divided. Personally, I find that it's best to have no attachments and to live from day to day. One night, when he was playing piquet with the curate of Saint-Merry... I mean the ex-curate, because he'd married the wife of Citizen Lancelot, who sold shoes and stockings in the Barillerie... the Lancelots had divorced, you see... and Lancelot was paying court, at that time, to the cousin of Monsieur Fouché, who had not yet bought his places of exile... Oh well! Footsteps were heard in the corridor–when there was no one there–and Mathieu Luneau, the brigadier of the Paris Guard, who went the same way as his mother and father, died suddenly within the week. I can testify to that: I've taken notes... Besides, the historians of antiquity are full of similar cases: the eve of Philippi, the eve of Actium... but you know all that as well as I do, Monsieur Séverin: I'm rarely mistaken in my appreciation..."

"Time's passing..." Jean-Pierre tried to stem the flow, having already consulted his large watch two or three times.

"Let me finish... I never talk at hazard. It was in order to tell you that, at this very moment, and in the middle of Paris, something deadly is abroad. Do you believe in vampires, my dear neighbor?"

"Yes," Jean-Pierre replied, without hesitation.

"Ah!" said Monsieur Berthellemot, rubbing his hands. "Have you seen one?"

"I've done better than see one," replied the Morgue-keeper, lowering his voice this time. "I've got one."

"What! You've got one! This is a subject about which I am particularly curious. Explain, I beg you–and please don't take offense if I make a few notes."

"Monsieur Senior Civil Servant," Jean-Pierre said, slowly, "every man has something which he does not wish to explain precisely. If I were interrogated under oath, I would reply according to my conscience..."

"Very well, Monsieur Sévérin, very well... You believe in vampires, that will suffice for the moment... I can assure you that at this very moment, in Paris, the capital of the civilized world, a hundred thousand people are convinced that a creature of that kind is prowling the streets by night."

"That's what I came to talk to you about, Monsieur Civil Servant," Jean-Pierre put in. "And if you would like me to..."

"Excuse me! One more thing–just a brief word! Do you not think that we are still in a state of complete ignorance on this matter, in spite of the learned works published in Germany? For myself, I read everything, without prejudice to my official duties–look how truly astonishing my organization is! Our idlers call the being in question the vampire, as if it were not well-known that the female of the vampire species is the oupire or succubus, also called a ghoul in the Middle Ages... I have already received eleven complaints... seven young men vanished, and four young women... But I will make the observation–and this is exactly what I say in my report to the prefect–that we have no need of a ghoul, nor a succubus, nor an oupire here. Paris herself is a monster that devours children."

"As of this moment, Monsieur Civil Servant," said Jean-Pierre, getting to his feet, "you have thirteen complaints, because I am bringing two more: one in my own name, one in the name of my comrade and companion-in-arms Citizen Morinière the horse-dealer, whom you have taken for Georges Cadoudal."

Berthellemot put his hand to his forehead in a theatrical manner. "I knew that I had something to ask you!" he said. "Notes must be taken. Have you any objection to telling me how long you have known Monsieur Morinière?"

"None at all. I met him for the first time two years ago. He came to my school in order to lose weight. He's a good fencer."

"Is it usual for horse-merchants to practice swordsmanship?"

"Not exactly usual, Monsieur Civil Servant, but the best swordsman in Paris–after me, who used to be a parish cantor– is François Maniquet, a poorhouse baker. One's profession is of no importance."

"And you have seen this Citizen Morinière regularly during the last two years?"

"On the contrary–I lost sight of him completely. His business does not permit him to remain in Paris for long."

Berthellemot screwed up his eyes and scratched the end of his nose. (No detail is superfluous when it concerns historical figures.) "That braggart Fouché," he muttered, "is scouring the entire country while overlooking the obvious; Monsieur Dubois is still floundering...but me, I hit the right track immediately, like a well-trained bloodhound." Raising his voice again, he said: "My dear Monsieur Séverin, under what circumstances did you renew the acquaintance of your comrade and companion-in-arms Monsieur Morinière?"

"At the Morgue."

"Recently?"

"Yesterday morning. He arrived in a state of acute anxiety, to make sure that the body of his son was not on display in the vault."

"But that's ridiculous!" Berthellemot exclaimed. "Georges Cadoudal has no grown-up son, to the best of my knowledge!"

Jean-Pierre made no reply.

Berthellemot went on: "I am entirely at your disposal in the matter of the abducted girl. You would not believe, neighbor, how much that kind of thing interests me and puts my imagination ardently to work. If Paris has a ghoul, it is necessary that I find her, examine her, describe her... You know that these individuals are given away by their lips... If I only had

184

one little lead to follow, I would arrive soon enough at the lair, cavern or tomb in which the monster is sheltering... It is the best part of the job, you see, offering refreshment from more serious work. Make your report in your own words, truthfully and precisely. I will take notes."

"Monsieur Civil Servant," Jean-Pierre asked, before sitting down again, "may I hope that I can do so without further interruption?"

"I don't think I've prevented you from speaking, my dear chap," Berthellemot replied, in a slightly piqued manner. "My only fault lies in being too reserved and too taciturn. Go on–I shall be as mute as a stone."

Jean-Pierre Séverin resumed his seat and began his story thus: "The new establishment on the Marché-Neuf of which I shall be the official keeper is nearly complete, and has already necessitated a great deal of work on my part. Bodies are still exposed in the old vault, but in a few days, the new Morgue will be usable for the first time...that's an amazing thing; I've been thinking about it for many weeks. I've been unable to help wondering who would be the first one to arrive there. It's not an occasion to which one can really look forward, of course, but there's a certain element of anticipation nevertheless. Who will be the first? A malefactor? A gambler? A drinker? A cheated husband? A deluded girl? The consequence of a misfortune or the produce of a crime?

"We live near the Châtelet, at the corner of the little Rue de la Lanterne. I love my wife as the desperate cherish consolation and the condemned mercy. At an unhappy time of my life, when I believed my heart to be dead, I discovered my wife at the end of an agonizing struggle, and my heart was given a new lease of life. Our home is very small; we live on top of one another. My son grew pale and weak because we had neither enough space nor enough air, but we thrived anyway. We are happy to be squeezed into a corner where our souls are in contact. We have three rooms: mine, where my son also sleeps; one in which my wife's family is accommodated, where the stove is lit in winter; and, lastly, the one in which Angela sews and sings so softly and so beautifully. That one is only a few feet square, but it is on the corner of the street and it gets a little sunlight. Yesterday the rose-bush outside Angela's window put out its first flower. She has not seen it... will she ever see it?

"On the other side of the street is a better house than ours, not as old. Its rooms are rented out by the month to young clerks and law-students. A little more than a year ago, a mere fortnight after my wife and I had said to one another, 'Angela is a young woman now,' a student took up lodgings in the house opposite. He had a room on the second floor–a very nice room, with two windows, as large on its own as our entire living-space. He was a handsome young man with curly fair hair. He seemed shy and gentle. He was doing a course at the law college–I found that out much later, because I don't take that much interest in the neighborhood; my wife knew him before me, and Angela before my wife.

"The young man was named Kervoz–or de Kervoz, for that was what people began to call him again, as they had before. He was the son of a Breton gentleman who died with de Sombreuil at Quiberon [74]..."

Monsieur Berthellemot made a note and said: "A bad lot!"

"As I have never changed my own views," Jean-Pierre said, "I never insult those who do not change theirs. The future will regret the blood that was shed there more than the injury that was done. May God stand by those who live according to their faith, and grant eternal peace to those who die for their faith.

"I don't want to tell you how pretty, happy and virtuous our daughter was. Although my son is my own flesh and blood, I don't think I love him any more dearly than Angela, who is only related to me by marriage. When she comes to offer her smiling face to my lips in the morning, I feel my heart lighten, and I thank God for keeping such a dear and adorable treasure in my humble abode. We love her too much. You have guessed the story, and I shan't spin it out. The street

186

is narrow; gazes and smiles are easily exchanged between one side and the other, and words too–one could almost reach out to touch hands.

"One night, when I came in late, having had to assist in a medical enquiry at the Châtelet, I thought I was dreaming. There was an object suspended above my head in the Rue de la Lanterne. It was the beginning of last winter, on a moonless night; the sky was blanketed with cloud, the darkness profound. At first sight, it seemed to me to be an unlit street-lamp, hanging in mid-air in a place where it did not belong. One end of the cord supporting it was attached to the young student's window, the other to Angela's casement."

"What do you expect," murmured the Secretary General. "There are plenty of angels of that sort. I'm taking notes."

"Personally, I didn't catch on at once," Jean-Pierre continued, "so sure was I of my little girl."

Berthellemot sniggered. "A fine love-letter you had there, neighbor." Jean-Pierre was as pale as a corpse. The Secretary General went on: "Don't get upset! No one deplores the dreadful immorality with which the Directory inoculated our fatherland more than I do. It seems to me that the Directory is comparable to the Regency so far as the relaxation of morals is concerned. Time will doubtless cure that leprosy, but we are living in the present, neighbor..."

"You certainly are, Monsieur Prefect," Jean-Pierre intervened, "or so, at least, it seemed when you left the Suckling Calf with a certain lady..."

"Shush!" said the Secretary General, blushing and smiling. "Some men attach I-don't-know-what moronic vainglory to their weaknesses; we are not made of bronze, Monsieur Séverin. Was it the manageress or little Duvernoy? She was launched, you know, at the Opera. She owes me a nice candlelit dinner."

"I don't know whether it was little Duvernoy or the manageress," Jean-Pierre said. "I don't know either one of them. I only know that you caught my attention for a moment as you passed by. Anyway, when I looked up again, there was noth-ing above my head."

"The street-lamp had crossed over?" said the Secretary General. "That's funny–a good story. Monsieur Picard [75] could make a nice little comedy out of that." Jean-Pierre was lost in remembrance. "I'm taking notes," Berthellemot reminded him. "Have you finished?"

"No," the official concierge replied. "I've scarcely be-gun. I went up our poor stairs unsteadily, my heart pressed and my head on fire. On reaching my room I opened my desk to take out a pair of dueling-pistols..."

"The devil you did! You had worked it out at last, neigh-bor?"

"I loaded them, and without waking my wife I went to knock on Angela's door."

Chapter XVI
The Three Germans

"There was no immediate response from my poor little Angela's room," continued Jean-Pierre Sévérin, called Gâteloup, "but the door was so thin that I could hear the noise of two people's hushed breathing.

" 'Save yourself!' whispered the frightened girl. 'Get away, quickly!'

" 'Stay where you are!' I ordered, without raising my voice. 'If you try to cross the street again, I'll open my window and put two bullets in your head.'

"Angela's voice had stopped trembling when she said: 'It's father. We must open up.' A moment later, with my pistols in my hands, I was inside the candlelit room. Angela looked me straight in the face; she didn't know how to look at me any other way. She was very pale, but she wasn't ashamed..."

"You don't say!" Monsieur Berthellemot put in.

"It's not for you to judge!" Jean-Pierre told him, calmly and authoritatively. "It's another matter on which I have come to seek your advice. The young man was standing at the back of the room, his back straight and his head held high. On the table beside him, there was a book of hours and a crucifix."

"What!" said the Secretary General. "Were they saying Mass?"

"I stood still for a minute, looking at them, because I was stirred to the depths of my soul, and could find no words. They were two beautiful, noble creatures: she spirited and half-defiant, he proud and resigned."

" 'What are you doing here?' I demanded."

The Secretary General burst out laughing at this point, but Jean-Pierre did not lose his temper. "Your occupation hardens the heart, Monsieur Civil Servant," was all he said. Then he went on: "Questions may produce laughter or tremulousness, according to the circumstances in which they are asked. No one there was in the mood for amusement–and yet, Angela's response will probably amuse you even more than my question.

" 'Father,' she said, 'we're getting married.' "

"A nice time for it!" Berthellemot exclaimed, cracking his fingers. "Hang on! I'll make a note of it."

"We are a religious household," Jean-Pierre continued, "although I had a reputation as an infidel when I sang vespers at Saint-Sulpice. My wife thinks about God frequently, like everyone possessed of a great soul and a good heart. It isn't necessarily the case that a Republican–and I was one before the Republic, Monsieur Prefect–has to be impious. Our little Angela prayed with us every morning and every night... for his part, young Monsieur de Kervoz came from a land where Christian ideals are deeply rooted. He is not devout, but he is a believer..."

"And a chouan," murmured Berthellemot.

"Jean-Pierre paused to fix him with a piercing stare. "And a chouan," he repeated. "I shall not deny it. If it is your police that have caused him to disappear, I beg you to tell me so frankly. That will put an end to one part of my search, and make the other easier."

Berthellemot shrugged his shoulders and said: "We are hunting bigger game, neighbor."

"Then I shall take it as read," Jean-Pierre went on, "that you have played no part in the disappearance of René de Kervoz and continue. So my poor little Angela said to me: 'Father, we are getting married.' René de Kervoz took a step towards me and added: 'I too have pistols, but if you attack me, I will not defend myself. You have the right: I have come into your house by night like a thief. You are entitled to assume that I have violated your daughter's honor.'

190

"I looked at him closely, and approved of the handsome nobility of his face. Angela said: 'Father does not want to kill you, René. He knows full well that I would die with you.'

" 'Don't threaten your father!' said young de Kervoz, in a low voice, placing himself between Angela and myself and crossing his arms in front of his chest."

At this point, Jean-Pierre interrupted himself to say: "You don't know me, Monsieur Civil Servant, and it's necessary that I should show you what God has made me: I had an impulse to embrace him, because I have a passionate admiration for all who are brave and proud."

"And besides," Berthellemot slipped in, "this René de Kervoz, chouan though he is, has estates in lower Brittany, and would not make too bad a match for a Parisian working girl [76]."

"I am Séverin, called Gâteloup," said the old master-of-arms, rudely, "and I have spent my life stamping out your petty calculations and expediencies. By the sarrabugoy!–as they used to swear in the old days–when I was the friend of many a marquis and many a countess, I had an income of no less than ten thousand *écus* in my wallet, Citizen Prefect, and the tenure of lands in lower Brittany in the corner of my eye! I had an impulse to embrace that boy because he pleased me, that is all... and don't interrupt me again if you want to know the rest!"

Berthellemot smiled politely while saying: "Now, now, neighbor, calm down. You didn't kill anyone, I suppose."

"No, I witnessed the marriage."

"So the little turtle-doves were married?"

"Provisionally, without the benefit of priest or mayor, before the crucifix... and I received René's solemn word of honor that he would not cross the street by tightrope again until the priest and the mayor had added their own blessing."

"Another love-token, neighbor."

"He kept his promise faithfully... too faithfully."

"Ah! There's more than one way to perjure oneself."

Jean-Pierre's fingers dug into his forehead, which was deeply furrowed. "My wife and I," he said, in a tone that was almost boastful, defiant of any mockery, "served as godfather and godmother when the baby came..."

"You don't say!" Berthellemot exclaimed, with an explosion of hilarity. "I knew full well that the deed was done! Was it a boy-chouan or a girl-chouan?"

"Monsieur Senior Civil Servant, you will pay me your respects and find my children, won't you?" Jean-Pierre demanded coldly, gripping him firmly by the arms.

"Neighbor!" said Berthellemot, seized by a vague anxiety.

But Jean-Pierre was already smiling. "She was a little angel," he said, "and we called her Angela, after her mother... Oh God, yes, as you understood perfectly well, the damage was already done. That night when I went into Angela's room with my pistols, René was there to make amends, or to promise that he would. All this was explained to us–for I never keep secrets from my wife, and my wife is no more inclined to strictness than I am. We accepted all the promises René de Kervoz made; we recognized the sincerity of the explanations he gave us. He could not marry for the moment, so the marriage was postponed, and we formed a family.

"It was good and sweet to see them so in love: that proud young man and that dear, tender young woman. Oh, I no longer forbid you to laugh. There are enough joyous and profound memories here in my heart to combat all the sarcasm in the universe! They stayed with us that night. I don't know which my poor wife loved more, her René or her Angela. It seems to me that I can see them, holding hands, smiling and confused: he anxious because Angela is so very pale; Angela, in spite of her ordeal, happy to be so adored. Then Angela recovered; she became beautiful again, and even more beautiful with her child in her arms."

It was Monsieur Berthellemot's turn to consult his watch: an elegant and valuable timepiece. "It's as well that I have a little time on my hands tonight," he murmured. "You aren't cutting things short, neighbor."

"From now on, I shall be brief, Monsieur Civil Servant," Jean-Pierre assured him, in a very different tone. "Anyway, the case I'm pleading is already won–your excellent heart is sympathetic, that's obvious!"

"Of course, of course," muttered the Secretary General.

"I'll skip the details and get to the catastrophe. One night, nearly a month ago, when our little angel was six weeks old and her young mother was breast-feeding her, René came to announce that nothing more stood in the way of his keeping his promise–and God knows, the boy was as happy as we were.

"There isn't much money coming into the house at present, and René is not wealthy for the moment, Even so, he agreed that the wedding should be magnificent. For once in our lives, my poor wife and I entertained ideas of luxury and folly; the great day of Angela's marriage was to be a celebration of everyone's happiness. It was set for thirty days afterwards, that wonderful occasion–which may not, after all, be celebrated. Angela and René were to be married the day after tomorrow.

"We set to work making preparations night after night–and as if Heaven were lavishing good omens upon us, our little angel smiled for the first time. A fortnight went by–then, one day, René did not appear at dinner time. When he finally arrived, much later, he was pale and anxious. The next day, he was even later. The day after that, Angela was also absent from the family meal. The baby girl began to suffer and grow thin; her mother's milk, which had nourished her so well until then, became overheated and then dried up. We were obliged to find a wet-nurse.

"What was happening? I questioned Angela and her mother questioned her too–all to no avail. There was nothing the matter with her, she said. Until the very last moment, she refused to answer us, and we didn't know what was wrong. It was the same with René. René offered plausible explanations

193

for his absences, and said that his sudden sadness was due to bad news that had come from Brittany. Angela was so changed that we could hardly recognize her. We were continually finding her with her eyes full of tears. Meanwhile, the day of the wedding got closer.

"Three times twenty-four hours have now passed since René de Kervoz last slept in his own bed. On the 28th February, he went to the Church of Saint-Louis-en-l'Ile, where he met a woman. Angela followed him, and I followed Angela. That night, Angela was brought to me, dying; she has refused to answer my questions. On the following night, weak as she was, she got out of the house, after having embraced her little daughter tearfully. René has not come back, and we have not seen Angela since."

Jean-Pierre Séverin fell silent.

During the last part of his narrative, related in a tone that was clear and curt, although profoundly sad, the Secretary General had seemed very attentive.

"I've taken notes," he said, finally, when his informant remained silent. "The course of my duties embraces little things as well as greater ones, and I have a particular gift for tackling ten problems at a time. More than that–I grasp connections with astonishing precision. This business, which seems at first glance so trivial, my dear neighbor, is connected with another, which touches upon the security of the State. I shall demonstrate my appreciation."

"Be careful!" Jean-Pierre began. "Don't be misled..."

"I'm never misled!" Berthellemot interrupted him, imperiously. "It's obviously a double suicide."

The official Morgue-keeper shook his head slowly. "In matters of suicide," he said, in a very low voice, "no one is more expert than myself. Only one of my two children could have had any reason to put an end to life."

"René de Kervoz?"

"No... our daughter, Angela."

"Then you haven't told me everything."

Jean-Pierre hesitated before replying. "Monsieur Civil Servant," he murmured, finally, "the mysterious being which is currently the talk of Paris, the vampire, is neither ghoul, nor succubus, nor oupire..."

"Do you know that for a fact?" Berthellemot demanded, excitedly.

"I've seen her three times [77]."

The Secretary General abruptly took up his paper and pencil.

"It's not blood for which the vampire thirsts," Jean-Pierre went on. "It's gold that she's after."

"What do you mean, neighbor? Explain yourself!"

"I've already told you, Monsieur Civil Servant, of our intention to push the boat out for the wedding of Angel and René. I reopened my fencing-school–and as soon as the door of the master is ajar, pupils flock in. A great many came. Among them were three young Germans from Swabia: Count Wenzel, Baron von Ramberg and Franz König, whose father owns the great alabaster mines at Würtz in the Black Forest. The people of Wurtemburg are all like their king: they love France and the First Consul... except for the comrades of Comment [78] ..."

"*Comment*?" repeated the Secretary General.

"That's the name of the Code of Fellowship of the University of Tubingen, whose mossy halls and ancient towers have something slightly diabolical about them."

"Now then, now then!" said Berthellemot. "What language are you speaking, neighbor? I'm taking notes. Just a minute. The prefect will see nothing in them but fire."

"I'm speaking the language of those good Germans, who are always acting in three or four fateful farces: the farce of dueling, the farce of conspiracy, the farce of suicide and that farce which Brutus performed so proudly, speaking at such length of killing Caesar–which Caesar understood in the end, and shut Brutus away in the bottom of a deep pit. One day, when I have the time, I'll tell you the story of von Burschenschaft and von Tugenbaud, which you don't appear to know..."

"How do you spell that, my dear Monsieur Sévérin?" asked the Secretary General. "Do you really think that they have had something to do with the infernal machine?"

"Posterity will know," Jean-Pierre replied, with an ironic gravity, "if time succeeds in solving the mystery. But let's get back to our three young Germans from Swabia: Count Wenzel, Baron von Ramberg and Franz König, who did not appear to belong to the League of Virtue and had no evil intentions. Count Wenzel was rich; Baron von Ramberg was very rich; Franz König was a multi-millionaire–that solid milk, alabaster, has been exceedingly fashionable for some time. Count Wenzel had spirit; Baron von Ramberg had abundant spirit; Franz König has as much spirit as the devil himself."

"You keep referring to the first two in the past tense, neighbor," the Secretary General observed. "Are they dead?"

"God only knows," said Jean-Pierre quietly. "We shall see. I have rarely encountered three such handsome cavaliers, the alabaster merchant most of all: fine and delicate features set upon the body of an athlete, with blond hair that a woman would envy. At any rate, all three were brave, adventurous and self-confessed pleasure-seekers. Count Wenzel was the first to leave for Germany, with unbelievable abruptness; Baron von Ramberg soon followed him, and–a truly remarkable thing in men of that sort–both went without settling their accounts with me. A fixed purpose completely changes one's character. I have spent my life neglecting my interests, but I needed money to welcome a son into our family–I would not have forgiven my best friend a single *écu*. I wrote to the Count immediately, for what he and the Baron owed. There was no reply. Next I wrote to the Baron, begging him to remind the Count. The same silence.

"Remember that I knew them as the most honest and most generous men on Earth. I liked them. I was worried. I sent a letter to the French Ambassador in Stuttgart, Monsieur Aulagnier, who was once a pupil of mine in music–I have a few friends everywhere–and he replied that not only had Count Wenzel and Baron von Ramberg not returned to Stuttgart but that their families were beginning to worry about them. No one had heard from them since a certain day when the Count had written to his bank, asking to be sent the sum of a hundred thousand florins, intended for a marriage-settlement. He was to be married in Paris, he said, entering into a considerable family. It was exactly the same story with Baron von Ramberg, except that instead of asking for a hundred thousand florins, he had asked for two hundred thousand.

"Both sums had been sent. And what alarmed the friends of my two pupils was that Count Wenzel and Baron von Ramberg were to be married to the same woman: Countess Marcian Gregoryi."

"Countess Marcian Gregoryi!" repeated Monsieur Berthellemot.

Jean-Pierre waited for a moment to see if he had anything to add. "Is that name known to you?" he asked, eventually.

"It is not unknown," replied the Secretary General, in that simultaneously meek and hostile manner which affects bureaucrats when speaking of that which concerns their superiors. "The Prefect must have mentioned it to me. I'm taking notes..." Jean-Pierre waited a little longer, but that was all. Berthellemot went on: "This business hasn't been brought to the attention of the bureaux. Nothing has been sent to us by the Ambassador to Wurtemburg."

"Nothing has been received," Jean-Pierre corrected him. "I went to the Ambassador. The messages must have been intercepted."

Berthellemot put on his professional smile. "That assumes such complicated ramifications..." he began.

"It assumes the infidelity of a single postal-worker," Jean-Pierre intervened, coldly. "And it has been known..."

"Occasionally," the Secretary General admitted, without losing his smile. "Administrative departments always grant one another a certain charity."

"In any case," Jean-Pierre went on, "I cannot pretend that this mysterious and bloody enterprise–to which public anxiety has begun to give, for its own reasons, the name of vampire–is devoid of extremely complicated ramifications."

"But does it exist?" Berthellemot exclaimed, getting up and pacing back and forth across the room in an agitated manner. "A man in my position is sometimes confounded by doubt, sometimes by excessive credulity. Ability consists..."

"Pardon me, Monsieur Senior Civil Servant," said Jean-Pierre. "I am the son of a poor man, who thinks a great deal and says little. Would you like to know how my father judged ability? He said: 'Go straight along the road, and you will never fall into the ditches on either side of it.' To which I, an old fencing-master, add: With sword in hand, stand straight and thrust straight; every feint opens a gap through which death might pass... You do not need to know where your interest lies in this, but only what your duty is."

The Secretary General stopped walking abruptly.

"Neighbor, you talk like a book. Continue, I beg you."

"I ought to tell you, Monsieur Civil Servant," Jean-Pierre resumed, "that I have seen Baron von Ramberg since his pretended departure for Germany, in very peculiar circumstances and in that same Church of Saint-Louis-en-l'Ile where my two children disappeared from my view. Ramberg was with Countess Marcian Gregoryi, and I believe that he was departing on a much longer journey than that to Germany..."

"Are you accusing this Countess?" Berthellemot asked.

"God help those that I shall accuse," Jean-Pierre replied. "Two of our Germans are already out of the way; there remains the alabaster merchant, the millionaire Franz König, heir to the quarries in Würtz. This one is neither a baron nor a count, but I don't know many sharp operators, French or not, who are as capable as he when it comes to playing the businessman. In pleasure he is fire, in negotiation, marble. He's lasted much longer than the others, although it has been evident to me for several days that a new element has come into his life. I sense that mysterious traps have been set for him, into which his two companions have probably fallen. Alas, I would have been better able to watch over him if I had not been watching over my two poor children, René and Angela. Franz König was still in attendance at my fencing-school today, but he will not be coming tomorrow."

"Because...?" murmured the Secretary General, who shivered and sat down again.

"Because, like the others, he has realized a considerable sum of money, and the time has come to dispossess him."

"You would make a remarkable agent," said Berthellemot. "I'm taking notes."

"When I do police work," Jean-Pierre told him, "it's on my own account. I've had to do it more than once in my life. I once sat in the office of Thirouz de Crosne, the police lieutenant who succeeded Monsieur Lenoir in that position, just as I am sitting today in the office of the Prefect Monsieur Dubois." (Sévérin, called Gâteloup, was alluding at this point to the bizarre adventure which was the subject of our earlier story, *La Chambre des Amours*; you will recall that he played an important role in that drama, under the name of Gâteloup, cantor at Saint-Sulpice and fencing-master.) "There is no need for a whole squad," he went on, "to follow one trail and conduct one hunt. I had to avenge the injury which poisoned my youth, and I had to safeguard the children that I loved. I was young then, bold yet prudent, although I was sometimes prone to look in the bottom of a bottle for a way to obliterate the sting of grief...

"Now I am nearly an old man, and that's why I have come to ask for help. Not much help: one man, or two, chosen by myself. That won't weaken your army, Monsieur Civil Servant, and it will be sufficient for me. Franz König had no need to write to Stuttgart to lay his hands on the considerable sum I told you about; he has unlimited credit at Mannheim and Company. At three o'clock this afternoon, he left my school; he went to Mannheim's and came back to his carriage with bonds to the value of two hundred and fifty thousand Prussian *thalers*. That, Monsieur, is why I haven't used the past tense in referring to Franz König, as I have in talking about Count Wenzel and Baron von Ramberg. The time of his death has probably not yet arrived, while the other two are surely dead already."

Chapter XVII
A Night on the Seine

After this speech, Jean-Pierre Sévérin remained silent for a little while.

The Secretary General played with his paper-knife nervously, reflexively cracking the joints of his fingers from time to time. "It would require twice as many men," he said, eventually, "or three or four times as many, to do even half the job required of me, and God knows where the Prefect is. I don't eat, I don't sleep, I don't socialize, and still the twenty-four hours of the day are far from sufficient. The First Consul has that remarkable eye which sovereigns have for picking useful men out of the crowd. I don't boast, that would be superfluous, since the whole world knows the services that I have rendered to my fatherland... The First Consul must have his eyes on me as I speak. My dear Monsieur Sévérin, my own inclination would be to devote my serious attention to your business... and I do not deny that if I were to do so, we would get to the bottom of it in a day...but the security of the State depends on me, and it would be wrong to abandon matters of such gravity for the sake of mere curiosity..." He interrupted himself to say: "I would like to see whether the lips of these sorts of individuals really do have a special quality. It's said that they're unusually vivid, and perpetually moist with blood... I've taken notes from time to time... and I once had the opportunity to talk with Fog-Bog, the flesh-eating English clown; he ate dogs with some pleasure, but he wasn't a vampire, because he died of an accidental blow from a megaphone struck by his master and didn't return thereafter to suck the blood of young people... what do you think, my dear Monsieur Sévérin?"

"Of Countess Marcian Gregoryi?" said Jean-Pierre.

"Didn't you say that you've seen her?"

"I've seen her."

"Tell me about her lips. I'll take notes. The lips of these individuals have a special quality."

"Her lips are clean and beautiful," said the official guardian, slowly. "In another face they might seem a little pale, but they are very well suited to the adorable whiteness of her complexion."

"Very good–pallor is a symptom. Go on."

"There are women of marble; this is a woman of alabaster..."

"Then the brave Wurtemburger, Franz König, has the opportunity to purchase one of his own products." The Secretary General seemed delighted with this joke, and let out a good-natured laugh after having cracked the joints of all ten fingers.

Jean-Pierre did not laugh.

"And her eyes?" Monsieur Berthellemot asked. "The eyes also present a particular appearance, in these individuals."

"She has dark blue eyes," the official keeper replied, "beneath the bold and clear line of eyebrows black as jade. Her hair is black too, strangely black, with flashes of bronze, as if one were looking into deep water mirroring a stormy sky. The contrast between daylight and the night-darkness of that hair is so violent that it wounds the eyes."

"That must be nasty, neighbor."

"It's magnificent! All the beauty in the world passes through Paris at least once. Without ever leaving Paris, I've seen the marvelous courtesans of the last days of the Monarchy, the goddesses of the Republic, the foolish virgins of the Directory; I've seen the daughters of England crowned with gold, the enchantresses of Italy, the spangled fairies who come from Spain, dancing as they descend from the Pyrénées; I've seen tableaux by Rubens arriving from Austria or Bavaria, Muscovites as charming as Frenchwomen; I've seen Circassian *houris*, Georgian sultans, Greeks like animated statues by Phidias–but I've never seen anything as magnificently beautiful as Countess Marcian Gregoryi!"

"Nice speech," said the magistrate. "What a pretty picture!"

"I was a painter once," said Jean-Pierre.

"You seem to have been everything."

"Almost everything."

"And do you know the address of this eighth wonder of the world?"

"If I knew that..." Jean-Pierre began, his blue eyes acquiring a black glimmer.

"What would you do?"

"That's for me to know," Jean-Pierre replied.

"Have you encountered her often?"

"Three times [79]."

"Where did you see her?"

"At the church... the second time."

"When was that?"

"The evening before last."

"And the third time?"

"On the Pont au Change, by the riverside."

"When?"

"The same night."

Berthellemot opened his eyes wide and said, impatiently: "Well–make your report!"

The official guardian automatically drew himself up to his full height.

"I beg your pardon, neighbor, I beg your pardon," the Secretary General said. "I'd like you to tell me your little story."

Before continuing, Jean-Pierre paused to collect himself. "I don't know whether it can be called a story," he thought aloud. "I don't believe so. To everyone except myself, the facts would seem so extraordinary and so insane..."

"Get on with it," Berthellemot interrupted. "My mouth is watering. I love improbable things..."

"It was at the Church of Saint-Louis-en-l'Ile," Jean-Pierre went on. "If I had not been there for my two children, perhaps Baron von Ramberg would still be numbered among the living. She was with Baron von Ramberg; she took him to the place from which Count Wenzel never returned... you have all the information you desire, I suppose, regarding the produce of the Quai de Béthune?"

"*The Miraculous Catch*!" Berthellemot exclaimed, laughing. "Are your newspapers still full of that, neighbor? The innkeeper Ezekiel keeps us up to date–he's one of ours."

"Monsieur Civil Servant," Jean-Pierre said, gravely, "those who have taken the trouble to put on that audacious and ominous comedy must have a considerable interest in it. The powers which recruit men like Ezekiel are twice deceived: once by Ezekiel and once by those who deceive Ezekiel. I have worked hard in recent days. The human remains found at the Quai de Béthune come from cemeteries, boldly violated over a period of weeks. The show put on there is to distract attention. At present, Paris is host to a whole chain of murders, and the point of all this mummery is to hide the charnel-house which devours the bodies of its victims."

"That's your opinion, neighbor," Berthellemot murmured. "I'm taking notes. Your profession must go to your head, a little."

Jean-Pierre pointed at the face of the large watch, whose hands marked eight o'clock. "The First Consul must be up by now," he murmured. "Perhaps he's started reading the letter I wrote to him yesterday... and I can't deny, Monsieur Civil Servant, that there have already been times when I would have thrown politeness to the winds, if I had not been waiting here for General Bonaparte's reply."

Berthellemot gave a little nod of the head, skeptical and submissive at the same time.

Jean-Pierre went on: "I could tell you a great deal about Ezekiel and the back of his shop. Thank God, I've begun to see the light at the bottom of that ink-bottle– but you would take me for a madman twice over, Monsieur Civil Servant, and that would be a pity. Have I mentioned Abbé Martel?"

"No, devil take you," growled the Secretary General, "and your method of giving information to the administration is not the clearest, you know."

"That's because I have no need to tell the administration everything; I intend to take care of some things for myself. Abbé Martel is a worthy priest who has become involved, unwittingly, in some diabolical affair. I returned to Saint-Louis-en-l'Ile yesterday and asked for him at the vestry. He had just been given the last rites. He had been struck down, during the night, by a stroke. I was able to get in to see him. I found him paralyzed and unable to speak–but when I whispered certain names in his ear, his eyes were reanimated by horror and terror."

"What names, neighbor?"

"Among others, that of Countess Marcian Gregoryi."

Monsieur Berthellemot lowered his voice to ask: "Do you really think, after all, that this Countess Marcian Gregoryi is a vampire?"

"I am almost certain of it," Jean-Pierre replied, calmly.

"But, the Prefect..." Berthellemot stammered.

"From this moment," Jean-Pierre added, decisively replacing his watch in his fob-pocket "I shall give myself another half-hour to await the First Consul's reply–and since we have the time, I shall get back to the beautiful Countess. This will amuse you, Monsieur Civil Servant: it is curious, like a charade. The very first time I encountered Countess Marcian Gregoryi, I saw her as I have described her: young, beautiful, with hair of ebony above a face of ivory..."

"And the second?" Monsieur Berthellemot asked. "Was she already old?"

Jean-Pierre fixed him with a strange stare. "There is a legend in the land of Hungary," he replied, "which my friend Germain Patou knows, as he knows many things. It is called the story of the Beauty with Changing Hair... I should tell you that Germain Patou is an orphan, the son of a drowned man, whom I have helped a little as he grew to be a man. He is not much taller than a thigh-boot, but he has more spirit than a dozen giants... and he has searched everywhere for a vampire to dissect or to cure, according to circumstance. He plans to go to Belgrade, once his thesis is accepted, to excavate the tomb of the vampire Szandor, which is on an islet in the Sava, and the tomb of the vampire of Uszel, as grand as a palace–where, it is said, there are more than a thousand skulls of young women..."

"What's all this, neighbor?" Berthellemot murmured. "I warned you that I'm losing patience. I don't dislike vampires, but there shouldn't be too many..."

"In German Patou's legend," Jean-Pierre continued, imperturbably, "the vampire or oupire of Uszel, the Beauty with Changing Hair, is madly in love with Count Szandor, her husband, who treats her harshly and will not make love to her unless she pays him extravagantly. It requires millions of florins to buy one kiss from a spouse so cruel..."

"And avaricious," the Secretary General put in.

"And avaricious," Jean-Pierre echoed, earnestly. "The Beauty with Changing Hair is thus named because of a particular circumstance entirely in keeping with the dark imagination of Slavic poetry. She sometimes appears brunette, sometimes blonde..."

"Of course she does," said Berthellemot, "if she has two wigs..."

"She has had a thousand!" said Jean-Pierre. "And every one of them cost the life of some dear young creature, beautiful, happy, beloved...."

At this point, Jean-Pierre recounted the legend which we have already heard from Lila's mouth, in the boudoir at Bretonvilliers Lodge. When it was finished, he took up his own story again: "The second time that I saw Countess Marcian Gregoryi, her hair was blonde, like amber."

Berthellemot sat back in his armchair. "That's a step too far," he muttered.

206

"I've almost finished, Monsieur Senior Civil Servant," said Jean-Pierre, tiredly. "Countess Marcian Gregoryi now has blonde hair, every bit as beautiful as the splendid black hair she had had before. In my entire life, I have only seen one head of hair to compare with that one: the gold ringlets which dangle over the forehead of our little Angela. It was the same shade, and it had the same richness and lightness when kissed by the wind. The truth of the matter, Monsieur Civil Servant, is that this time, even though it was two o'clock in the morning, I went up to Countess Marcian Gregoryi, thinking that she was my Angela.

"I should tell you that I labor as long by night as by day. You thought a little while ago that my job had addled my brain. Perhaps it has. At any rate, it disturbs my sleep. When there is a fever in the air, whether it be sickness or chagrin; when nerves are bad, agitated, aching; when it is difficult to breathe, I say to myself: this is one of those nights when unhappy people weaken in the fight against despair; the Seine is carrying some naked sorrow towards the Pont de Saint-Cloud. Then I untie my boat, which is always moored under the rampart of the Châtelet, and take up my oars. This is what I did yesterday. The atmosphere was heavy, Angela was missing from home, and there was a great deal of disquiet in my heart. René was missing too...

"I don't know why, but René was further from my thoughts than Angela. René is a young man, brave and bold; he had fallen prey to seduction some days before; he could have been caught up in one of those adventures that have carried youth away since time began. But how could the absence of Angela–our little saint, the purest soul that God ever made; Angela, who loved and respected us so much–be explained?

"I left my wife, who was worn out by her tears, and I went down below the tower of the Châtelet. It was a stormy night. The rain had stopped, but turbulent clouds were racing across the sky, hurrying northwards like an immense army, passing furiously across the face of the moon, which seemed to flee in the opposite direction.

"The Seine was high, wild and roaring as it swept under the bridge, but I know the currents well, and my old arms still know how to combat the river's wrath. I found a backwash and I floated towards the Iles. The Quai de Béthune had been drawing me like a magnet for some days, and I was certain that one of these nights I would discover some deadly secret there.

"I passed the Pont Notre-Dame under the arch of the Quai aux Fleurs, where the current isn't as strong because of the curb provided by the Ile de la Cité. When I came out from beneath the arch, the moon lit both branches of the river brightly. Listen to me, Monsieur Civil Servant: I have a clear head and good eyes; I drink nothing but water nowadays, and I'm not mad, whatever you may think. I saw, as distinctly as in broad daylight, something that I could not believe immediately, because it was contrary to all the laws of nature.

"I saw a body–a dead body–which emerged from the shadow of the bridge at the same time as me, but over on the far side, from the last arch on the Rue Planche-Mibraie side. And this body, although it was quite inert, like the cadaver it was, was travelling upstream instead of following the dictates of the current, just as I was–and I had to use all my strength to gain a length a minute. When a cloud passed in front of the moon, I lost sight of it, and I said to myself: 'I'm dreaming.' But the cloud hurried on, the moon's rays fell upon the muddy tumult, and once again I saw the cadaver–long, rigid, as stiff as a statue laid on its side–following the same route as me on the other side of the river, gaining exactly as much ground as I was.

"I called out, as it finally occurred to me that this might be a living being–but no response was returned, in the disquieting fashion of the sentries of the Place de Grêve. I plied my oars, trying to pull upstream before crossing over; but even though I had the advantage of the backwash, my boat could scarcely keep pace with the corpse. As far as cutting across the current was concerned, it could only be done by walking on the water like Our Lord. The six rowers of the First Consul's

208

pleasure-boat, which I've seen at Saint-Cloud, could not have beaten the current–but my desire to see more became almost passionate; my head became feverish. I redoubled my efforts, and having got upriver as far as the Archbishop's palace I launched myself into a cross-current which flows from that point towards the right bank.

"When I reached the middle of the river–losing, unfortunately, all the ground that I had gained–there was a sudden flash of light. The moon was crossing a pool of blue, and every wave on the river was set alight, as if it had been showered with sparks all the way to the horizon. The corpse, shrunk by the distance, appeared to me one last time, still going upstream, before it was lost in the shadows of the tall trees bordering the Quai des Ormes.

"Just there, not far from the Pont Marie, along the riverbank under the Quai des Ormes, there is a place which is sacred to us–I mean, to my wife, to Angela, to me, and hopefully to René de Kervoz. Angela told us everything. She once took us there to tell us how her heart and René's were united, on the lawn among the flowers, with God as their witness, on a beautiful evening in spring, on that very spot. I went there often, and since unhappiness had descended upon us I sometimes prayed there.

"I don't know why my heart was so painfully affected by the sight of that cadaver entering into the shadow cast over the site of our tender memories. I put all my effort into reaching the right bank, because it was now obvious to me that I could not achieve my objective while remaining in my boat. To get out on the bank and run as fast as I could towards the Pont Marie seemed the only reasonable plan. I put it into action, and after hastily mooring my boat I set off for the gardens of the Quai des Ormes.

"My legs lost their strength, as if I were paralyzed, and progress became impossible. The wind that froze the sweat on my face thrust me back. I had the kind of weakness in my limbs that marks the onset of a serious mental disturbance, under the threat of great unhappiness.

"I was still some distance away. How, then, could I see so far, and so distinctly, in the darkness beneath those trees? But I saw it; I definitely I saw it, for I let our a cry of anguish as I hastened on my way, in the interval of a lightning-flash.

"Beside the river, there among the flowers and the grass, I saw a young girl kneeling: as desperate, doubtless, as those for which I am always searching, and sometimes find, by the grace of God. I can recognize them among a thousand. They nearly all pray like that before losing their poor blind souls. And do you think that God's eternal mercy can find no pity for that heart-rending folly?"

At this point, Jean-Pierre Sévérin, called Gâteloup, passed his hand over his moist brow. The words caught in his throat. So entirely had emotion overtaken his thoughts that he was speaking far more to himself than to his interlocutor, who was now immobile and mute.

Monsieur Berthellemot had discretion enough not to reply to the last question that had been put to him, even though it was a philosophical question that might have served as the theme of a long discussion–and if the reader is astonished by that excessive reserve on the part of such a determined inter-rupter, we confess that Monsieur Berthellemot, like many other senior civil servants, had the useful talent of sleeping profoundly while remaining upright in his chair and retaining all the appearances of vigilant attention. He was, in fact, asleep, perhaps dreaming of the fortunate hour when, the penetrating eye of the First Consul having finally distinguished his true and unparalleled merit, *The Monitor* would publish that eloquent and brief sentence: Monsieur Berthellemot is appointed Prefect of Police.

Jean-Pierre, for his part, was in no need of any reply. He continued regardless. "There is a sublime contradiction that I have encountered ten times over on my way through life. Every human being who has decided to kill herself could probably be stopped at the very brink of the abyss by the hope of saving someone in a similar situation. A man who is going to commit suicide is always ready to prevent someone else from committing suicide. In this way, two desperate souls, perched on the lip of the abyss, could discover the counsel of courage and resignation that would lead to their mutual salvation.

"The young woman on the Quai des Ormes had made the sign of the cross, and I was saying to myself 'It's no use hurrying, I'll get there too late' when I suddenly perceived that the corpse that had come up the Seine, hugging the right bank, was in front of her. It shone, that corpse, with its own light, and it seemed to me that the tableau was lit by the rays emanating from it. All my blood ran cold. Why? I can't put it into words.

"The young woman leaned forward and reached out her arms. Another arm—the cadaver's—also reached towards the young woman. My hair stood up on my head as my view was interrupted.

"I caught sight, as if through a fog, of something unheard of, impossible. It was not the young woman that drew the corpse towards her, but the corpse that drew the young woman towards itself. Neither the corpse nor the young woman was yet in the water because the corpse, which had risen to its feet, stopped for a moment.

"One dead hand plunged into the abundant tresses of the young woman, while the other described a rapid circle around her forehead and temples.

"Then the corpse climbed up the bank—living, agile, young—while the poor infant took its place in the tormented water; but instead of going upriver, like the corpse, the girl was carried downstream by the current, twisting and turning as it plunged beneath the surface.

"I threw myself head first into the Seine, and I did my best. After swimming for half an hour, in vain, I found that the furious current had carried me all the way back to the Place du Châtelet, above which was my own house.

"The young woman had vanished.

"At the moment when I climbed back on to the quay, vanquished, exhausted and desolate, a woman passed before me along the steps of the new Morgue: the woman who had Angela's hair.

"I stopped her. When she turned round, I recognized Countess Marcian Gregoryi, gloriously radiant with beauty and youth, but with blonde hair.

"I don't know why, but the sight made me think of the livid corpse which had moved up the stream of the river a short time before.

"I didn't say anything; astonishment shut my mouth.

"Countess Marcian Gregoryi pronounced a foreign name, which I believe was Yanusza. A carriage, drawn by two black horses, came out of the shadows at the corner of the Marché-Neuf. The Countess got into it, and the rig went off at a gallop in the direction of Notre-Dame..."

The sudden loud sound of a bell made Jean-Pierre jump and woke the Secretary General with a start.

"Present!" said Monsieur Berthellemot, blinking his eyes furiously. As he looked around, wondering what the noise that had interrupted his peaceful sleep signified, the main door was thrown open. Charlevoy, one of the agents who had been on sentry duty earlier, came in, saying: "An urgent message from the Tuileries, with the First Consul's seal."

Berthellemot got up unsteadily, still dazed.

"For Monsieur Séverin," Charlevoy added.

"Ah! Ah!" said Monsieur Berthellemot. "Monsieur Séverin. I've taken notes... the man who said Your Majesty while the National Convention ruled... Give it to him!"

The bell rang again, and Berthellemot, now wide awake, exclaimed: "It's the Prefect!"

Having recovered the use of his legs, he was about to hurl himself towards the door that connected with the office of his superior, when Jean-Pierre stopped him and handed him the letter that had come from the Tuileries, open.

It was not long, saying only: Order to put at the disposition of Sieur Séverin the agents he requires [80]. It was signed Bonaparte, First Consul.

"Monsieur Despaux!" shouted Berthellemot, "put all the agents we have at the disposal of this excellent man... Pardon me for leaving you, neighbor... the Prefecture is yours... Needless to say, your story was most interesting... You can bear witness to the fact that I don't need to seek the advice of the Prefect before obeying the orders of the First Consul... What am I saying? Between the First Consul and Monsieur Dubois, one cannot hesitate...."

When the Prefect rang the bell for a third time the bell-cord broke. Berthellemot hurled himself head first through the door, like a rider in the Olympic Circus leaping through a paper-covered hoop. When he arrived in the Prefect's office, the Prefect was kissing the hand of a radiantly beautiful young woman with blonde hair.

Monsieur Dubois seemed very animated, and was playing the administrative big wheel to perfection. "Monsieur Secretary General," he said, severely, "I called three times." He interrupted the apology stammered by his subordinate to add: "Monsieur Secretary General, understand that the Prefecture of Police is entirely at the disposition of Countess Marcian Gregoryi, here." And when Berthellemot recoiled in stupefaction, Monsieur Dubois drew himself majestically up to his full height and said: "By the signed order of the First Consul!"

Chapter XVIII
Countess Marcian Gregoryi

Monsieur Berthellemot was not an ordinary man; we have seen that he possessed the piercing gaze of Monsieur de Sartines, the irony of Monsieur Lenoir, and I don't know what tic belonging to Monsieur de la Reynie. His conversational banter was elegant and he knew how to crack his fingers like an angel. It only remains to be added that he was loquacious, self-satisfied and envious of his superiors.

Foreigners and malicious persons claim that these agreeable virtues have been appreciated by the French Administration in every era; it is these virtues, and others too, that have won it the reputation of being able to accomplish in three months, with sixty employees, all of them university graduates, work that would be done in London in three days by four petty bureaucrats. It is only fair to add, though, that the English military establishment is always ready to boast of having saved the French army at Inkermann when it retreated, raked by gunfire, into the bottom of a ditch, and that it is common knowledge in Turin that Sebastopol was taken by the Piedmontese Infantry without any help at all [81]. We must beware of believing the impudent bragging of rival nations, and trust in our Administration, which could provide a perfectly adequate encumbrance to all the bureaux in the entire universe.

Monsieur Berthellemot, in spite of his talents and his experience, was immediately dumbfounded by the sight of the beautiful person, insolently blonde, who was looking at him in a slightly mocking fashion.

Although he did not like his Prefect, Monsieur Berthellemot was at least wholeheartedly fearful of him. How could he tell him that this charming woman was a vampire, an oupire, a ghoul, a hideous collection of desiccated bones whose tomb, situated somewhere on the banks of the Seine, was full of skulls belonging to unhappy young girls whom she had scalped for the benefit of herself, Countess Marcian Gregoryi, the ghoul, the oupire, the vampire?

The insinuation would have seemed improbable.

I will go further: by what means could it be established that this monstrous creature, whose dimpled cheeks were smiling wonderfully, nourished herself on human flesh? How could one accuse her of having been brunette yesterday, when her radiant child-like face was dressed in such a profusion of golden curls? You could have cried "She is bald!" as loudly as you please; no one would have believed it.

Monsieur Berthellemot sensed this. More than that: he doubted it himself, so naturally rooted did those amber tresses seem to be. He was not very far from believing that his "neighbor" had made him the victim of an audacious practical joke. "Monsieur Prefect," he stammered, in the end, "I beg you to be assured that I have taken notes... and I am the Countess' most faithful servant."

"A signed order, Monsieur," Dubois repeated, loftily, "drawn up in a manner which seems to presage the great events for which the auguries were favorable... in brief, the matter is understood. I do not suppose that you have any need to know State secrets."

Berthellemot bowed deeply.

"Listen to this, please," the Prefect went on, unfolding a small piece of paper covered in bold and slightly irregular writing. In a voice entirely saturated with unctuousness he read:

"We instruct M.L.N.P.J. Dubois, our Prefect of Police, to listen with the greatest care to the intelligence that will be furnished by the carrier of this item.

"Countess Marcian Gregoryi is a noble Hungarian lady who has already rendered us a signal service during the Italian campaign. We have personal experience of her devotion.

"Whatever instructions she gives should be carried out to the letter.

"Signed: N.

"Yes indeed!" exclaimed Monsieur Dubois, who put the paper in his pocket in order to crack his fingers, though not as adroitly as the Secretary General. Yes indeed–I am *his* Prefect of Police; *his* to the death! This is private, Monsieur–confidential, even. I know arrogant men who would trample me underfoot, who would be made to tremble by this little piece of paper. My position is my destiny. One cannot always hide one's light under a bushel–isn't that so? Merit will have its day... and remember that the eye of an eagle is fixed upon us." Berthellemot timidly opened his mouth, but Monsieur Dubois silenced him with a capacious gesture and said: "Remain silent, if you please, Monsieur." He glanced sideways at the Countess to see what effect that firm statement had produced.

Countess Marcian Gregoryi was sitting down, gracefully arranging the pleats of an exquisite dress. She was so young, so beautiful and so charming that one was disposed to wonder how old she could have been in 1797, when she had rendered such signal service to General Bonaparte.

Monsieur Dubois continued: "It is signed only with an N, but it is a capital N. I feel a sincere joy, Monsieur, and I cannot hide it. My opinions are known, they have never varied. He who is the destiny of France and of the world has sounded, I hope, the depths of my heart... and Madame the Countess will inform him directly, I am sure, of my eagerness, of my... in a word, the aspirations of our fatherland are manifestly monarchical."

Berthellemot placed his right hand on his breast in order to make a premature acclamation, but the Prefect said to him again: "Remain silent, if you please, Monsieur." He went on, solemnly: "Madame Countess, my Secretary General awaits your orders."

The delectable blonde had not yet spoken. Her voice emerged like a song. "The most urgent," she said, "is to arrest the evil-intentioned person who, in spite of his very subordinate position, is the most dangerous enemy of the First Consul. I refer to the official keeper of the vaults at the Châtelet where the dead are displayed to the living."

"My neighbor!" murmured Berthellemot, with a groan.

"His name is Jean-Pierre Sévérin, called Gâteloup," the Countess concluded.

"But, Madame Countess... Monsieur Prefect," Berthellemot said, in a strangled tone, "this Gâteloup is a friend of the Emperor!"

Monsieur Dubois was embarrassed, not by the fact but by the word. "No one wishes or desires more than I do," he said, emotionally, "to devote all his vows, all his aspirations... and Madame the Countess must not have the slightest doubt... but in the end I must protest, in the name of the Head of State..."

"Time is pressing," the adorable blonde interrupted him coolly, delicately raising her eyebrows. "Every minute lost makes the situation worse... and I'm afraid that the Secretary General might have blundered."

This plain statement did not surprise the Prefect in the least. He murmured, in a tone of commiseration: "Well, the poor fellow is certainly capable of it... if those in high places only knew how pitifully we are supported..."

For the first time in his administrative career, Berthellemot, who was red with anger, lost control. "A nice thing to say!" he cried. "In whom should one believe? You, Monsieur Dubois, or the First Consul? I, too, have received an order! A signed order!"

"A signed order!" the Prefect repeated. "From him to you?"

"To me," Berthellemot riposted, firmly mounted on his high horse. "That is to say... in the final analysis, my personal opinion has been that I ought not to be disobedient to Napoleon Bonaparte."

"And what did this order say?" asked the Countess, who had paled slightly.

"The order put the Prefecture of Police at the disposition of Monsieur Jean-Pierre Sévérin, who was once the First Consul's fencing-master."

"The order must be false!" exclaimed the Countess. "This Sévérin is the most dangerous accomplice of Georges Cadoudal."

The two functionaries were quite overwhelmed. Monsieur Dubois fell into his armchair rather than merely sitting down, and Berthellemot, performing his circus trick-riding act for a second time, leapt head-first through the doorway.

He was only gone for three minutes. He spent those three minutes with Monsieur Despaux, who had–acting under the orders of Monsieur Berthellemot–given Jean-Pierre Sévérin one peace officer, equipped with his sash, and four selected agents, among whom were Laurent and Charlevoy.

"And they've all gone?" demanded the unhappy Secretary General.

"In a tearing hurry," Despaux replied. "That Sévérin gave the impression of having the devil at his heels."

"Where did they go?"

"No one told me to ask them that."

"You've kept the order, I suppose."

"What order?"

"The First Consul's order."

"I didn't even know they had an order from the First Consul. I was only obeying you, my immediate superior."

Berthellemot stared at him, anger fighting distress within his expression. "So you say!" he cried. "You're under suspicion! It wouldn't take much for me to make an example of you! I leave the choice of adjective to you: incompetent or criminal."

"Whenever Monsieur the Secretary General wishes," Despaux replied, taking off his hat, "I am a hunter, and Monsieur Fouché can make very good use of beaters on his estate at Pont-Carré."

"Monsieur, Monsieur," Berthellemot grated, "you will answer to me for the life of the First Consul."

Despaux saluted, laughing derisively, and went out backwards.

"When Monsieur Berthellemot went back into the Prefect's office, he was cringing like a beaten dog.

Far from cracking his fingers, he twiddled his thumbs with an air of consternation. "All that I can do," he muttered, "is put Monsieur Despaux in prison..."

The Prefect cut his speech short with a razor-like gesture. "Remain silent, please," he said. "You're under suspicion."

Berthellemot's legs became weak beneath the weight of his body.

"Incompetent or criminal, Monsieur," Dubois went on. "I leave the choice of adjective to you. I am constrained to tell you that you are not worthy to be the lieutenant of the man who, by virtue of his zeal and clear-sightedness, has known how to prevent the disastrous consequences of various conspiracies directed against a precious life... of the man who stands like an impenetrable barrier... of the man who laid hold of Pichegru and Moreau... of the man who will lay hold of Georges Cadoudal this very day!"

"Ah...!" said Berthellemot, his mouth agape.

Dubois clasped his hands behind his back. He dazzled his Secretary General. "Monsieur Despaux," he went on, "does not seem altogether unsuitable to fulfill duties which now seem to me to be beyond your capability. It wouldn't take much for me to make an example of you..."

"Oh, Monsieur Prefect," said Berthellemot, "after all the misfortune that I have suffered... *Sic vos non vobis!* [82]"

"Are you trying to pretend that you have something to do with the continual success of my efforts?"

"Nice words," the Secretary General riposted, bravely, discovering a sprig of courage in the depths of his distress. "Just discharge me, and you will see that I have my tongue in my pocket... I've taken notes, thank God... Monsieur Fouché will have his hands on me in a matter of days, thanks to this same Despaux..."

Fouché was the terror of every policeman. It was understood that there was a small domestic dispute between him and the First Consul, but that there would be a reconciliation sooner or later. Monsieur Dubois paced back and forth within his room. "You may go, Monsieur," he said, eventually, in a slightly less haughty tone. "I need to be alone with the Countess, thanks to whom I shall accomplish a deed that will be the pride of my public career... We have awkward contingencies to overcome. You have made a mistake–endeavor to repair it. I order you, at all costs, to find this Jean-Pierre Sévérin, who is a villainous bare-faced liar, and to bring him in dead or alive... If you can do that, you have some hope of regaining my confidence..."

"Oh, Monsieur Prefect...!" Berthellemot exclaimed, with tears in his eyes.

"One last thing!" Dubois interrupted, cutting short this impassioned plea. "I hold you personally responsible for the life of the First Consul. Get out!"

Dubois went back to the Countess as soon as the door had closed behind Berthellemot. "You see what I have to work with!" he said. "It's essential to take that kind of line with men of inferior quality. Only God and the Head of State understand the prodigious extent of the difference between a Prefect of Police and a Secretary General!"

Berthellemot was of the same opinion as God and the Head of State–but he, of course, considered the difference from an inverted perspective. "Despicable brute," he thought, as he re-entered his office with his head bowed. "Miserable weathercock, turning with every wind! I'll have your job or die trying! Everything that adds luster to your career is down to me–me, and me alone! I'm as far above you as the free-flying bird is above the fowls in our chicken-runs... nicely put, you must grant me that! And when I became the head of the administration, the whole world will hear of your stupidities!"

The song says that beggars are happy men, and that they love one another, but it has nothing at all to say about those who administer us. If you wish to see hatred at its very finest– its most concentrated, most vitriolic and most venomous–go to

220

ts most concentrated, most vitriolic and most venomous–go to the bureaux.

While he was drawing up and giving out the orders which launched an army of agents on the trail of Jean-Pierre Sévérin, called Gâteloup, however, Monsieur Berthellemot's thoughts were dominated by the image of the Countess Marcian Gregoryi. "A pretty little thing," he said to himself, "to say the least! It's claimed that vampires have lips sticky with blood, but her mouth is a rose... But when all's said and done, one of these two orders signed by the First Consul is certainly false... if it's his..."

Meanwhile, the Prefect of Police was sitting beside the adorable blonde. "Now, if you please, Madame," he said, "we must get on with our work, starting with Georges Cadoudal..."

"No," the Countess interrupted. "The first necessity is to arrest all the Brothers of Virtue... if even one of them remains at liberty, I shall say nothing more." From a Russian leather wallet, richly ornamented in an Arabesque fashion, she took a long list which contained, among many others, several names familiar to us: Andrea Ceracchi, Taïeh, Caernarvon and Osman. Each name was supplemented by an address.

"I have come a long way," she said, "and my journey had but one purpose: to save the man whose glory has already dazzled our half-savage lands. The seeds of his devotion were sown in me beyond the Danube, in the plains of Hungary, where the League of Virtue has begun to recruit poniards. I joined that bloody organization for the express purpose of opposing it. I did not know, to begin with, how perilous that enterprise would be. It has cost the lives of three of my dearest friends: I speak of the brave Count Wenzel, the brilliant Baron von Ramberg and finally of Franz König, whose future seemed so bright..."

Dubois quickly pulled open his desk-drawer and consulted a note. "Count Wenzel," he murmured, "Baron von Ramberg.... it's the first time I've heard mention of the third..."

"You have only once heard mention of the other two, Monsieur Prefect," the Countess said, sadly, "and I was the one who caused news of their death to be brought to the Prefecture. The third met the same fate as his two companions today. You can add his name to your list. He's from Stuttgart too."

The Prefect's eyes were lowered, and his eyebrows drew together as if he were thinking hard.

"But for those young German knights errant," the Countess continued, "I would have done what I am doing today three months ago. I would have come here, where denunciations are made, and I would have made my denunciations. But Wenzel, Ramberg and König said: 'We can win this fight this ourselves, with our own forces: we shall crush the vampire'..."

"The vampire!" Monsieur Dubois echoed, astonished.

Countess Marcian Gregoryi was smiling. "It's a name which has often been spoken in Paris of late," she said. "I know that Monsieur Dubois, the rational and enlightened man of science, to whom the future imperial government promises such high office, cannot believe, I must suppose, in the poor fables of Eastern Europe... Paris's Prefect of Police does not believe in vampires..."

"No, certainly not!" Dubois stammered. "My education, my knowledge..."

"The vampire of which I speak," Countess Gregoryi put in, her voice clear and firm, "is the secret society that calls itself the League of Virtue, and which is nothing but a bunch of scoundrels, united in criminal intent."

"Of course," said Monsieur Dubois, innocently. "I never doubted it!"

"An association of owls," the beautiful blonde went on, animatedly, "assembled by night to halt the flight of the eagle... a tangle of hatreds, envious desires, lax ambitions. The real vampire, the league of assassins, has invented the other vampire: the fake, the fantastic and impossible monster that has frightened all the grown-up children of Paris. The fable was intended thus, to confound those who would have wanted

222

to pursue the reality... even that comedy of the Quai de Béthune, *The Miraculous Catch*, had the object of attracting public attention away from a charnel-house which is, alas, only too real, where the human remains of so many victims, already immolated, are decomposing!"

Dubois had put his hand to his forehead. "That explains everything!" he murmured. "And it corresponds with a series of hypotheses that I have submitted more than once to the test of my rationality... for nothing escapes me, Madame, nothing... as you will soon see. The people who come here, all mealy-mouthed, to tell me to watch out, to pay attention to this or to that, are petty busybodies..."

"You are the Minister of Police of the future!" said Countess Marcian Gregoryi, solemnly.

"Except," Monsieur Dubois replied, "that I have no support. A flock of geese, Madame, that's my army... without taking account of several others who are always trying to thrust a stick in my wheel, so to speak, whose names are Savary, Bourrienne, Fouché and the devil... do you take my meaning? And also without taking account of the fact that above me–yes, Madame, above me–there is a senator of cardboard, a mannequin, a stuffed turkey-cock, Monsieur Supreme Justice, if you please, who can put the brakes on the most well-oiled machine all by himself... Without them. I would already have stuffed that vampire in my pocket twenty times over, whether it be a secret society or a ghoul pulled out of the gutters of the Tour de Saint-Jacques-la-Boucherie [83]... I give you my word, Madame."

"I said as much to the Emperor," the Countess murmured, as if she were talking to herself.

"Shush!" said Dubois, "Let's not abuse that term. Fouché has spies even in the bureaux... Please, Madame, don't tell me what I don't need to know, but only what is necessary to my appreciation of that which, according to you, is the ultimate purpose of these numerous murders."

"The ultimate purpose is threefold, Monsieur Prefect: to stir up the populace, to make enemies disappear and to raise money..."

"Ah! Are these Virtue fellows thieves?"

"To attack a Head of State requires money, Monsieur Prefect."

"That's true, Madame. I admire your perspicacity." At this point, Dubois fixed her with the stare borrowed from Monsieur de Sartines–which Berthellemot had adopted in his absence, much as a good valet puts on his master's old boots from time to time. "And permit me," he said, changing his tone, "to give you the proof that I promised you a little while ago... the proof that nothing escapes me, no matter how badly supported I am. My personal clear-sightedness is entirely sufficient... almost... there is a dossier here relating to you, Countess."

The beautiful blonde leaned forward.

"You were engaged to be married to Count Wenzel?" the Prefect said.

"News travels fast, Monsieur."

"A record of it was made at the sacristy of Saint-Eustace."

"Nothing can be hidden from you, in truth."

"You were also engaged to be married to Baron von Ramberg."

"So it's said."

"I have extracted the information from the register at Saint-Louis-en-l'Ile."

"That's marvelous, Monsieur Prefect! What an institution your police force is! But you don't seem to know that I was also affianced, in the same fashion, to the valiant and handsome Franz König."

Monsieur Dubois let out an exclamation of astonishment. "If I ventured to ask you for an explanation..." he began.

"I fully intended to offer you one," put in the Countess–whose large eyes seemed, in truth, to have momentarily taken on an expression of religious penitence. "Wenzel, Ramberg and König were the dearest of my friends, to say the least: they were my brothers, and I make no secret of the fact that my ardor to continue our communal mission has been redoubled by the hope of avenging them. We were a league within a league: a league of good against a league of evil. I had exhausted my own fortune in the preliminary phases of the struggle; for good as for evil, necessity is the sinews of war. My three beloved companions were rich but young; they needed an excuse to obtain large sums from their trustees in their own country. There was no need to vary the excuses, because each of us believed that the end of the war was close at hand. Wenzel sent the extract from the register at Saint-Eustace to Stuttgart, signed by Abbé Aymar; Ramberg sent a similar document signed by Abbé Martel at Saint-Louis-en-l'Ile; König..."

"Only the first two documents are here," said the Prefect. "Do you have the money?"

"The vampire," the Countess replied, her voice becoming gloomy, "has won almost a million francs in this game."

Monsieur Dubois shut his drawer with a bang.

"Now, Monsieur," the charming blonde went on, her tone becoming as sharp and deliberate as it had been at the commencement of the interview, "permit me to anticipate your question, because the night's getting on and everything must be concluded by tomorrow morning. There's one thing you don't yet know, of which you need to be apprised without further delay, and which will explain the audacious move attempted by this Jean-Pierre Sévérin, with the aid of the First Consul's forged signature."

"Forged?"

"Forged," repeated the Countess, with assurance. "The First Consul will leave for Fontainebleau at seven o'clock this evening."

"Without giving me any warning!" Dubois exclaimed, jumping from his seat.

"The last person that the First Consul saw in Paris was me, and I was instructed to warn you."

Dubois rang his bell vigorously. Monsieur Despaux came in almost immediately.

It would have required a more penetrating gaze than that of the Prefect of Police to catch sight of the rapid glance exchanged between the new arrival and Countess Marcian Gregory.

"To the Tuileries at once, as fast as you can," the Prefect ordered. "The First Consul will be leaving for Fontainebleau tonight!"

"The news has just arrived," said Despaux, "and I was on my way to tell Monsieur the Prefect." He went out again at a sign from his superior.

"The fact with which I need to acquaint you," the delectable blonde resumed, calmly, "is one confided to me privately by a young law student named René de Kervoz, the future son-in-law of Jean-Pierre Sévérin..."

"What the devil has he to do with this?" said the Prefect, in a heartfelt tone.

"...and the nephew of the chouan Georges Cadoudal," the Countess concluded. Monsieur Dubois brightened, and became more attentive. "A child, Monsieur Prefect, to whom all political conspiracy is as foreign as it is possible to be, and whom I am keeping prisoner precisely to keep him away from the violent scenes which will take place tomorrow morning."

"And it was from him that you learned Georges Cadoudal's hiding-place?" Dubois asked.

"From him."

"He's a traitor, then."

"He loves me," Countess Marcian Gregoryi replied, blushing–not with shame, but with pride. After a pause, she continued: "Now that we have said everything we have to say, Monsieur Prefect, let's agree to the facts. I remind you that I have nothing to ask of you. It is for me to dictate conditions. The first condition is that today, at midnight, an adequate force will surround the house situated on the Chemin de la Muette, in the Faubourg Saint-Antoine, of which this is a plan." She placed a piece of paper on the desk. "All the affili-

226

ates of the League of Virtue will be meeting in that house. This is how you must be introduced in order to lay your hands on them: one of your men will present himself at the door facing the Rue de la Muette and knock six times, spaced thus and not otherwise: three, two, one. Someone will open it and ask: 'Who are you?' He will respond: 'In the name of the Father, the Son and the Holy Spirit, I am a Brother of Virtue.'

"At the same time, if possible, or immediately afterwards, your agents will enter the house which bears the number seven in the Chaussée des Minimes, at Marais. There you will seize all the conspirators' papers, which will furnish you with all the proof you need. My name is frequently to be found in those papers–under what entitlement you now know. I have howled with these wolves in order to have the right to follow them into the depths of their lair.

"In the conservatory, situated to the left of the drawing-room, the third pot you come to after the glass door, containing a yucca plant, can be pushed aside to uncover a trap-door. Beneath that trap-door is a sepulchre: the vampire's real charnel-house.

"No harm is to come to young René de Kervoz when he reappears among the living.

"In the meantime, you will prepare my passports for Vienna. I shall be travelling with a woman by the name of Yanusza Paraxin, who is my nurse, my coachman and my valet. I shall leave tomorrow, as soon as I have delivered Georges Cadoudal into your hands. Until that moment, I shall remain in Paris as a hostage."

"And how will you deliver Georges Cadoudal?" Dubois wanted to know.

"All this is acceptable?"

"Yes, it's all agreed."

Countess Marcian Gregoryi got up–and Monsieur Dubois, who was a connoisseur, could not help admiring the exquisite gracefulness of her figure. "This is how I shall deliver Georges Cadoudal to you," she said. "Before daybreak, your men, all in plain clothes, will set an ambush in the Rue Saint-

Hyacinthe-Saint-Michel, between the Rue Saint-Jacques and the square. Some will be around the corner of the Rue Saint-Jacques, others forming a line along the Rue de la Harpe, thus surrounding the block of houses on the southern side.

"At eight o'clock in the morning, a hired cab will come to a halt in front of one of the houses in that block–I don't know which, because Georges Cadoudal knows how to maintain a hiding-place like a fox's earth, which has ten different exits. The arrival of the cab will be the signal to watch the windows. A veiled woman will appear at one of them; when that veiled woman shows herself, Georges Cadoudal will emerge from his doorway and get into the cab. The rest is up to the agents."

The Countess inclined her head slightly, great lady that she was, and went to the door. She was escorted, at a respectful distance, by the Prefect of Police, who thanked her profusely.

Chapter XIX
The Last Night

Left alone, the Prefect struck a meditative pose in order to demonstrate to himself, sincerely, that no magistrate since the invention of the police force had ever given evidence of greater perspicacity. Thanks to his talent, he would bring down three magnificent birds with a single stone, confiscating the success of the vampire to his own advantage, revealing to a dazzled Paris the existence of the League of Virtue and ensnaring that wolf Cadoudal. A triple triumph! He regretted, while rubbing his hands, that there was no such thing as a deputy emperor, for he felt worthy of a little throne.

Meanwhile, Countess Marcian Gregoryi's carriage and horses were waiting in the Rue Harlay-du-Palais. It was exactly the same elegant carriage, hauled by two beautiful black horses, that we once saw stationed at the threshold of the Church of Saint-Louis-en-l'Ile.

"To the house!" ordered the Countess as she stepped up into the carriage.

When she closed the carriage door, a shadow detached itself from the corner of a neighboring house and slid noiselessly towards the rig. The shadow was almost as broad as a full-grown man, but it was no taller than a twelve-year-old child. When the carriage departed at the gallop, the light of the next street-lamp might have revealed to an observer the figure of our friend Germain Patou, crouched in the footman's seat.

The beautiful horses eventually came to a halt at the stable-door of an old and magnificent house situated in the Chaussée des Minimes: number 7. Countess Marcian Gregoryi went up a grand flight of steps. An old woman with a mannish figure was waiting in the hallway on the first floor; there was an enormous dog sprawled on the tiles in front of her. As the Countess entered, the dog got up on its four legs and extended its neck as if it were about to howl.

"Quiet, Pluto!" said Yanusza, in her barbarous Latin.

Pluto evidently understood Latin, because he squatted down again, then stretched himself out and groveled before the newcomer, sweeping the tiles with the fur of his belly.

"Did Franz König come?" the Countess asked.

"He came," Yanusza replied.

"At the appointed hour?"

"Before the appointed hour."

"Has he got the five hundred thousand *thalers*?"

"He has the five hundred thousand *thalers* and three jewel-cases. The wedding-presents are coming tomorrow morning."

The Countess smiled bleakly. "He's waiting for me?"

"Undoubtedly," the old woman replied.

"Who with?"

"With Taïeh, the Negro, and Osman, the infidel."

"Do you think the business is concluded?"

Just as Yanusza opened her mouth to reply, a harrowing and long-drawn-out cry pierced the thick wall of the hallway. The Countess gave a faint shudder and Yanusza made the sign of the cross, murmuring: *Requiescat in pace!*" The huge dog let out a long plaintive howl.

"Pack the bags, Paraxin," ordered the Countess, having already recovered her coolness. "Don't waste any time."

"The bags are packed, mistress," the old woman replied. "Is it absolutely certain that we'll be leaving tomorrow?"

"As sure as it is that you're a good Christian, Yanusza. This is the last night. Franz König completes the million ducats demanded by Count Szandor. I'm going to live and to die–I, who am privy to life and death at one and the same time. *In vita mors, in morte vita!* Szandor, my adored spouse, will grant me an hour of love before burning my heart!"

Her ardent passion transfigured her beauty in the same way that the varnish on an old master sometimes glimmers with strange reflected light. She took a step toward the door that gave access to the interior apartments, but stopped before touching the handle. "And the poor boy..." she murmured, hesitantly.

"He threatens, he prays, he blasphemes, he weeps," the old woman replied. "This evening, he called out to his Angela."

"But he hasn't pronounced the name of Lila?"

"Certainly–to curse it."

The Countess' eyebrows contracted slightly, as if silken fringe above her eyelids had been delicately lowered. "Have all his needs been attended to?"

"All of them: I took in his meal while he was asleep."

"He slept?"

"As you know, mistress, since..."

The Countess smiled and put a finger to the servant's lips. "You did not forget to put the wine of dreams on his bedside table before you left?" she said, in a low voice.

"No," Yanusza replied, "I did not forget."

The Countess opened the door and went through, while the old woman crossed herself for a second time, mumbling a Latin prayer.

The rooms within were framed and decorated in the style of Henry IV, with deeply-molded wood panels on the walls and ceilings, tall fireplaces sculpted in wood and tapestries whose colors had not faded with age. Having passed through a dining-room, whose walls seemed to buckle beneath their burden of painted game-birds, fruit, flowers and flagons, a sitting-room with high, sleek silver-framed hangings and a bedroom fit for the use of the beautiful Gabrielle [84], Countess Marcian Gregoryi opened a rear door and passed into a chamber that was immediately recognizable as the one in which René de Kervoz's wound had been tended on the day after his visit to the isolated house on the Chemin de la Muette. Everything was in the same state, save for the four-poster bed, whose curtains were closed, and the lamplight which had replaced the daylight.

The conservatory, whose door was open, exhaled the scents of tropical flowers, mingled with the smoke of the corn-cob pipe which Taïeh was smoking. He was at his post beneath the huge yucca plant–not lazily stretched out, as he had been on the former occasion, but occupied in knotting the four corners of a sheet of ticking that was wound around a sinister form. Outside, the nocturnal wind stirred the naked branches in the garden. Andrea Ceracchi, the white-haired young man whose complexion was as pale as a corpse, was sitting in the same armchair in which we saw him previously; since then he had become even thinner, and more like a phantom. He was propping up his head with both hands. The Negro was humming a creole song while he worked.

"Victory!" cried the Countess, as she crossed the threshold. "Cadoudal is with us, and in a few hours our brothers will be avenged!"

Taïeh pulled out a curtain which masked the interior of the conservatory. The sound of the pot grating as it slid across the pavement could be heard, and then the noise of the trap-door opening.

Andrea Ceracchi had lifted his head. All that remained of his vitality was in the fervor of his eyes. The Countess clasped his hand and said: "I have followed your advice, Andrea. Delivering Cadoudal would win us several days of safety–but what does that matter, if we only need a few hours? Cadoudal is worth more than that. Instead of selling him, we shall use him. Tomorrow. Caesar will be in the company of the gods, with his throat cut."

"I want to strike him down!" said Ceracchi, in a somber voice. "I promised my brother that I would strike him down."

On the other side of the curtain, the trap-door closed heavily.

"The third has gone to join the other two!" the Negro called out–and he pulled back the curtain in order to come out, saying: "Me too! I want to strike him down. I have promised my master that I would strike him down."

"All those among you who wish to strike will strike!" said the Countess. "There is room for a thousand poniards in this glorious enterprise. I hate the man even more than you, because I admire him and because I have knelt before him lovingly; I hate him as much as I abhor God himself! I too want to strike him down! I have made no promise to anyone, but I have sworn it to myself!"

The doctor and the Negro lowered their eyes before her crushing stare.

"When you are here, Addhema," Ceracchi murmured, "doubt vanishes and one is tempted to believe in you. The blood that has been spilled is a weight upon my conscience, but if my brother is avenged, joy will cure remorse... what must be done?"

"What must be done?" echoed the Negro, handing the Countess a portfolio and three jewel-cases.

"The last drop of innocent blood has been shed," she replied, "and you have kept your hands clean, Andrea Ceracchi. It's taking a share that determines complicity. You remain poor in the midst of your enriched brothers. The supreme hour is upon us. Go to our meeting-place once more. The lamp of our council will be lit for one last time in the isolated house, to which history may yet give a name. All the Brothers of Virtue will be present; they are being summoned this very day. You must take the chair, because I shall not arrive until the time comes to act, with Georges Cadoudal himself..."

"Will you do that?" exclaimed Ceracchi. "Will you bring the bull of Morbihan?"

"I pledge my faith that I will bring him before three o'clock in the morning sounds. While waiting for the signal that will announce our arrival, this is what you have to do. It is as well that our family secrets are not confided to Georges Cadoudal.

"You have to say to our brothers that I have taken, this very day, drafts for a million ducats to Jacob Schwartzchild and Company in Vienna. If the familiar spirit that watches over this Bonaparte protects him from our blows, the rendezvous will be in Vienna; the association will have lost nothing but time and blood; it will be rich and it will be able to start again. If, on the other hand, we are successful, those among us who love Liberty will have enough profit from their victory to raise to their idol a throne so high and vast that no tyrant will ever be able to scale the same height. They must be prepared; they must have faith: tomorrow's sun will not set without having seen events which will change the face of the world."

She gave one hand to Ceracchi, the other to Taïeh. The black man pressed his lips upon the hand he held, while Andrea Ceracchi said: "Where is Lila?"

"Lila," the Countess replied, "no longer has parents; she is under my protection. My first duty is to ensure that she is safely sheltered when the hour of danger arrives."

Andrea, in his turn, kissed the hand that he held. "Till to-night, then," he said, "at three o'clock." And he went out, accompanied by Taïeh, bound for the appointed meeting-place.

"Three o'clock," the Countess repeated. "You shall wait no longer than that!"

She opened the jewel-cases one by one, and then the portfolio, to verify their contents. Then she moved toward the door, without a sideways glance at the conservatory.

Scarcely had she vanished from sight when the two frames of the window were cautiously pushed back, and the slim figure of the medical student Germain Patou appeared astride the balcony.

"A bone-breaking job!" he growled. "I must be very fond of Papa Jean-Pierre. Look how she lives, this adorable blonde! But knowing that doesn't get me much further forward."

He leapt down from the balcony and took a few steps into the room.

"Someone's been smoking here," he mused. "She's got a nice place, damn it. A regal bed, like the ones at Meudon [85]... let's take a peek."

He parted the curtains, then leapt back as if he had been struck in the face. The bed was disordered and the curtains were dripping blood.

"Thank God!" he thought. "It's not my blonde's blood, I can be sure of that... but it's quite fresh... someone's been killed here!"

His piercing gaze, glimmering with bold intelligence, made a tour of the room and plunged into the depths of the conservatory. For an instant, one might have thought that a kind of divination had enabled him to unravel the mystery of that place... but a clock chimed in the next room and he bounded to the window, climbing on to the balcony again.

"The boss is waiting for me," he said. "I've accomplished what I was told to do. I know where Countess Marcian Gregoryi lives... and perhaps I've divined the denouement of that comedy whose first scene was played out at the Church of Saint-Louis-en-l'Ile."

He lowered himself down as he had pulled himself up, by the strength of his slender but wiry arms. At the moment when his head reached the level of the balcony-rail, his last glance into the room encountered, above the bed, the enameled plaque which fixed the pleats of the curtains. There was a coat-of-arms on it, on which all the radiance of the lamp seemed to be focused–and there was a motto engraved in black Gothic letters on a field of gold, which read:

In vita mors, in morte vita...

Countess Marcian Gregoryi was nonchalantly stretched out on the cushions of her carriage when the coachman–following orders given in advance–brought his horses to a halt at the corner of the Pont-Marie and the Quai d'Anjou.

The Countess got out, saying: "Wait!" She set off along the Quai towards the eastern part of the Ile. The wall enclosing the Bretonvilliers gardens formed the far point of the spur. It was a bulge as solid and thick as a rampart. Not far from the corner of the Rue Saint-Louis, which faced Lambert House, the half-ruined steps of an ancient building stuck out a little further than the wall. There was a subterranean postern gate in the wall–which still existed a few years ago, its deep recess serving to shelter the little establishment of a foreign tinker. Countess Marcian Gregoryi had the key to this postern, which she opened in order to enter a damp and very dark space. When she had shut the door behind her, the darkness was absolute.

The properties of phosphorus have been known to adepts since the time of Cagliostro [86], and perhaps even a hundred years before him. Fearing an accusation of anachronism, we do not venture to say that Countess Marcian Gregoryi had a box of matches in her pocket, but a light scraping sound within the obscurity gave instantaneous birth to a vivid gleam. The candle of a muffled lantern was lit, illuminating the salt-peter-encrusted walls of a long corridor. The Countess immediately began walking along it.

When she had gone fifty paces or so, her face met a sudden gust of fresh air. There was a rather large crack in the left-hand wall, though which air and a ray of moonlight passed from outside. The Countess paused, tilting her ear attentively. She covered up the lantern by pressing its face against her breast and rapidly glanced outside. She was looking into a dark, overgrown, badly-maintained garden. "Was that the sound of footsteps?" she murmured. "Or voices...?"

She regretted the absence of Pluto, the giant dog, who normally roamed freely among those black shadows. No matter how hard she stared, though, she could not see anything but tangled branches swaying in the wind.

She continued on her way. "Even Ezekiel must have betrayed me..." she mused. "Then again, what does it matter? He will not have time..."

The corridor ended in a subterranean flight of steps, which the Countess climbed. At the top of the stairway, there was a narrow landing, on to which a cleverly-concealed door opened. The Countess opened it, still keeping the lantern hidden within her clothing, then closed it again and listened hard. Her ear caught the faint noise of even respiration.

"He's asleep," she murmured. Then she uncovered her heavy lantern, by whose light we could have recognized that room where René de Kervoz and Lila ate supper on the evening of the day on which our story began: the room without windows.

It is worth mentioning that many tales were told in the quarter about the old d'Aubremesnil House and its even older outbuildings: Bretonvilliers Lodge and the house on the riverbank. Paris had many such legendary corners in those days. One such tale told of a marvelous hidey-hole that President d'Aubremesnil–a friend of Abbé Gondi and companion of Monsieur de Beaufort, the king of the market place–had caused to be constructed in his home in the days when Cardinal de Mazarin returned victorious to his favorite city [87]. It was hastily added that President d'Aubremesnil never employed this hidey-hole against the queen mother or her favorite minister, but that he put it to much more amusing uses. Along that narrow corridor which led to the Seine came pretty bourgeois girls and lively working girls, to defraud Madame la Présidente of her legitimate entitlements...

Countess Marcian Gregoryi went straight to the table, where several dishes of food were placed. They had hardly been touched. Beside the dishes were a flask of wine and a carafe; only the carafe had been opened. The Countess removed the stopper, sniffed the contents and smiled. She went to the bed then and turned the face of her lantern towards the pale and handsome head that was on the pillow.

We do not know exactly what witchcraft of Yanusza's was signified by the words the wine of dreams, but it was certain that René de Kervoz was asleep, for he was smiling.

Countess Marcian Gregoryi's large eyes were brimming with compassion and tenderness. "You shall be free tomorrow," she murmured. She planted a kiss on his forehead.

René de Kervoz stirred in his sleep and pronounced the name of Angela.

The charming blonde frowned, but only momentarily.

"I love none but the great Count Szandor," she said, lifting her head proudly. "What does the caprice of a few hours matter? This is not my destiny." She extinguished her lantern and the room was plunged into total darkness again.

A voice was raised in that darkness, saying: "René, it's Lila..."

René did not wake up.

And the voice changed, this time speaking in a tone softer than a song: "René, my René, it's Angela... only run your hands through my hair, and you will recognize me."

René's lips rendered up a murmur that was cut short by a kiss.

Outside, the city was silent. From further within, strangely enough, something was audible: something like the confused echoes of footsteps and whispering voices.

An hour passed; then Countess Marcian Gregoryi leapt suddenly to her feet. Footsteps had sounded in the next room. She cocked her ear avidly, but nothing more could be heard. Had it been an illusion?

The beautiful blonde went silently to the hidden door and left as she had entered. It was not until she was in the corridor that she relit her muffled lantern. The candlelight illuminated an object that she held in her hand: a black ribbon, bearing a silver medal of Sainte-Anne d'Auray [88].

Countess Marcian Gregoryi went back to her carriage, which was still waiting at the other end of the Quai d'Anjou, near to the Pont-Marie. It was nearly two o'clock in the morning. "The Brothers of Virtue are judged!" she said. Then, addressing her coachman, she added: "The Rue Saint-Hyacinthe-Saint-Michel, at full speed!"

Her last thought, as she stretched herself out on her silky cushions, was: "The wolf of Brittany has done me no harm, but I need him to get my passports... Tomorrow, I shall sleep in my own bed."

In the Rue Saint-Hyacinthe-Saint-Michel, the carriage stopped in front of a little closed alley. The Countess knocked on the door. There was no response. She told the coachman to get down and ordered him to knock with the handle of his whip, which he did.

After a ten minute wait, a widow opened on the mezzanine floor, immediately above the door to the alley.

"What do you want, good people?" asked the reedy voice of a fat woman, who seemed to be in her night-dress.

"I want to see Citizen Morinière, the horse-dealer," the Countess replied.

"Oh," said the reedy voice, "it's a woman... Madame, nobody buys horses at this hour."

"Then Citizen Morinière is here?"

"Listen... the dear man stays here when he comes to Paris, but at present he's looking at some Percherons in the Loire valley, the other side of Chartres... come back in a week, at a decent hour."

The window was closed again.

"Knock again!" the Countess ordered her coachman.

The coachman showered the door with such loud blows that after three minutes the mezzanine window was opened again.

"By all the devils in Hell!" said the fat woman's voice, which was not so reedy now. "Will you let us sleep or not, my good people?"

"I want to see Citizen Morinière," the Countess replied.

"Since he's not here..."

"I believe that he is."

"So I'm a liar, by God...!"

"Yes, you're a liar, Monsieur Morinière..."

The fat woman withdrew, and there was the click of a pistol being cocked. "Woman," grated a voice that was no longer in the least reedy. "Tell me your name and what you want..."

"I want to talk about a matter of life and death," the Countess replied. "I am Angela Lenoir, daughter of Madame Sévérin of the Châtelet and *fiancée* of your nephew René de Kervoz..."

A muffled exclamation interrupted her, but she went on: "I am here on behalf of your nephew, who is in prison because of you, and I have brought as a token the medal of Sainte-Anne d'Auray which his mother, your sister, put around his neck on the day he left Brittany."

The mezzanine window closed for a second time, but almost immediately afterwards the door of the alley opened. "Come in!" someone said.

The Countess obeyed without hesitation.

In the sudden darkness which fell after the door had closed, the voice, tremulous with anger, resumed: "You're playing a crooked game, lady. I know my nephew's fiancée. You're not Angela Sévérin."

"I am Constanza Ceracchi, the sister-in-law of the sculptor Giuseppe, who died on the scaffold," the countess replied, boldly.

"Ah! An audacious rogue!" said the voice. "Although the dagger is a coward's weapon... I've nothing but my sword, by God! But how do you know my nephew?"

"Let's go upstairs," said the Countess.

Her hand was taken and she was led up a staircase as narrow as a ladder, at the top of which was a room lit by a nightlight. She went in. Her companion, who was the fat woman who had appeared at the window, but whose chin had the dark shadow of a beard when seen at close range, repeated: "How do you know my nephew?"

240

The Countess took the Saint-Anne d'Auray medal from her bosom and gave it to the bearded woman, saying: "Monsieur Cadoudal, your nephew is in love with me."

"My God!" exclaimed Georges—for it was he, in person—"Is my disguise no better than that? The lad has reason, for you're as pretty as a heart, my busybody... and I've already heard tell that he has had his escapades... but did you mention prison?"

"Monsieur Cadoudal," repeated the fake sister-in-law of Giuseppe Ceracchi, "I am in love with your nephew."

"It seems that it's scarcely worth the bother!"

"I have come because René de Kervoz is in deadly danger... the one he has betrayed has taken revenge on him..."

"Angela!" murmured Georges, going pale. "But then, I too... for Angela knows what her father and mother do not."

"Let's sit down and discuss the matter, Monsieur Cadoudal," Countess Marcian Gregoryi interrupted him, gravely. "I don't have all night to talk to you about that which you could hope for in future, and that which you ought to dread... There is a bond between you and the sister of Ceracchi: it is hatred... When day breaks, you will know whether you ought to strike or run away..."

"Run away!" cried Cadoudal. "Never!"

"Then, you will strike?"

"In God's name, lady," Cadoudal replied, laughing and sitting down next to her, "you said it! Just give me the means of getting to the Corsican in the midst of the consular guard, and I swear to you by Sainte-Anne d'Auray that he'll never be Emperor!"

Chapter XX
The Empty House

It was a clear, cold night. The street-lamps on the Ile Saint-Louis were not in use, allowing the moon to do their work for them. All manner of chimeras were abroad in Paris, even the most absurd. The spot where we once saw so many fishers for diamonds sounding the blanched current of the Seine was deserted now. The fame of the Quai de Béthune had been short-lived; no more signet rings had been caught beneath the sewer of Bretonvilliers and its prestige was now defunct. The men with rods and nets had begun to jeer at the miracle; as eleven o'clock approached, poor Ezekiel's inn–closed and extinct–offered mute testimony to the contempt which falls upon all abandoned Eldorados. The river's turbulent flow was at the full height of its banks.

Some minutes before eleven, rapid footsteps sounded in the Rue de Bretonvilliers–but did not wake the neighboring households, which were sound asleep. Jean-Pierre Sévérin, called Gâteloup, was going to war at the head of his squad of policemen. We know that the guardian of the Châtelet Morgue had a well-established reputation throughout that quarter of old Paris where chicanery and the police crossed swords. He was a man with a head on his shoulders, as the citizens of the Marché-Neuf would have put it.

There is always an element of adventurous vocation in the police agent, so it is said–and for my own part, I am often astounded when I read about the prodigious acts of implacable courage coolly accomplished on a day-by-day basis by such men, whose service is not rendered under the spur of fame. On a battlefield, there is the intoxication of the point of honor, the call of the drum, the deafening roar of the cannon, the fever of gunpowder–but in the gutters, by night, there are terrible struggles of which no newspaper sings loudly: struggles during which, most of the time, the armed bandit seeks to kill, and in which the man of law must hit back in self-defense. What can they do, these muddy heroes, as robust as any in Homer, to ensure that their accumulated prowess might one day redeem the opprobrium commonly attached to the way they earn their crust?

There were four such agents, accompanied by a peace officer–a young man, rather well-dressed, who had a cigar in his mouth and his hands in his pockets. They were all delighted to be following Gâteloup, on the scent of some curious affray. The peace officer, in keeping with the seriousness of his rank, listened to all the anecdotes recounted in a low voice by Laurent and Charlevoy in praise of the vigorous sword of Monsieur Séverin. The third agent applauded generously but the fourth, an ugly fellow whose face was masked by a voluminous black beard, and who was marching a little behind the others, grumbled: "I've seen him do better than that! He hits hard, there's no doubt about it."

When Jean-Pierre stopped at the corner of the Rue de Bretonvilliers and the Quai, the fourth agent laughed behind his beard and said: "What a farce! Is this where we've been headed? Perhaps he's after more bad wine."

Jean-Pierre knocked loudly on the door of *The Miraculous Catch*. There was no response from inside.

"Boys," said Jean-Pierre, "we'll have to break down the door."

"Before you do that," the peace officer observed, "I'll have to run through the formalities."

"No need for that, Monsieur Barbaroux," said a voice from the rear which made Jean-Pierre prick up his ears. "That farce is played out. The proprietor has moved on."

"Is that you, Ezekiel?" Jean-Pierre demanded.

"At your service, Monsieur Gâteloup," replied the fourth agent, who came forward with his cap in hand, "if there's anything I can do for you. I put this little bit of beard on my

243

chin so that no notoriety attaches to me when I come back to fish in the neighborhood. I have my everyday face for everyday business, and my professional physiognomy for work: does that hurt anyone?" While he was speaking, he put a key into the lock and turned it. The door opened immediately.

There was nothing to be seen in the cave-like space that had formerly served as an inn but four blank walls.

"Oh, it's all in order, Monsieur Gâteloup," said Ezekiel, in response to Jean-Pierre's astonished expression, as he picked up a tallow candle and lit it. "I've made my report–and besides, *The Miraculous Catch* has served as a trap. The times are hard and one lives as one can."

"It wasn't the Prefecture that provided your living," Jean-Pierre said, with a frown, "any more that it was your trade as an innkeeper. Don't play games with me, or you'll be in trouble. You were paid by Countess Marcian Gregoryi!"

"Damn you!" groaned Ezekiel. "So you already know that, Monsieur Gâteloup? Well, what if it's true? I have to put a little money by for my old age... you know very well that one can't see anything clearly in these affairs, at first... and it took a long time for me to figure out why the Countess had put the machinery in place on the Quai de Béthune."

"And is that reason in your report?"

"Certainly–but the inspector didn't wish to believe me. I'm sorry that I no longer have a bottle of wine to offer you, boys–although it wasn't up to much, was it, Monsieur Gâteloup? One must cater to all tastes... When I told them down at the Prefecture that bodies were being carried from Bretonvilliers Lodge, near here, to a vault somewhere in the Marais, out towards the Chaussée des Minimes, all I got was sniggers. I don't know why."

The peace officer threw his cigar away. Ezekiel went on: "As there was talk of the vault, and the vampire too, throughout Paris–it was common knowledge that something was wrong–the Countess said: 'A false trail must be set for the dogs.' "

"What was the inspector's name?" the peace officer demanded, impetuously. He had visions of a coup that would make him commissioner.

"Despaux, damn it!" said Ezekiel. "He'll be Secretary General when Monsieur Fouché has got rid of Monsieur Dubois."

"What's the number of the suspect house?" the peace officer asked.

"As far as that's concerned, Monsieur Barbaroux, the most beautiful girl in the world couldn't say that she'd found that out..."

"We'll know it soon enough," Jean-Pierre put in, having listened to the discussion impatiently. "We're here for another reason... can you get us into Bretonvilliers Lodge?"

"I can get you as far as the door," Ezekiel replied, "and these chaps must have a way to get past the locks."

Agent Charlevoy patted his pocket, bringing forth a jingling sound, and said: "I have my tool-kit."

"But as for finding the magpie in the nest," Ezekiel went on, "that's another thing entirely. The Countess hasn't been back since the evening when the lads brought that pretty little blonde in here...do you know, Monsieur Guardian, that I've been told that a young man went into the Lodge that evening?"

"Who said so?"

"That mare of Satan, Madame Paraxin."

"And was he brought out like the others?"

"I didn't hear any mention of it."

Jean-Pierre's expression brightened. "There's still a glimmer of hope," he murmured. "Let's go!" And he marched off towards the sunken door at the back of the inn. Ezekiel let him lead the way.

As soon as the door was open, Jean-Pierre found himself facing a pile of earth and rubble, which seemed to seal the passage hermetically.

"You were the cause of this," Ezekiel said. "On the day when you pulled away the goods that were stacked in front of the door, the Countess had spies here. The following day, the passage was blocked...but they counted without old Ezekiel, who has learned all sorts of things since his school-days. Stand aside, please, and let me pass."

Still clutching his burning candle, the ancient innkeeper slid into a narrow gap which remained on the left-hand side, and led to the stairway in his cellar. Jean-Pierre and the agents followed him. The cellar was as empty as the hovel above, but at its eastern extremity there was a heap of debris surrounding a recently-made opening. Ezekiel shone the light upon it; it was wide enough to accommodate a man of moderate girth. "The night when I made this hole," he said, reddening with anger, "the old witch set her dog on me. If that four-footed devil had been able get through, I'd be a dead man. I carried a tooth away with me, not from the dog but from the woman– and did you know, Monsieur Gâteloup, learned man as you are, that one can only put an end to such creatures by plunging something hot into their hearts?"

Charlevoy and Laurent went very pale. "So, is there really a vampire?" they murmured, in unison.

"Let's get on with it!" ordered Jean-Pierre. He was the first to push forward into the opening–but Ezekiel caught his arm and stopped him.

"Monsieur Gâteloup," Ezekiel said, "you're a brave man, and I've seen you take on ten with a wooden stick. I'm on your side, and I don't want you to come to any harm. It's only fair that you go first, since you're the most enthusiastic to go, but before putting your head through that hole, be on your guard. Look and listen. If the dog's there, it'll bark, and if it barks, watch yourself–it's the kind of beast that can chew up a man as if he were a chicken."

Séverin disengaged his arm, muttering his thanks and squeezed through the hole without too much difficulty. There was a moment's pause, which was terribly tense. Ezekiel had sweat on his brow.

"It's all clear," said Gâteloup, from the other side. "Are you coming?"

"The dog's gone for good, apparently," said Ezekiel. "It would have kicked up a row already if it were there. Let's go!" He went through before the others, not without a certain residual anxiety. The other three agents and the peace officer followed.

Beyond the hole there was a sort of pit, which communicated with the gardens by a stairway made of earth and wood. The gardens were completely deserted. The little troop moved on right away, going through the grounds in both senses of the word. Charlevoy and Laurent were two first-rate bloodhounds, and the industrious Ezekiel knew what was what.

Eventually, they came to the high wall that bordered the two Quais, closing the spur of the Ile Saint Louis like a rampart. The night was bright. Although this part of the garden resembled a virgin forest, Laurent and Charlevoy, after searching through it, declared that no human creature could have remained hidden there. The door on the river bank, by which Countess Marcian Gregoryi would enter an hour later, did not escape their notice, but having seen the state of the lock, they believed it to be sealed shut.

Jean-Pierre managed to get through the breach in the wall into the corridor that connected the riverside door to the windowless room. He went along its length, taking it for one of those secret passages constructed in troubled times which astonish the curious and remain enigmatic to the keenest researchers. The corridor branched at one point; the narrower passage led to President d'Aubremesnil's ancient hidey-hole while a broader one descended directly to the kitchens of Bretonvilliers Lodge. Jean-Pierre only noticed the latter passage. He called Charlevoy, and set him to work opening a door, solidly clad in iron, that would have delighted an antiquary.

The kitchens were as empty as the gardens. There were, however, signs of the recent presence of one or more occupants, for the floor was littered here and there with vegetable peelings and partly-gnawed beef-bones. On the table there was a woman's cap made of thick fabric and decorated with tarnished tinsel; its Hungarian origin was evident at first glance.

"This is Mother Paraxin's lair," Ezekiel said, "and here are the remains of Pluto's last supper. I've a suspicion that the horrible beast eats the bones of Christians more often than the bones of cattle."

"Did the people who were carried here pass through the corridor that we used?" asked Gâteloup.

"Never," Ezekiel replied.

"Then they must have passed through your shop!" Charlevoy exclaimed. Ezekiel reddened, and looked at him in annoyance.

A large stone staircase, which long neglect had left in a badly-worn state, led from the kitchens to the ground floor. When the ground-floor doors had been opened with the aid of Charlevoy's "tool-kit," they passed into a series of bare rooms, damp and decrepit, which had obviously not been occupied for many years. There were a few faded portraits and ragged tapestries on the walls.

The peace officer, Monsieur Barbaroux, was a utilitarian. He remarked, reasonably enough, that there was a lost opportunity here, in that a great many people presently sleeping in the streets could have been accommodated in these rooms.

"Let's go upstairs," said Jean-Pierre. "There's nothing for us here."

The first floor, which was much better preserved, presented signs of recent occupation. It was to a room on this floor that René de Kervoz had been introduced on the evening when our story began. Charlevoy's tool-kit having worked its magic again, Jean-Pierre went into the room where René had waited dreamily for the arrival of his mistress, using the cool windows to refresh his fevered brow.

Facing the window, on the other side of the Rue Saint-Louis-en-l'Ile, was the boundary-marker where Angela had sat down to endure the cruel torture which would bring about her death. It was there that she had recognized, or divined, the silhouette of her fiancé by the last rays of moonlight. It was there, when the lamp lit within had projected two shadows on the curtain, that she had seen those two heads coming together, in a kiss that had stabbed her in the heart. It was there that she had despaired of God's goodness.

There were no curtains at the window now, nor any screens at the doors, nor a carpet on the floor. There was no furniture at all; everything had been removed. The decrepitude of the old house showed through everywhere–or almost everywhere. A withered bouquet, a scrap of female attire and a book remained as witnesses to the passage of the migrants who had briefly animated the solitude.

In the second room, which we once saw decorated in an Oriental style, where Lila elected to relate her story–true or fabulous–to the young Breton, the abundant heaps of cushions and Bohemian lamps had vanished like everything else. This second room seemed to extend as far as the house itself; the wall opposite the door offered no evident opportunity to go further. It was, however, that wall that had opened forty-eight hours earlier to display to René's dazzled eyes a charming retreat, at the back of which was the silk-draped bed-alcove: the boudoir where supper had been served; the room without windows; in a word, the love-nest that had transformed itself into a prison.

It would be an insult to the intelligence of the reader to explain why a room constructed and installed for the specific purpose of serving as a hidey-hole, at the time when the art of accommodating hidey-holes was at its apogee, showed no exterior trace of its existence.

Jean-Pierre Sévérin and his squad remained on the first floor for nearly an hour, ferreting and rummaging around–but their search was fruitless. There was nowhere left to go but the second floor, which they found in a state of desolation even worse than the ground floor. The ceilings were coming down and the partition-walls were in ruins.

"Let's go down to the cellars," said Jean-Pierre. "I'll tear the house apart if I have to, but I'll find my daughter's fiancé, alive or dead."

The policemen were there to follow his orders. Barbaroux, the peace officer, restricted himself to muttering: "Madame Barbaroux is waiting for me, all alone."

When they heard that, Laurent and Charlevoy exchanged an incredulous smile. "Waiting, is she?" Charlevoy said. "All alone?" Laurent added. Alas, it is said that nothing is hidden from the hundred eyes of Argus, son of Avestor–the patron saint of police forces–except the petty mysteries of his own household.

As Jean-Pierre and his squad, coming down the stairway, passed the open door on the first floor, a sudden noise coming from the interior of the apartment brought them to an abrupt halt. Jean-Pierre immediately threw himself forward, followed by his agents. They arrived in the room with two windows just in time to see a hand pass through a broken window-pane and turn the catch dexterously.

Germain Patou jumped into the room, shaking his sweat-soaked head.

(While not seeking to excuse this habit he had for climbing over balconies in this manner, we might offer several extenuating circumstances in his defense. In the first place, the walls of Bretonvilliers Lodge were constructed in a monumental style which, in leaving a considerable gap between the stones, made the use of ladders superfluous. In the second place, he was impelled by good intentions–and in the third place, he was not yet a fully-fledged doctor. If he had passed his final examination at this point, we would of course regard his conduct as inexcusable.)

"Evening, boss," he said. "It only took me four minutes thirty seconds, watch in hand, to get here from the Chaussée des Minimes, but I lost more than a quarter of an hour prowling around the house. Then, as the door was shut, I came in by the window. The pane was broken, and I wanted to know what all these little bits of paper here on the balcony had to tell me. There's a pebble in every one of them... bring the light."

"What have you found out?" asked Jean-Pierre Séverin.

"I've found her lair," Patou replied, unfolding one of the pieces of paper that he had mentioned, "but the she-wolf has fled."

"The she-wolf?" Jean-Pierre repeated.

Patou took his hand and squeezed it firmly. "Boss," the medical student whispered in his ear, "there's blood inside. There'll be a newcomer in the Marché-Neuf Morgue tomorrow; I suspect that your new showroom might be too small. Franz König was murdered this evening."

Jean-Pierre put his hand to his pale forehead, his fingers clenched. "And my daughter?" he said, shivering. "And my poor René?"

Charlevoy came up to them with the light. Gâteloup's gaze fell upon the paper that Patou was holding in his hand. "That's Angela's writing!" he cried, snatching the letter.

"There's no shortage of it," the medical student said. "I found at least half a dozen of them outside the shutter...Hold on! Here's one that got into the room. That's what broke the window!" He picked up a piece of paper, wrapped around a pebble like all the rest, that had fallen on the floor. "Oh!" he said, lowering his voice in spite of himself. "This one is speckled with blood."

Jean-Pierre took the lighted candle from Ezekiel's hand. "Get out, all of you!" he said, in a low voice. "But don't go far–I'll have need of you soon enough."

Chapter XXI
Poor Angela!

Jean-Pierre Sévérin, called Gâteloup, and Germain Patou were alone together. They were no longer in the drawing-room but in the room which contained the hidey-hole. Jean-Pierre wanted to put one more door between them and the curiosity of the agents.

They were seated one beside the other, on the step or window-box which is customarily placed in front of the window in all old houses. This was the only seat that now remained in the room. Each of them had in his hand one of those pieces of paper that had contained pebbles. The candle was on the floor and they had to lean over it in order to read. The Morgue-keeper's white hair, tumbling forward, inundated his face. His breath could be heard rattling in his throat. Tears were running down on to the piece of paper he held in his trembling hand.

"Poor Angela!" murmured Germain Patou, whose voice was also tearful.

"Poor Angela!" Gâteloup echoed, in a deep voice. "She had no thought for her mother!"

"She had no thought for you, boss," added the medical student. "You loved her as much as her mother did."

"Do you think she's dead, Germain?" asked Gâteloup.

Instead of replying, Patou read:

" 'René, my dear René, you promised to love me forever. I did not doubt it, for there is no one on Earth as noble or as loyal as you. And then, we had our little Angela. How could anyone abandon a cherub in her crib?

" 'I have had a dream, René; listen to me, I want to tell you everything; I'm sure that it is a dream.

" 'You are in this house, that I know; I saw you go in and you have not come out again–but perhaps you are being kept prisoner.

" 'Oh, she's beautiful, it's true! I have never seen such beauty! But does she love you as I do?

" 'René, she is not the mother of our little angel.

" 'I shall throw this paper at the window of the room where I have seen you; you will read it if you return to that window to think and look out into the darkness.

" 'Poor beloved, you are suffering; I might add that your suffering is mine; I would want to make you happy even at the expense of my own unhappiness.

" 'I am here, on the boundary-marker that faces the window on the other side of the street. Look at it. I believe that you will see me. What ideas come into one's head when the soul lurches! My God! If you have seen me, perhaps we might both be saved!

" 'I was wrong not to call out to you, not to kneel down with my hands pressed together in the middle of the street. You are good; you would have had pity on me.

" 'I was there; I saw you. I have seen everything, and I love you as before, my René. Our little Angela was your gift to me. I love you...' "

Germain Patou stopped reading, and the paper slipped from his fingers. "The Breton devil!" he muttered. "If I get my hands on him, he'll have a nasty quarter of an hour."

"Shut up!" said Gâteloup, darkly. "Didn't she love him well enough?"

"She was an angel of the Good Lord!" said the student. "Oh, that Breton swine!"

Jean-Pierre was thoughtful. "That one must be the first letter," he said, his eyes fixed on the damp scrap which he was re-reading for the second time. "Perhaps this is the second:

" 'I have thrown the paper at the window; it has stayed there after falling back many times. You have not answered me, René, you have not read it! How long the hours are! My poor mother has no idea how desperate I am; I have said nothing to my father, who will perhaps avenge me.

" 'I have only spoken to our child. I tell her everything, because she is not yet able to understand me. At times, that much-loved little creature seems to divine my suffering; at others, her smile tells me to hope.

" 'My God! To hope!

" 'Well, yes! I still hope, while I am not dead. I have not read many books, but I know that there are distractions, sicknesses of the soul.

" 'You are distracted, you are sick, and this enchantress has not given a single moment's thought to your child.

" 'It was at Saint-Germain-l'Auxerrois, wasn't it? I saw nothing, but something disturbed my prayer. I felt something inside, like a dull ache. My heart was squeezed; the thought of our wedding no longer filled me with joy.

" 'She was there; I'm sure of it!

" 'Our wedding! The day I've looked forward to so much, and look what has happened! Oh, René, René, you once said to me: "It would be a crime to bring a single tear to the eyes of an angel."

" 'The angel is fallen. Was that your punishment?

" 'When I came back from the church, I had already lost track of you. I wondered what you were thinking. I wept as we went upstairs.

" 'The whole night went by, René. I was lost.

" 'Answer me, if only with a single word. What are you doing in that dark house? Do you want me to tell you what my last hope is? That you are, perhaps, involved in some conspiracy.

" 'Neither my father nor my mother will hear anything from me; it is your secret. I have heard talk of arrests today... if I have slandered you in my thoughts, René, my dear René, if you were only unhappy...!' "

Jean-Pierre broke off, then said: "What do you think of that?"

254

"Kervoz is a Breton," Patou said. He added: "Wasn't the fat horse-dealer at the Church of Saint-Louis-en-l'Ile his uncle?"

Jean-Pierre slapped his forehead. "Morinière!" he said. "And the Secretary General of the Prefecture told me..." He trailed off, as his thoughts went off on a new track. "Morinière seemed a good man," he murmured. "It's impossible..."

"Perhaps the third letter will tell us something," said the medical student. "The writing changes."

Jean-Pierre seized the piece of paper that was held out to him and kissed it. He read:

" 'Nothing from you, René! You have not received my messages. You would never have been so cruel to me...

" 'Our little girl is growing thinner and becoming very pale now that my own dried-up milk can no longer nourish her. I looked at her this morning. Perhaps God will take both of us together.

" 'What a night! Would a year be enough to say all that one thinks in the space of a single night?

" 'I have seen my father and mother for the last time. All day long I had been prowling around after you, and all the following night too. I saw you, I want you, I will talk to you...

" 'They were asleep! I have kissed the white hair of my adoptive father, who loves me as much as if I were his own daughter. I have pressed my lips to my mother's forehead. She too has suffered a great deal, but she has had the courage to live! I have also kissed my young brother–a good, kind child, who will weep for me. He already has the heart of a man. Father often says that he will not have a happy life. Then I went back to my daughter and I dressed her in white. I put the garland that you gave me on my birthday in her hair. Our daughter is very beautiful.

" 'I need to laugh and sing. I don't know if that's the way it is when one goes mad...' "

Gâteloup's arms slumped. His face expressed a torture so poignant that tears came into Patou's eyes.

255

"You must be strong, Jean-Pierre," he said. "We haven't finished."

"No," Gâteloup replied, his voice altered. "We haven't finished." Stifling a sob in his throat, he added; "They were to be married tomorrow. My poor daughter won't survive that long!"

His feverish hand unfolded another piece of paper.

" 'I wanted to see your room, which I know so well, although I was never allowed to go in. I had a childish hope; I thought that I might find you there. The porter let me in. I'm writing to you from your home: this will bring me luck.

" 'I'm on the spot where I saw you sitting, when I looked out of my window. It was here that your eyes spoke to mine for the first time. I have before me the portraits of your father and mother. How your mother must love you! And how much I love her! There is the beginning of a letter in which you mention me to her. Am I really so dear to you, René? Then why have you left me? What have I done? Am I not everything to you?

" 'There is also a bloody handkerchief here, with a coat-of-arms and a crown... I can't stay here; I must go to you, search for you... Besides, there is another place where I'm better able to speak to you than here, near the Pont-Marie, under the Quai des Ormes–there, where we sat down between the lawn and the flowers and listened to the wind murmuring in the foliage of the great trees.

" 'I'm not mad now; I'm hopeful again, since seeing the picture of the Virgin Mary above your bedside. You haven't forgotten me; you are being held prisoner somewhere; I shall rescue you.

" 'René, my René, my life! I've kissed your mother's portrait...' "

Gâteloup broke off again. "Is that the last?" he asked, faintly.

"No," said Patou. "There's the one that's written in blood."

"Read it," murmured the old man. "I have no strength left."

Germain Patou wiped his moist eyes, whose lids were hot.

" 'All day again, all the long day! Where are you? The people in the neighborhood know me, and are already calling me the madwoman. I threw two letters before dawn. Haven't you heard the pebbles rattling on the window-panes? I've looked. Nothing to be seen. I've called out. You haven't replied. Then the passers-by arrived with the sun, and I went prowling around the evil house.

" 'I've gone around it ten or a hundred times. I've knocked on the door where you went in. An old woman came, who spoke a foreign language. She chased me away, showing me the long teeth of an enormous dog with bloodshot eyes.

" 'I'm on the bank near the Pont-Marie. The trees are murmuring, as they did that other time. The Seine flows at my feet. How deep it must be! I'm writing to you with a little of my blood, on a blank page of my missal, which I brought so that I might pray.

" 'I can't pray.

" 'My thoughts are not very clear in my head. I'm suffering too much. There is, however, one thought in my head that is clear and which keeps coming back. I no longer try to chase it away. I won't kill myself all alone. I'll hold my little Angela in my arms, with her white dress and her crown. I'll take her with me. What would she do without her mother?

" 'This time, I'll throw my letter through the window. Perhaps you'll receive it. Then I'll come back here, to the bank.

" 'In the morning, if I haven't had a reply, I'll go to get my little Angela from her crib...' "

The medical student suddenly asked: "Is the little girl still at home?"

"Yes," said the guardian, bleakly. Then, as if talking to himself, in a voice brittle with anguish, he went on: "It was she! She didn't have the time to double her crime by sacrificing her child..." He broke off, but resumed with sudden vehemence: "Her crime! When an excess of misery has given rise to delirium, is it still a crime? I'm an old man, but I never encountered a soul as gentle or as pure... It was she! You don't understand me, boy, and I don't have the strength to make you understand... It was she! It was she that I saw in the very spot that she describes, distraught in the grip of the demon of suicide... Before my very eyes, do you hear, as I see you now... and the rest is so far beyond the bounds of possibility that the words catch in my throat... A monster, a foul creature, has stolen her life for itself–her angelic life!–and the most shameless of all prodigals... the vampire!"

Patou's eyes shone. "I read the most astonishing of all books last night," he said, in a low voice. "*The Legend of the Ghoul Addhema and the Vampire of Szandor*, printed in Baden in 1736, by Professor Hans Spurzheim, doctor of the University of Pressburg [89].

"The oupire Addhema took the life of her victims at a discount, so to speak, living one hour for each of their years, while ceaselessly roaming the world collecting treasures for the king of the living dead, Count Szandor. She loved him adoringly, under a curse, and he sold her his kisses for the price of a gold piece each."

"And how did she inoculate herself with the life of others?" Jean-Pierre demanded, despite the shame he felt to be investigating the mysteries of Oriental dementia.

"By applying the hair of murdered girls to her bald head," Patou replied.

The Morgue-keeper let out a dull cry, and leaned back against the window to stop himself falling. "I have seen the vampire Addhema face-to-face," he stammered. "I have seen the hair of my own daughter, my poor Angela, on the skull of Countess Marcian Gregoryi!"

The student moved back, stupefied. He looked Gâteloup in the eyes, fearful of the eruption of a sudden madness.

Gâteloup's eyes were staring into infinity. Perhaps he saw that inert corpse moving upriver along the banks of the

Seine, against all the laws of nature: the corpse that had reached out its arms to seize the indecisive young girl leaning over the water near the Pont-Marie.

The demon of suicide!

In the silence that followed, a noise could be heard coming from the seemingly-solid wall that formed the eastern part of the room. It was like a door grating on its hinges. Jean-Pierre and Patou pricked up their ears avidly. The door grated a second time, and then was closed again with evident care.

"There's something there!" exclaimed Germain Patou.

Jean-Pierre put his hand over his companion's mouth. He listened for another minute; then, when the noise was not re-newed, he said: "René de Kervoz is on the other side of this wall. I'm sure of it! We must get through it."

Chapter XXII
Similia Similibus Curantor

In the story which began this series, *La Chambre des Amours*, we met Jean-Pierre Sévérin, called Gâteloup, when he was very young. Although he was already tormented by somber dreams, he was a wise man, and strong. Even in the exceedingly humble sphere in which fate had placed him, he had been able to see at close range the struggle of modern philosophers against the beliefs of the past. In becoming involved in that struggle, he had done battle with his own self. A Christian, he found impiety repulsive; but, as a freethinker and comrade of the great men of ancient history, he remained loyal to the Republic at the very hour when the Republic was tottering. He was not a superstitious man–he had been born in Paris, the first city to have defeated superstition–but he was a traveler by night, a solitary man, and perhaps, without being aware of it himself, a poet. Nocturnal life educates the mind in strange thoughts.

When Jean-Pierre Sévérin was on watch, bent over his oars, listening to the eternal murmur of the river and seeking the mysterious enemy that he had fought for so many years– suicide–who could divine or follow the roads where his dreams became lost?

As soon as Jean-Pierre had said, "We must get through the wall," Germain Patou threw himself into the sitting-room, calling for the agents at the top of his voice. These men, well-used to never letting their time go to waste, were already asleep–except for Monsieur Barbaroux, who was smoking his pipe. Ezekiel, who thought he knew the house by heart, had announced formally that the expedition was finished.

Gâteloup, left alone in the other room, set about testing the wall, slapping it here and there with the palm of his hand. At first, the wall sounded solid, but Gâteloup arrived soon enough at a panel which sounded hollow, reverberating under his hand like a drum. That was the door, very cleverly concealed in the moldings of the woodwork. Gâteloup, in circumstances of this sort, had no need of lever or crow-bar. He stood sideways, took a step back, and rammed his shoulder into the panel, which splintered and burst asunder.

When reinforcements arrived, Gâteloup was already inside the windowless room. "Are you there, René de Kervoz?" he demanded. He listened hard, but the beating of his own heart seemed deafening, and got in the way. Even so, he thought he could hear the respiration of a sleeping man.

The light of the tallow candle, suddenly penetrating the hidey-hole, showed him that René was indeed stretched out on a bed, fast asleep, his hair wildly disordered.

"What!" said Ezekiel. "She hasn't killed him!" He examined the hidden compartment carefully. "A nice double wall," he added.

"Get up, Monsieur de Kervoz!" Gâteloup ordered, shaking the sleeper vigorously.

Laurent and Charlevoy started ferreting around. Monsieur Barbaroux said: "At least we can arrest this fellow!"

René, meanwhile, would not wake up no matter how rudely Gâteloup shook him.

German Patou uncorked the two vessels one at a time, sniffing their contents as he passed them back and forth beneath his flared nostrils. He had a keen sense of smell, sensitive to many kinds of chemicals. "Turkish opium," he said. "Belgrade hashish: the concentrated sap of *Papaver somniferum* [90]. Don't tire yourself out, boss–you'll kill him before you wake him up."

Everyone wanted to see then, and Monsieur Barbaroux himself put his large nose above the bottle-neck like a snuffer over a candle. "It's a mediocre white, sweetened with sugar," he declared. Charlevoy and Laurent would have liked to taste it.

"We have to wake him up," said Gâteloup. "He's the only one who can put us on the track of the vampire now."

"What!" said Monsieur Barbaroux. "You've found your lost boy. It's bedtime now." Charlevoy and Laurent, on the other hand, were very keen to see the thing through to the end. They were agents by vocation.

"Have you means to wake him up, boy?" Jean-Pierre asked Patou.

"Perhaps," the student replied. Then he added, drawing closer and lowering his voice: "Perhaps we don't need all these men any longer. When the young man wakes up, he'll want to talk, and he won't be fully conscious of his first words. It might be better, for you and for him, if there weren't so many indiscreet listeners around."

"Messieurs," Gâteloup said, immediately, "I am indebted to you. Monsieur Barbaroux is right: we've found what we were looking for, and I have no further need of you."

The peace officer had, however, reconsidered his opinion. It is never useless for an administration to have in its ranks a man as complete as Monsieur Berthellemot. The image of that superior employee passed before Barbaroux's eyes as he said: "That's easy for you to say, friend; haven't you got orders to give us? I've been ordered to follow you and to give you a hand. I have to submit my report to the Prefect, so I'm staying." He had not quite finished this prudent speech when the sound of knocker on the main door, handled with considerable expedition, broke the silence of the night.

It was an utterly unexpected interruption. At first, no one could figure out what it was. But a voice was raised soon enough in the street, which said: "Open up, in the name of the law!"

"Monsieur Berthellemot!" cried the policemen, in unison.

Monsieur Barbaroux was the first to respond, followed by the four agents, and the Secretary General made his solemn entrance a few moments later. He had a whole army behind him. In order to present himself, he had set up the well-known smile of Monsieur Talleyrand, to which he had added the stern expression of Monsieur de Sartines. "Ah, neighbor," he said, carefully sharpening the statement with fine irony, "nothing escapes me. We have had some trouble following your track, but we are not novices at that game. This is some business! A serious business! I can't go into detail prematurely with regard to its ramifications, but you can be assured that I've taken notes... I demand that you show me the pretended order of the First Consul, if you have not already destroyed it."

"Why would I destroy it?" Gâteloup asked, putting his hand into his pocket.

Monsieur Berthellemot favored the company with a look of self-satisfaction, and clicked some of his fingers. "One never knows, neighbor," he replied. "One never knows."

"I knew there was something shady about this from the start," Barbaroux murmured.

In the next room, the Secretary General's followers and Barbaroux's agents began to chatter animatedly. The falsity of the order signed by Bonaparte, of which Séverin had made use, was no longer a secret to anyone. Charlevoy said: "The chap has a funny way of doing things. If he has to be carried off, it must be done speedily, for he has supporters in the neighborhood and this will stir things up."

"Dig down," Ezekiel added, "and you will find that he has a heart–which proves that there are chouans and chouans!"

Meanwhile, Germain Patou was busy with René, who was still asleep.

Jean-Pierre gave the order to Monsieur Berthellemot, who had a torch brought and studied it minutely through his spectacles. When he had turned the paper over, in every sense, and examined the signature, he coughed. Even the cough of certain eminent men has a doctoral significance. "The Prefect sees no further than the end of his nose," he grumbled. "Myself, I see the situation at first glance. There is an affair of State here or the devil knows nothing at all. It's definitely the

First Consul who scribbled these fly-tracks. What would that rascal Fouché do in similar circumstances? It's a matter for God rather than the saints..." He broke off, then took Gâte-loup's hand and shook it vigorously before continuing on in a loud voice and a resolute tone: "The Prefect is my immediate superior, but above the Prefect there is the sovereign master of the destiny of France... I want to talk to the First Consul. You will bear witness when the need arises to my political senti-ments... what is your personal opinion regarding this Countess Marcian Gregoryi?"

Jean-Pierre hesitated before replying. "Monsieur Senior Civil Servant," he said, eventually, "take a good escort and go to number 7, Chaussée des Minimes. Search the house from top to bottom."

"Not forgetting the conservatory," added German Patou. "There's a trap-door in the conservatory under the third pot you'll come to, counting from the sitting-room–it contains a *Yucca gloriosa*."

"When you've done what needs to be done there, Mon-sieur Civil Servant," Jean-Pierre concluded, "you'll no longer be in doubt as to what Countess Marcian Gregoryi is."

"Follow me, men," cried Berthellemot, inflamed by sud-den zeal, "and remember that the First Consul has his eyes on you." To himself, he thought: "This is quite a trick to play on the Prefect."

The double squad departed at a rapid pace, but once they were in the street, Monsieur Berthellemot stopped and called out: "Monsieur Barbaroux!" The peace officer came up to him. Berthellemot took him aside. "For some time, Monsieur Barbaroux, I have entertained the gravest suspicions in regard to that woman–who was, alas, protected in high places. In particular, I have specific reports signed by Ezekiel, who was blindly following a trail of intelligence provided by me. I have all the notes. Without necessarily believing in vampires, Mon-sieur, I reject nothing that might be admitted by enlightened skepticism. Nature has profound secrets; we are only in the infancy of the world... I charge you to keep watch on Monsieur Sévérin, cleverly and without arousing his suspicion. He has connections... If events turn out as it is permissible to anticipate, we shall have changes at the Prefecture, Monsieur Barbaroux, and I shall not forget you when those changes transpire." The peace officer opened his mouth to offer a brief statement of his entitlement to a position in the commissary of police, but Berthellemot cut him off. "I shall be taking notes," he said. "Report to me regarding this Monsieur Sévérin. You would not believe me, Monsieur, if I assured you that all this intrigue is as clear as daylight to me." Then he left, accompanied by Ezekiel and his own escort.

Charlevoy and Laurent remained on observation duty in the Rue Saint-Louis, under the orders of Monsieur Barbaroux, who murmured: "You only see a little more clearly than the Prefect, who sees exactly as clearly as me, who cannot see anything at all!" This was addressed to the absent Monsieur Berthellemot. When have subalterns ever appreciated the merits of their superiors?

Meanwhile, in the windowless room, Jean-Pierre Sévérin and his protege Patou were leaning over the sleeping René de Kervoz.

"How changed he is" murmured Jean-Pierre, "and how he must have suffered!"

"The last forty-eight hours," the medical student replied, "have been a long dream to him, or a sort of intoxication. He has not suffered in the way you mean, boss."

"His forehead's flooded with sweat, and it's running down his sunken cheeks."

"The opium's made him feverish."

"Can't you wake him?"

Germain Patou hesitated. "The disciples of Samuel Hahnemann are so funny," he murmured, eventually. "One dares not say too much to reasonable people. It's good for burning brains like mine... *Similia similibus*... If I were alone, I'd take a chance on the formulas of the wizard of Leipzig."

"What are these formulas? Don't talk Latin."

"I'll speak French. There are a great many formulas, because the system of Samuel Hahnemann is as precise and mathematical as a musical scale–the most mathematical thing in the world–and it varies and harmonizes according to the vast spectrum of ills and medicaments. All the thousands of formulas are, however, unified in the formula *Similia similibus curantor*. Or rather, for the rule itself is expressed in a loose and inadequate fashion, this is cured by this–in place of the old dictum, this is cured by that.

"These are mere words," murmured Jean-Pierre Sévérin, "and time's passing."

"They're things, boss–great, noble things! Time's passing, it's true, but it won't be time lost for your young friend. Monsieur René de Kervoz is already under the influence of a Hahnemannian preparation. I have given him a treatment appropriate to his condition."

Jean-Pierre's eye searched the night-table for a phial or a glass which might confirm that medicine had been given. He saw nothing.

"You have dared...?" he began.

"There's no need for audacity here," Germain Patou put in. "You could take what he has taken at a thousand times, or a hundred thousand times the dose, without any impact on your constitution."

"A hundred thousand times!" Jean-Pierre repeated, indignantly. "What can the dose be...?"

"A million times!" Patou interrupted, in his turn. "That's the miracle, and the motive that will delay the popularization of the greatest medical system that has ever dazzled the scientific world. When the school of Sangrado [91] runs out of arguments with which to fight the new system, it cries: Lies! Mummery! Imposture! Hahnemann prescribes nothing but inert and neutral matter: sugar, milk and clear water. Indeed, in that which Hahnemann distributes, chemical analysts can discover nothing at all!"

"But then..."

"But then, do you know a chemist who has discovered by ordinary analysis the life-giving principle of good air, or the evil principle that infests the atmosphere in times of epidemic? If anyone tells you that he know what it is, reply stoutly: 'You're a liar!' Free air always renders the same elements to analysis... and yet there is an air that gives health, an air which produces sickness... I mean the air which is under the sky, for the miasma concentrated in a confined space can be chemically detected... You are therefore able to kill or cure by means of something infinitesimal, escaping instruments that easily detect, for example, the millionth part of a dose of arsenic, which would not be sufficient to give you a stomach-ache."

René de Kervoz shifted abruptly on his bed.

"He moved," said Jean-Pierre.

Patou took from his coat pocket a flat box, a little larger than a snuff-box, and opened it. "I've spent many a night making this up," he said, with an innocent pride. "I'll do better, but it's not bad for a first effort." Twenty little flasks, each one bearing a label, were arranged within the box. Patou chose one, continuing: "At present, our pharmacy is not very elaborate, but the master seeks and finds... if I ever find out for sure whether this man is a madman or an impostor, I'll be able to manufacture a disease!" Having uncorked one of his little flasks, he pulled out a granule which he put on the point of a needle, kept for that purpose in the silk which lined the box.

René de Kervoz had parted his lips to murmur a few indistinct words. Patou took advantage of an instant when the teeth of the sleeper drew apart to introduce the globule dexterously on to his tongue.

"What are you giving him?" Jean-Pierre asked.

"Opium," the student replied.

"Opium! You said a little while ago that this lethargy was produced by opium."

"Exactly!"

"Well?"

"Well, boss, it'll need time and trouble to accustom the world to that apparent contradiction. The system of the man from Leipzig has been subject to long and rigorous testing; reason is opposed to it and it is often mocked. How can one thing kill and cure? Soon I'll demonstrate to you the amazing effect of a dose that is invisible, imponderable... infinitesimal if you want the technical term. Is it necessary to prove to you now–to you who have experience of life–that the same thing can and must produce entirely contrary results, according to the mode and the quantity employed? In the moral order, the passions that are God's supreme gift and the source of all grandeur also engender all shame and all misery–pride degrades; ambition brings down; love manufactures hate—while, in the physical order, wine exalts or stupefies according to the dose."

"I know that," said Jean-Pierre, nodding his head.

"The good La Fontaine, in a fable that isn't for children, has a satyr reproach a man for blowing hot or cold, employing one and the same thing–his breath–to cool his soup and warm his fingers. It's a vulgar but striking image from nature. Everything down here blows hot and cold; the universe is homogeneous; there is not in the whole of creation, so full of contrasts, two atoms that are different. The physician who will extrapolate this axiom will change the face of every natural science within a few years. Thanks to this new principle, the century we have just entered will invent more, explain better and produce as much, within its own span, as all the other centuries put together."

"His eyes are trying to open!" murmured Gâteloup, whose anxious gaze was still fixed on René de Kervoz.

"They will open," Patou replied.

"If you give him another one of those little pills?"

"Bravo, boss!" said the medical student. "You are converted to the opium which revives! In spite of the *facit dormire* of Molière, it is the plain truth. I have had no need to quote you the most extraordinary and simplest of the scientific facts of our time: Edward Jenner's cow-pox–a vaccine which is the same virus as smallpox, but which protects against smallpox."

"Give him a pill, boy!"

"Patience! The dose alone will not suffice; it requires time... one can get drunk even on these playthings, tiny glasses though they are, if one empties them too often."

Jean-Pierre wiped the sweat from his brow. Patou took the hand of the sleeper and felt his pulse.

"But in the end," muttered Gâteloup, whose stubborn rationality was still rebellious, "if you find me, one fine morning, lying on the bedroom floor with a stomach full of arsenic..."

"Boss," the student interrupted, "you have no need to go so far. I will answer you. The day when the truth struck me like a thunderbolt was one on which, with no hope remaining in ordinary medication, finding myself beside an unfortunate poisoned by arsenic, I chanced to try the master's prescription: I gave arsenic to the dying man..."

"And did you save him?"

"Unfortunately, for it was our friend Ezekiel–but yes, I saved him, damn it!"

Gâteloup squeezed his hand violently. René's lips had breathed out a sound. They both fell silent. After a few seconds, René's mouth opened again, Faintly, he pronounced a name:

"Angela!"

Chapter XXIII
The Awakening

The town halls of Paris now give three francs to every family which has its children vaccinated. It's not dear, but it pays handsomely nevertheless for the twenty years of suffering, envenomed by sarcasm, that Jenner endured between the invention of his vaccine and its triumphant acceptance. In much the same way, the several thousand *thalers* it cost to found the bronze statue erected to Samuel Hahnemann is glorious payment for the rocks which previously pursued the much-stoned master. That is the way of the world, decrying at first that which it will later come to adore.

Homeopathy will be counted henceforth among the number of systems made illustrious by triumph. It is in vogue, its adepts rolling in gold while they splash mud upon the formerly-illustrious methods, which protest in vain from the height of their academic thrones. Mockery is blunted now, disdain exhausted, and hatred–that providential consecration of success–has arrived.

This is not a science book, by any means; so much the better for the reader to be able to discover herein, along the way, a few pages detached from its curious account of the contradictions of the human spirit. We should like, therefore, to add a few words regarding the doctrine of the great doctor of royal Saxony. Sometimes, the homeopath seems suddenly to be arrested in his triumphant march by a wild rumor: one is accused of having killed some illustrious person, or having opened to some princely heir the succession to a throne. It is, indeed, generally the treatment of the wealthy and great which attracts attention; medical practitioners are ever-ready to minister to artworks on public view and take the pulse of a hand which rests on a scepter, while throwing the doors of its dispensaries wide open to work and misfortune. Those that it 'kills,' according to popular rumor–the natural-born enemy of all doctors–make a noise as they fall. But then, even the best medal has its reverse side. Samuel Hahnemann, who has invented so many specifics, did not leave in his will any formula capable of exterminating charlatanism. There are charlatans everywhere–and charlatans, according to their nature, would far rather practice in palaces than thatched cottages.

In sum, we merely wished to display herein the first attempts of an original practitioner who–under the Restoration, fifteen years later–would pass for a sorcerer, so marvelous were his cures.

After pronouncing the name of Angela, René de Kervoz fell silent again; but his pale face somehow acquired the power to express his thoughts. A fugitive reflection of the dreams which troubled his sleep could be traced in his face. Jean-Pierre Sévérin and Germain Patou both examined it attentively. At one time, the face brightened, betraying a vague ecstasy; at another, a somber cloud descended upon its features, which suddenly expressed poignant suffering.

The student consulted his watch several times, and only gave the third drop of the medicament when the hands marked the appropriate hour. Some minutes after the globule was placed on the tongue of the dreamer, his eyes opened again, this time all the way–but the eyes saw nothing.

"Lila!" he said, in a changed voice. Then, with a sudden anger that made the veins in his temples stand out: "Go away! Go away!"

"Can you hear me, Monsieur de Kervoz?" Jean-Pierre demanded, unable to contain himself.

It was as if the spell were suddenly broken. René's eyelids fell again, while he stammered: "It's a dream! Always the same dream! Sometimes Lila, sometimes Angela...the hot breath of the demon; the soft hair of the angel!" His hand made a sudden movement under the covers, as if it were stroking someone's hair.

271

"Angela is dead!" Jean-Pierre thought aloud. "I understand everything he says... everything!" His cheek was whiter than the invalid's, and his eyes expressed an indescribable terror.

René suddenly opened the palms of his hands. "*In vita mors*," he murmured, "*in morte vita*. Always the same dream. Death in life, life in death! No... no... He's the brother of my poor mother... I shall not give you the means to destroy him!"

The witnesses redoubled their attentiveness.

"Who's he talking about?" asked Patou, after a moment's silence.

"His mother's brother," Gâteloup replied, "is a Norman horse-merchant, near the border with Brittany. I don't know what he's trying to say."

René sat up in bed. "It's you, it's you!" he cried. "The living and the dead! It's you who is Countess Marcian Gregoryi! It's you who is Addhema the vampire!" He was halfway to standing up, but he slumped back exhausted.

Jean-Pierre passed a hand over his sweat-bathed forehead. "I don't believe that," he said, between clenched teeth. "At least, I don't want to believe it. It's impossible!"

"Boss," the student said, gravely, "I'm not yet old enough to know exactly what must be believed. There is only one thing in all this that I deny, and that's the impossible." And his extended finger pointed to the Latin motto running around the scroll mounted above the fireplace, which reproduced exactly the same words that had escaped René's sleep. Patou went on: "Man has said for a long time: this is not, because this cannot be–but some years ago Benjamin Franklin played with the lightning; that poor devil the ci-devant Marquis de Jouffroy made a boat move with neither sail nor oars... You can talk to me if you have something to say; I know the legend of Count Szandor the vampire king, and his wife the oupire Addhema."

"Myself, I know nothing," Jean-Pierre said, rudely, "The world is growing old and going mad!"

"The world is growing old and becoming wise," the student riposted. "Old Republicans like you belong to the past just as much as the old aristocrats. The day will come when one will be ashamed to doubt that which one still blushed to believe yesterday."

The tallow candle, almost entirely consumed, bronzed the copper of the candlestick with its dying flame. It gave out the bright but intermittent light of a lamp on the brink of extinction–but the end of night had arrived, and the first rays of daylight were visible through the open door.

René de Kervoz, sitting up in bed, was supported by Jean-Pierre while Germain Patou was shaking a glass half-full of what seemed to be pure water.

René had the air of a fever-victim, or a drinker laid low by overindulgence. "Don't ask me anything," he said–and those were his first words. "I don't know whether I'm thinking or dreaming. The least question will send me back into the depths of delirium."

"Drink," Patou instructed him, bringing a spoon to his lips.

The young Breton obeyed mechanically. "How long has it been since you last saw me?" he asked, addressing himself to Gâteloup.

"Three days," was the answer.

René made an effort to clear the darkness from his brain. "And I haven't seen Angela since then?" he asked.

"No," said Jean-Pierre.

"Three days," René repeated, counting painfully on his fingers. "Then this is the morning of the wedding-day."

Jean-Pierre lowered his eyes.

"It's true, it's true," stammered the young Breton, whose features became distorted. "Angela's dead!" Two huge tears rolled down his cheeks.

Jean-Pierre stood up straight, as stern as a judge. "How do you know that, Monsieur de Kervoz?" he asked, in his turn.

René cried like a child, but made no reply. Jean-Pierre repeated his question in a darkly menacing tone.

"I don't know anything," René stammered. "But I feel that my heart has been murdered, as if someone had said to me: 'She is dead.' "

"She is dead..." Jean-Pierre intoned, like an echo.

"Who told you?" said René.

"No one."

"Have you seen her?"

"Her last letter... written in blood, which said: 'I'm going to die!' " the old man said, haltingly, through flowing tears.

René drew himself erect and placed his bare feet on the floor. "Perhaps there's still time!" he said, recovering his youthful vigor as if by magic.

Jean-Pierre shook his head, and tried to take hold of him to prevent him from falling–but Germain Patou said: "It's over; the crisis has passed." And, indeed, René's legs were quite steady.

"Tell me everything," René said, in a voice that was faint but firm. "I don't know anything. These last three days have been ripped out of my life... and many others before them. I swear on my honor that I know nothing! I have never stopped loving her! I have been insane rather than criminal, and that gives me the right to avenge her."

Jean-Pierre clasped him to his breast. "We would have been so happy!" he said, thinking aloud. "My poor wife has often said to me: 'I am so joyful that it frightens me!' She and I are both old, Monsieur de Kervoz; we have not known suffering for a long time now... Promise me that you will be a brother and friend to the child who will soon be alone."

"Your son will be my son!" René said.

"A double portion!" said German Patou. "But you're not going anywhere, boss, not for all the devils in hell. Hahnemann also has remedies for chagrin. Your dear wife has her Christian resignation, and the son of which you speak: she will transfer all the love in her heart to him."

Jean-Pierre shook his head for a second time, and murmured: "Her heart was Angela."

"But if Angela isn't dead?" said the student. "We have no proof..."

This time it was René who shook his head, repeating without his knowledge: "Angela is dead!"

Germain Patou, as obstinately hopeful as all men are when they must overcome some great obstacle by the power of their will, replied: "I'll believe it when I see it!"

Jean-Pierre briefly related the story of the naively heart-rending letters found on the window-sill, the last of which–the one written in blood–had broken the pane. René de Kervoz listened. His strength abandoned him for an instant and his legs shook again under the weight of his body. He fell back on the bed, groaning: "I've killed her!"

Then, as his reason rebelled against this conviction, which had no natural basis and resembled the stubbornness of his dementia, he cried: "Hurry up! Let's search...!" The words caught in his throat, and his expression became haggard. "It's already been a long time," he said, in a voice which did not seem to be his own. "A long time. I saw and heard everything in my dream, everything that she wrote... her poor plaint came to me from on high... and I've been in the garden on the Quai des Ormes, beside the river... one night when the Seine was in full flow... she was kneeling... and Despair took her by the hand, drawing her gently into the freezing bed from which one never wakes... never...!" A convulsive sob rose within his breast. "The rest is horrible!" he continued, as if in spite of himself. "She came to me... my lips knew that soft hair so well... I'm certain that I kissed her dear curls, I would swear it... Who, then, told me the hideous story of the monster gaining one hour of life for each year of existence that she stole... of youth, of beauty, of love..." He answered that question with an exclamation. "Lila!... It was Lila who told me...the vampire could not avoid the law which required her to tell her own story..."

René launched himself away from the bed, as if contact with its covers had burned him. "I remember! I remember!" he gasped, seized by a spasm which shook him from top to toe, as the hurricane shakes the trees before stripping them of their foliage. "There are things which cannot be said... my heart is branded by that sepulchral kiss... the lair of the animated cadaver is here... the lair of the monster which lives in death and dies in life!" A forefinger extended from a clenched fist pointed to the Latin motto, vaguely illuminated by the daylight which slipped through the narrow doorway. He tottered. Jean-Pierre and Patou ran to support him, but he pushed them back violently. "Everything is clear, now," he said, slapping his forehead. "My memory's coming back. I've betrayed my mother's blood... so much the better! Do you hear me? So much the better! My treason will put me on the track of Countess Marcian Gregoryi. Angela will be avenged!"

He threw himself headlong through the apartment and went the stairs in a few furious bounds. Jean-Pierre and the student hurled themselves in pursuit without having time to consult one another.

By the time they reached the street, René had turned the corner already, running with extraordinary speed towards the bridges to the right bank. Our two friends went in the same direction, as fast as they could. Behind them, the agents posted by Monsieur Berthellemot immediately joined the chase.

Chapter XXIV
The Rue Saint-Hyacinthe-Saint-Michel

On the left bank, the Boulevard de Sebastopol–passing majestically between the Pantheon and the railings of the Luxembourg–now flattens the western rump of the Montagne Saint-
Geneviève. All is open and clear in the newly-rejuvenated
university district. Its bizarre foreign physiognomy, so curious
and picturesque, has disappeared, to make way for broader
vistas. Paris, the predestined capital, never loses beauty without gaining splendor. Was it beautiful, though? It was certainly strange. The view told lively and singular stories. It is
permitted even to those who sincerely admire New Paris to
regret the loss of the original and garrulous aspect of Old
Paris. What anecdotes were inscribed on the black walls of
those gables, and how well those antique cottages told their
dramatic tales!

Take a few steps away from the young boulevard and
you can still encounter horrible yet charming coverts where
the Middle Ages dribbled into the beard of our civilization; the
newly-opened spaces still give easy access to mysterious cav-
erns. Behind the College de France, steeped in modern philosophy, you have only to follow that narrow thoroughfare
which seems to be a drain of open sky: here are houses to the
right and the left which have seen Montaigu's *capettes* [92] lying
on beds of straw; here is the debris of the cloisters where the
League [93] plotted; here the chapels, transformed into ware-
houses, at whose portals Claude Frollo [94] made the sign of the
cross while out and about–and where his brother Jehan, a
charming, perverse and precocious creature, played some
wretched farce for him from the height of a worm-eaten balcony, which already had an evil appearance when the royal

vampires were sucking the blood of captains at the Tour de Nesle [95]. It is melodrama itself that says: melodrama, yet another vampire, drinks the glory of kings and the honor of queens from its pewter tankard.

In 1804, at the place where the boulevard now widens out into a vast misshapen square, overlooked by the Pantheon, the Luxembourg and the thick-set back of the Odeon, there was the narrow and winding Rue Saint-Hyacinthe-Saint-Michel, more misshapen than square, where everyone turned a blind eye to depravity. The house in which Georges Cadoudal had established his retreat was notorious in those days as the very model of a conspirators' den. I have a map of it before my eyes as I write these lines. Some years previously, it had accommodated Gensonné the Girondin [96], who, it is said, made a passage under the next house to one which had an exit to the Rue Saint-Jacques (via the third stable-door in the direction of the Quais). This is not to say that the passage had been dug with a view to evading, should the need arise, some political hazard.

Another passage ran in the opposite direction, connecting the Fallex house–that was the name of its owner–to the courtyard of a brick building that stood at the corner where the Rue de la Harpe enters the Place Saint-Michel. This second passage, whose origin is unknown but must date back to a far more distant era, extended across no less than thirteen house-numbers. Among that number, it communicated with five houses that had exits to the Rue Saint-Hyacinthe and one opening on to the Place Saint-Michel. It was for this reason that Georges Cadoudal's retreat had nine exits, some of them situated at a considerable distance from the others. He had the habit of saying to himself: "I am a lion lodged in a fox's den." Knowing full well that the majority of his neighbors were ignorant of these connections, Cadoudal hardly ever used the two most extreme exits, and the others only rarely. Usually, according to the people of the neighborhood–who knew him very well under his assumed name of Morinière–he came and went by the door of his own house. The police, therefore, had no inkling of the exceptional facilities that the disposition of his retreat gave to Cadoudal.

On the ninth of March 1804, at seven o'clock in the morning, a hired cab stopped outside the door of the chouan chief in the Rue Saint-Hyacinhe, and waited.

Agents were stationed all along the street, in accordance with the measures put in hand the previous evening in the office of the Prefect of Police. Others were at the window of houses. The cordon of surveillance extended to the right and the left as far as the Rue Saint-Jacques and the Rue de la Harpe.

No one had made a move towards the concierge of the house–who, at the request of the cab-driver, went up the steps to the first floor, rapped at Georges' door and shouted, as was apparently his habit: "Monsieur's carriage is waiting."

Georges was fully-dressed and very abundantly armed, although none of his weapons could be seen. He was arm-in-arm with a young and adorably beautiful woman, who was sitting on the settee in his drawing-room. This was a blonde whose dark blue eyes seemed black in the meager light that entered by the low-set windows.

"All right!" Georges said to the concierge, who went back down the steps.

"I believe," said the charming blonde, whose beautiful eyes were bathed by a kind of ecstasy, "that it is permissible to kill by any possible means the man who is an obstacle to God... but I like you even more, my valiant Breton Knight, for disdaining vulgar assassination and throwing the gauntlet in the face of the tyrant."

"I don't disdain assassination," Georges replied. "I detest it." He was standing up, making the most of his tall figure–which was robust and majestic, in spite of its excessive stoutness. Despite his weight, which must have been considerable, he had a reputation for extraordinary agility in his native Brittany. His face was open and round. He wore his hair short and–a truly strange thing, consistent with the cavalier temerity of his character–he wore on his hat a bronzed clasp combining a cross and a heart, which was the distinctive a cross and a heart, which was the distinctive and well-known badge of the chouans.

Countess Marcian Gregoryi raised Georges' hand ceremoniously to her lips, but he withdrew it.

"No foolishness," he said, brusquely. "Now that day has broken, I'm General George, and I no longer laugh."

"You are the last of the knights," replied the blonde enchantress. "I shall never know how to tell you how much I admire and love you."

"You can tell me some other time, lovely lady," Georges Cadoudal replied, laughing. "There's time for everything. Today, if your information is correct and your men have beards on their chins, I shall force the future Emperor of France to cross swords with a simple peasant of Morbihan... or to exchange pistol-shots, for I'm a good sport and I'll leave the choice of weapons to him. But I swear on my faith that the pistol will not win him any better result than the sword, and the poor devil will kill the First Consul." He took two swords out of a leather case and put them under his arm. He went on: "Tell me again, please, the address and the exact itinerary."

"Are you going straight there?" asked the Countess.

"No, I'm obliged to pick up captain L*** at the Buci crossroads. He's my second."

"A Republican!"

"It's the way the world is going. The captain and I will fight one another the day after the victory."

"Oh well," said the Countess, clapping her pretty little hands together. "That's what I love about you, Georges. Your attitude to the saber is as playful as that of our young Magyars, who are always laughing in the face of death... At the Buci crossroads, you take the Rue Dauphine, the Quais, then straight ahead into the Faubourg Saint-Antoine, keeping to the right–and don't turn until you reach the corner of the Chemin de la Muette, two hundred paces from the Trône barrier. There you'll see an isolated house, an ancient building surrounded by marshland... You knock on the main door and you say to the person who comes to answer it: 'In the name of the Father, the Son and the Holy Spirit, I am a Brother of Virtue.' "

"Damn," said Georges. "Your Welshmen won't come to it by four roads! And must they sing a Tyrolean dirge?"

"It is necessary to add," the blonde said, smiling as if his insouciant merriment amused her, " 'I come by the will of the Rose-Cross of the Third Kingdom, sovereign of the circle of Buda, Gran and Comorn [97]; I want to see Andrea Ceracchi.' "

"And after that?"

"After that, you will be allowed into the sanctuary... and our brothers will see to it that you will meet this very day, in an appropriate place, your enemy General Bonaparte."

"A masterful man," Georges muttered, "who would have made a great chouan, if he had wished!" He shook the Countess' hand heartily and went towards the door. He paused on the threshold to add: "There's a little place on the other side of the town of Brech that I would have liked to see again. Everyone has some memory that returns to him in times of peril, and I'm sure that the dance will become rough today. It says to me: Be true to God and the king, and I swear to you... well, I'm sixty years old, and I've always kept my promises. The captain often says, 'Georges, if you'd been born in the Rue Saint Honoré, you'd be shouting, "Long live the Republic!" '– but these Parisians drivel on like the Bretons. Who knows what the last word will be...? Lovely lady, don't forget to take the corridor to the left: you'll come out in the Place Saint-Michel. And if anyone asks you about Citizen Morinière, you answer: 'I never heard that name.' "

There was admiration and respect in the Countess' smile.

Georges opened the door and went down the steps, singing.

As soon as he had gone, the Countess' features changed, expressing hard, cold sarcasm.

As Georges leapt up into the cab, his driver said to him in a very low voice: "The road looks bad, and so does the entire neighborhood."

A rapid glance had already apprised the clever chouan of the situation. "Take your time, my good fellow," he said, sitting down next to the driver. "While it seems that they haven't been seen, these birds will rest content... is your animal a good one?"

"It's one of yours, Monsieur Morinière."

Georges laughed heartily, and pretended to raise the cab's hood an extra notch. "Collect yourself," he said, "and get your horse underway very suddenly... don't spare the whip... head for the Rue Monsieur-le-Prince as if the devil were after you."

It seems that the policemen did not even have a description of Georges Cadoudal. We find fault, to a greater or lesser extent, with all our servants, but heads of State are no better served than we are. All along the road the agents exchanged glances, and hesitated.

The cab was on the point of moving off, and yet again Georges was about to pass like a thunderbolt through the badly-dressed pack, when a young blonde woman appeared at one of the first-floor windows, which had opened quietly, directly above his head. Her blonde hair, exposed to be daybreak, sparkled in the first rays of the sun. She leaned gracefully over the sill, smiling–and although Georges could not see her, she blew him a kiss.

It was a signal. All the agents moved in at the same time. At the same moment, the cab-driver roused his horse, a robust and lively animal, which set off immediately, knocking half a dozen men to the pavement.

Countess Marcian Gregoryi stayed at the window, following the cab with her eyes as it went down the street like a tornado. When the cab disappeared as the Rue Saint-Hyacinthe curved away, the charming blonde leaned out of the window and closed the shutters. "By this time," she said, "there can't be a single one of them left in the Faubourg Saint-Antoine. I've won my ransom, I'm free, and I leave nothing behind me... tomorrow, I'll be fifty leagues from Paris."

She suddenly turned round, astonished because a footstep had sounded on the floor of the room, which had been empty a moment before. Although her heart was made of bronze, she let out a loud exclamation: a cry of fear and distress.

René de Kervoz was standing before her. He was haggard and disheveled, but his eyes were burning. "I've come too late to save anyone," he said, "but I have time for vengeance."

He grabbed her by the hair, without any resistance being offered, and put the barrel of a pistol to her head.

The shot echoed terribly in the confined space.

The bullet made a round, dry and lipless hole, from which not a single drop of blood flowed. It was as if it had pierced a page of parchment.

Countess Marcian Gregoryi fell, and remained quite still, like a beautiful recumbent statue.

Chapter XXV
An Embarrassment of Carriages

René de Kervoz was accustomed to going into his uncle's house from the Rue Saint-Jacques. He had a key to the secret passage. Georges Cadoudal had arranged matters thus in order that his sister's son should not be compromised if things went wrong.

In leaving the Rue Saint-Louis-en-l'Ile, René had launched himself full tilt towards the Pont de la Tournelle, without worrying about being followed. Fever gave him wings.

Jean-Pierre was getting old and Germain Patou had short legs. Although they both did their best they lost sight of René in the vicinity of the Hôtel-Dieu. Monsieur Berthellemot's agents were behind them, followed at an even greater distance by the peace officer Monsieur Barbaroux, who was in a pitiful condition, nursing a legitimate fear of having contracted some nasty rheumatism that very night.

Day had now broken.

When they arrived at the place where they had lost sight of René, Gâteloup and the student separated, each taking one of the two routes presented to them. Jean-Pierre went along the Quai and Patou went up the Rue Saint-Jacques. It was the latter route that René had taken, but he was already so far ahead that Patou could not catch a glimpse of him.

René let himself in, as we have said, by means of a key that he was carrying about his person. From the direction in which he came, the room where Countess Marcian Gregoryi was to be found was the third that he came to. Two loaded pistols were set on a pedestal table in the second–the entire house was full of weapons. René picked one of them up as he passed by, and cocked it before opening the last door.

When German Patou, still running, reached the top of the Rue Saint-Jacques, he saw a big crowd of people massed in the Rue Saint-Hyacinthe. This mob was in the process of piling into number 7, where a scream had been heard, followed by the crack of a pistol. Germain Patou went in with them.

René was still standing there with the pistol in his hand.

Patou knelt down beside the blonde, who was splendidly beautiful and seemed to be deeply asleep. He felt her heart. His own was beating as if it might burst through his ribs. "Does anyone know this woman?" he asked. When no one replied, he added: "She must be taken to the Marché-Neuf Morgue, which opens for the first time today." Then, in the hope of saving him, he said to René: "Citizen, you must follow me." His final glance was, however, for Countess Marcian Gregoryi, and he thought: "Would I have loved her? Would I have hated her? Now my scalpel will go in search of her secret, delving into the depths of her being!"

At the end of the Rue Monsieur-le-Prince, another crowd was spilling into the Rue de l'Ancienne-Comédie, rolling along like an avalanche, crying: "Get the chouan! Get the chouan! Arrest Georges Cadoudal!" Although it seemed that every house was vomiting its inhabitants on to the pavement, the windows were overflowing with curious faces.

Georges Cadoudal's cab had run into its first obstacle at the top of the Rue Voltaire. Two carts loaded with vegetables were crossing its path.

"Carry on!" said Georges.

The two carts tipped over, depositing the poor devils who were driving them into the gutter, and the cab was through. The people in front of it were beginning to get excited, even though they had no suspicion of what was happening. Assuming that a runaway horse had got the bit between its teeth, a helpful crowd assembled to bar the way. It was a bad mistake.

"Make way!" commanded Georges, who was standing up in the cab. When they did not hurry to obey him as quickly as he would have liked, he snatched the whip from the coachman's hands and slashed rudely to either side of the road–and was free again in an instant. But the racket coming from behind was now so loud that it could be heard at some distance.

"We can't go on like this for long, Monsieur Morinière," the coachman muttered.

"We'll go all the way to Rome if I say so," Cadoudal replied. "Do you think that a man like me can be arrested by Parisian losers?" Then, handing back the whip, he said: "Set them alight, my lad, and have no fear!"

Approaching the Odéon crossroads, the driver was obliged to rein in. There was a heavy carriage crossing over.

"Pass in front or behind," Georges cried, looking behind–and he put on a smile, raising his hand to salute those who were following as they called out: "Get the chouan! Get the chouan! Stop the assassin!"

From the Odéon crossroads to the place where the Rue de l'Ancienne-Comédie forks into the Rue Dauphine and the Rue Mazarin, there was no further obstacle, but there a veritable embarrassment of vehicles was gathered, blocking the way completely.

"Stop," said Georges. "The play might as well reach its last act here as somewhere else. Pichegru and Moreau are out of it–both alive, having given themselves up–but I shall only fall when I'm dead, and I'll have done my best." He stood up again and unsheathed his two swords. Then he took three pairs of pistols from his clothing and arranged them on the seat beside him.

His pursuers drew closer.

"Get away, lad," he said to the coachman, good-humoredly. "The rest needn't concern you. If the road becomes clear, I can steer a course just as well as you–they won't take me then!"

The coachman hesitated. "I've got three kids," he said, in the end. He jumped down to the pavement and vanished into the crowd.

The crowd was growing, already anticipating an extraordinary spectacle.

Georges lifted the cab's hood all the way. At that moment, seeing him thus in the middle of that crowd, you might have taken him for a carnival barker about to go to work.

His work was, indeed, about to begin. He threw off his overcoat to display a kind of jacket–in good cloth, admittedly, but precisely reproducing the cut of the waistcoats worn by the men of Auray. There was a silver heart embroidered on the left side.

"Get the chouan! Get the chouan! Stop the chouan!"

This time, there was a great clamor which came from every side at once. Georges took the whip in his hand; it had served him well–and it must be said that a whip, when wielded by a Morbihanian hand, becomes a weapon not to be disdained. I have seen duels fought with whips in the town of Gacilly, on the river Oust: bizarre and savage tourneys which leave wounds every bit as deep as those inflicted by expertly-plied sabers in duels fought in German universities.

Georges' whip cleared a large circle around him.

"What do you want with me, gentlemen?" he asked, imitating the accent of Normandy to perfection. "My name is Julien-Vincent Morinière. I sell horses for a living; I have done no harm to anyone."

"Chouan!" Charlevoy called out, from a distance–a distance he was careful to keep. "You've stripped off too soon!"

"Perhaps that's true," Georges murmured, laughing. It goes without saying that he did not lose sight of his horse, and was still keeping watch on the traffic-jam that blocked his way. On the far side of the jam, in the Rue Dauphine, the crowd of sightseers was still growing. There came a moment when the pressure of its curiosity broke through the blockade and opened a gap in the middle of the road. Georges twirled around to check behind him–then, touching the horse's ears lightly, he shouted: "Hey, Bijou! Go on through! We have business at the fair!"

The spectators had the same spirit as the audience at a comedy. Paris is entertained by everything, and among every hundred gawkers there were less than ten prepared to believe that Georges Cadoudal was really before them. In spite of the Breton waistcoat, and in spite of the chouan heart, nine-tenths of the audience were in doubt. The stout and hearty fellow seemed like such a nice fellow–and the police were so often deceived!

"Look out, chaps! I won't be responsible for breakages!"

The horse went through the gap easily enough, but the cab was caught between the body of a *fiacre* and the wheel of a huge cart that was in the process of turning the corner.

"God damn it!" said Georges. "We're stranded now–but we're inside a redoubt of sorts."

A pistol-shot–the first–came from behind and carried away his hat. "Lower!" he shouted, turning to fire at the man who still had the smoking gun in his hand. The agents re-treated once again, while the sight-seers, in trying to get away, produced a murderous crush. No one paid the slightest atten-tion to the appeals of women and children.

Georges opened his clasp-knife and cut the two leather straps that attached the horse to the shafts of the cab, and calmly said to the people gathered in the Rue Dauphine: "Citi-zens, would you care to make way for a brave man?"

There was a moment's hesitation on the part of the curi-osity-seekers. Georges turned to make a face at the agents who were trying to clamber into the two neighboring vehicles. He fired two pistol-shots, and three projectiles came back at him, one of which was a bottle hurled from the inn at the corner of the Rue de Buci. When he looked in front of him again, the crowd was noticeably thinner, but those who remained seemed determined to take him head-on. Among others, a group of soldiers had drawn their sabers. Then the sound of shots was heard in the Rue de Buci. Captain L*** and three of his asso-ciates were attacking the agents from behind. At the same time, a tall white-haired man was cleaving a way through the crowds pressed in the Rue Saint-André-des-Arts. He leapt on to the scene brandishing a saber, which intercepted the thrust of a soldier–who turned on him, shouting.

We have observed that Jean-Pierre Sévérin, instead of taking the Rue Saint-Jacques like his companion Germain Patou, had continued along the Quai. All that we have just described passed with such great rapidity that Jean-Pierre had only just arrived, although he had been marching at a good pace. From the Rue Saint-André-des-Arts, he had recognized René de Kervoz's uncle in the very heart of the scuffle, standing up in his cab and firing a pistol. It had suddenly occurred to him that this must be a consequence of Monsieur Berthellemot's error, which had confused the inoffensive horse-dealer Monsieur Morinière with Georges Cadoudal, who wanted to kill the First Consul. None of us is perfect; it is said that every man, in his own opinion, is first and foremost a knight errant, and Gâteloup really was a knight errant. He had spent his life defending the weak against the strong. It was in his mind, perhaps–for he was a subtle man, after his fashion– that Morinière's danger had come about because of some trap set by Countess Marcian Gregoryi. Hadn't he too been mistaken for one of the Head of State's would-be assassins in *The Miraculous Catch*?

Gâteloup pacified the soldier by announcing his name, which was known in every armory of every regiment, and saying: "Put up your weapon, comrade. Be a good boy and give me five minutes, will you?" Then, quickly pinning the heart of gold to his breast, he called out: "Hey! Is there anyone here who'll take a stand beside Papa Gâteloup?"

Ten voices spoke up from the crowd: "Here, Monsieur Sévérin! Here I come!" And all the soldiers barring the way on the Rue de Dauphine side sheathed their swords.

Gâteloup, meanwhile, approached the cab from the front. He took the situation in at a single glance and completed the unharnessing of the horse. Georges stared at him in stupefaction. A few men were already climbing up the back of the cab, where the police agents were feebly resisting the pressure of the crowd.

"Why, comrade," said Georges, pointing his finger at the heart which the Morgue-keeper wore on his breast, "are you too for God and the King?"

"For God, yes, Monsieur Morinière," Gâteloup replied, "but to the devil with the king! Climb on that horse and get out of here–I'll take care of the people who are after you."

Georges frowned.

Gâteloup looked him in the eye. "Well, well," he growled, "you seem a little odd today, comrade. Are you really Georges Cadoudal?"

"Old man," said Georges, who was no longer laughing, "I thank you for what you wanted to do for me. Look after my nephew, who has no cause, and may even approve of that against which we fought in former days, near my noble birth-place of Saint-Anne-d'Auray. I am no Norman; I am a Breton. I am not Morinière the horse-dealer; I am Georges Cadoudal, general of the Catholic and Royal Army. I am not an assassin; I am a champion arriving all alone, with head held high, to do battle with a man who has millions of defenders... Get out of my way–your road isn't mine."

Gâteloup lowered his head and stood aside, without saying a word.

Georges stood up, tucked two of the four pistols that were still loaded into his belt and kept the others in his hands. "It's the truth!" he shouted, at the top of his voice. "I'm the chouan Georges Cadoudal, and I've come to fight the man who would be Emperor!"

It was not merely the police agents but the entire crowd which rushed him. All Paris loved the First Consul.

Georges fired his four pistols and grabbed his two swords. The first broke before anyone had got the better of it. When he finally fell, covered in blood from head to toe, he no longer had anything with which to defend himself but the broken stump of the second. The last wound that he received was inflicted on him by a tradesman butcher, who struck him with the cleaver from his stall–but he was not yet dead, and the agents dared not approach.

It was the same butcher who threw the first rope around his neck.

Five minutes later, as the cart that had stopped Georges Cadoudal's cab carried him away, garroted, to the Conciergerie [98], a man appeared in the midst of the agents who formed the core of the vast crowd assembled at the Buci crossroads.

"See how I manage things!" said this man, rubbing his hands wholeheartedly.

"What?" said Charlevoy. "You haven't been sighted throughout this business, Monsieur."

"I'm well aware that I wasn't actually here," said Monsieur Berthellemot, pushing through the crowd, "but it was all my doing. Boys, I'm proud of you. We've done good work here. All it needed was a level head. I've taken notes, you mark my words!"

Monsieur Berthellemot was in the process of making his finger-joints crack when another, even more majestic, organ sounded these words: "Nothing escapes me. The eye of a master was needed here. I have come, at the risk of my life."

"Monsieur Prefect," stammered the Secretary General.

These two functionaries seemed, in truth, to have sprung out of the ground. While they were looking at one another–the Secretary General crestfallen and envious, the Prefect triumphant–a third *deus ex machina* passed between them, swaggering.

"My dear fellows," said the great Judge Régnier, amiably, "I have taken care of everything. I thank you for not having put any spokes in my wheels. I'm off to the Tuileries to make my report to the First Consul... Oh, my dear friends, you need to be quick off the mark to fill a position like mine."

But when Régnier, the future Duc de Massa, went into the castle, he found Fouché, the future Duc d'Otrante, waiting in the antechamber–who greeted him politely, and said to him: "The First Consul knows everything, my friend. I had to take a

291

hand in the matter myself, of course–without me, you'd never have sorted it out."

Chapter XXVI
A New House

Paris was in a fever that day, from morning till night. The news of the arrest of Georges Cadoudal ran like lightning from one end of the city to the other, crossing the path of other dramatic and terrible items of news. The newsvendors had no idea what it all meant.

Ordinarily, when reality speaks, fantasy shuts up. In the midst of great upheavals of public opinion is not, in truth, the time to tell fireside stories. We should nevertheless take note of the fact that Paris was even more occupied with the vampire than it had been before. I mean Paris high and low: Paris the great and Paris the little. That morning, the First Consul had discussed the vampire with Fouché, and while the future minister of police gave very forcible expression to the idea that the existence of vampires ought to be relegated among the absurdities of another age, the man who was to be Emperor had smiled. No diplomat ever boasted of having translated that brazen smile easily.

Did the First Consul believe in vampires?

A silly question. Nobody believes in vampires. And yet, a muffled and sinister rumor slid sinuously through the great riot of political news. The word "vampire" was on the tip of every tongue. Dissertations, commentaries and explanations were freely offered. Strong-minded men, forced to reconsider the underpinnings of the idea that had been before them for such a long time, claimed to know that "the vampire" was actually a gang of thieves. That way of seeing things enjoyed a certain success, but the great majority clung to its monster and used the word literally: the vampire was a vampire, and her name was Countess Marcian Gregoryi. She was miraculously beautiful, young and seductive. She pretended to be very pious; it was mainly in churches that she cast her nets, without neglecting the theatres and the promenades. The fact that she sometimes had blonde hair and sometimes had black hair was carefully noted–but nothing can change the nature of Parisians. Even their superstition makes room for laughter. The miracle of the changing hair was for them simply a matter of wigs.

And, indeed, perhaps that was the secret, in its entirety.

Her traps were, after all, set for foreigners. She maddened them with love and steered them towards marriage. As civil marriage is undignified and one can only be married once at the town hall, she had introduced herself, under the cover of good works, or even politics, into the confidence of certain holy priests who were so unworldly that they did not know what hour was marked by the hands of the clock of history. They were numerous, and easy to deceive. She deceived them. She invented fables which made secret religious marriage indispensable. These fables always had a partisan streak; persecution explains so many things!

For her, provisionally at least, a religious marriage, celebrated according to that simple form that a recent case has illuminated–a mass heard and the mutual consent murmured at the appropriate moment–sufficed to satisfy her conscience. After the mass, the two newlyweds got into their carriage, the husband having announced his imminent departure on a long journey–and he did indeed depart for a country from which no traveler returns.

Note that each of the priests had an interest in keeping the secret, in addition to the respectable reasons she provided. Although it might be an exaggeration, people say nowadays that Countess Marcian Gregoryi had been married in most of the parishes of Paris. Her three final victims were the most widely cited: Count Wenzel, Baron von Ramberg and Franz König, the wealthy heir to the alabaster mines of the Black Forest. You might say that these mysteries, so long and so deeply hidden, had suddenly burst forth into the light of day.

And as the details were repeated back and forth, they corroborated one another. They were no longer suppositions; they were certainties. There were official reports. By some means which no one knew, but about which everyone talked, the vampire found herself mixed up in recent criminal activities directed towards the First Consul. She had had a hand in the infernal machine, in the conspiracy hatched at the *Théâtre Français*, and–last but not least–in the Cadoudal conspiracy.

These rumors spread like the wind. By midday, the vampire was the mistress of Georges Cadoudal, having formerly been the mistress of the Roman sculptor Giuseppe Ceracchi. Then a new flood of intelligence arrived: Countess Marcian Gregoryi was dead, killed by a pistol shot in the chief chouan's own home. Then another: she had been killed by a young man who was still miraculously alive, even though she had drunk all his blood. This young man had been found in a dark dwelling in the Marais, in the depths of a veritable dungeon with neither door nor window, deep in deathly sleep. And the dwelling in question communicated by subterranean passages with that famous inn, *The Miraculous Catch*, which had maintained these sinister connections for weeks and months, while human remains had been carried down to the Seine by the Bretonvilliers sewer. The violated cemeteries were not forgotten, and people asked themselves fearfully why they had been confronted by this luxury of horrors.

In the afternoon, a third wave of news broke: a house in the Chaussée des Minimes, stormed by the police, had revealed excesses so hideous that words could hardly describe them. There was a vast hoard of corpses there, and that whole dismal comedy of the Quai de Béthune had no other objective but to lead the dogs astray. A hole opened in the conservatory of that house in the Chaussée des Minimes–a delectable place where the traces of orgies of pleasure still remained–a noxious hole where literal heaps of human remains were rotting, corroded by quicklime.

All this was so improbable and so powerful that as the evening approached, Paris began to have doubts. But just as

Paris, its redoubtable appetite having been defeated by the mad abundance of the menu, asked for permission to leave the feast, a new course arrived to crush that impulse, so appetizing that it was essential to return to the table. This was no mere matter of more-or-less improbable gossip; this was a fact, inscribed in visible and tangible flesh, no less: the residue of an appalling tragedy; the bloody remains of a veritable massacre!

Paris would have run full-tilt to the theatre where this exhibition would be put on had it been ten leagues outside the suburbs–but the theatre was in the very heart of the city, between the palace and the cathedral.

Do you remember that little partly-constructed building whose stonemasons had greeted Jean-Pierre Sévérin, calling him "Boss," when he passed over the Marché-Neuf on the evening when our story began?

The building was finished. It was the theatre of which we speak. It was opening that very day–and the terrifying solemnity of its opening would not be forgotten for a long time.

It was the Morgue, a virgin still to all exhibition.

And the final news affirmed that for the baptism of the new Morgue, there were twenty-seven cadavers accumulated in the showroom. All Paris rushed towards the Ile de la Cité.

Sometimes Paris gets all excited like this for nothing. One often sees obscene crowds, having run to the spectacle of the guillotine, coming back with heads down because the performance has not taken place. Where do they come from, these women who resemble wives, miserable creatures that they are? What do they do, these women returning with pouting mouths? They have reserved their "good seats" in vain, although they will keep their coupons for another time.

To be sure, those who ardently desire that abstention from crime might abolish the scaffold would have nothing but a profound pity for these creatures, male or female, who form the executioner's claque–but they cannot blame popular anger too severely, nor be too loud in jeering human perversity. And no one will take the trouble to be unduly indignant if some of these couples, marrying blasphemous gaiety to elegant shame, who come to savor a bloody *sorbet* between their soup and main course, arrive one fine day to be whipped in the gutters of the Rue Saint-Jacques; only chastisement will moderate these filthy pranks.

But Paris, today, did not have to be deceived in its hope.

This is what happened.

On the previous night, Monsieur Dubois, the Prefect of Police–acting on information provided by Countess Marcian Gregoryi–had sent men to surround the isolated house in the Chemin de la Muette, in the Faubourg Saint-Antoine, where the Brotherhood of Virtue was meeting.

No matter what one may think of the merits of Monsieur Dubois as Prefect of Police, it's certain that he was never a man for extreme measures. He was not in any way the cause of the events we are about to relate.

At about one o'clock in the morning, the Brothers of Virtue were assembled in their usual meeting place, awaiting the arrival of Countess Marcian Gregoryi, who was to bring Georges Cadoudal with her. The general mood was very heated, because the majority of the members had intensely personal reasons to fuel their hatred. All the members of that Parisian Tugenbund [99] were thirsty for the blood of the First Consul. At about half past one, a message arrived from the "sovereign," as Countess Marcian Gregoryi was known. The message consisted of a single line: "You are betrayed. Flight is impossible. Choose between treason and death." Andrea Ceracchi gave the order to uncork the barrel of gunpowder that was kept in the meeting-room. A vote was taken on the question of whether, in case of misfortune, it should be set off. There were thirty-three members in attendance; the affirmative vote was unanimous.

Six brothers were sent outside as scouts. There is no way of knowing whether they were thinking more of their own safety than the security of the whole company; the only certain thing is that they never came back. One of these six scouts was Osman, the slave of Mourad-Bey. A quarter of an hour after their departure, the house was surrounded. The sentry at the main door came to tell them, as two o'clock chimed, that there were more than four hundred men–troopers and police–in the marsh. Ceracchi went up to the next floor to check the accuracy of this intelligence.

They were heavily armed. They would have been able to put up a desperate fight–but Ceracchi was more a dreamer than a man of action. Going back down, he said: "Brothers, the hand which desires to execute the arrest of God must be clean, Our hands are not clean. That woman has drawn us into her crime, and there is a voice crying within me which says: 'She is the one who has betrayed you!' We know how to die like men."

He lit a fuse, which the Illyrian Donaï tore from his hands, saying: "Men die in combat!"

At that moment, the sound of rifle-butts hammering against the main door rang out. Two or three of the conspirators attempted to run away, but there was no more time. A single musket-shot fired from without blasted the lock on the front door, while the back door was attacked with a hatchet.

Taïeh, the Negro, took the latter position with five resolute men, while the Germans, led by Donaï, took up their battle positions around the front door. The two doors opened simultaneously. All the rifles were fired at the same time, within and without.

Then there was a great explosion, which brought the ceiling down and ripped the walls apart. Andrea Ceracchi had shaken the torch above the powder-barrel.

Twelve of the assailants were killed, and everyone inside the room perished, without exception.

The new Morgue had these twenty-seven mutilated cadavers–among which that of Taïeh, the Negro–for its opening. They excited considerable curiosity. There is not a theatre in Paris that can boast of having had such a long and constant run of success as the Morgue; its mute and ominous showroom, has always been the same, for more than sixty years, with three hundred and sixty-five performances a year–and the pit has never tired of it. Nevertheless, the Morgue would never recover the feverish vogue of its original debut, to which the city and the suburbs alike crowded, madly stuffing themselves in for two days running.

After going out, the mob–terrified but not yet satisfied–took the road to the Marais and sought out the Chaussée des Minimes, hoping to provide an audience for an even more curious spectacle. Imaginative men were talking up the marvels of the hole filled with the vampire's victims–and if some speculator had been able to establish a turnstile at the door of the house recently inhabited by that vampire, he would have made an enormous fortune in a week. But that was one fruit they were forbidden. For several days, a cordon of troopers guarded the approaches to the house formerly occupied by Countess Marcian Gregoryi. Paris, disappointed, had to be content with the Morgue.

We must now return to our main characters.

Jean-Pierre Sévérin had been at his post since eight o'clock in the morning. Although he had to run all the way from the Buci crossroads to the Châtelet, he was present, calm and serious, at the ceremony which transferred his old office to the new. He remained at his duties throughout the day, and it was he who received the mortal remains of the unfortunates struck down in the Chemin de la Muette. When the time came to close his doors, he left his post and went home.

His wife and son were kneeling in Angela's room, before a little bed on which something was outstretched. In a crib at the foot of the bed, a child was sleeping.

The hideous injury which had mutilated Angela's forehead was hidden by a bandage of white muslin. She was beautiful, with a celestial purity, and she seemed beneath her makeshift crown to be a sixteen-year-old nun, dreaming of Heaven.

To his son, who was weeping silently, Jean-Pierre said: "You shall doubtless be neither powerful nor strong, but you will be good. Look at this and learn. I have saved a few others, but I could not save her. Later, I shall tell you the name of the enemy which drew her into the gulf of suicide–and you will do as I do, my son; you will fight against them."

Wiping away his tears with a gentle and trusting gesture, the boy replied: "I will do as you do, father."

In the next room, Germain Patou was at René's bedside. René was in the grip of a terrible fever; he was delirious. He called out to Angela and swore that he would love her forever. When the Châtelet clock chimed seven, the medical student came to the door and said: "Boss, I have to go. The medicine's made up; give him a dose every quarter of a hour. I'll be back tomorrow."

He left.

On the Quai Saint-Michel, he knocked at the booth of a second-hand bookseller, which was already closed.

"Father Hibault," he said to him, "you've offered me twelve *louis* for my books. Come to collect them and I'll sell them to you."

Father Hibault made the familiar grimace of a dealer in old paper who sees a chance to exploit necessity. "I can't give you more than eight *louis*," he replied.

"Ten or nothing," said Patou, firmly.

The bookseller took up his hat.

Germain Patou lived in an attic in the Rue Serpente. His room contained a bed, a table, two chairs, a bookcase and a very nice skeleton. The bookseller handed over the ten *louis* and carried away his cargo of books.

Germain sat down and waited, thinking: "What shall I know, in the end?"

After ten minutes or so, heavy footfalls sounded on the steps of the spiral staircase leading up to the attic. "Is it she?" he murmured. Young people anxiously awaiting lovers' rendezvous speak thus. Germain Patou, a keen researcher, his nature hardened by necessity, had never been to a lovers' rendezvous.

There was a light knock on the door. Germain opened it immediately. The sly and decrepit figure of Ezekiel appeared in the doorway. He was carrying a heavy burden: a sack which seemed to be full of straw, but whose weight made it obvious that it must also contain something else

"I've gone to some trouble, Monsieur Patou," Ezekiel said. "I've risked my position at the Prefecture, and you know that the funny business down at the Quai de Béthune is over and done with. Give me three hundred francs."

"I only have ten *louis*," Germain told him. "Take it or leave it." Indicating the shelves which had formerly been filled with his books, he added: "I've sold everything I had to get these ten *louis*."

Ezekiel's gaze made a circuit of the room.

"I would have been able to get as much down there, maybe more," he grumbled. "The pool-players down at the Café de la Concorde in the Place Saint-Michel would love to see how she is doing in there... and they would have paid a lot to burn her heart."

"If you don't sell her here," the medical student countered, "you won't sell her at all. I'll come down with you and make sure that she's deposited in the Morgue."

Ezekiel threw his burden on the bed, which creaked. He accepted the ten pieces of gold and went off in a bad temper. When he had gone, Germain closed and locked the door. The blood rose to his cheeks and his eyes shone strangely. He lit the second lantern that was on the mantelpiece; then, having placed candles in the mouths of two empty bottles, he lit them too. Never had the room been so brightly illuminated.

Germain took a large and exceedingly sharp scalpel from his instrument-case and slit the sack along its side. Having done that, he parted the cloth and the straw with two tremulous hands.

In this way he uncovered the pale and marvelous beauty of a young woman, recently deceased.

It was Countess Marcian Gregoryi.

Chapter XXVII
Addhema

Her beauty was, as we have already established, marvelous. I do not know quite how to put this, but the strands of straw that polluted her disordered hair seemed somehow to be a suitable ornamentation, and her sagging clothes accentuated the perfection of her figure. She was pale, but her face and bosom had none of that ghastliness which denotes the absence of life. The wound that had killed her was a round hole in the temple, surrounded by a bluish circle so small as hardly to be visible. Her gaze still seemed to glide between her half-closed eyelids.

Germain looked at her contemplatively. Her thoughts seemed to be written in her physiognomy, upon which a lively intelligence had set its seal. And her thoughts–or, rather, the impression of them which he conceived–were so subtle and so complex that perhaps even he would have had no idea how to express them. At least, he would not admit them to himself.

He felt greatly troubled. The fundamental conflict–perhaps the first great trial of his life–was between science and emotion. His pulse was feverish, and he was astonished by the oppression which bore down upon his breast. After several minutes, without quite knowing what he was doing, he picked out the straw that was tangled in her hair and caught in the folds of her garments, piece by piece. It took a long time to complete this toilette; when it was done, he let out a great sigh.

"There is no woman as beautiful as this in the whole world," he murmured.

He appropriated the Countess' own handkerchief–a fine piece of batiste whose edge protruded from the pocket of her dress–to wipe her brow amorously. That first contact provoked a sensation so violent that he was afraid that he was ill. She was cold–she was dead–and yet the young man's entire body thrilled to that touch. In spite of himself, Germain lifted the handkerchief to his lips. It exuded a subtle and mysteriously intoxicating perfume. The folds of the handkerchief parted to display an embroidered coat-of-arms, around which ran a motto, glossily inscribed on a mat background. Germain read: *In vita mors, in morte vita.*

The handkerchief fell from his fingers. His legs were giving way beneath him and he moved towards a chair. He sat down.

The March wind was blowing outside, shedding its tears upon the window-panes. The shrill sound of lively music drifted upwards from a neighboring pleasure-garden, where students were dancing. Germain, momentarily enfeebled, searched for a train of thought that was fleeing his mind. That train of thought was science. He had sacrificed his books–his beloved books–in order to get to the bottom of a strange secret: all of his books, even Samuel Hahnemann's *Organon*, whose reading had been, for him, a rebirth.

He firmly believed that his motive was scientific, and he repeated, as one is sometimes compelled in spite of oneself to murmur a stubborn refrain: "What shall I know? What shall I know, in the end?"

He reopened his instrument-case with a great sigh, and selected the sharpest of all his scalpels. Contact with the steel made him shiver. "Life in death," he said, "death in life! Is there nothing in it but decrepit error, or is it a prodigious reality? The mystery is there, beneath that silk, behind that adorable breast, within that heart which no longer beats and yet conserves a terrible latent vitality. I can slice into the life, open the breast, interrogate the heart..."

And that, remember, was for him a very simple thing, an everyday occupation. Anatomy had, by this time, no more secrets from him. Why, then, were his temples bathed in cold sweat? Without being aware of it, he staunched the moist flow with the same piece of batiste with which he had mopped the beautiful face of the dead woman.

It is said that a king of France fell madly in love in the same fashion, having breathed in the subtle perfumes of a veil which retained the emanations of the divine body of Diane de Poitiers [100].

Germain closed his dazzled eyes. But he was a resolute individual; he was ashamed and gripped the handle of his scalpel convulsively.

"I want to!" he said. "I want to know!"

He sliced the silk dress open with a brisk sweep, then cut through the chemise to expose the exquisite perfection of the bare breast. He stood up, swaying like a drunkard, in order to make the first cut.

But the tint of the unveiled flesh was so emphatic, and so vibrant, that the scalpel leapt out of his fingers. He clutched his head in both hands, terrified by his own passion...

"Am I in love?" he asked himself, thinking aloud.

A voice, which did not come from the immobile lips of the dead woman–a feeble voice which seemed very distant, yet distinct–replied.

"You love me!"

The student's blood ran cold.

He thought he had gone mad.

"Who said that?" he asked.

The voice, more distant and not so clear, replied: "It's me, Addhema..."

The March wind shook the window-frame, and strident bursts of laughter could be heard in the pleasure-gardens down below. Germain, brought to his senses by these external sounds, made a violent effort to collect himself, and placed the hollow of his right hand upon the woman's breast, at the place where a heartbeat ought to have been tangible.

The breast was cold. The heart was no longer beating.

Germain felt nothing, except for the extravagant pulsation of his own arteries. He felt nothing, insofar as the verb "to feel" signifies a clear and positive fact–but he experienced something extraordinary and powerful, which he could only liken to a profound magnetization. His entire being became unsteady, as if his soul had been split from his body. For the first time since his life had begun–and perhaps for the last, until the hour of his death–he was conscious of the two principles comprising the entity that was his existence. He perceived, fleetingly but quite distinctly, the division of his material and spiritual selves. The process by which they were torn apart was painful, but also somehow voluptuous.

It only lasted for a moment: the time that it takes for a lamp to emit the last flare of light that precedes its extinction. Then everything became vague. He sought to recover his soul, just as he had sought to recover his train of thought a short while before. He wanted to pull his hand away, but he could not; the muscles in his arms were set in stone. That heart was not beating; that flesh was inert and cold; but a slow fluid wave was spreading therefrom.

Germain realized that he was going to sleep while standing up, falling into a cataleptic trance. He tried to resist, but an irresistible and ironic force opposed his effort, subjecting it to a crushing defeat. His eyes were already seeing that white and magnificently beautiful statue differently. She seemed to him to be rising from the bed and floating in space.

The light which glimmered between her closed eyelashes became brighter, reaching out and climbing towards him like a stare.

And the voice–the voice that had said "You love me"– came from everywhere at once, enveloping him like a voluble atmosphere, murmuring within and without his being words that required a considerable time to make their meaning clear.

That voice said: "Kill me! Kill me! I implore you, in the name of the Father, the Son and the Holy Spirit! The most terrible torment of all is mine, to live within this death and to die within this life... Kill me!"

These strange words seemed to come and go, mockingly.

Nothing could now be heard outside: neither the plaint of the wind nor the gaiety of the tavern. Everything within the

305

room began to move, as if it were the cabin of a ship tossed upon a wave. The dead woman alone remained immobile, in the serenity of her ultimate sleep, suspended above the bed by an occult power which supported nothing else.

She was ascending very slowly, rising into the void.

Germain realized that her mouth would soon reach the level of his lips.

And the voice, ever more distant, said: "To kill me, it is necessary to burn my heart. I am the vampire whose death is life, whose life is death. Kill me! My torture is life; death will be my salvation. Kill me! Kill me!"

These words echoed like bitter laughter in the student's ears.

And the white statue continued its ascent.

When the face of the dead woman was at its closest to his own, Germain saw a single crimson drop of liquid blood emerge from the bullet-wound, and he felt a hot breath strong upon his cheek—and his lips were touched by that mouth, which seemed to him to be made of fire.

He was overwhelmed by a shock, whose violence no words would be adequate to describe. It was his last sensation. He caught a glimpse of the bottomless pit which is called Eternity, widely agape and he fell into it...

And he woke up the following morning in broad daylight, lying across his bed, his face buried in the bedclothes.

The body of Countess Marcian Gregoryi had disappeared.

The idea that he had been the victim of a frightful nightmare tried to take possession of him—but he still had his scalpel in his hand. The sack of coarse cloth was there too, as was the straw, and the batiste handkerchief, whose glossy thread spelled out the Latin motto—and on the sheet in which the body had been wound, at the exact spot to which her lips had been applied, there was a round red stain.

It was a drop of blood.

When harvest-time arrives in the huge fields of maize that stretch out from Semlin, as far as Timisoara and Szeged, they tell the tale of the great nocturnal orgy that takes place in the ruins of Bangkeli.

Our story has already reached its real denouement. This is, perhaps, its fantastic denouement.

Bangkeli was a Christian citadel flanked by eight Turkish towers, which looked out over the Sava from the heights of a bare mountain. Its ruins testified that it had been as large as a town. Throughout the centuries that have passed while the water of heaven has inundated the magnificent halls through fallen roofs, it has been the place of the vampire orgy.

Lila had lied when she told René de Kervoz that the last count was a general in Prince Charles' army during the Napoleonic war. The last count was a famous and powerful voïvode in the time of Matthias Corvinus, the son of John Hunyadi [101]. He was killed by his wife Addhema, who betrayed him for the rebel Szandor. And for many long years, Szandor and Addhema were masters of a vast domain that was terrorized by the clamor of their crimes.

Both of them were vampires. In the ages which followed, the misfortune that emanated from their tombs spread terror and sorrow throughout the land. Collectively and individually, they were legendary all along the banks of the Sava.

One night–the exact date is unspecified, but it was around the beginning of the present century–the Serbian boatmen saw the reflections of the sun grow redder in the broken windows of the ivy-clad dwelling, as if they were on fire. When the sun set upon the plain which stretched away towards the Adriatic, however, the windows of the antique fortress were still red, or even redder: the great fire was inside. The boatmen crossed themselves, saying: "Count Szandor is selling a night of love to his wife Addhema." And they plied their oars to send them hurrying downriver to Belgrade. No one would have approached the accursed fortress, even for a fortune. Who, then, told the tale of what passed there that evening? Who was the first? No one knows, but it was told never-

307

theless. That is always the way with popular traditions–and perhaps you will find therein the origin of the faith they inspire. They are believed because no one can name the liar who invented them.

The great hall of the citadel of Bangkeli was illuminated in a grandiose fashion. The painted walls, faded and soiled, seemed to revive in the fire of the chandeliers. The old suits of armor reflected clusters of dull sparks, and the Saracen galleries added to the ancient Roman building displayed the lightness of their polychromatic lace coquettishly. A cloth-covered table was abundantly furnished with the most exquisite dishes, mingling with bottles of wine from Hungary, Greece and France.

The climate in those parts is like Italy's, perhaps even more benign. The golden apricots climb in pyramids among the hills of citrus fruits, oranges and grapes, while the watermelons in their green envelopes bleed beneath the knife. No one can say whence came the silken cushions and the magnificent carpets that ornamented for a night that lordly domain, abandoned and deserted for centuries. Beside the table, where the untidy plates and uncorked bottles advertised the end of a feast, a young man and a young woman, both stunningly beautiful, were stretched out on the cushions. Not far from where they lay, a heap of gold pieces stood beside an empty chest.

"My lord," said the young woman, as she offered up her soft forehead, crowned with blonde curls, to the kisses of her companion, "that gold cost a great deal of blood."

The young man replied: "Blood is necessary to the acquisition of gold, and gold that one spends lavishly causes bloodshed in its turn. There is a mystical bond between blood and gold. That stupid herd which populates the word, humankind, calls us vampires. They are horrified by us, and offer, unsuspectingly, their veins to those other vampires they name the clever, the happy and the strong, never dreaming that the opulence, the power and the glory of any one of them can only be made with the blood of all: blood, sweat, marrow, intelligence, courage. The thousands work, but only one profits..."

"You are eloquent, my lord," the young woman murmured. "You are handsome, my lord. Your are like a god, my lord–but deign to spare a downward glance for your little servant Addhema, who is languishing for love of you."

The superb Szandor did indeed spare her a glance. "You are entitled to one night of pleasure," he replied. "You have purchased that. I am here to win that heap of gold. But when you are dead again, Addhema, I shall take that gold and buy a harem of princesses with it. I shall dazzle Paris, whence you have recently come, London, Vienna, or Naples the divine; I shall dispute with cardinals in Rome, with padishahs in Istanbul, with the ailing consuls of English conquest in Mysore. Everywhere I go, other vampires will grow pale in being eclipsed..."

There was a strange gleam in Addhema's beautiful eyes.

"One kiss, Szandor, my love! One kiss, Szandor, my lord!" [102]

The superb Szandor gave in to her; it was necessary that their business should be concluded.

The storytellers of the Sava's shores say that this embrace, whose price was several millions, was audible all along the river, in the plain and in the depths of the forests. The love-making of tigers is a battle; it makes a great deal of noise. There were howlings, and grindings of teeth; the red glow intensified; the ancient fortress was shaken to its foundations ten times over.

Then, the two monsters with the faces of angels lay still, exhausted by voluptuous fatigue.

Wine ran freely, tinting their pale lips with ruby droplets.

Addhema's eyes burned with suppressed fire.

"I find you beautiful tonight, my bride," said Szandor contentedly. "Tell me the story of those golden curls crowning your forehead."

"I always find you beautiful," the female vampire replied. She put her charming head upon her lover's breast, and

309

went on: "There was a beautiful little girl on the road, who asked for bread. I met her between Vienna and Pressburg. She smiled so nicely that I took her into my carriage. For two days she was extremely happy, and I heard her thank God for having found such a beautiful and generous mistress. That night, before coming here, I sensed that my blood was growing cold again within my veins. I needed to be young and beautiful. I had taken the child in my lap; she was asleep; I killed her..."

While she spoke these words, her voice was as smooth as a song.

Szandor's hands bathed in that soft and silky hair, which was the price of a murder. The tale seemed piquant to him, and reawakened his dormant caprice. The savage love-tussle began again, similar to the revels of ferocious beasts which disturb the solitude of thickets.

They explored every orgiastic opportunity–and then did it again, and again...

The first light of dawn illuminated the conclusion of the battle, among broken bottles, scattered gold, carpets soiled with wine and filth. A fire was burning in the hearth; an iron bowl set over the fire contained molten metal. Within the burning charcoal, an iron bar was glowing red.

Addhema said: "I don't want to see the sun come up. You, whom I have loved, both living and dead–Szandor, my king, my god–promised me that I should die by your hand when this night of delights is over. You know how to put an end to my suffering, for my torment is to live and I long for the blissful sleep of death."

"I have promised, my ultimate beauty, and I shall keep my promise," replied Szandor, without much emotion. "It's as well–the day is here and I have to be on my way. There are beautiful girls in Prague. I want to be in Prague before nightfall. Are you ready, my love?"

"I'm ready," Addhema said.

Szandor moistened a silk handkerchief to wrap around the end of the red-tipped iron bar. Addhema followed his every movement with a somber and troubled gaze, watching his features for the slightest trace of emotion–but Szandor was thinking of the beautiful girls of Prague while he smiled and hummed a drinking-song.

Addhema's eyes burned.

Szandor withdrew the iron bar from the fire, which spat out a shower of sparks. "It's just right!" he said, with a sinister gaiety.

"It's just right," Addhema echoed. "Goodbye, Szandor, my beloved."

"Goodbye, my delight..."

Szandor lifted his arm, but Addhema said to him: "I don't want you to see me struck down, light of my life. Give it to me; I shall pierce my own breast. You will only pour out the molten lead."

"As you please," Szandor replied. "Women are fickle." And he passed her the red-hot iron.

Addhema took it, and plunged it into his heart so violently that the hot shaft went right through his torso, from front to back.

The monster fell, stammering an incomplete curse.

"The girls of Prague will have to wait," murmured the female vampire, drawing herself up gloriously to her full height, smiling with triumph. She withdrew the iron bar from his flesh, leaving an enormous hole, into which she poured the molten metal from the bowl. Then she kissed the livid forehead of her monstrous lover and thrust the iron bar–which was still red hot–into her own heart.

That morning, there was a thunderstorm whose like had never before been seen in Hungary. Of the citadel of Bangkeli, struck by lightning twenty times, not one stone remained set upon another. In the thick undergrowth which grew among the debris, two skeletons were found, whose bones were interlaced in a funereal embrace.

Afterword

Nineteenth-century Vampire Fiction
Before and *After* The Vampire Countess,
with some Further Observations
on Hesitations and Inconsistencies in the text.

The Vampire Countess was probably the sixth full-length vampire novel to be published, following *Der Vampyr* (1801) by Ignatz Ferdinand Arnold, *Lord Ruthven, ou les Vampires* (1820) by Cyprien Bérard, *La Vampire, ou La Vierge de Hongrie* (1825) by Etienne-Léon Lamothe-Langon, the anonymous *Varney the Vampyre* (1846-7) and *La Baronne Trépassée* (*The Late Baroness*) (1853) by Pierre-Alexis Ponson du Terrail, but it is difficult to be certain because the bibliography of 19th century vampire fiction is exceedingly problematic. The Arnold novel seems to have been lost and there does not appear to be any detailed account of its contents. Like the text on which it was based, John Polidori's short story "The Vampyre," Bérard's novel was misrepresented by its first publisher; whereas Polidori's work was falsely attributed to Lord Byron, Bérard's was falsely credited on its title page to "l'auteur de *Jean Sbogar* et de *Thérèse Aubert*"--i.e., Charles Nodier. The anonymous "penny dreadful" serial *Varney the Vampyre* was long misattributed to Thomas Peckett Prest, although its true author was probably James Malcolm Rymer. Ponson's novel is a deeply ambiguous text whose use of the motif of vampirism is teasingly elliptical. *The Vampire Countess* is problematic in the same way as its immediate predecessor, and also because of the means of predation employed by its eponymous anti-heroine; a pedant might reckon that it is not a vampire novel at all, no matter how promiscuously the word is bandied about in the text. Nevertheless, *The Vampire*

Countess certainly warrants consideration as a historical curiosity, and it is an interesting text in its own right.

The first time the word *vampire* appeared in French as a feminine rather than a masculine noun was under rather peculiar circumstances. "La Vampire" was the title attached–by mistake, as it happens–to a translation of a story extracted from *Die Erzählungen der Serapionsbrüder* (1819-21) by the German writer E.T.A. Hoffmann. This three-volume work is a long dialogue between the eponymous brothers, interspersed with stories, some of which have their own titles and some of which do not. At one point in their long conversation, the brothers discuss the phenomenon of vampirism–a discussion to which a German editor subsequently added the gloss "*Vampirismus*." The discussion is followed by a story, which is not represented by either its notional teller (Cyprian Serapion) or its actual teller (Hoffmann) as a vampire story, but when French translators stripped out the tales for a collection of Hoffmann's *Contes Fantastiques* they borrowed the gloss that had been attached to the preceding discussion by the German editor. The story is actually about a female cannibal, or ghoul. (Alexander Ewing's 1892 English translation of *The Serapion Brethren*–which includes the introductory discussion on vampirism–follows the example of the French translator in titling the story "The Vampire," but when Christopher Frayling reprinted it in his 1991 anthology *Vampyres*, he substituted "Aurelia").

The consequences of this confusion are partly responsible for the fact that Féval's Monsieur Berthellemot is so insistent that the "female of the vampire species" ought to be distinguished from the male, in terms of her habits as well as her nature, and ought more properly to be called a *ghoul* or *oupire*. *Oupire* is derived from the Russian word for vampire, *upyr*; it is highly unlikely that Féval had read Alexei Tolstoy's "Upyr" (1841), which appears to be the second significant vampire story written in Russia, after Nikolai Gogol's "Viy" (1835)–which also features a female vampire–but he may have heard tell of it, and would in any case have encountered

313

the word in the one scholarly work on vampires to which he certainly had access, Dom Augustin Calmet's treatise, *The Vampires of Hungary and Neighboring Regions*, first published in Paris in 1746 (and reprinted several times).

In addition to Hoffmann's story, however, Féval must have read Lamothe-Langon's similarly-titled *La Vampire*, in which a young officer serving in the Napoleonic wars promises to marry a young Hungarian although he is already engaged to a Frenchwoman; when he returns to his homeland, he reverts to his original plan, but when the Hungarian girl turns up at his new home, he welcomes her as a guest. The household then suffers a long catalogue of disasters, including the deaths of his wife and child; finally, in desperation, he agrees to honor his broken promise–but the church ceremony reveals that his new bride's true form is skeletal. There are ironic echoes of this story in the account of her origins that Countess Marcian Gregoryi (disguised as Lila) offers René de Kervoz before she too is revealed as a skeleton. One of many famous individuals whose memoirs Lamothe-Langon faked (the most famous by far was Louis XV's mistress the Comtesse du Barry) was the Comtesse d'Adhémar, a minor figure in the French court who is nowadays best-remembered for conversations she reported with the Comte de Saint-Germain, on which his reputation as a magician is partly based; it is probably from her name that Féval derived the name Addhema. Lamothe-Langon's penchant for rewriting and sensationalizing history endeared him to many *feuilletonists*, who regularly mined his work for inspiration; his *L'Espion de Police* [*The Police Spy*] (1826) may well have influenced Féval's use of police agents as plot devices and his attitude to that dubious profession.

Two other writers who had taken note of the story from Hoffmann were among the most significant French predecessors of Féval. Théophile Gautier used Serapion as the name of the vampire-vanquisher in his novella *La Morte Amoureuse* (1836, usually known in English as "Clarimonde"); Féval had certainly read this story, which was by far the most prestigious example of vampire fiction available to him, and *The Vampire*

314

Countess follows Gautier's example in making its vampire an irresistible femme fatale. Indeed, there is much in *The Vampire Countess'* visionary sequences which seems to be attempting, consciously and methodically, to outdo Gautier, in terms of erotic symbolism as well as melodramatic verve. In *La Morte Amoureuse*, the beautiful vampire crumbles into dust when doused with holy water by Serapion, but Féval's disintegration scene is much more graphic and has far more in common with the "rapid aging" scenes beloved of modern cinema; even the scenes of lovemaking between Clarimonde and her victim pale by comparison with the extravagant account of vampiric coupling offered in the final chapter of *La Vampire*. A more obvious follower of Hoffmann's accidental example was, however, Alexandre Dumas, who imported a female vampire into *Le Vampire* to serve as a counterpart to the second-hand villain, describing her in the cast list as "*la goule.*" This example also left its mark on *The Vampire Countess*, along with certain aspects of Dumas' play that had been carried forward from its predecessor.

Although Féval gives the primary credit for the 1820 version of *The Vampire Countess* to Achille de Jouffroy, it is nowadays listed among the works of the much more famous Charles Nodier. It was the first of three plays–none of which he acknowledged at the time–on which Nodier worked with the director of the Porte-Saint-Martin Theatre, Jean-Toussaint Merle. The extent of his involvement is unknown, but it seems probable that the idea to produce a stage adaptation of John Polidori's short story (which was then misattributed to Lord Byron) was Merle's and that Nodier was brought in as a "script-doctor" when Jouffroy's preliminary efforts needed further work. Merle and Nodier tried to repeat the trick in their second collaboration, *Le Monstre et le Magicien* (1826), an adaptation of Mary Shelley's *Frankenstein*, after Nodier had adapted a tragedy by another British Gothic novelist, Charles Maturin, for another director (*Bertram ou le Pirate*, 1822, from an 1816 original).

In Polidori's original story, a young aristocrat named Aubrey falls in with the older Lord Ruthven while taking the grand tour. While they are in Greece, the horrified Aubrey concludes that his companion is a "vampyre" when Ruthven appears to be rejuvenated after the death of a young girl; the two part company, but not until Ruthven has wrung a solemn oath to remain silent from his companion. When Aubrey returns to England to discover that his sister's fiancé, the Earl of Marsden, is actually Ruthven, his inability to warn her drives him mad. The two items from this story that were eventually carried forward as cornerstones of modern vampire fiction were the self-rejuvenating aristocratic male vampire (clearly based on Byron and embodying Polidori's deeply ambivalent attitude toward his former employer) and the description of his Greek victim: "upon her neck and breast was blood, and upon her throat were the marks of teeth having opened the vein." This vampiric *modus operandi* recurs in *Varney the Vampyre* and *Dracula*, but its omission from the 1820 French drama resulted in its omission from all that work's French successors, thus clearing the way for the unique but very striking method of predation featured in *The Vampire Countess*.

In the 1820 dramatization, Lord Ruthven becomes Lord Rutwen (the English surname Ruthven is pronounced "Riven" but none of the French dramatists appear to have known this) and Aubrey's sister is named Malvina. The play's first act is, however, preceded by a prologue in which Ituriel, the Angel of the Moon, and a second symbolic character–named in one manuscript as Abdiel, Angel of Love, and in another as Oscar, the Genius of Marriage–introduce the audience to the notion of the vampire. This prologue introduced the idea that the vampire's permission to operate in violation of the natural and divinely-ordained distinction between life and death is constrained by certain rules, whose violation results in severe penalties. These rules determine exactly when he can operate, and exactly how he may be subjected to the permanent annihilation to which death has failed to deliver him.

The purpose of this preliminary disquisition is to establish the means by which this Aubrey, unlike Polidori's, will be able to save Malvina and thus contrive a more crowd-pleasing ending. The device of subjecting the vampire's sojourns on Earth to arcane sets of rules was so useful that it was built into many subsequent variations on the theme, although the rules themselves remained very variable until Bram Stoker formulated the definitive set. The most important item in the set devised by Merle, Jouffroy and Nodier is that Rutwen has to work against a deadline while claiming his victims–if he delays too long, he is doomed. All Aubrey has to do, therefore, is persuade Malvina not to go with her fiancé when the time comes for him to carry her away to his tomb. Despite its relative lack of melodramatic flair, this device was faithfully copied in several subsequent versions of the story, most notably the opera *Der Vampyr* (1828) by Heinrich Marschner (which Féval might have seen). It was reimported into English fiction in Upton Smyth's prose version of the opera, *The Last of the Vampires* (1845), but that remains a very obscure work. A similar device is effective in *The Vampire Countess*, where Addhema's own account of herself emphasizes that she must work relentlessly against the clock to achieve serial rejuvenation.

In the final scene of the 1820 drama, the shades of Rutwen's previous victims emerge from obscurity as he goes to his doom (crying "*Le Néant! Le Néant!*"). They are young women clad in veils, which are sufficiently flimsy to reveal wounds in their breasts from which blood is still flowing. Because these wounds were clearly symbolic, they did not set any precedent regarding a vampire's actual method of predation–Rutwen is never seen in action during the play.

When Dumas came to produce a new version of *Le Vampire*, he had far more experience of the narrative mechanics of melodrama to draw upon. (His version was also a collaboration, with his long time associate Auguste Maquet, but Maquet, like Jouffroy, has been airbrushed out of the picture by subsequent literary historians.) Although the five-act drama of 1851 retains the same villain as the three-act play of 1821, whose name is here spelled Ruthwen, almost everything else is changed.

Aubrey, who became a Scot in the 1820 play, is replaced by a Breton named Gilbert de Tiffauges. This is a highly significant choice of surname because the Château de Tiffauges was a real place: the once-luxurious residence of Gilles de Rais, the Marshal of France and associate of Joan of Arc who became the subject of the most sensational sorcery trial of the 15th century. It was still standing in 1851, but quite deserted, stripped of every vestige of its former finery.

Gilbert is said to be a descendant of the fairy Mélusine, the central character in one of the most famous Breton folk-tales, a local variant of the lamia story from Philostratus' *Life of Apollonius of Tyana* which had inspired both John Keats' poem "Lamia" (1820) and Gautier's *La Morte Amoureuse*. In a dream sequence (one of several symbolic interludes modeled on the 1820 prelude), Mélusine actually appears, stepping out of a tapestry in order to tell Gilbert the awful truth about Ruthwen. In a key passage of Act II, the relatively amiable supernatural beings of Breton folklore are sharply contrasted by a traveler with the superstitious apparatus of northern Greece, whose key figure is neither "the benevolent fairy, the inoffensive elf nor the mischievous goblin" but "the terrible, maleficent ghoul: the spectral female, reinvested with the appearances of beauty and youth in order to bait her snares more attractively, who attacks young men–especially the most handsome and virile–and drinks their blood with relish!" The exact method of the ghoul's predation is not specified, but it is described as "*un baiser mortel*"–the word "*baiser*" here implying far more than a mere kiss, just as it does in the final chapter of *The Vampire Countess*.

In the 1851 play, Ruthwen claims three victims, the first being a Spanish girl named Juana, murdered (in an unspecified fashion) in the haunted castle of Tornemar. Gilbert avenges Juana by killing Ruthwen, but obeys the dying man's request to lay his body on a rock beneath the rays of the moon instead of burying him. Gilbert is understandably surprised, therefore, when he discovers in Act III that the Baron de Marsden to whom his sister Hélène is engaged is none other than Ruthwen, although Ruthwen quickly convinces him that he had only seemed to be dead and had made a swift recovery from his wound. Despite Mélusine's warning, Gilbert fails to save Hélène in Act IV, because Ruthwen manages to convince her, temporarily but effectively, that Gilbert is mad. Again, however, Gilbert avenges the crime, this time by hurling Ruthwen into an abyss.

By this time, Ruthwen has realized that there is a supernatural force working against him: a being of his own ambiguous kind, whose clandestinely-offered advice prompted Gilbert to dream of Mélusine and heed her advice. When Ruthwen returns yet again in Act V, this time in pursuit of Gilbert's fiancée Antonia, he expects trouble, but does not anticipate that his rival–"*la goule*," here masquerading as Antonia's friend Ziska–will go so far as to tell Gilbert how he can be destroyed, because such treason would consign her to the same extinction as himself. Alas for Ruthwen, the ghoul has fallen in love with Gilbert, and sacrifices herself in order that he may have his heart's desire. In the final scene, when Ruthwen has been rendered harmless (by sealing him in a tomb), the shades of Juana and Hélène reappear, like the shades in the 1820 version, to wish the lovers every happiness.

The central character of Féval's *The Vampire Countess* obviously owes as much to Dumas and Maquet's ghoul as to Lamothe-Langon's Hungarian bride and Gautier's "amorous corpse," although Féval is careful to reserve explicit credit for the most significant literary predecessor of Dumas' self-sacrificial demon: Jacques Cazotte's *diable amoureux* Biondetta (see note 45). Like Cazotte, Féval obviously had difficulty figuring out how to resolve his account of a she-demon deflected from her evil purpose by infatuation, but whatever he came to think of the novel in later years, he obviously became entranced while he was actually writing it with the power of this delectable central image. Even though he could never quite bring himself to believe wholeheartedly in her reality, neither could he let her dissolve entirely into a mere vulgar trickster. Although *The Vampire Countess* mingles ironic comedy with its melodrama, according to what was rapidly becoming Féval's standard recipe, the sequences which feature the vampire in action have a raw power that overrides the apologetic hesitancy with which they are introduced.

The two subsequent novellas Féval wrote in which vampirism plays a part–*Le Chevalier Ténèbre* (1860; book version 1862; tr. as *Knightshade*) and *La Ville-Vampire* (1867; book version 1875; tr. as *Vampire City*) are both comedies with flamboyant melodramatic intrusions. They provided distant foundation-stones for the modern subgenre of horror-comedy, but in themselves they provide further evidence of Féval's inability to take the idea of vampires seriously. *The Vampire Countess*, on the other hand, is a remarkable example of the infectiousness of the idea; its hesitations and comedic intrusions could not, in the end, either defeat or detract from the splendid force of its melodramatic flourishes.

Although certain key features of the image of the vampire constructed in *The Vampire Countess* recur in *Vampire City*, Addhema's *modus operandi* remains unique in the annals of supernatural fiction. Some readers might consider that this disqualifies her from being considered a vampire at all, but when it is properly placed in the context of prior works, *The Vampire Countess* is obviously not as far apart from the tradition as it may seem to modern readers. It is, in essence, a tale of irresistible and catastrophic sexual seduction–and that is what really entitles it to its title. The novel did, however, contribute two crucial images to the evolving literary lore of vampirism, the first contained in the very striking "rapid aging" scene, and the second in the way it dwells so lasciviously on the device of destroying a vampire by impaling the heart.

There are, of course, numerous previous references to staking vampires; they are common in treatises on vampire folklore, although the purpose of the wooden stakes is usually to pin down corpses that might otherwise get up and walk rather than to perforate their hearts. Hoffmann's Lothar Serapion was probably the first literary character to recommend a wooden stake through the heart as a reliable means of destroying a vampire, so Féval's preference for a red-hot iron bar might be regarded as an unfortunate sidestep–but the purpose of Féval's instrument is to make the sexual symbolism more violent and more obvious, and in that respect he was definitely ahead of his time. Even the studied eroticism of *La Morte Amoureuse* and J. Sheridan le Fanu's "Carmilla" (1872)–the next significant *femme fatale* vampire story after Féval's–pale slightly by comparison with the hectic carnality of the final chapter of *The Vampire Countess*.

It is also interesting to compare Féval's scene in which a beautiful vampire is seen to wither into a crone after a sexual tryst with the imagery of "Les Métamorphoses du Vampire" by Charles Baudelaire, one of the poems that was removed from *Les Fleurs du Mal* (1857) following its prosecution on a charge of outraging public morality. The similarity is striking, all the more so because it must surely be a coincidence; the manuscript of Baudelaire's poem dates from 1852, and it had no publication prior to 1857. Unless my estimate of the date of *The Vampire Countess*' serialization is wildly inaccurate, neither author could have seen the other's work; perhaps Baudelaire, like Féval, had seen the 1851 version of *Le Vampire* and had been similarly impressed by the metaphorical potential of the amorous ghoul. Given Féval's moral stance and slapdash methods, it is hardly surprising that "Les Métamorphoses du Vampire" became a much more famous work than *The Vampire Countess*, or that Féval played little part in the inspiration of the Decadent Movement of 1887-1900–but when *The Vampire Countess* was reprinted in 1891, the Decadents must surely have recognized it as a work that, in spite of itself (to borrow one of Féval's favorite phrases), was definitely one of theirs.

Paul Féval did not believe in vampires. Nor do I. While my incredulity is no barrier to reading and writing fiction about vampires, however, Féval's seemed to him to be a serious problem. We are products of very different literary eras.

No modern reader or writer has any difficulty in reconciling world-within-texts in which the existence of vampires is taken for granted with a lived-in-world in which their non-existence is presumed, even when the imaginary worlds within the relevant texts include among their *dramatis personae* actual historical figures. In 1995, Tom Holland could write a book like *The Vampyre*, in which Lord Byron and John Polidori are vampires–even though the remainder of the text is carefully respectful of known historical facts–without feeling the slightest pang of conscience, and his readers could enjoy the story without the least disquiet. With even greater insouciance, and equal success, Kim Newman launched a whole series of alternative histories in 1992, stemming from a revised version of Bram Stoker's *Dracula* in which Dracula, having thwarted Van Helsing and Jonathan Harker, goes on to marry Queen Victoria and "convert" a substantial fraction of London high society. All three of my own vampire novels–the historical fantasy *The Empire of Fear* (1988), the psychological melodrama *Young Blood* (1992) and the literary conceit *The Hunger and Ecstasy of Vampires* (1996)–present the takeover of the world by vampirekind as an accomplished fact or a future inevitability. No one nowadays has any difficulty reading such fanciful texts, or entering wholeheartedly into the imaginary televisual worlds of *Buffy the Vampire-Slayer* and *Ultraviolet*. But it was not always thus.

In the 1850s, when Paul Féval wrote *The Vampire Countess* for serialization, no one in France knew for sure how tolerant the reading public might be of fictions which brought vampirism into the "real world." All the French literary works in which vampires had previously been featured had been calculatedly fanciful romances drawn from foreign sources and set in faraway places. A tale of Paris in the final days of the Consulate, which pretended to be true to the facts of history

322

and employed a cast mingling real and fictitious individuals, must have seemed a different matter.

There were good reasons to doubt the propriety of placing a "real" vampire in such a setting. The victory of science over superstition, if not yet entirely secure, seemed inevitable. French readers had thrilled to the dark delights of German and English Gothic novels, but French novelists had not been nearly so willing to dabble in such absurdities. The 1820 play that had established vampires as a consistent presence in Parisian theatres had inspired as many scathing parodies as reverent imitations.

Because it was intrinsic to the nature of newspaper serials that they were made up as the author went along, the sensible thing for Féval to do, having been asked to write a story about a vampire at large in Paris, was to begin ambiguously, carefully refusing to specify whether the vampire was real or merely a device invented to mask a wholly naturalistic but intricately deceptive criminal conspiracy. It was sensible, too, for him to conserve his options as long as possible, reserving the possibility of resolving the climax in either fashion. It is perhaps understandable that he never did make up his own mind one way or the other, and fudged the issue even in the final chapter.

Reader response to the slowly-expanding text of *The Vampire Countess* presumably provided some evidence that the French public was not only willing but enthusiastic to accept a real vampire haunting the streets of a Paris that many of them still remembered, but it is unlikely that the response was unanimous. Perhaps Féval tried to give the majority what they wanted, within the limits that his own conscience would permit, but it is equally likely that he did his best to please everyone by conserving ambiguity as carefully as he could. At any rate, by the time the final decision as to the reality of the vampire had to be made, the ambiguity of the text was very deep-seated indeed, and its resistance to firm resolution could not be easily overcome.

There is no doubt that, in purely aesthetic terms, the vampire wins the contest within the text hands down. The three chapters in which she is seen at work in Paris, from the separate viewpoints of the three principal characters, are by far the most vivid in the novel. However, the fact that they are all couched in more-or-less hallucinatory frames—and clash so discordantly with the chapters featuring mundane criminal activity and woeful police incompetence—gives the whole work a quasi-paradoxical hesitancy that is almost unparalleled in the history of vampire fiction.

The central question of the text is, of course, who (or what) is Countess Marcian Gregoryi? Is she really the vampire Addhema, or is she merely a confidence trickster intent on looting the fortunes of her various suitors for more vulgar purposes? Although the question seems to be settled in favor of the former hypothesis, the text carefully leaves room for doubt, and renders some encouragement to skeptical readers who might prefer the latter.

Of the four passages in the novel in which the vampire Addhema is revealed, three are obviously problematic. The vision in which René sees her turn into a bald crone is an opium dream; the fact that he finds what he takes to be a scrap of flesh and hair when he wakes up cannot constitute convincing proof that his vision was anything more than a nightmare induced by the pack of lies that Lila had told him beforehand. The vision which Germain Patou experiences in the final chapter is equally suspect; although he has not been dosed with opium, he is clearly in a highly abnormal mental state, and what he sees has all the hallmarks of a hallucination. The fact that the body has vanished when he wakes up is insignificant; the text has carefully provided Ezekiel with an incentive to sneak back and steal it, so that he may sell it elsewhere. The subsequent account of Addhema's tryst with Szandor is not even afforded the status of a vision; it is explicitly represented as a tale told in the relevant locality, to whose alleged events there could not possibly have been any human witness.

The only vision of the vampire at work which carries any real hint of authority, therefore, is the one which Jean-Paul Sévérin describes to Monsieur Berthellemot–and it is surely significant that the novel's narrator chooses to render this particular tale as a second-hand account rather than describing it as it happens. Sévérin is certainly not a liar, but he is a simple man, capable not only of making mistakes but of failing to draw conclusions that seem obvious to the reader. One of the most curious thing about Sévérin's vision of the vampire is his failure to realize that the girl he sees by the riverside is his beloved Angela. Given the significance that the spot has for both of them, he would surely leap to that conclusion even if he could not see her clearly. Is it not possible, therefore, that he did recognize her, but found the thought of her committing suicide so appalling that his already-disturbed mind retrospectively constructed an elaborate fantasy which made her a victim rather than a sinner. We know already that Sévérin believes himself to be a visionary, who distinctly remembers having seen Bonaparte as an emperor long before any such conclusion was remotely plausible, so it would not be entirely surprising if his vision of the vampire were, indeed, exactly that.

It is worth recalling that *The Vampire Countess* was planned as an item in a series about the victims exhibited in the Morgue, and that the preface of the novel establishes that the novel began as Angela's story rather than Marcian Gregoryi's. The seed of the story was the notion of confronting the Morgue-keeper with the body of his own adopted daughter–a circumstance made all the more tragic by his personal crusade to save would-be suicides from hurling themselves into the Seine. Angela never sees herself as a victim of vampirism; she alone, among the main characters, sees René's seductress as a perfectly ordinary human being.

While the narrative is tracking Countess Marcian Gregoryi, however, she never actually does anything that suggests that she really is Addhema. Nor, with the exception of one cryptic comment to Yanusza in chapter XIX and one equally-unclear aside while she is alone with René, does she ever actually say anything to give that impression–everything she tells René while pretending to be Lila has to be regarded with the utmost suspicion.

If Séverin's story of the corpse in the river is set aside, therefore, the only circumstance that lends any real credence to the Countess' supernatural status is the fact that she contrives to fascinate René before he has seen her face. If it required a literal spell to do that, her supernatural ability is proven–but was it really magic? Féval, in his capacity as narrator, surely protests a little too much, as well as far too ambivalently, about its unnatural status. Again, there is an explanation available to anyone who cares to read between the lines with a sufficiently cynical eye.

The plain fact is that René's love for Angela, however strongly he proclaims it, is more than a little suspect. His liaison with her is initially secretive, and when he finds out that she is pregnant, his immediate response is to persuade her to go through a "marriage" which anyone else would regard as a hollow and rather shabby sham. It is not until Séverin confronts him, guns in hand, that he condescends to come clean–and no matter how much we may admire Séverin and loathe Monsieur Berthellemot, we surely have to admit that Berthellemot's innuendoes are not without a certain force.

The narrator, while assuming the privilege of looking into his thoughts, assures us that René really does love Angela–but one does not need to be a psychoanalyst to wonder whether René's insistence on that point results from a determination to persuade himself. Perhaps, deep down, he was looking for a way out long before the date of his marriage became imminent–and perhaps, as that date approached, his need became desperate. Bewitched he may have been, but there may have been nothing supernatural in the fascination he developed for the veiled woman, or the intensification of that fascination when he first saw Lila's face.

There are, of course, other problems afflicting the plot apart from the question of Countess Marcian Gregoryi's true nature–problems so awkward that one cannot, in the end, see how the story can possibly make sense. What is the point of the elaborate pretense mounted in *The Miraculous Catch*? Why is any distraction necessary–and why, if it is, should it take this peculiar form, which surely calls attention to the fact that something nasty is afoot? Why has Countess Marcian Gregoryi involved herself with the League of Virtue? What do they do for her that she could not do more economically and less obtrusively for herself, given that she seems to have no compunctions about committing murder herself? Why is she so intent on finding Georges Cadoudal, since she has no use for him other than to betray him along with the League? Why, given that she has such power over men, could she not obtain a passport from the Prefect without paying such a price and taking the absurd risk of forging a note from Bonaparte? Why does Séverin waste so much time at the Prefecture when he really does not need the agents at all? (The only one who makes a useful contribution is Ezekiel, whose presence in his party is entirely accidental and could not possibly have been anticipated.)

It is probable that all these puzzles arise as a consequence of the fact that Féval was making up his story as he went along–perhaps alongside two or three other serials–and that he never managed to make up his own mind as to what the answers to these questions actually were. Perhaps, in view of the generally chaotic nature of the story, it is ridiculous to search for elaborate psychological explanations of seemingly-supernatural incidents, all the more so when the supernatural interpretations are clearly preferable. But we should not forget that whether literary vampires are taken literally or not, their power to move and disturb us is vested in their metaphorical significance. It is what vampires stand for that is really important, in the final analysis, not whether they are "real" or merely hallucinatory.

The tremendous success of Bram Stoker's *Dracula* as a generator of cinematic images has caused modern commentators to concentrate on the vampire as a sexual symbol. Dracula is, above all else, a primal force of nature which threatens to turn prim young Victorian maidens into lascivious nymphomaniacs; if his descendants are more often heroes than villains in today's vampire literature, it is because that seems to be a much more desirable result nowadays than it did in Victorian times, when sexy sluts were a significant reservoir of venereal disease. Vampire stories featuring femmes fatales are even more obviously about sex; *La Morte Amoureuse*, "Les Métamorphoses du Vampire" and "Carmilla" are all explicit commentaries on various paradoxes of passion. *The Vampire Countess* certainly belongs to that company–and it is at least arguable that its commentary on the paradoxicality of passion is a good deal more wide-ranging than any of its obvious rivals–but if we are to get to the bottom of Addhema's significance, it may be profitable to remember that there were other metaphorical vampires in the 19th century as well as those who symbolized sex. It is easy to forget them today, because they were not as easily transmutable into cinematic imagery, but at least one of them was very readily available to the 19th century imagination.

Another metaphorical vampire which has been handed down to us from the rhetoric of 19th century is the "blood-sucking capitalist." Capital, Karl Marx informs us in chapter 10 of Volume One of *Das Kapital*, is "dead labor which, vampire-like, lives only by sucking living labor, and lives the more, the more labor it sucks." A note to chapter 14 assures us that "the capitalist devours the labor-power of the worker, or appropriates his living labor as the life-blood of capitalism." And so on. Féval probably never read Marx, and would not have approved of him if he had, but he read Eugène Sue, and although he did not altogether approve of him, Féval was certainly prepared to be contemptuous of the myriad ways in which the rich lived as parasites upon the labors of the poor. It is, therefore, highly significant that Countess Marcian Gregoryi is not primarily interested in sex, but in money. Whether or not she is Addhema (all the more so if, as seems likely, she is not), she is definitely a vampire of sorts: a ruthless predator upon the wealth of her victims, who sucks them dry and leaves them for dead. It is in this respect that Paris itself seems somewhat vampiric–and when Féval intrudes into his story, in his capacity as narrator, to compare the Paris of old with the Paris of the present day, it is often to call attention to industrial and commercial "progress" and their human cost. Alongside its feverish eroticism, the last chapter takes the trouble to remind us, in Count Szandor's ringing voice, that we are all more-or-less willing victims of the gold-hungry vampires in our midst.

Perhaps, unlike the various reincarnations of Lord Ruthven–not to mention Clarimonde, Addhema and Carmilla–Countess Marcian Gregoryi is only masquerading as an aristocrat. "Count Marcian Gregoryi" is, after all, a figment of her vivid imagination, even if Addhema is not. We are never given a reliable clue as to who she really is, if she is not Addhema, but that hardly matters–we know what she is. Like the brothers Ténèbre of *Knightshade*, she is the embodiment of a deadly sin–but she is like the elder brother, not the younger; she is avarice, not lust. Indeed, lust is her eventual downfall; as with Dumas and Maquet's ghoul, it is the fact that she becomes enamoured of René that seals her doom. Sex is her snare, but it is a snare she falls into herself; unlike the brothers Ténèbre, who will always be together no matter how much they quarrel, and will always come back no matter how fervently they are hunted down, Countess Marcian Gregoryi is damned the moment she takes her eyes off the real prize–and it is surely best to read Addhema's final confrontation with her own vampire-master as a symbolic summation of that damnation, akin to the prelude and final scene of the 1820 version of *Le Vampire* and the interludes of the 1851 version, but not quite as blinkered in its accounting of the necessities of life. At any rate, Féval, unlike the vast majority of his predecessors and successors, never lost sight of the vampire-as-symbol-of-wealth-and-power. He took the trouble to extrapolate it in the gloriously grotesque symbolism of *Vampire City*–even though he never lost sight of the vampire-as-symbol-of-sex either.

There is also a third vampire which is of some significance in French literary history, and which Féval might have
had peripherally in mind as he penned *The Vampire Countess*,
and that is the vampire-as-muse. Although the explicit imagery of the literary muse who claims her reward in blood has
only recently been restored to vampire fiction–in such novels
as Tim Powers' *The Stress of Her Regard* (1989) and Federico
Andahazi's *The Merciful Women* (2000)–it was once a com-
monplace of French Renaissance poetry.

The idea of the creative imagination as a cruel and
bloodthirsty mistress lies at the very heart of the literary myth
of the *femme fatale*; the reason the *femme fatale* came to such
prominence along with the French and English aesthetic
movements is that their followers embraced–and did their best
to embody–a notion of art as self-sacrificial ordeal, leading in
extremis to martyrdom. The names of the martyrs in question
are too numerous to require extensive listing here–interested
readers might start with the case-studies included in *Les
Poètes Maudits* (1884) by Paul Verlaine and *The Romantic
Agony* (1933) by Mario Praz–but my own reverential trinity
has always consisted of Edgar Allan Poe, Charles Baudelaire
and Oscar Wilde.

Paul Féval may not be an obvious candidate for inclusion
in this number but it is probably not the case that most "hacks"
suffer any less in the process of creation than their more prestigious counterparts. The common opinion that prolific writers
find their work simple, and that they do it merely as an easy
way of making money, is obviously ludicrous when one examines the extent of their sacrifices and rewards. It makes
more sense to regard prolific writing as a form of obsessive-
compulsive behavior, which exacts its toll irrespective of financial recompense–although logic dictates that prolific writers who cannot make enough money to live on will usually be
forced to redirect their obsessive-compulsive tendencies into
another behavioral channel. The fact that Féval's literary
products were not held in high esteem by his contemporaries
does not mean that his muse was any less exacting than theirs,

or that he shed one less drop of metaphorical blood in answering her demands.

If, as seems likely, Féval began work on *The Vampire Countess* shortly after recovering from a breakdown, having received ironically paradoxical treatment from a homeopath, there is surely likely to be a personal meaning in the novel's account of the trials and tribulations of René de Kervoz–for it is certainly René, far more than Jean-Pierre Séverin, in whom Féval sees something of himself. It would, of course, be extremely impolite to wonder whether Féval was ever guilty of the same sorts of crimes and misdemeanors that led René de Kervoz into what he took, retrospectively for a vampire's embrace, but we know that Féval was a man capable of looking back in anguish and demanding laborious acts of contrition from his own repentant soul.

Paul Féval never believed in literal muses any more than he believed in literal vampires–but how else, if called upon to do so, could he have characterized his own personal muse? He might not have been a great writer, but he was by no means a stupid reader, and he had read Gautier as intelligently as any other admirer of the doctrine of "art for art's sake" set out in the prologue to Mademoiselle de Maupin (1835-36). Féval undoubtedly understood all the subtexts of *La Morte Amoureuse*, including the one in which the victimized priest represents the harassed author, and the visionary sequences of *The Vampire Countess* are certainly trying as hard as their author was capable to match–and, where feasible, to surpass–Gautier's example.

If this interpretation is accepted, then Addhema is really three vampires in one. She is, first and foremost, the vampire-as-libido-run-wild, but she is certainly the vampire-as-gold-digger too, and she may well have something of the vampire-as-muse to complete her mystique. There is a sense in which vampires do not benefit from being too well-rounded, any more than they benefit from being too crudely literal or too conscientiously metaphorical, but anything that Addhema might lose in being reckoned an overloaded and self-confessed figment of the imagination she surely makes up in sheer flamboyance.

After 1856, it would be a long time before any other writer or movie maker contrived a vampire as perversely charismatic as Addhema; and, whether it is a false memory or not, no one but Féval has ever produced another scene like Jean-Pierre Sévérin's horror-stricken account of the manner in which his adoptive daughter came to fulfill her appointment with the icy heart of the Morgue.

Notes

[1] Louis-Antoine Fauvelet de Bourrienne (1769-1834) was Napoleon's secretary, who continued to hold political office after the Restoration. His *Mémoires* are a significant source of information about the period, although Féval may be right to suggest that they are no more reliable than the general run of self-serving and self-glorifying autobiographical fictions.

[2] Gâteloup translates literally as "wolf-spoiler." Wolfbane sounds better but might give the wrong impression; I can find no evidence that the label was ever applied to the plant that bears that English nickname–the French name, *aconit*, corresponds to the English aconite and the Latin *Aconitum*.

[3] I have translated *"va montrer"* as "will display" rather than substituting a term more usually employed in explaining what stories will do because Féval is clearly drawing an analogy between his story and the expositions of the Morgue. When he wrote this prelude, he presumably intended to write more stories in this series–including, one infers, the stories of two more Angelas whose fates were bound to Jean-Pierre Séverin's family by his adoption of the first (one of whom we shall encounter in the course of the narrative).

[4] Pierre Baour-Lormian (1770-1854) was the French poet who translated the two epic poems attributed to the Scottish bard Ossian but actually fabricated by the Scottish poet James Macpherson (1736-1796). Despite widespread doubts about their authenticity, the Ossianic epics were widely praised throughout Europe and were a considerable influence on the Romantic movements in Germany and France.

[5] The English Gothic novelist Ann Radcliffe (1764-1823) was later to serve as the heroine of Féval's horror-comedy *La Ville-Vampire*, my translation of which is currently available from Black Coat Press under the title *Vampire City*.

[6] It is not inconceivable that there really was a Parisian legend of this kind, but the likelier alternative is that Féval was mischievously appropriating the tale of Sweeney Todd, the demon barber of Fleet Street, as related in the penny dreadful serial *The String of Pearls*.

[7] The "*récit de Théramène*" can be found in Racine's famous tragedy *Phèdre* (1677). It describes the death of Hyppolytus, dragged by horses, after a battle with a sea-monster.

[8] I have re-translated the French titles of Radcliffe's novels in order to conserve the symmetry; *The Confessional of the Black Penitents* (1797) is also known in English as *The Italian*. The actual English title of *The Mysteries of the Pyrenean Castle* is *The Romance of the Forest* (1791) and that of *The Mysteries of the Apennine Cavern* is *A Sicilian Romance* (1790); *The Mysteries of Udolpho* was published in 1794.

[9] The title almost certainly evades Féval's memory because he invented the text in question. The only plausible candidate among actual German texts is the fabulously rare *Der Vampyr* (1801) by Ignatz Ferdinand Arnold (1774-1812), but was never translated into French. Féval's casual plot summary is much more closely akin to the 1820 and 1851 versions of *Le Vampyre* (for further details of which see the afterword).

[10] Robert Lovelace is Clarissa Harlowe's despoiler and effective murderer in Samuel Richardson's novel *Clarissa* (1748-9). Richardson had a greater reputation in France than in his own country.

[11] The 1891 edition and the Marabout text both have Dumolard, which was the name of an early 19th century French dramatist specializing in comedy, but Féval must be referring to the infamous Martin Dumollard, described in the 1872 *Larousse*–in an article much longer than the one devoted to Féval!–as an "*assassin des servantes*." The Dumollard case was a *cause célèbre* involving an alleged serial killer specializing in female servants, who was allegedly active in the environs of Lyons for a period of eight years. Whether Dumollard was actually guilty of the crimes laid at his door remains something of a mystery–the initial accusation brought against him seems to have been fabricated, and the allegations that he had a private cemetery where he buried his victims after drinking their blood were probably products of the overactive imagination of his accuser–but he was found guilty and guillotined, instituting a legend to compare with that of Gilles de Rais. Significantly, the case only came to light in 1861, five years after the first book publication of *Les Drames de la Mort*, so this reference must have been freshly inserted into the 1865 edition (whose text the 1891 and 1968 editions of *La Vampire* presumably reproduced). It is easy enough to understand why Féval was so enthusiastic to incorporate the reference into his story, even though he failed to spell the name correctly.

[12] The statue of the commander is the vengeful revenant which drags the great lover Don Juan down to hell in the oft-retold tale first recorded by Gabriel Téllez in *El Burlador de Sevilla* (1630). Féval would have been familiar with Molière's comedy *Dom Juan* (1665) and Mozart's opera *Don Giovanni* (1787) as well as versions by Pierre Corneille and Alexandre Dumas, although the linkage made here between Don Juan and Faust recalls Christian Dietrich Grabbe's German drama *Don Juan und Faust* (1828).

[13] However famous the vampire of "Debreckzin" and Professor Hemzer may have been in the 1850s–and Féval may, of course, be indulging in sarcastic fantasy–there seems to be no record of either of them in modern accounts of the literature of vampirism.

[14] A goffering-iron was a device for crimping cloth or paper; its nearest modern equivalent is probably the kind of device used to curl hair.

[15] Vampire is rendered here in Féval's text as a feminine noun rather than a masculine one, despite the fact that the anecdotal account which has just been given is of a male vampire: a "Faust" who draws blood from the breasts of a series of Marguerites. Plainly, however, the kind of creature which might be responsible for a flow of human body-parts from a sewer-outlet would be more akin to a ghoul.

[16] The terms "Vendeans" and "chouans" are interchangeable; les guerres de Vendée, named for one of the main départements of Brittany, were the conflicts between the Breton rebels and the Revolutionary forces. Babouvistes were followers of François Babeuf (1760-1797), a proto-communist who agitated for land reform before and during the Revolution and duly went to the guillotine. Louis-Joseph, Prince de Condé (1736-1818) was another famous opponent of the Revolution, who left France in 1792 to form an army at Coblentz, on the Rhine.

[17] The Directory was the body of five men who held executive power in France from November 1st, 1795, when it succeeded the Convention, to Brumaire 18 (November 9), 1799, when it was overthrown by Napoleon's *coup d'état*. It was modified halfway through its career by the coup of Fructidor 18 (September 4), 1797, when the Republicans wrested control from the reactionaries.

[18] The *noblesse de robe* was a sector of the French aristocracy whose position of privilege was entirely dependent on the King, because they had no hereditary estates.

[19] "*Ci-devant*" means "formerly"; the word acquired a particular significance after the Revolution of 1789, when everyone became a Citizen, and all aristocratic titles were prefaced *ci-devant*.

[20] William Pitt the younger (1759-1806) was the English Prime Minister in 1804. Friedrich Josias, Prince of Saxe-Coburg (1737-1815), was an Austrian general who had won a significant battle against the French in 1793 but had been comprehensively defeated at Fleurus in 1794.

[21] Christian Friedrich Samuel Hahnemann (1755-1843) announced his new system of medicine, homeopathy, in 1796. Strictly speaking, Professor Loysel cannot have been lecturing on Hahnemann's *Organon der rationele Heilkunde* in 1804 because it was not published until 1810–nor could Germain Patou have owned a copy (as is alleged when he sells his books in chapter XXVII).

[22] There is no trace of any story by Féval called *Numéro Treize* [*Number Thirteen*] in the catalogue of the *Bibliothéque Nationale*. It may have been a story that was never reprinted in book form, or one whose title was changed.

[23] "*Trois-quarts-du-monde*" is, of course, a sarcastic extrapolation of "*demi-monde*;" there is no point in translating it as "three-quarters-of-the-world." The English equivalent of "*la Baronne de N'importe quoi*" would be something along the lines of Lady God-knows-what.

[24] Edouard Benazet was an impresario who took over the casino at Baden-Baden in 1838 and made it one of the most important gambling venues in Europe. In 1855, a team of French architects outfitted the casino in the style of a French royal palace (decor which has been retained to the present day). If, as seems highly likely, the latter news item was what prompted Féval to include the reference, it provides further evidence that the novel was written and serialized in 1855.

[25] The Pactolus was a river in ancient Lydia, in Asia Minor, which was celebrated as a source of gold, although the relevant field was soon exhausted.

[26] Auvergne was an ancient province in the south of France, reclaimed by the Crown in 1610. Its mountains had once been infested by bandits.

[27] Paul Niquet was a famous Parisian *cabaretier* whose establishment was near Les Halles. I have not been able to ascertain exactly what went on at his "nights" but am tempted to speculate that they were among the ancestors of the "theme nights" occasionally featured in modern pubs and clubs.

[28] "Spiritshops" and "gin palaces" are both rendered thus by Féval. There is no such English word as "spiritshops," but as its meaning is obvious I have let it stand.

[29] *Foutreau* and *bouillotte* belong to a set of gambling-games whose best-known French version is *brelan*. They are similar to the vast set of Anglo-American games which are variants of poker.

[30] Hippodamia was the real name of Briseis, whose seizure by Agamemnon after her capture by Achilles caused the rift between the two recorded in *The Iliad*.

[31] A *liard* was a quarter of a *sou*–a very small denomination indeed.

[32] Christianity was officially abolished in Revolutionary France in October 1793, a mere fortnight before the Vendean insurgents suffered a heavy defeat at Cholet, and the insult must have strengthened the resolve of the Anti-Revolutionary forces. Freedom of worship was, however, restored in February 1795. Like René's father, Jean-Pierre Sévérin–a cantor at Saint-Sulpice–must have strongly disapproved of the closure of the churches no matter how strong his Republican sympathies were. One suspects that Féval, even before his ostentatious conversion, felt much the same.

[33] A brave man, ready for anything.

[34] Harmodius and Aristogiton were two Athenian youths who killed the Hipparchus in 514 B.C.

[35] Tsar Paul I of Russia was the son of Peter III and Catherine II (the Great), who succeeded his mother in 1796. He joined the coalition against France but withdrew from it in 1800. He was assassinated in March 1801, the victim of a conspiracy. The references to Caesar in this little digression carry a multiple meaning, of course, which embraces Napoleon III as well as Bonaparte.

[36] Armide is a seductive enchantress in Torquato Tasso's epic *Gerusalemme Liberata* (1581)–a favorite work in 19th century France–who beguiled crusaders into breaking their vows until her powers were defeated by a Christian talisman (after which she was converted by her former captive Rinaldo).

[37] Circé is the enchantress who turned Odysseus' men into swine in Homer's *Odyssey*, although he eventually got the better of her.

[38] Jean de La Fontaine (1621-1695) was the most famous French fabulist.

[39] Féval actually wrote "*Let us knock down the damned rascal!*" but I have taken the liberty of making his English more plausibly colloquial. Admittedly, a real cockney would have been far more likely to say "bastard" rather than "bleeder," but Féval never permits himself any expletive stronger than "*damné*" so that would be out of keeping with the manner of the text. Féval also added a parenthetical translation of his English phrase into French, which I have omitted.

[40] Madame de Staël (1766-1817) was one of the most important French writers of her day, an essayist, novelist and literary critic who was one of the founders of what is nowadays called "cultural studies;" her novel *Corinne, ou, l'Italie* (1807) is a tale of the doomed love of a female poet for a Scottish aristocrat.

[41] *Horaces* (*The Horatii* in English) is a tragedy by Pierre Corneille, first produced in 1640. The plot involving Ceracchi, Aréna and Diana was sometimes given that label because that was the play which Napoleon was watching while the conspirators attempted to gain access to his box, but its plot has a particular significance with respect to the fictitious Andrea Ceracchi's recruitment to Féval's story, because the play retells the story of three legendary Roman brothers, one of whom avenged the others after they had been defeated by the Curiatii.

[42] Dominique-François Toussaint-Louverture (or L'Ouverture) was born a slave in Haiti in 1743. After the 1789 Revolution, he fought for the Royalists before switching sides in 1794 and decisively tipping the balance in favor of the Republicans. When the British abandoned the island in 1798,

they surrendered their positions to him rather than hand them over to the French, and he eventually took control of the whole island, establishing himself as its president in July 1801. Napoleon sent a large force to depose him, and Toussaint-Louverture capitulated in May 1802, after a series of bloody battles; he was sent back to France shortly thereafter and died a prisoner in the Castle of Joux, in April 1803.

43   A tincture of the rhizome and roots of the herb *Arnica montana* was a common medicament often applied to bruises and swellings; it thus qualified (albeit dubiously) as a vulnerary–something useful in assisting wounds to heal.

44   Achille-François Jouffroy d'Abbans (1785-1859) was one of three writers who allegedly had a hand in a three-act melodrama called *Le Vampire*, that was first produced at the Théâtre de la Porte-Martin in 1820 (for further details of which see the afterword). Jouffroy did indeed go on to become an ingenious inventor, working on the development of some of the earliest steamships and steam locomotives. Patou's reference to the play is, of course, anachronistic–more flagrantly so than his references to Samuel Hahnemann's *Organon*.

45   *Le Diable Amoureux* by Jacques Cazotte (1719-93), translated into English as *The Devil in Love*, is an enigmatic and frustratingly ambiguous work in which a young student summons the Devil in the form of a beguiling young woman named Biondetta, who apparently becomes enamored of him and eventually passes up the chance to secure his damnation. The novel was hugely popular in France in spite of–and partly because of–its ultimate failure to make much sense; Féval was not the only feuilletonist who treasured that precedent.

46   Presumably Charles le Téméraire (the Bold), the last Duke of Burgundy, who was killed before the Battle of Nancy–fought against the forces of René II, Duc de Lorraine–in 1477.

[47] Féval is writing before Rosicrucian lifestyle fantasies became popular in Paris; I have translated his "*palais*" and "*royaume*" literally rather than substituting terms which became more familiar at a later date. Buda was one of the two cities that were united into Budapest in 1872. This passage is slightly inconsistent with the only other reference to Countess Marcian Gregoryi's Rosicrucian status (see note 97).

[48] Seïd was the slave and first convert of Mahomet. Voltaire used his name as a synonym for blind, fanatical devotion.

[49] Féval has "Kaërnarvon" here, but reverts to the usual spelling on the only other occasion he uses the name. He must have known perfectly well that there was a world of difference between cockneys and Welshmen, but was always calculatedly casual in his representations of the British.

[50] Mourad Bey was the famous leader of the mamelukes, who was defeated by Napoleon at the Battle of the Pyramids in 1798.

[51] Aristides the Just was an Athenian general and statesman in the 5th century B.C., who was ostracized in 483 but returned thereafter to fight at Salamis in 480 and lead the Athenian army at Plataea in 479.

[52] Lucullus was a Roman general of the 1st century B.C. who became notorious for the wealth he accumulated and the luxurious lifestyle he adopted when he retired from active service. The "Lucullus of the Directory" is not a reference to a particular individual but to the tendency of the men who served in that government to come out of it far richer than they went in.

[53] Gabriel Honoré Riquetti, Comte de Mirabeau (1749-1791) was the greatest orator of the 1789 Revolution, who was

briefly president of the National Assembly before his death (of natural causes). Unlike "the Lucullus of the Directory," Mirabeau did not gain any financial advantage from the Revolution, thus providing a complementary exemplar.

[54] Coblentz, a town situated at the confluence of the Rhine and Moselle, became a rendezvous for French *émigrés* in 1792, before being occupied by the Revolutionary forces in 1794.

[55] The last three Kings of legendary Rome–the fifth, sixth and seventh–were Tarquinius Priscus, Tarquinius Sextus and Tarquinius Superbus. This literal reference is to the last, whose reign is said to have ended in 510 B.C., but the metaphorical reference is, of course, to Napoleon. The next paragraph, overtly admonishing Napoleon I, must have been calculated to make contemporary readers reflect on the wisdom of Napoleon III.

[56] The *Vehmgerichte* were tribunals which flourished in Germany in the 14th and 15th centuries. Their sessions were open when they concerned civil matters but secret when they concerned murder, robbery, heresy and witchcraft.

[57] The Jagellon dynasties descended from Jagello, the Grand Duke of Lithuania who became King of Poland in 1386 as Wladislaw II.

[58] "*Ban*" is a Serbo-Croatian contraction of the Turkish "*bajan*," meaning ruler. It was a title once given to the warden of the southern marches of Hungary, and subsequently attached to provincial governors in the same region (whose lands thus became "banates").

[59] The French word "*baiser*," here translated literally as "kiss," can imply much more; this is one case in which it obviously does.

[60] I have not been able to determine what a "jatspka" is, or was.

[61] The Tagliamento is a river in northern Italy. The banks of the river provided the site of a subsequent French victory in November 1805, when Masséna's forces defeated an Austrian army led by Archduke Charles.

[62] Chiusa San Michele, northeast of Turin, is the site of a famous Benedictine Abbey.

[63] A *torsade* is a twisted cord, or an ornament shaped to resemble one.

[64] A treaty signed in 1797 between France and Austria which ceded Belgium and the Ionian islands to France.

[65] Jean-François Rewbell (1747-1807) was President of the Directory in 1796. He was born at Colmar, hence the subsequent reference to "Colmar's advocate."

[66] Egeria was a nymph or minor goddess. The second King of Rome, Numa Pompilius, claimed that she was his adviser.

[67] The *Conseil des Cinq-Cents* (i.e., The Council of Five Hundred) was one of two lawmaking assemblies created by the new constitution of Revolutionary Year III (1795); its role corresponded roughly to that of the English House of Commons, while the *Conseil des Anciens* had a role similar to that of the House of Lords.

[68] Marshal Jean Lannes, Duc de Montebello, was one of the most distinguished French generals of the Napoleonic Era.

[69] The *Angelus* is a devotion commemorating the Incarnation, said every morning, noon and evening in Roman Catholic churches, after a bell has sounded.

[70] Charles-Maurice de Talleyrand-Périgord (1754-1838) was one of the most famous French statesmen of his era, surviving numerous changes of government.

[71] Nicolas-Gabriel de la Reynie was the first occupant of the post of Lieutenant of Police, created by Louis XIV. He was appointed in 1671 and his post was redesignated Lieutenant-General of Police in 1674. His responsibilities were even greater than those attached to the position of Prefect. Among his 18th century successors, two who achieved particular renown were Antoine-Gabriel de Sartines and Jean-Charles-Pierre Lenoir. Berthellemot would have seen all three of them represented on the stage because Anti-Royalist satire became a popular genre of comedy after the Revolution of 1789. De Sartines was more widely featured than the other two because he had some dealings with the Comtesse du Barry, the notorious mistress of Louis XV, who had become a favorite object of this kind of satire in scurrilous Pre-Revolutionary literature.

[72] Louis-Gustave, Comte de Pontécoulant, was a Girondin member of the Convention.

[73] Aeolus was the mythical keeper of the winds, who briefly entertained Odysseus in Homer's *Odyssey*.

[74] Quiberon is a coastal town on a peninsula in the Morbihan département of Brittany. A party of French Royalists landed there in 1796, supported by the chouans and the English fleet, but were comprehensively defeated in July 1795. One division

was commanded by the *émigré* Charles Virot de Sombreuil, who was among several hundred captives executed by firing squads after the battle.

[75] Louis-Benoît Picard (1769-1828) was a prominent comic playwright of the period.

[76] The French "*grisette*" (referring to the grey clothes worn by Parisian seamstresses, milliners, etc) carries a similar double meaning to the phrase I have used, so Berthellemot is, as usual, heaping one insult atop another–thus prompting poor Sévérin's long-overdue response.

[77] The text has "*deux fois*" (twice) rather than three times–and repeats the phrase subsequently, as observed in note 79–but the subsequent text clearly establishes that there were, in fact, three occasions: once when the Countess was with Count Wenzel (when she had black hair), once when she was with Ramberg (when she had blonde hair) and once on the bank of the Seine, at the conclusion of the episode related in the next chapter.

[78] *Comment* is, of course, French for "how"; this is why the Secretary General becomes confused.

[79] Here, as in the last chapter, Féval has "*deux fois*"; this time the inconsistency is compounded in the following lines by Sévérin's contention that he saw the Countess at the church for "*la première fois*" and Berthellemot's consequent inquiry as to where he saw her for "*la seconde fois*." There are several hypotheses which might explain the inconsistency, but I suspect that when Féval was writing the serial version, he forgot that the Countess had blonde hair when she first appeared; this chapter seems to me to have been written under the misapprehension that when Sévérin saw her at Saint-Louis-en-l'Ile she had black hair, and that the first time he saw her as a blonde

was after his terrible experience on the river. If so, having realized his mistake, Féval presumably amended the proofs of the book to include a passing reference to an earlier encounter in the episode at the church, but seems to have neglected to make similar repairs to this chapter. Whether this is the true reason for the inconsistency or not, it seemed to me that it would be best to make a further correction here, so I have altered these two references to "second" and "third" respectively.

[80] Sieur is a familiar contraction of Monsieur, whose use by Bonaparte indicates the closeness of his relationship with Sévérin.

[81] The Battle of Inkermann (fought in November 1854) and the Siege of Sebastopol were key events in the Crimean War. Féval is, of course, being sarcastic; the French army came to the aid of the British when they were attacked at Inkermann and played the leading role in storming the citadel. These references support the assumption that *The Vampire Countess* was written and serialized in 1855, although–bearing in mind the Dumollard reference (see note 11)–they might conceivably have been freshly inserted into the 1865 edition.

[82] As you (i.e., in your place) and for you.

[83] The Tour Saint-Jacques-la-Boucherie was the bell-tower of the Church of that name, situated not far from the Châtelet.

[84] Gabrielle d'Estrées (1573-1599) was one of Henri IV's mistresses.

[85] The Castle of Meudon, five miles from Paris, was a famous royal residence.

[86] Count Alessandro di Cagliostro was the assumed name of
the notorious charlatan Giuseppe Balsamo (1743-1795).

[87] President d'Aubremesnil is fictitious. "Abbé Gondi" is
Jean-François de Gondi, Cardinal du Retz (1613-1673), who
continued a family tradition by becoming Archbishop of Paris;
he and "Monsieur de Beaufort"–François de Bourbon, Duc de
Beaufort (!613-1679)–were close associates of Cardinal de
Mazarin (Guilio Mazarini, 1602-1661), one of the most famous diplomats serving Louis XIII and Louis XIV in the 17th
century.

[88] Cadoudal was born near Auray in Morbihan, so Sainte-
Anne d'Auray–a famous local place of pilgrimage–would
have a special significance for him.

[89] This source is entirely fictitious, but the mention of Pressburg–now Bratislava, the capital of Slovakia–would have had
a certain resonance for contemporary readers because of the
Treaty of Pressburg of 1805, signed after Napoleon's victories
at Ulm and Austerlitz, which completed the humiliation of
Austria begun in the Treaty of Campo-Formio (the subject of
note 64). The terms of the Treaty of Pressburg included the
secession of several significant possessions, and the payment
of an indemnity of forty million *francs* in gold–a much greater
sum than the million *thalers* which Countess Marcian Gregoryi has exacted from her string of short-lived husbands, allegedly to purchase the favors of her own vampiric lord and
master. Féval used the name Johann Spurzheim in *Les Compagnons du Silence* (1857) as an alias of the villainous David
Heimer, the machiavellian chief of the secret police of the
Kingdom of Naples (who prefigures the infamous Colonel of
Les Habits Noirs).

[90] *Papaver somniferum* is the opium poppy.

[91] Doctor Sangrado is a character in *Histoire de Gil Blas de Santillane* (1715-35), usually known as *Gil Blas*, a classic comic novel by Alain René Lesage. Sangrado's favorite prescriptions were copious blood-letting and drinking lots of hot water; in an era where such procedures could still pass for orthodoxy, Samuel Hahnemann's prescriptions were definitely more respectful of the Hippocratic principle that the first responsibility of a doctor is to make sure that his treatments will do no harm.

[92] This reference is unclear. Montaigu is a town in the Vendée where two important battles in the Vendean wars were fought, but it seems probable–given the progression of the passage and the occasional carelessness of Féval's spelling–that the reference is actually to Gilles de Montagu or Jean de Montagu, both of whom were prominent 14th-century statesmen. The literal meaning of "*capette*" is "little cape" but I have been unable to locate a more specific use of the term that would clarify the type of uniform indicated, or its likely wearer.

[93] Numerous "*Ligues*" are featured in French history, but the *Ligue* is the *Saint-Ligue* formed by the Duc de Guise in the 16th century, ostensibly for the defense of the Catholic faith against the challenge of Calvinism, but actually to further the political ends of his family, which was ambitious to claim the French throne.

[94] Claude Frollo is one of the principal characters in Victor Hugo's *Notre-Dame de Paris–1482* (1831), which was the most important model text for the Paris-set *roman feuilleton*. Frollo is the Faustian priest who becomes besotted with the gypsy Esmeralda, leading him into fateful conflict with his protégé Quasimodo. (Quasimodo presumably helped inspire the eponymous hero of *Le Bossu*, Féval's most popular novel.)

[95] The Tour de Nesle, in the southern wall of ancient Paris, obtained its name by virtue of its proximity to the Hôtel de Nesle. It is the setting of *La Tour de Nesle* (1832), a lurid and very successful play by Alexandre Dumas, whose main character is Marguerite de Bourgogne (1290-1315), a notorious Queen of Navarre who was executed after allegedly disposing of the bodies of several of her lovers in the Seine. The play and the character may well have played some part in the inspiration of *La Vampire*.

[96] Armand Gensonné was a member of the Legislative Assembly and the Convention before being guillotined in 1793.

[97] Buda, Gran and Comorn (or Komorn) were all regional capitals of Hungary. The earlier reference to Countess Marcian Gregoryi's Rosicrucian credentials (see note 47) referred to the thirty-third kingdom rather than the third but the discrepancy may be deliberate, emphasizing the fact that she is improvising.

[98] This fortress-like building on the Ile-de-la-Cité, built by Philippe the Fair (1284-1314) now makes up much of the *Palais de Justice* complex. Its history as a place of imprisonment, torture, and death is is significant. Among its famous prisoners were Marie Antoinette, Charlotte Corday and Danton.

[99] The Tugenbund (Féval has "*Tugenbaud*") was an association formed in Königsburg in 1808 for the ostensible purpose of cultivating patriotism, reforming the army and promoting education, although its real agenda was to resist and overcome French domination; although it was officially disbanded in 1809, it continued to operate in secret for several more years.

[100] Diane de Poitiers (1499-1566) was a famous mistress of Henri II.

[101] Matthias I, Corvinus, a.k.a. "The Great" (1443-1490), was King of Hungary from 1458-90. He was perennially engaged in wars against the Turks, the Bohemians, the Poles and the Holy Roman Emperor. His father, John Hunyadi (1407-1456), was the scion of a noble Hungarian family who became *voïvode* of Transylvania and Captain of Belgrade, in which capacity he too waged war against the Turks.

[102] As observed in note 59, the French word "*baiser*" can imply much more than "kiss"; given the subsequent none-too-subtle reference to multiple orgasm, this is another case where it obviously does. For this reason, I have translated "baiser" as "embrace" on its next appearance, and in the last line of the text.